Fractured

A Family, A Nation, A Dream

Martina Reilly

Claire Joyce

Brendan Farrell

Joe Bergin

Cover – Gerard O'Shea as Joseph Hughes and Sarah Murphy as Mary
Barry. Photo by Andy Keegan

ABOUT FRACTURED

We might not have called our project 'Fractured' had we known what a perspicacious name that would turn out to be. Fractured by name and fractured by the freak of nature that is Covid 19. However, having picked up and rearranged the broken pieces of our dream – twice! – the team from Down at Heel Productions has finally completed our project – albeit in a vastly reimagined format.

So what is – or was – Fractured?

Essentially, 'Fractured' is Kildare's commemoration of the War of Independence. Funded by Creative Ireland through Kildare County Council, it was originally planned as a live, immersive, episodic soap opera that would run for two years in the shops/houses and on the streets of Maynooth, telling the story of a fictional family who lived, loved and lost during the very turbulent times of 1920-1922.

All shows were to be ticketed and free. Audiences would follow the Barry family who live and work in a Maynooth pub as they navigate the politics and divisiveness of the time. Each episode (one 40 minute show per month) was to be filmed and available online for audiences to follow.

Fractured follows all the of historical events of the time – the elections, Bloody Sunday, local ambushes, Treaty negotiations – and mixes it up with raw human drama to create an addictive mix that would hopefully have encouraged loyal audiences month after month.

More than 60 cast members – all local actors from Kildare – had been recruited, and were happy to spend the next two years of their lives performing in our live shows. A further ten directors were enlisted, as well as costume designers, stage hands, prop masters and stewards. It was going to be epic!

And then Covid hit and it all fell to pieces.

After many false starts and changes to plans, the team finally decided to record our series in podcast format, and we are thrilled to have finally achieved this. Fractured is now available across all platforms, and has been streamed by listeners all over the world. We're thrilled that this fascinating period of Irish history can now be accessed by a far wider audience than we ever anticipated.

Our four writers – Martina Murphy, Claire Reilly, Joe Bergin and Brendan Farrell – have created a nail-biting, emotional, tense, fractious, tender and often hilarious roller coaster ride through history.

We hope you enjoy it!

ACKNOWLEDGEMENTS

FRACTURED is the biggest, most ambitious creative project conceived by Down at Heel Productions to date. Even in its new podcast format, it could not have happened without an enormous amount of help from an enormous amount of people.

Thanks to Lucina Russell in Kildare Arts Office who championed the idea from the beginning. As a result, finance to breathe the Barry family into life was secured from Creative Ireland, Kildare Arts and the Department of Tourism, Culture, Arts, Gaeltacht, Sport and Media under the Decade of Centenaries 2012-2023 initiative. Thanks also to Lorna Kenna, Kevin Murphy, James Durney and Mario Corrigan in Kildare County Council.

Thanks to Martina Reilly, Claire Joyce, Joe Bergin and Brendan Farrell for writing the episodes.

Meadhbh Fitzgibbon-Moore for our FRACTURED logo / poster design.

To the wonderful Des Nealon for launching FRACTURED in January 2020.

Elaine Bean and her team in Maynooth College Library for our launch venue, Cairdeas band for lovely launch music and Rody Molly for videoing the event.

To the actors who read at the launch but were unable to be in the podcast – Tom Brady-Connor, Geraldine O'Brien and James Freeney.

For Patricia O'Malley and Edel Hutchinson for steering the project through the stormy logistical nightmare it became with Covid.

To Boyne Dental and Intel for their help with the project.

To all our actors, to all those who offered to direct and never got the chance, to those people who offered props for when FRACTURED was to be a play and then a film – Declan Kennedy (Brady's Maynooth), Anthony Lee, Laurence Kelly (Kelly's Hardware), Scout's Den Maynooth, St Mary's BNS Maynooth, Maynooth Soccer Club, James Roche (Roches Donadea), Connolly's Public House, Donadea.

Declan O'Connor for his pub memorabilia and knowledge.

Photographs were provided by the talented Andy Keegan. Thanks to Mary Doolan and her late aunt Ria Young for providing us with a fabulous house for pictures, Prof. Michael Mullaney, President St. Patrick's College, Maynooth for allowing us take pictures and also Breda Konstantin for facilitating pictures.

Geraldine O'Brien, Orla Gildea and Mary Power-Cooney for sourcing us talented young actors from their Youth Theatre Groups.

For publicity – thanks to Vincent and Aideen Sutton (Liffey Champion), Jack Gilligan (Dublin City FM), Aine Toner (Woman's Way), Henry Bauress, (Leinster Leader), Caoimhe Murphy (poster designer, ad creator social media).

Colm Murphy for designing and making our 'pods'. To all those who lent us the equipment to record - Anne Kelly and Pete Butler. To Brendan Farrell for his knowledge and expertise in recording, directing and editing the podcast.

Maeve Townsend (Townsend School of Music and Leixlip Community Youth Band) for the music in episode 28.

For Maynooth Campus and Accommodation and Leixlip Musical and Variety Group for allowing us to record.

Joe Bergin for managing the podcast site, recording and editing our 'Meet the Cast' videos on our FB page. And for compiling and editing this book.

Martina and Colm Murphy for their vision and passion to drive the project along.

And to you, the listeners, for tuning in and spreading the word.

CONTENTS

CAST LIST

(alphabetical by character name)

Alan O'Toole	Matt DeBarra
Andrew Hughes	Brendan Farrell
Anne Kilbride	Hilary Madigan
Annie Cahill	Martina O'Connor
Assassin (Peter)	Daniel McCarthy
Assassin (Peadar)	Bob Tysall
Betty Dwyer	Eilish Rafferty
Brigid Barry	Mary Power-Cooney
Cameron	Tony Joyce
Catherine Long	Clare Enright
Cissy Boland	Caoimhe Murphy
Frank Boland	Pete Butler
Civic Guard	Brendan Farrell
Colm (eps 2)	Colm Durkin
Colm O'Sullivan	Stephen Ball
Con O'Sullivan	Daire Keogh
Cons. Curran	Peter Ronayne / Tony Joyce
Cons. Perry	Daire Keogh
Cons. Stiff	James O'Haire / Noel Wade
Domhnall UaBuachalla	Brian McCabe
Eoin eps 2	Eoin Durkan
Farrell	Rian Glynn
Fran Murphy (Judge)	Sadie O'Reilly
Fr. Dempsey	Noel Wade
Girl in eps 11	Lucy Finn
Girl in eps 12	Elyza Levins
Girl in eps 43	Grace McDonald
Got-Me	Peter Ronayne
Joe O'Reilly	Conor Hogan
Joseph Barry	John Bean
Little	Callum Maxwell
Lizzie O'Neill	Meadhbh Fitzgibbon Moore
Love	Bob Tysall

Madge (midwife) .... Orla Gildea
Maggie O'Donoghue .... Patricia O'Malley
Margaret .... Eileen Larkin
Mary Barry .... Sarah Murphy
Maureen O'Leary .... Martina Murphy
Moll Barry .... Beth Joyce
Mossie Kinsella .... Tom McGrath
Paddy Dooley .... Joe Bergin
Paddy Mullaney .... John Fitzgibbon Moore
Patrick Colgan .... Paul Keogh
Peadar Doran .... Sean King
Polling station campaigner 1 .... Tony Joyce
Polling station campaigner 2 .... Sean King
Polling Station campaigner 3 .... Daire Keogh
Poor Brid (Mrs O'Sullivan) .... Karina Power
Rebel 1 .... Ciaran Walker
Rebel 2 .... Catherine Joyce
Rebel 3 ....John Heveran
Reporter .... Marc Cheevers
Seamus McCullough .... George Hogan
Sean Barry .... Aaron O'Connor
Sgt. Blake .... Tony Joyce
Sgt. Joseph Hughes .... Gerard O'Shea
Sgt. Tom Dwyer .... David Murphy
Shiela .... Eithne Rankin
Teresa .... Ann Kelly
Tim Farrell .... Tony Joyce
Tomas Barry (S1) .... Dean McPartlin
Tomas Barry (S2 & S3) .... Oran O'Rua
Union Man (eps6) .... Brendan O'Sullivan
Voiceovers .... Claire Joyce
Volunteer (eps 25) .... Marc Cheevers
Volunteer leader (election) ....Brendan O'Sullivan
Volunteer Ryan .... Conor Lanigan
Williams .... Benjamin Reilly

EPISODE 1 - TOWN HALL BOMBING, MAY 1920

Scene 1 – Outside Maynooth Town Hall

Night time sounds. Three men running, shallow breathing. After a moment we hear a match being struck. The fizz of dynamite.

SEAN: And now...

We hear footsteps receding and the loud boom of an explosion. Glass shattering. Dogs howling.

VOICEOVER: Fractured. A soap drama set in Kildare, Ireland during the War of Independence. May1920.

Scene 2 – Barry's pub

Sound of Brigid sweeping up glass from the floor of her pub.

BRIGID: I'd string them up, so I would. It's not enough destroying buildings they've to destroy livelihoods. *(She calls)* Tomas, get up! There's a window needs fixing. *(Back to muttering)* Oh, isn't it fine for him snoring away -

The pub door opens, sounds of the street fade in. Sean enters.

SEAN: Good morning, Mammy.

BRIGID: Are you only coming in from last night, Sean?

SEAN: *(Beat)* Not at all. I was up from the crack of dawn.

BRIGID: And you didn't think to sweep up this glass or pick up a few chairs?

SEAN: It was just, I heard all the commotion last night and wanted to see what had happened. That was a fair bang, ey?

BRIGID: A fair bang and them that did it should be ashamed of themselves.

SEAN: The way I heard it they had no choice.

BRIGID: Of course they had a choice. Blowing up buildings in the middle of the night!

SEAN: It'd be alright with you if the RIC took over the Town Hall as a barracks, would it?

BRIGID: The RIC are Irishmen too. It's them Tans you'd want to be watching out for.

SEAN: There's a lot of people says the RIC are traitors.

BRIGID: There's a lot of people talks a lot of rubbish. If your father -

SEAN: *(Sound of glass)* I'll put this glass outside, Mammy, alright.

Scene 3 - Yard

As Sean is disposing of the glass, we hear a door opening from the pub. Tomas approaches.

TOMAS: *(In a low voice)* What happened you last night?

SEAN: Shush, will you? *(Beat)* Pat needed to get rid of the guns and –

He is interrupted by Poor Brid entering from the back gate.

POOR BRID: Hello, hello, hello? I thought I heard voices. Have ye seen the main street, boys? I got up early especially to look at the destruction.

SEAN: Aw now, Mr. O'Sullivan is not that bad surely?

POOR BRID: *(Laughs)* You cheeky whelp. I'm talking about the town Hall, a hole blown through it the size of a camel and enough smoke coming out of it for ten volcanoes. Is your mother inside?

SEAN: She is.

Poor Brid bustling in, calling out Brigid's name. As her voice fades..

TOMAS: *(Whispering)* Go on so.

SEAN: Pat needed to get rid of the guns but sure, once the explosion went off, everyone scarpered.

TOMAS: We were told to run.

SEAN: Not that soon. Me and Pat turned around and all the lookouts were gone.

TOMAS: Sorry.

SEAN: We had to lug the guns and the explosives up under our jackets and not a lad on the road between here and Leixlip to help.

TOMAS: Christ.

SEAN: A lorry of Tans went by at one point and over into a ditch with us. I'm telling you, one of them guns went somewhere it shouldn't.

TOMAS: *(Laughing)* Christ.

SEAN: I'm still walking funny.

TOMAS: Stop!

SEAN: I thought I'd need Dr Grogan to help me out.

TOMAS: Aw stop, will you?

They share a laugh.

SEAN: Anyway, I spent the night in a safe house in Leixlip. Came back this morning.

TOMAS: Did Mammy catch you?

BRIGID: *(Distant)* Tomas! Tomas!

SEAN: I told her I was up and out already.

4

TOMAS: And she believed it?

SEAN: I suppose.

BRIGID: *(Distant)* Tomas.

TOMAS: *(To Brigid)* Coming! *(To Sean)* She'd never get over it, I'm thinking, you know, if something were to happen…

SEAN: She's as tough as Mick Collins.

TOMAS: Still and all…

SEAN: Still and all, it was a great blast, wasn't it?

TOMAS: My ears are still ringing.

SEAN: Dong! Dong! Dong!

TOMAS: And the way the stones flew all down the street, I wasn't expecting that.

SEAN: And right through Lynch's shop window -

TOMAS: - destroying everything in the place.

SEAN: Couldn't happen to a nicer chap.

They laugh again. Then serious.

TOMAS: Still and all…Mammy's not…

SEAN: I know, alright?

Brigid: *(Distant)* Tomas, there's a customer needs serving. And Sean, get in here and help me clear up.

TOMAS: Coming!

Footsteps retreat as the two boys go back inside.

Scene 4 – Inside pub

POOR BRID: The story I heard is that one man had his head blown clean off and … aw, double my usual ham there, Tomas please. I was just telling your mother, they say four people were killed last night.

Sound of Tomas dropping the ham.

BRIGID: That's a fine waste, dropping that ham.

TOMAS: Sorry, Mrs. O'Sullivan.

POOR BRID: It's grand, a bit of dirt will do no harm. I should be dead long ago, God knows. Wrap that up there now. I was just saying to your mother that the story I heard is that one man had his head blown clean off. Shot off his shoulders, up into the air like a firework, then landed and rolled along the street and Mossy Kinsella kicked it, thinking for all the world it was a rugby ball. Then there was another lad -

SEAN: No one was killed last night, Mrs. O'Sullivan.

POOR BRID: There was, Sean. I heard -

SEAN: Sure, the Town Hall and Courthouse would've been unoccupied that time of the morning, the streets deserted, how would anyone be dead?

BRIGID: That's true

POOR BRID: But I heard -

BRIGID: You must have heard wrong.

POOR BRID: So, no one died?

TOMAS: It's very unlikely.

POOR BRID: Right. So, the building was just blown up?

BRIGID: Isn't that enough?

POOR BRID: It's just that what with all the things happening around the country, we have nothing happening here. My letters to my sister in Cork are very boring so they are. Down there, sure they are being murdered left, right and centre.

TOMAS: *(Teasing)* Are you disappointed no one died?

POOR BRID: Indeeden, I'm not. That's a fierce accusation to make.

TOMAS: Because it sounded for a minute there like you were.

POOR BRID: I'm glad no one died. Taking a life is a mortal sin.

SEAN: I would have thought being the best looking woman in Kildare was a mortal sin.

POOR BRID: You're fierce so you are. And I'm not, so I'm not. *(After a beat)* I'm not, amn't I not?

TOMAS: You're not far off it, is she Sean?

SEAN: I thought you only had eyes for Lizzie O'Neill.

Brid whoops. Sean laughs. Brigid smiles. Tomas is mortified.

TOMAS: Shut up!

POOR BRID: She's a fine girl, is Lizzie.

TOMAS: I wouldn't know.

SEAN: It's not from the want of trying, though.

TOMAS: Shut up, I said.

BRIGID: Tomas, stop shouting. Honestly Mrs. O'Sullivan, you know how to get my boys riled up and no mistake.

POOR BRID: Sure, don't I remember feeding them and changing them? Tomas there had the shittiest arse there ever was.

TOMAS: Remember that when you're eating the ham.

POOR BRID: I will. And I suppose you'll all be wondering why I'm wanting the extra ham? *(They haven't)* It's because I'm having a new lodger next week.

SEAN: You're finally getting rid of Mr. O'Sullivan then?

POOR BRID: Go away out of that! The best man that ever lived, he is. No. (*A slight hesitation*) Me and Mr. O'Sullivan are getting a nurse child. (*No response*) I know what you're thinking and sure, I was the same myself. But then, Mr. O'Sullivan said to me that many a boy he met came from the workhouse and that some of them were the hardest working people you could imagine.

SEAN: And some of them would rob you blind, you'd want to take care there, Mrs. O'Sullivan.

POOR BRID: 'Tis only a little lad, I'm getting. Five or thereabouts. He'll be grand.

BRIGID: And his beginnings?

POOR BRID: I didn't ask. Better off not knowing we thought.

BRIGID: Ah, Mrs. O'Sullivan.

POOR BRID: What odds? He's a little boy. (*Growing emotional*) And you know, Mrs. Barry, how me and Mr. O'Sullivan would have loved a little lad and what with them closing the workhouses and -

TOMAS: You keep feeding him ham, he'll love you so he will.

POOR BRID: I hope so, Tomas. What do you think, Mrs. Barry?

BRIGID: (*After a moment, holding back reservations*) I think he's a very lucky boy.

The two women share a moment.

POOR BRID: He will be. (*Beat*) Anyway, I'll be off. Tell your little Moll to come and play with my new little lad. She'll be welcome.

She leaves, calling out her goodbyes. The door closes behind her.

BRIGID: Bye Brid. Tomas, make a start on those tables and -

Paddy Dooley, Joseph's friend, arrives in.

PADDY: Hello Mrs. Barry, I wonder could I, eh, leave some leaflets here on behalf of my election candidate, Mr. UaBuachalla?

BRIGID: You can, Mr. Dooley but there's no guarantee I won't throw them out.

SEAN: Mammy! You can leave them, Mr. Dooley.

PADDY: Thank you, Sean. As you know Mr. UaBuachalla is very active in local politics, having been elected to the first Dail in -

BRIGID: We do know and as you know, my friend, Mrs. O'Sullivan's husband is also going up for the elections and -

SEAN: He's not, Mammy.

BRIGID: He is.

SEAN: No, Mr. O'Sullivan told me that Poor Brid…eh…Mrs. O'Sullivan begged him not to. She's afraid he'll get his head blown off. Like that lad in Cork.

PADDY: Marvellous thinking. Domhnall's wife died there last year so she's free of all that worrying.

BRIGID: I'm sure that was a relief to her on her deathbed.

PADDY: I never know whether you're joking me or riling me, Mrs. Barry. Anyway, keep Domhnall UaBuachalla in mind when you go to the polls next month, ey?

BRIGID: Be hard to forget him seeing as it's his lot blew the courthouse up last night.

PADDY: Ah now… *(Uneasy laugh which tapers out)* Is himself within?

BRIGID: He is. Had a skinful too much last night. Slept clean through the explosion.

PADDY: He always was the soundest sleeper, mind you. I'll go in and wake him for you, will I?

BRIGID: Tell him we've run out of drink, that'll get him up.

PADDY: Aw, you're an awful woman and no mistake. *(Calling)* Joseph, Joseph!

Footsteps fades as he exits.

BRIGID: I'm going out to see if anyone needs a hand. Sean, keep an ear out for Moll if she wakes and get Mary out of that bed. Tomas, pick up those chairs and polish those tables.

Brigid leaves.

SEAN: Mary! Mary! Up!

He runs from the room, pounding up the stairs. Footsteps fading off.

TOMAS: *(Calling after him)* Don't go annoying her, Sean. Jesus.

Door to the pub opens. O'Reilly enters.

TOMAS: What's up, O'Reilly?

O'REILLY: I'm looking for Sean.

The muffled conversation is blended throughout the Tomas/O'Reilly exchange.

MARY: *(Muffled)* Get out of my room, Sean Barry. Get out!

TOMAS: He'll be down in a minute. Can I –

O'REILLY: No. I'll wait.

SEAN: *(Muffled)* But mammy says you have to move your lazy arse out of the bed and -

MARY: *(Muffled)* I'll tell her you used that word in front of Moll.

8

SEAN: What? Lazy? I –

The sound of something being thrown hard against the door. Sean laughs. We hear footsteps on the stairs. Sean enters.

O'REILLY: Jaysus! That's some sister you have, Sean.

SEAN: How are you. Good night last night, ey?

O'REILLY: Yes. Come on with me. Best leave out the back way.

TOMAS: Can I come?

BOTH: No.

They leave, the door slamming behind them.

TOMAS: *(To himself)* Feckers.

He continues to clean up, whistling softly. The door leading to the hallway, creaks open softly. We hear stealthy footsteps approach Tomas.

MARY: Stick 'em up, you bloody Irish.

Tomas jumps, realises it's Mary. She falls about, laughing.

MARY: Your face! Sorry…sorry…sorry…

TOMAS: You witch. Jesus, you put the heart crossways in me.

MARY: You must have something to hide so.

TOMAS: No!

MARY: You don't have anything to hide, do you Tomas?

TOMAS: No.

MARY: Because it's all very well digging ditches and trenches but blowing things up and -

TOMAS: Don't be concerning yourself.

Street noises float in as Brigid re-enters.

BRIGID: *(To Tomas)* Have you not done those tables yet, Tomas? Mary, here's two loaves, I want you to butter up some sandwiches, there's a good girl.

MARY: Now?

BRIGID: No, next year. Yes, now.

MARY: But I'm going to Dublin with Cissy. We're off work today and we're getting the train in and -

BRIGID: -and there's poor unfortunates whose windows were blown out last night and haven't a bite to eat between them. Sandwiches, please. *(Walking off)* Joseph!

MARY: I hate her sometimes.

TOMAS: She's only trying to help.

MARY: Why is it you always stick up for her and yet -

She doesn't finish. Awkward beat.

TOMAS: I'm only saying…she's just trying to help.

MARY: *(Long pause)* I'm not meeting Cissy.

TOMAS: No?

MARY: No.

TOMAS: Who are you meeting so?

MARY: A friend.

TOMAS: As in -

MARY: A boy.

TOMAS: You kept -

MARY: It's our first proper meeting and now she's gone and spoiled it.

TOMAS: Ask him to come and help with the sandwiches.

MARY: Don't be ridiculous.

TOMAS: You'll just have to keep him dangling so.

He resumes cleaning, whistling.

MARY: Will you make the sandwiches for me? Please Tomas.

TOMAS: No! What would I be making sandwiches for? That's for women. No.

MARY: I'll tell Lizzie O'Neill you're a great chap, so I will if you do this for me.

TOMAS: Why would I want you to do the likes of that?

MARY: You're soft on her, we all know it.

TOMAS: I am not and even if I was, I wouldn't want my sister interfering.

MARY: Please Tomas. I'll do your shift later on tonight. I'm not working today and I'll do your shift and I'll love you forever and I'll tell everyone you're my favourite brother so I will and I'll give you a hug and -

TOMAS: Get off. All right so. But be back by six, because that's my shift.

MARY: I will. Oh, thank you.

She dances off. We hear Paddy and Joseph descending stairs.

PADDY: Right-oh. I'll be off. Thanks for the lend of the book, Joseph. See you at the rally.

BRIGID: *(Muffled from off)* Is that fella not gone yet?

JOSEPH: Ignore her. I'll see you there, Paddy.

Paddy leaves. Sounds of Joseph unscrewing a bottle of whiskey and pouring himself a glass, then downing it. And again. Enter Sean.

10

SEAN: Morning, Daddy. I'm just getting my cap for work.

JOSEPH: You didn't come back last night.

SEAN: I did, I -

JOSEPH: You'd want to be careful, d'you hear me?

A moment as Sean wonders whether to deny but in the end he joins his father at the bar.

SEAN: I thought you'd be proud.

JOSEPH: I'm worried is what I am.

SEAN: No need.

JOSEPH: Pour me a drink there, I could do with one to start the day. And sure, one for yourself. *(Sound of pouring)* Your mother can't be pleased.

SEAN: I'm not sure she knows yet.

JOSEPH: 'Tis only a matter of time.

SEAN: I can face the Tans alright, I'm just not sure about Mammy.

They share a laugh for a moment.

JOSEPH: Take care of each other, you and Tomas, won't ye?

SEAN: You know we will, Daddy.

JOSEPH: And I am proud of you, son but never do anything that you might regret later, d'you hear me?

SEAN: Yes, Daddy.

JOSEPH: *(Raising his glass)* Then all I can say is, to Ireland.

SEAN: Slainte.

Glasses clink.

END OF EPISODE

EPISODE 2 – ELECTION RALLY, MAY 1920

Scene 1 - Maynooth street. Rally.

A political rally. We hear the sound of a busy street, Maynooth Brass Band are playing a rousing tune.

PADDY / JOSEPH: Vote Sinn Fein. Vote Domhnall UaBuachalla. Vote Sinn Fein. Vote Domhnall UaBuachalla.

Voices fade.

VOICEOVER: In May of 1920, elections were held. In Kildare, Sinn Fein were pushing hard.

Scene 2 - Maynooth street. Rally.

The political rally. Paddy and Joseph's voices in the background.

BRIGID: *(Calling)* Anne, Anne! Have you seen Joseph? He's meant to be minding the pub.

ANNE: No, but I saw Tomas handing out leaflets a while ago, I must say, I was surprised, a lot of auld rabble rousing. There must be a law Brigid against -

BRIGID: Joseph will be with Mr. Dooley, have you seen him?

ANNE: No and you'll have to excuse me now for I'm in hurry. Myself and Mr. Kilbride are off to Dublin today. To the Shelbourne.

BRIGID: To see Donnacha, is it?

ANNE: That's right, it's months since he's been home. Very busy you know what with -

BRIGID: His course. Yes. Tell him I was asking for him, will you?

ANNE: If I remember. Mr. Kilbride thinks that being in the Shelbourne will make us forget ourselves altogether.

We hear Joseph and Paddy, clearly at that moment.

BRIGID: Would you look at the cut of them. Joseph!

Her voice fades out as she makes her way to the two men.

Scene 3 – Barry's pub

Mary is minding the bar.

MARY: Moll, stay up there, do you hear? I've a lot of work to do in the bar.

MOLL: *(Distant)* I'll come down and help.

MARY: *(Panicked)* No! Stay up there. I'll buy you a toffee so I will if you behave.

MOLL: *(Distant)* Fine so!

The door opens. Mossie enters.

MARY: Sorry, we're closed.

MOSSIE: What?

MARY: *(Loudly)* I said, Mr. Kinsella, that we are closed.

MOSSIE: Ah, now you wouldn't be taken agin me like?

MARY: We are closed Mr. Kinsella on account of the rally. We'll be open after.

MOSSIE: Are you sure you're not just closed to me?

MARY: And why would I just be closed to you?

MOSSIE: On account of me owing your father's very good friend, Mr. Dooley, a small sum of money which he hasn't the common decency to wait for.

MARY: I know nothing about that Mr. Kinsella and I'll thank you to leave.

MOSSIE: But sure, Joseph Barry is not your real father, is he?

MARY: Mr. Kinsella -

MOSSIE: Your real father took the British coin, didn't he?

MARY: We are closed, Mr. Kinsella.

MOSSIE: I want a pint and I want it now.

MARY: Well, you'll have to go somewhere else for it.

Scuffle as Mossie grabs her by the arm, pulls her towards him.

MOSSIE: Now, I said.

MARY: *(Frightened)* Then you'll have to let go my arm, won't you?

The door opens once more and Hughes comes in.

HUGHES: I saw your mother leave and - *(Realising)* what's going on here?

MOSSIE: Nothing for you to concern yourself about. Traitor. *(To Mary)* A pint, I said.

HUGHES: Miss Barry, is everything all right?

MARY: I was just informing Mr. Kinsella that we're closed on account of the rally and he wasn't very happy about it.

MOSSIE: That's not true now, is it? You were taking against me because of a debt owed -

MARY: I was not.

HUGHES: If the place is closed, the place is closed. I think you should leave.

MOSSIE: I'm taking no orders from an RIC man.

HUGHES: You'll take my orders so you will or you'll see the inside of a cell for yourself.

MOSSIE: You and your like - your days are numbered.

HUGHES: That they may be but in the meantime, I'm the one holding the keys to the jail, so hop it.

MOSSIE: I won't forget this.

HUGHES: Neither will I. Your card is marked.

Mossie spits and leaves with a slam of the door. Beat.

HUGHES: Are you all right, a stor mo chroi?

MARY: I'm grand, so I am.

HUGHES: You're looking grand.

MARY: Just grand?

HUGHES: Beautiful so.

MARY: Just beautiful?

HUGHES: Just the most beautiful girl I ever set eyes on.

They kiss.

Scene 4 - Maynooth street. Rally as before.

PADDY: Domhnall UaBuachalla for the Council. Vote your number one for Domhnall.

JOSEPH: A vote for Domhnall is a vote for nationhood.

PADDY: A vote for Domhnall is a vote for freedom.

JOSEPH: I like that one Paddy, I may steal it off you.

PADDY: Steal away.

JOSEPH: A vote for Domhnall is a vote for freedom.

PADDY: Number one for Domhnall. Number one for - oh, hello there, Mrs. Barry. Joseph! *(More urgent)* Joseph!

BRIGID: *(Sarcasm)* After Domhnall gets us all freedom, d'you think he might give us a hand in the pub?

JOSEPH: Eh...hello...Brigid!

14

BRIGID: Don't 'hello Brigid' me. You were meant to be serving in the pub today and here you are faffing about with leaflets.

JOSEPH: Mary said 'twould be alright.

PADDY: That's right, she did now.

BRIGID: The last time I looked, Mary wasn't the one in charge.

PADDY: With all due respect now Mrs. Barry, 'tisn't you in charge either.

BRIGID: That doesn't sound very respectful, Mr. Dooley. But seeing as I'm not in charge, I'll stay about a bit and see what's what.

JOSEPH: You mind your tongue now, d'you hear me?

BRIGID: If I want a say, I'll have my say.

Teresa arrives up. A taciturn woman, speaks when necessary.

TERESA: Mrs. Barry.

BRIGID: Teresa.

PADDY: Vote UaBuachalla for nationhood, Teresa. He's your only man.

TERESA: I thought I could vote for more than one person now with this new voting system.

PADDY: Well, that's true certainly, but sure why would you want to?

TERESA: Maybe I want to vote for the other Sinn Fein fellow as well?

BRIGID: Maybe she wants to vote for a home ruler.

PADDY: Ah now…

JOSEPH: Brigid!

TERESA: Maybe I want to vote for all of them.

PADDY: Well … then you can.

TERESA: And that's what proportional representation means, isn't that right?

PADDY: You seem very well informed for a woman. We'll be explaining it all in the rally.

TERESA: I'll look forward to that. Good day.

She leaves.

PADDY: That woman could suck the joy from the Second Coming.

JOSEPH: Aye. So, you're well up on this new voting system then?

PADDY: I'll be honest, I haven't much of a clue about it. It's just the Brits, trying to complicate things as usual.

BRIGID: I'm sure saying that will make it crystal clear when you're explaining it, Mr. Dooley.

JOSEPH: Brigid! For God's sake… oh, here's the man of the hour. Up you go, Paddy and introduce him.

The band strikes up again as the cheering increases. Fade.

Scene 5 - Barry's pub

We hear the muffled sound of the band from outside.

MARY: I wish we could stay here forever.

HUGHES: In a pub? With a rally going on outside and people queuing up to have a go at me and a man who wants to get served a pint and can't?

MARY: *(Laughing)* Stay here with you, you fool.

HUGHES: Aye, it's nice, isn't it?

MARY: It is. 'twas a lovely day in Dublin, we had, wasn't it?

HUGHES: Aye. And did no one suspect?

MARY: No, though my mother kept asking me questions about Cissy and how did Cissy like Dublin and what did Cissy buy. *(Pause)* What?

HUGHES: I don't like you lying on account of me.

MARY: Then I'll tell them the truth.

HUGHES: No. *(Beat)* They're tarring and feathering girls down in Cork for being with crown forces.

MARY: Those girls are with the Tans. You're an Irishman.

HUGHES: I'm doing the same job.

MARY: You are keeping order. You're one of our own.

HUGHES: Then why will no one serve us in the shops? Or deliver our post? Or let their daughters go out with us?

MARY: It's not as bad as that.

HUGHES: It's worse. One of our lads walked into UaBuachalla's yesterday, years they know him. He wanted a half pound of butter for the barracks and everyone in the place turned their backs on him.

MARY: Half a pound of butter is it? I can give you half a pound of butter.

HUGHES: Mary, you know that's not the point I'm making.

MARY: I know that this country is full of fools that go about making targets of innocent people.

HUGHES: I'm not innocent. I choose to do this job. But I don't want you being one of those targets.

MARY: I won't.

HUGHES: You don't know that.

MARY: And neither do you. *(Beat)* I'm disappointed with you, Constable Hughes. I see what you're at. You had your way with me and now you want to be rid of me.

HUGHES: It isn't like that and you know it.

MARY: I know no such thing. *(Chair scrapes back as she stands)* Now, if you'll excuse me, I've work to be getting on with. You can leave.

HUGHES: Aw now, Mary….

MARY: I said 'go'

HUGHES: I won't. I'd be remiss in my duties if I didn't wait to be sure that that Mossie character isn't coming back

MARY: Suit yourself.

She takes up the sweeping brush and begins sweeping. Fade.

Scene 6 - Maynooth street. Rally.

The band plays out, we hear Paddy call out over the crowd sounds.

PADDY: …Gaelic League, he's a staunch supporter of our native language. Those of you familiar with this man will know that his love of the cupla focail has led to him being prosecuted by the crown forces and those in league with the crown forces. *(Booing)* That's right, Irishmen doing England's bidding. In 1916, this man led fourteen other brave souls into Dublin to fight for a free Ireland, he was imprisoned in the most terrible conditions, but his spirit remained unbowed. Now, with your help, he hopes to lead, not fourteen men, but the whole of Kildare into a free Ireland. Ladies and gentlemen, I give you Domhnall UaBuachalla. *(Cheering, clapping)*

UABUACHALLA: Go raibh mile maith agat, Padraig. Go raibh mile maith againn. The fact that so many of you are here today can only mean one thing - Victory. Not just for me but for you. I am not doing this for personal gain but for the gain of every citizen of this land, I am doing it for the same reasons the men of '98 and '16 did it. Freedom. The great question we must ask ourselves is, do we want to be a nation or a province? *(Referencing the Union Jack)* Do we want to be forced to live under that flag?

EOIN: No mister, down with the English.

COLM: We'll tear the flag down for you, mister.

Speech fades as the action moves to the flagpole.

UABUACHALLA: Do we want Irishmen enforcing British law under the mane of that flag? I said in 1916, the RIC do not count with us anymore.

We will have our land back, we will have our laws back. And we will do it from Ireland. *(More cheering)* The British fought in 1914 for the small nations. What about our small nation? I want to say to Mr. Home Ruler O'Connor, never trust an Englishman! *(Continues underneath the following action)*

DWYER: Boys! Come on now boys!

EOIN: What mister?

DWYER: Leave the flag alone now, there's a grand lad.

COLM: We are grand lads, you're the traitor.

STIFF: *(English accent)* Now, now, no need for that.

EOIN: Why don't you go back to that horrible place you came from and leave us be?

DWYER: Do you want a skelp about the ear? Do you?

EOIN: Ow! Let me go! Let me go!

EOIN: You leave my friend alone! You're a traitor! Turncoat!

BRIGID: That's enough now, you cheeky brat. This man is only trying to do his job.

COLM: And you're a traitor too, sticking up for him.

Boy yowls.

BRIGID: I'll kick you so far up your backside, you won't sit for a week.

Slap. Boy yowls.

DWYER: Let's all calm down, now.

UABUACHALLA: *(Distant)* What's going on down there?

BRIGID: More wanton destruction at your command. Are you happy?

JOSEPH: *(Distant but grows closer)* Brigid! What are you doing!

BRIGID: You two children should be ashamed. Talking to an officer like that. Talking to me like that. Where is your respect? *(To the crowd)* And well may you all watch. This is not some sort of a game. Lives will be lost. And I know all about that.

Jeering.

JOSEPH: Let the lad go, Brigid. Now. *(To boys)* Off with you boys, home now. *(The boys run. Beat)* You best get off home too Brigid.

BRIGID: And do what? Work in your pub, like you are? I'll stay here, thank you very much.

JOSEPH: Well, don't you go making a show of me. *(To Domhnall)* It's all under control, Domhnall.

UABUACHALLA: Thank you, Joseph. And thank you, youngsters, your day will come! Now, I'll hand you back to Mr. Dooley to explain this new voting system to you all. Mr. Dooley.

Clapping.

PADDY: Right … eh … Go raibh mait agat. Well, now, Proportional Representation. What a mouthful, ey? This means that, eh, your vote will get represented proportionally. For instance, on your voting card, there will be nine candidates and, if you like, you can vote for them all, in order of your preference. So, for instance, number one, which is the top vote will go to Domhnall and number two for Thomas Harris because he's a Sinn Fein man too and three for whoever you want or you might just stop at number two. It's up to you. Do you get me?

TERESA: But when the votes are counted out? What happens then?

PADDY: When the votes are counted all the number ones are put together and if you reach the quota you'll get elected. But if not -

TERESA: And who decides the quota?

PADDY: Who decides it?

TERESA: I heard it was decided by the number of votes cast divided by the number of seats plus one and then add one to your answer.

PADDY: What?

TERESA: And if a candidate has more votes than they need, how do you decide which of their votes is used as surplus?

PADDY: What?

TERESA: Is it true that you go through all the votes of that person and get the percentage for the other candidates and then determine how much of the surplus this percentage is and then -

PADDY: Do you want to get up here or something?

TERESA: I'm only asking a few questions.

MOSSIE: *(In distance)* Out of my way there. I'm on urgent business. Out of my way.

TERESA: I'm only asking a few questions.

PADDY: And if you give me time to think, I'll answer them. Now, on your ballot paper there will be nine candidates. You can -

TERESA: What I'm asking is what happens after I cast my vote? I'm not just going to *(She is pushed sideways by Mossie)* Watch it.

MOSSIE: *(Ignoring Teresa)* Hey. Tomas, Tomas Barry, have I got something to tell you!

19

Scene 7 - Barry's pub.

As before, muted crowd sounds. Mary is sweeping the floor.

HUGHES: Can I not help you with the sweeping? *(Beat)* Are you just going to pretend I'm not here? Jesus Christ, Mary, don't you know that if the country wasn't exploding the way it is, I'd be hounding you day and night to be with me.

MARY: Hounding me, is it?

HUGHES: Yes. And I'd be saying to you that when I get promoted to maybe Sergeant, that I will marry you.

MARY: And I'd be saying we hardly know each other.

HUGHES: And I'd be saying, I feel like I know you forever.

MARY: And I'd be saying you can't just tell a girl you're going to marry her, you have to ask her.

HUGHES: And I'd get down on my knees *(He kneels)* like this and I'd say 'will you marry me?'

MARY: And I'd say, I have to think about it because I'm not sure I want to be with a man who's scared to be with me in the middle of all this trouble.

HUGHES: And I'd say, the only thing I'm scared of is something happening to you Mary. The only thing I care about is you.

MARY: You care about your job.

HUGHES: Yes, I do.

MARY: And your family in Wolfhill, you care about them.

HUGHES: Yes.

MARY: And your dog you had on the farm, you cared about -

HUGHES: Stop making fun, Mary. It's you I care about most of all.

MARY: Well, then I'd probably say 'yes', I will marry you. *(Beat)* If you were asking …

HUGHES: I'd like nothing better, but … I'd worry, Mary. I'd never forgive meself if -

MARY: You can't go about forgiving yourself, not without taking holy orders. *(They share a laugh)* It'll all be grand, you'll see.

The door is shoved in. It's Mossie with Tomas.

MOSSIE: I told you, thrun me out of your pub, he did, and your sister wouldn't serve me.

MARY: You threatened me, Mr. Kinsella, caught me by the arm and this Constable was only trying to help.

TOMAS: We don't need help from the likes of him, Mary and you'd do well to remember it. Out with you.

MARY: Tomas!

TOMAS: Out!

HUGHES: I'm on my way. Are you sure you're all right, Miss Barry?

MARY: I am Constable, thank you, but I still can't serve you that half pound of butter.

HUGHES: Grand, miss.

Footsteps as he makes his way out.

TOMAS: Don't come back, empire lover.

The door closes after Hughes.

MOSSIE: *(To Tomas)* Well done, you. Well done. Now, I'd like -

TOMAS: Did you threaten my sister?

MOSSIE: She wouldn't serve me and -

TOMAS: Then neither will I. Get out! *(Sound of scuffle, the door opens again and Mossie is thrown onto the street)* Out!

MOSSIE: *(Distant)* You'll rue the day. You'll rue –

The door is slammed closed on him.

END OF EPISODE

EPISODE 3 – WOMENS GROUP MEETING, JUNE 1920

Scene 1 - Maynooth Main Street

Street sounds – horses and carts, footsteps, chatting etc.

COLGAN: It's a chance for us to show what we're made of. Is your brother up to it?

SEAN: He is Pat. We won't let you down.

COLGAN: See that you don't.

VOICEOVER: Fractured – a family, a nation, a dream.

Scene 2 – Barry's Parlour

Sound of Brigid placing cups, saucers and cutlery on the table.

BRIGID: Mary! Can you bring in the good milk jug? And those nice biscuits that Auntie Nora sent from England?

More sounds of laying the table.

BRIGID: Mary! For the love of God, they'll be here soon.

TOMAS: Is this the one you mean Mammy?

BRIGID: Does that look like a good milk jug to you Tomas?

TOMAS: Emmm…

BRIGID: Oh for Heaven's sake! Do I have to do everything myself. Mary!

She exits. Sound of Tomas eating a piece of the cake. Brigid's voice comes from the kitchen, getting louder as she re-renters the room.

BRIGID: Get your hands off that cake Tomas Barry! It's for the visitors. And where are those nice biscuits that Auntie Nora sent?

Sean enters.

SEAN: Did somebody mention biscuits?

BRIGID: Sean! Get out of my good room. You'll have oil everywhere. Your dinner's on the stove. We ate early today because of my meeting.

SEAN: What meeting?

BRIGID: Does nobody pay any attention to me at all around here? My ladies meeting.

SEAN: Ah yes. The housecoat gang.

BRIGID: What? Go on away with you. Housecoat gang indeed. *(She laughs, despite herself)* Your sister is going to be a member of this housecoat gang, I'll have you know. Where is she anyway? I told her seven on the dot.

TOMAS: I eh..think she went out earlier.

BRIGID: Out? What do you mean, out? Where's she gone?

TOMAS: There was…some emergency with Cissy, I think.

SEAN: That's right! She got a ladder in her stockings, didn't she? It was all over the local papers.

BRIGID: The little rip. I'll murder her, so I will.

SEAN: I'd offer to climb up and repair it myself -

BRIGID: There'll be nobody here. It's going to be disaster.

SEAN: - but I believe Donnacha Kilbride is the only man for that job!

TOMAS: Donnacha Kilbride? Cousin Donnacha?

SEAN: The very man.

TOMAS: Holy God. Auntie Anne won't be impressed with that.

Anne Kilbride enters.

ANNE: Auntie Anne won't be impressed with what?

BRIGID: Anne – you're here! Right on time. I was worried you wouldn't make it.

ANNE: What am I not going to be impressed with Tomas?

TOMAS: Em…the biscuits.

ANNE: I beg your pardon?

TOMAS: The nice biscuits that Auntie Nora sent from England.

ANNE / BRIGID: Yes…

TOMAS: We .. eh .. we used them as a raffle prize for Domhnall UaBuachalla's election fund. Sorry Mammy.

BRIGID: Oh for the love of God. Can I have nothing at all in this house?

SEAN: Ah you can have a big hug Mammy. A big hug from the handsomest, oiliest railway worker in North Kildare.

BRIGID: Go on out of that! It's not much of a railway worker that's on strike half the time. Get out of here the pair of you.

SEAN: How about you Auntie Anne? I bet I can give Uncle Denis a run for his money!

ANNE: Please!

BRIGID: Sean!

SEAN: Alright! I'm going. Come on Tomas. The Housecoat Gang is in session. No men allowed! Mmmm. Nice cake Mammy!

Sean plants a kiss on both women's cheeks before leaving. He laughs.

23

ANNE: Sean! That's highly inappropriate!

BRIGID: God I'm terrible sorry Anne.

ANNE: Yes…well. I'm not one to criticise – you know that Brigid. But really. That lad needs a firm hand.

BRIGID: His heart's in the right place.

ANNE: Tomas now, he's a good lad. But then, he's a real Barry isn't he?

Scene 3 – Barry's pub.

SEAN: We're in Tomas! We're on duty for the elections.

TOMAS: The elections? Next week?

SEAN: Just got word from Colgan. We're to report to the polling station at 10. Full uniform.

TOMAS: What polling station? Not Maynooth?

SEAN: What's wrong with…? Oh right.

TOMAS: Mammy'll kill us. Ask for Naas would ye?

SEAN: I can't just go telling Colgan…

Door opens. Maggie enters.

MAGGIE: Yoo hoo! Only me boys! Is your mammy inside?

SEAN: Yes Mrs. O'Donoghue. Go on through.

MAGGIE: Bless us and save us but that's fierce wind out there. June how are ye!

Sound of her footsteps exiting into parlour.

SEAN: We've only just signed up. I can't be asking for favours already.

TOMAS: But…

Door opens again. Teresa enters. Footsteps walk past the boys.

SEAN: We'll get what we're given and just deal with the consequences. Hello Teresa!

TOMAS: I'll ask Colgan myself.

SEAN: You can't do that.

TOMAS: Watch me.

Scene 4 – Barry's parlour

MAGGIE: Couldn't eat his breakfast, spent half an hour on the toilet…

TERESA: Hello everyone. I'm five minutes late. Couldn't be helped. What have I missed?

MAGGIE: I was just telling the girls about Father Dempsey…

BRIGID: You haven't missed anything Teresa. We haven't started yet. Will you have a cup of tea?

TERESA: No thank you. *(Sound of chair)* When are we going to start?

BRIGID: Soon. We're just waiting on a few others. *(Silence)* Will you have cake Teresa?

TERESA: No.

Further silence, becoming more awkward.

BRIGID: Anne?

ANNE: What?

BRIGID: Cake?

ANNE: Oh Good Lord no! We were in the Shelbourne this afternoon you know. A little treat. Donnacha couldn't come. Very busy with his studies. My son. Doing Law you know Teresa. UCD. *(No response)* Yes, well. The Shelbourne was packed. Their hor d'oeuvres are absolutely delicious. Mr. Kilbride and I would thoroughly recommend them.

MAGGIE: Their what?

ANNE: Hor d'oeuvres Mrs. O'Donoghue. Little mini-appetisers.

MAGGIE: Appetisers?

ANNE: Yes. Like a snack. You eat it before your meal.

MAGGIE: Why in God's name would you eat a snack before your meal? Sure that would ruin your appetite altogether. The Father wouldn't have any of that nonsense. Eats like a horse so he does. Just last week - now don't tell anyone this – but…

TERESA: Who are we waiting on Brigid?

BRIGID: Oh. Yes. Let me see. Mrs. Delaney from the haberdashery.

MAGGIE: Oh she won't be here. God no. Wasn't she in Phelan's this morning getting medicine for Donal Og? He has the runs.

TERESA: Who else?

BRIGID: Mrs. Dwyer.

ANNE: Betty Dwyer?

BRIGID: Yes

ANNE: You can't ask her.

BRIGID: Why not?

ANNE: Oh for goodness sake Brigid. You know why not.

BRIGID: No I don't.

ANNE: Her husband is RIC.

BRIGID: And what's that got to do with anything? Wasn't I in school with Tom Dwyer. He's a gentleman.

ANNE: He's taking the English coin.

BRIGID: There's worse things in this world than taking the English coin.

ANNE: Ah now Brigid you would say that.

TERESA: Who else?

BRIGID: Pardon?

TERESA: Who else is coming?

BRIGID: Oh...Mrs. O'Sullivan.

ANNE: Poor Brid?

BRIGID: Yes. *(She stresses the name)* Mrs. O'Sullivan. I think I hear her now.

ANNE: God help us. As long as she doesn't bring that workhouse brat along with her.

BRIGID: Anne! He's only a child. He's had a terrible time. Give him a chance, will you.

ANNE: She'll rue the day, mark my words.

Poor Brid enters.

POOR BRID: Come on love. We won't be long. And then we'll go home to Daddy. Daddy's looking forward to seeing you.

ANNE: Daddy! Did you ever hear such nonsense?

POOR BRID: Hello Mrs. Barry. Hello everyone. Sorry we're late. Come on in pet. Say hello to everyone. *(Silence)*

BRIGID: Hello Colm! Would you like to go upstairs and play with Molly? *(Silence)* Would you like some cake is it? Is that okay with Mammy?

ANNE: Mammy!

POOR BRID: Would you like some cake pet?

Sound of Colm grabbing the cake, eating noisily and burping.

ANNE: *(Under her breath)* Little savage.

POOR BRID: Say thank you Colm. *(Silence)*

26

BRIGID: Would you like to go upstairs love? Me and your mammy and all these ladies are just going to have a little chat. My little girl would love to play with you.

POOR BRID: Or you could stay here sweetheart. Whatever you want. What would you like to do?

TERESA: Oh for Christ's sake! *(Stunned silence)* If you want to go, go. If you want to stay, stay.

We hear Colm's footsteps leaving the room and the door closing.

POOR BRID: Teresa – how did you…

TERESA: Can we get on with the meeting now?

Scene 5 – Maynooth main street

Street sounds. Voices, horses and carts going by, footsteps, laughter.

COLGAN: I gave you orders to report to Maynooth polling station next week. What part of that have you a problem with?

TOMAS: Mr. Colgan, sir – it's just, me and my brother, we're well known here, and…

COLGAN: If you've a problem following orders, then you shouldn't be in the Volunteers.

SEAN: We've no problem Pat. No problem at all. My brother…he's…well – young.

COLGAN: *(With menace)* 10am. Maynooth Poling Station.

Sound of Colgan leaving.

SEAN: 10am Pat. We'll be there.

TOMAS: But…

Sean grabs Tomas and gives him a belt. Tomas curses.

Scene 6 – Barry's parlour

Sounds of the women chatting. Anne bangs the table with a spoon.

ANNE: Order! Order!

MAGGIE: Hor d'oeuvres? Ah now come on Mrs. Kilbride. You're not in the Shelbourne Hotel now. You can't expect Mrs. Barry to be providing you with hor d'oeuvres. She's already made us a lovely sponge cake.

ANNE: For goodness sake. I'm calling this meeting to order. I'm not looking for hor d'oeuvres. Oh you weren't here Mrs. O'Sullivan. Hor d'oeuvres are little mini appetisers. I had them…

TERESA: *(Getting very frustrated)* The meeting?

BRIGID: Yes. Sorry Teresa. We were just saying Mrs. O'Sullivan that some people can't make it today.

MAGGIE: Is Mary not joining us?

BRIGID: No. She had an appointment.

ANNE: An appointment it is? Very important appointment by the cut of her jib walking down Main Street earlier.

BRIGID: We're just waiting on Mrs. Dwyer now.

POOR BRID: Oh she won't be here. With the good wind and everything she decided to do her laundry today instead of tomorrow.

MAGGIE: I should have done that. The Father's sheets are in a terrible state.

BRIGID: Laundry?

POOR BRID: Yes, she told me..

ANNE: Objection! Heresy!

POOR BRID: What?

ANNE: Heresy!

BRIGID: Heresy? What do you mean, heresy?

ANNE: You can't provide as evidence something that someone else has said. It's called heresy. It's won't stand up in a court of law.

POOR BRID: But she told me to tell you...

ANNE: Objection! Mrs. O'Sullivan, I don't think you understand. Mrs. Dwyer has to give us this information herself.

POOR BRID: But she can't. She's not here.

ANNE: Well then I'm afraid that what she said is inadmissible. It's heresy. Not a bit surprised really. Given that her husband is RIC.

MAGGIE: Lord save us. Heresy is a terrible thing altogether. The Father is always giving out about it.

BRIGID: Anne, I really don't think...

ANNE: I do believe it's my son that's studying Law in UCD at the moment Brigid. I think I may have a little more knowledge of legal matters than anyone else here present, ad nauseum, ecetera.

Scene 7 – Barry's pub

Sound of Sean and Tomas entering the pub.

SEAN: Jesus, you're after making a right show of us and no mistake. Didn't I tell you…

TOMAS: You didn't have to say I was young.

SEAN: What should I have said huh? That you're afraid of what your mammy might say?

TOMAS: I'm not joking Sean. I'd rather take my chances with the Tans.

SEAN: If I had my way right now, I'd hand you over to them. Eejit!

Sound of Sean walking away.

Scene 8 – Barry's parlour

Sounds of the women chatting. A chair is pushed back.

TERESA: Look. I've had enough with the lot of you. I'm going.

BRIGID: Teresa, please. Stay. I know we're after delaying you but I promise this won't take long. I could really do with your help, so I could.

Pause. Sound of Teresa's chair moving again.

BRIGID: Thanks Teresa. Thanks to all of you. I just – I had this idea. It might not be..women like us – with skills – there's so much we can do. There's other women out there in desperate situations. Sick children, husbands locked up, strikes, women and children who have been abandoned…

MAGGIE: Infidelity! Puts heresy into the ha'penny place, according to Father Dempsey. Those men should be strung up, so they should!

Awkward silence. Sharp intake of breath from Anne.

BRIGID: I'd like to set up a group of women who are prepared to help other women. All women. Forget about politics. This is non-political. Non-judgemental. Politics causes nothing but trouble. It's just women. Women helping women.

TERESA: I can help with the broken windows.

BRIGID: Oh Teresa I knew you would. You run that hardware shop single handed. And look…I've been keeping the books in this place for years. I know how to save a bob or two. I can help the women with money, give advice… And Mrs. O' Sullivan, I thought you might be able to organise a sale of work. Raise money for food parcels, clothes, whatever we need.

MAGGIE: I'll talk to the Father about getting the parish hall for the sale of work. Who knows? Might even sweet talk him into donating a few bob from the Sunday collection to the cause.

BRIGID: I knew I could count on you all.

ANNE: I'll take care of the legal side of things.

BRIGID: The legal side of things?

ANNE: Yes. It's very important to have good legal advice in times of hardship. I'll be there to offer wise counsel – don't worry, it'll all be completely sub judas.

MAGGIE: Sub judas?

ANNE: It's a legal term Mrs. O'Donoghue. It means private and confidential.

BRIGID: Well…maybe you can ask Donnacha to help you.

ANNE: Oh for goodness sake. I've been reading his legal books all year. I'm quite capable of making judicial reviews. Dominium. De Facto. *(Pause)* Look, I'll pay a visit to the Volunteer Courts next month. Get some experience. It'll be absolutely fine.

BRIGID: *(Sighs, unsure)* Right. Thank you Anne. I thought we could also run courses for women. We might run one on first aid next month.

MAGGIE: First aid? Why first aid?

BRIGID: Well…it's important isn't it? All the children who were cut by glass in the explosions last month? There's women with children out there who could be sick, and they might not know. Maybe they can't spot the signs. The children could be in pain, and they just think they're hungry or something. They might have breathing problems and not know…

There's a sympathetic silence.

MAGGIE: I think that's a great idea Mrs. Barry.

Silence for a moment.

TERESA: I'm going.

BRIGID: Bye Teresa! Thanks for coming.

Teresa exits.

MAGGIE: Well…she's a barrel of laughs.

BRIGID: She'll get the job done, that's all that matters.

There is a roar from upstairs. The sound of Moll crying.

MOLL: *(From upstairs)* Give that back! You're a bold boy so you are. I'm telling my Mammy on you. Mammy!!!

POOR BRID: Oh God! Colm love! I'll go Brigid. What's the matter pet?

Sounds of her leaving.

ANNE: Rotten seed. Bad blood in that lad, no doubt about it. I'll be off Brigid, before he sets fire to the place.

MAGGIE: Me too Mrs. Barry. The Father's undies won't wash themselves!

Sounds of the women exiting. Poor Brid enters with Colm.

POOR BRID: You need to share love. *(To Brigid)* He took her toy. Wouldn't give it back. I don't think she'll be playing with him again too soon.

BRIGID: Give it time love. He'll come round.

POOR BRID: Con bought a football for him last week. He just looked at it and walked away. Didn't know what to do with it.

BRIGID: He's not used to kindness Brid.

POOR BRID: I wasn't too used to it myself, until you took me in.

BRIGID: Ah go on out of that.

POOR BRID: It's true. I didn't know what a family was until I came to work for you Mrs. Barry. I don't know what I was thinking. I can't be a mother. I've no idea what to do.

BRIGID: Now you listen here to me Brid O'Sullivan. We would have been lost without you in this family over the years. When poor Joseph Junior passed away – Lord have mercy on his soul – you were mother and father to my children. Mother and father. I sometimes think young Tomas..I was…lost..for a long time Brid.

Silence. She pulls herself together.

BRIGID: That young lad is the luckiest child in Maynooth! Isn't that right Colm? Aren't you a lucky boy? And I'd say you'll feel even luckier with another slice of cake inside you! Go on son. Enjoy!

Sounds of the women laughing as Colm noisily eats another slice of cake.

END OF EPISODE

EPISODE 4 – VOTING DAY, JUNE 1920

Scene 1 – Sean and Thomas' bedroom

Sound effects of Sean getting dressed.

SEAN: Come on Tomas. We're to be there in ten minutes! Would ye get up!

TOMAS: Oh God Sean. I think I'm going to be sick.

SEAN: Get your arse out of bed and into that uniform or I swear to God I'll tell Lizzie O'Neill you're mad about…

BRIGID: *(From downstairs)* Sean! Tomas! I'm going off to vote now. Someone needs to look after the shop!

SEAN: Yes Mammy.

TOMAS: Can we not just wait until she gets back. We'll say we got delayed.

SEAN: How are ye ever going to fight for your country when you can't stand up to your own mother!

VOICEOVER: Fractured – a family, a nation, a dream. Local elections. Friday, June 4th 1920.

Scene 2 – Outside polling station

Sounds of excited crowds, chattering, etc. The supporters speak over the noise.

SUPPORTER 1: Take a leaflet will ye? Tom Harris, Sinn Fein. He's a great fella. Been my neighbour for twenty years. Give him a vote. Honest, loyal – marched up to the GPO in 1916.

SUPPORTER 2: Michael Fitzsimons. Best man for the job in my opinion. A strong Independent voice is essential, especially in these times – you know yourselves.

SUPPORTER 3: I'm canvassing for JJ Flanagan from Labour. He's a popular man – favourite to top the poll today they say. But look, every vote counts, and I promise yours won't be wasted if you give it to JJ.

UABUACHALLA: Domhnall UaBuachalla, Sinn Fein. The local man, as they say! If you want Maynooth represented at county level, then I'm the man for the job.

SUPPORTER 1: Harder times are coming and we need to make sure the agricultural sector is supported at local level. Tom Harris is your only man!

UABUACHALLA: You're going to get two sheets of paper in there. One is for the County Council and the other one is for the Urban District

Council. So if it's your first time to vote you get to do it twice! Just put me in at number one and don't worry about anything else!

SUPPORTER 3: We need different voices in there. Sinn Fein is taking over. The working man has to be represented. And JJ is the man for that job.

Scene 3 – Inside polling station

Murmur of people talking. Shuffling of papers. Footsteps.

VOLUNTEER LEADER: Ladies and gents! Ladies and gents. The polling station is open now. If you'd like to make your way through these doors – that's it. Line up just over here – very good folks. Lovely to see ye all. If you all proceed in an orderly fashion towards Mrs. O'Donoghue over here. She'll take your polling cards and get ye all organised. Our polling booths are over there. If anyone has any difficulty with reading just make yourself known to me and I'll do everything I can to assist.

MARGARET: Hey Mister! What are ye Volunteers doing here?

VOLUNTEER LEADER: Security madam.

MARGARET: Security? Are ye jokin' me? Sure isn't it youse fellas who blew up the Town Hall? What kind of security is that?

VOLUNTEER LEADER: Now madam. Let's not be casting aspersions.

MARGARET: I'll cast any aspersions I want. Here, Mrs. O' Donoghue. Give me those papers and let's get this over with.

MAGGIE: Here ye go, love. How's Josie? Did you manage to get rid of her head lice? Oh those nits are a terrible curse.

She walks away, embarrassed. Maggie continues to shout after her.

MAGGIE: You tell her from me that I had them for six months – six months – when my three were small. Listerine was the only thing that worked, tell her – and those combs. I have one I can give her – don't be wasting money on one now. As good as new. I'll drop it over when I'm finished up here. Next please!

Sound of whispering.

MAGGIE: Don't worry about that in the slightest Sheila. We'll get that sorted for you. And all in the strictest confidentiality. (*Shouting*) Mr. O'Brien! Sheila here can't read or write! Can you help her with her voting?

VOLUNTEER LEADER: Mrs. O'Donoghue! Please. Discretion! Discretion! Yes Mrs ...O'Rourke. I'd be delighted to help. This way please.

Enter Sean and Tomas, dressed in their Volunteer uniforms.

VOLUNTEER LEADER: Men! What time do you call this? You're late. Man the ballot boxes immediately.

SEAN: Sorry Sergeant.

TOMAS: Yes sir…it's just…we're very well known here.

VOLUNTEER LEADER: All the better lads. Build up our profile. We're being put in a position of serious trust today. We have to be professional at all times. Don't let me down.

MAGGIE: Tomas! Sean! Don't ye look very handsome in your new uniforms? And to think I remember changing your dirty nappies like it was yesterday! When did ye join the Volunteers? I can't believe your mother never told me! I'm going to have words with her when she comes in later!

TOMAS: Oh God. Who put Mrs. O'Donoghue in here? It'll be all over town in ten minutes.

SEAN: Mammy was going to find out sooner or later.

TOMAS: She'll kill us.

SEAN: Just keep your head down. Turn your back. There's a lot of people here. She might not notice. We'll break the news to her later, in private.

TOMAS: Yeah. Hopefully no one else will notice us.

Fade to another area in the room.

SHEILA: I might not be able to read but I'm not a complete eejit, ye know!

VOLUNTEER LEADER: But Madam…I…

SHEILA: Who's my number five? Number five? Every gobshite in the country knows you only get one vote. I'm not staying here to be made a fool of. I'll be telling Domhnall UaBuachalla about you!

Sound of her footsteps marching out.

MAGGIE: Discretion Mr. O' Brien…discretion. Oh there's another vote. Good man Jim. I wouldn't have taken you for a Labour man. JJ Flanagan? He wouldn't be my first preference now. Or the Father's, come to think of it. I'll say no more. Discretion…discretion.

Anne Kilbride enters.

MAGGIE: Woohoo! Mrs. Kilbride! Over here! There's no queue over here.

ANNE: Mrs. O'Donoghue. I didn't expect to see you here.

MAGGIE: Well, they need people they can trust to do this job you know. Very responsible. The Father put my name forward. 'Off you go Mrs. O'Donoghue", says he. 'Your country needs you more than I do.'

ANNE: How very self-sacrificing of him.

MAGGIE: He models himself on the life of Our Lord, doesn't he? Always making sacrifices that man. Beggoden, it's no wonder his trousers are falling down around his arse.

ANNE: My voting papers please.

MAGGIE: Here you go Mrs. Kilbride. Between you and me now there's no point voting for yer man Lawler. Nobody's voting for him. You'll be wasting your time. O'Connor is doing well at the moment, but then all the farmers have been in. From what I've seen so far, Domhnall UaBuachalla has it sewn up. He's a good bet.

ANNE: Thank you Mrs. O'Donoghue. Good to see the secret ballot in operation.

MAGGIE: Discretion Mrs. Kilbride…discretion. Next please!

Fade to another area in the room.

MARY: Janey Mac, it's black in here.

BRIGID: Mary, what are you talking about?

MARY: Oh, that's what they all say in Dublin Mammy. 'Janey Mac'. I kept hearing it when I went up there the other day with……Cissy.

BRIGID: Yes, well you're not in Dublin now.

MARY: Who are ye going to vote for Mammy? That engine driver fellow is a real smasher. He looks lovely in his photo. Will ye vote for him? I'd love to see him getting in. Do ye think Sean knows him, with him working on the railways and all?

BRIGID: I've no idea Mary. You know love, there's so much more to life than finding a man…

Fade to another area in the room. Anne has finished casting her vote and walks towards the ballot box where Sean is standing with his back to her.

ANNE: Is this where I put my vote? *(No response)* Excuse me young man. Is this where I put my vote? Could you please turn around and speak to me? *(Silence again)* Oh for goodness sake. Young people these days. Is it too much to request a verbal reply? Or have all Irish Volunteers recently taken a vow of silence? You weren't too silent last month when you blew up half the town.

VOLUNTEER LEADER: Is there a problem Madam?

ANNE: I'm simply asking this young man if this is the correct location for my vote, and he seems unable to answer.

VOLUNTEER LEADER: Apologies Madam. Yes that is the correct place.

Anne posts her vote and turns to leave. The Leader speaks to Sean and Tomas.

VOLUNTEER LEADER: For Christ's sake Sean and Tomas. Turn around and face the crowd. You've got one job to do. Act professional.

Fade to another area in the room.

ANNE: Hello Brigid. What are you doing here Mary?

BRIGID: Hello Anne

MARY: Hello Auntie Anne. I just came to see what all the fuss is about. I'd love to have a vote. I'd vote for that smasher railway man.

ANNE: Good God. Just as well you have to wait until you're 30. And 21 is far too young for men, in my opinion. Votes are wasted on the young. We need to get the professional classes into power. These farmers and labouring men have absolutely no idea how to run local government.

MARY: But he's gorgeous Auntie Anne. Did you not see him? I think I'll call for Cissy on the way home. Get her to come down. She'd be mad about him.

BRIGID: Mary, move up the queue there.

MARY: So who did you vote for Auntie Anne? Go on. Tell us.

ANNE: *(Tapping her nose)* Jurisprudence Mary my dear. Jurisprudence.

MARY: Juris who?

ANNE: *(Anne sighs)* Oh Brigid. Just to let you know. I'll be going along to the Volunteer Court next week. Brush up on my legal expertise. For the Women's Group. I expect to be able to dispense legal advice in the coming weeks. Ipso facto. Dictum.

BRIGID: Great – thanks Anne. We might get on with that First Aid course in the meantime.

ANNE: Hmmm. I'd seek an adjournment on that one if I were you. Habeas corpus Brigid. Let the buyer beware!

She exits.

VOLUNTEER LEADER: Apologies for the wait ladies. If you'd like to go to that table over there, we'll ensure you get your vote cast in no time.

MARY: Who are those fellows mister?

VOLUNTEER LEADER: What fellows young lady?

MARY: Those fellows over at the ballot boxes. Are they Volunteers too?

VOLUNTEER LEADER: Yes Miss, they are. By request of the Government.

BRIGID: And what's wrong with the RIC? They've provided a perfectly good service for years.

VOLUNTEER LEADER: True Madam. Changing times though. Given all the troubles around the country, it was thought that our lads would be better able to provide the security we need on a day like today.

BRIGID: Better security than the RIC? Thugs the lot of ye. It's a sad day when gangsters and layabouts are given free reign. Look at them, with their backs turned on us all. Ashamed to show their faces no doubt. Either that or just no respect for honest hardworking people. What kind of homes did they grow up in at all, with no decency or manners between the pair of them?

VOLUNTEER LEADER: I'm sorry Madam?

BRIGID: Look at your recruits for God's sake. Ashamed to even show their faces in public. If they really believe in what they're doing let them own up to it. Let's see exactly who we're dealing with here.

MARY: Mammy. This is embarrassing. Can you not just vote like everyone else.

VOLUNTEER LEADER: Christ lads. This is the third time I've had to speak to you in the space of ten minutes. What are ye doing with your backs to the ballot box? You're supposed to be protecting it. Turn around and act like the soldiers you're supposed to be.

BRIGID: Sean! Tomas! *(Silence)* Home. Now. The pair of ye.

SEAN: Mammy!

VOLUNTEER LEADER: What? No! Stay where you are men. We have a job to do.

MAGGIE: Mrs. Barry! There ye are now. Would ye look at the cut of your two fine boys in their smart uniforms. Oh if I was only twenty years younger...

BRIGID: I said home. Now.

SEAN: Just go and vote Mammy. Stop making a show of us.

BRIGID: I'm the one making the show? I'm the one making the show? I'm not the one dressed up in a ridiculous costume pretending to be a soldier.

VOLUNTEER LEADER: Can we please deal with this situation at a later stage?

SEAN: Nobody's pretending Mammy.

VOLUNTEER LEADER: Preferably in private?

SEAN: I am a soldier. Tomas is a soldier.

37

BRIGID: You've no idea what it's like to be a soldier.

SEAN: And you do?

BRIGID: I know what's it's like to love one.

SEAN: Oh for God's sake.

MARY: Sean…

VOLUNTEER LEADER: Look, we have a job to do here..

BRIGID: I know what it's like to be married to one … I know what it's like to have two children by a soldier. I know what it's like to be widowed by a soldier.

VOLUNTEER LEADER: Can we all please just get on with the voting?

MAGGIE: Yes boys. Listen to your mammy. It's very difficult to be widowed. I should know.

SEAN: That's different Mammy and you know it.

MAGGIE: It's not different at all.

BRIGID: How is it different? If your father could see…

MAGGIE: My Jack was no soldier. But he had a traumatic death none the less.

SEAN: Joseph already knows. So there.

MAGGIE: Fell off the barn on Mossie Kinsella's farm. God rest him.

BRIGID: I'm not talking about Joseph. I'm taking about your real father.

SEAN: Joseph is Tomas' real father.

BRIGID: Well he's not yours, so you should know better.

VOLUNTEER LEADER: This is getting out of control. Men – back to your station. Mrs. O'Donoghue, get on with your work. Madam, if you can't control yourself I'm going to have to ask you to leave.

SEAN: I should know better, should I Mammy? I'm not the one fighting for the enemy am I? I'm not the one selling my soul to the British Army.

MAGGIE: Ah Sean! Now there's no need..

SEAN: I'm not the one betraying my own people. I'm not the traitor!

A horrible, uneasy silence settles over the room.

BRIGID: Your father…your father was the bravest, strongest most honourable man I have ever known. He 'sold his soul' as you call it so that you and Mary could have food in your bellies and clothes on your back. So you could be educated. So you would never be forced like he was to fight in someone else's pointless war.

VOLUNTEER LEADER: Madam .. I realise you're upset but really…

SEAN: It's not pointless Mammy.

BRIGID: And what have you done with that opportunity? That life that your father wanted you to have so badly that he got killed for it. What have you done Sean? What have you done?

SEAN: Look…I'm sorry Mammy. I really am. But… my father fought for what he believed in. I'm fighting for what I believe in too. I'm only doing the same as what he did.

BRIGID: And you're going to get killed son. Just the same as he did.

VOLUNTEER LEADER: Nobody is going to get killed madam. Now if you could just…

BRIGID: And what would you know about it mister, with your fancy uniform and your shiny shoes? It's not the like of you that'll be sent to do the dirty work anyway is it? No – it'll be my two sons in the firing line, my two sons at the end of an RIC rifle, and my two sons bleeding to death in the gutter. So don't tell me that no one is going to get killed because I've heard it all before mister, from a man far better than you. It wasn't true then, and it's not true now.

TOMAS: Mammy…I'm really sorry.

MARY: Come on home Mammy. Everyone's staring at us.

TOMAS: We can't leave Mammy. We've a job to do.

MARY: This way Mammy. Please. Can we just leave?

BRIGID: I believe I'm entitled to a vote. And I'm not leaving this bloody place until I've had my say on Sinn Fein.

MAGGIE: Good woman Mrs. Barry! Here's your voting sheet. *(Sound of the voting paper being torn)* I'd say you're probably wasting your time, given the number of people that don't agree with you. But never mind!

Sound of a pencil writing.

BRIGID: Come on Mary. We're wasting our time here.

Sound of footsteps exiting. Sighs from the two boys.

END OF EPISODE

EPISODE 5 – VOLUNTEER COURT, JUNE 1920

Scene 1 - RIC Station

DWYER: You'd better get a move on, Constable Hughes.

HUGHES: Are you sure about this, Sarge?

DWYER: No, but orders are orders. Take Stiff and Perry with you in case you run into trouble.

HUGHES: These courts are legal according -

DWYER: My hands are tied. It'll take you twenty minutes to get there. Go – shut it down.

HUGHES: *(Resigned)* All right, Sarge.

VOICEOVER: Fractured – a family, a nation, a dream. June 1920. And after the success of Sinn Fein in the polls, the Volunteer courts are in full swing.

Scene 2 - Volunteer Court

PADDY: Evening, Sean. I see Mossie over there. I'll be getting justice, today, what?

SEAN: I can't comment, Paddy, I'm on duty.

PADDY: Of course, of course. When is your father arriving?

SEAN: Daddy's coming?

PADDY: Aye, to support me. Does he not know you do the Courts?

SEAN: He, eh – well…

PADDY: Sure, it'll be grand once your mother doesn't show up.

He laughs. Laughter from the other Volunteers.

SEAN: Shut up, you lot. *(Bigger laughter)* Paddy, sit down. I shouldn't really be talking to you.

PADDY: Where do I sit?

SEAN: Beside Mrs. Cahill. Her case is the first one on the list.

PADDY: What's up with her?

SEAN: Paddy, please, just sit down.

PADDY: I'll have to ask her myself so.

We hear Paddy cross and sit in beside Annie Cahill.

PADDY: *(To Annie)* Evening Ma'am.

ANNIE: Hello Mr. Dooley

PADDY: What brings you here?

ANNIE: You'll hear all when the court starts. I'm in an awful state.

PADDY: I've heard they're fair. Nothing like Irishmen giving Irishmen justice, isn't that right.

ANNIE: I hope so, Mr. Dooley, I really do.

We hear footsteps approach, it's Joseph and Anne Kilbride.

PADDY: *(Moving to make space)* Aw, Joseph, sit in here. And Mrs. Kilbride, come to support me, have you? Or are you up yourself?

ANNE K: Indeed I'm not, Mr. Dooley. Not wishing to offend anyone but washing my dirty linen in public is not my style. I'm here as an observer of the legal process. Ad infinitum.

We hear a door opening and a hush descends on the murmuring.

SEAN: Order please. This Court is now in session presided over by Mrs. Frances Murphy, Chairwoman.

Scene 3 - Road

The sound of marching. Stops.

HUGHES: Constable Stiff, can you keep up!

STIFF: *(Running to catch up)* I got a bad feeling about this. I want to go back.

HUGHES: Just do as I say and there'll be no trouble.

STIFF: I fought in the trenches, I thought coming here would be better.

HUGHES: You're lucky you're not in Cork. Now come on, get a hold of yourself. Men!

The marching begins again.

Scene 4 - Court as before

ANNIE: My husband died eight months ago. We had a small farm in Mooneycooley and as we had no children and he had no brothers or sisters or anyone nearby, I was left to run the farm. A month after my husband died, Mr. Lennon who has land bordering our farm offered to buy the land.

LENNON: And I offered a good price!

MURPHY: *(Holding a hand up to Lennon)* Mr. Lennon. Proceed Mrs. Cahill.

ANNIE: It was a good price. We agreed the sale. It was only for the land. After the land was sold, Mr. Lennon agreed that we had a week to move the cows. My brother-in-law was going to take them.

LENNON: That was more than fair.

ANNIE: Then my brother in law came to pay me for six cows …. Sure I knew my husband had seven but my brother in law insisted that he only found six. I'm not one to make trouble so I left it at that. But a week later, what do I see but my cow grazing in my old field along with Mr. Lennon's cows.

MURPHY: You're sure about this?

ANNIE: All my husband's cows had the same mark. There's no mistaking it.

LENNON: May I speak?

MURPHY: Proceed, Mr. Lennon

LENNON: I think the court will agree that a week to clear the land is more than fair. They had free access to the land for all that time. If one of their cows happened to break through the ditch onto my land, I can't be held responsible for that.

Laughter in the Court.

MURPHY: Let me clarify Mr. Lennon. Are you admitting that one of Mrs. Cahill's cows is in your possession?

LENNON: I found the cow wandering on my land after the time I gave them to clear the land.

MURPHY: It took you over a week to realise that you had gained a cow?

Laughter.

LENNON: Yes

MURPHY: And on discovering this extra cow, did it not strike you to inform Mrs. Cahill?

LENNON: I thought maybe they didn't want it or that there was something wrong with it. It was on my land so I took possession.

MURPHY: I am not a farmer Mr. Lennon but even I know that a cow is a valuable asset. Would you agree?

LENNON: Yes but …

MURPHY: And does it make sense that the owner of such an asset would just give it up … let it go?

LENNON: Well .. no … but

MURPHY: Mr. Lennon. You knowingly held on to the cow thinking you could profit at the expense of a poor vulnerable widow.

LENNON: That was not my intention.

MURPHY: Moreover, if you had shown some common decency, this is a case that should have been resolved without resort to the courts. I find for the plaintiff, Mrs. Cahill and order that the cow be returned immediately. Furthermore, I order that you will pay Mrs. Cahill the sum of £5 in compensation.

LENNON: But ..

MURPHY: I will hear no more Mr. Lennon. I will assign a Volunteer to ensure that the Court's orders are carried out.

(Lennon storms out of the Court – door opens, slams shut.

MURPHY: Mrs. Cahill. You're free to leave the court if you wish.

ANNIE: Thank you madam. *(Looking after Lennon)* I think I'll stay for a while.

MURPHY: As you wish. Next case concerns an unpaid debt. The plaintiff is Mr. Patrick Dooley and the defendant is Mr. Maurice Kinsella. Are both parties in court?

PADDY: Yes. Patrick Dooley.

MOSSIE: Mossie, I mean Maurice Kinsella.

MURPHY: And the nature of your case, Mr. Dooley?

PADDY: I've been running a general merchants business in Maynooth for the past 20 years. I'm a fair trader. If my customers were unable to pay, I'd always allow them credit. They were fair with me, I was fair with them. I had been dealing with Mossie Kinsella there for years without any trouble. At the end of last year, he owed me £100. When I went to him looking for some of the bill to be paid off, he told me that times were hard and he had no money. He never even offered to pay a small amount back.

MURPHY: Why have you waited so long to make a complaint?

PADDY: I didn't. I took a case against him in the … other court, the petty sessions and won but when the decree was handed to the Sheriff, he said it was useless for him to proceed at that time as he could not execute it

MURPHY: Were you given any reason?

PADDY: None. Then it came to my attention that Mossie here had recently given £100 to the Irish National Loan. And him saying that he had no money to pay me!

KINSELLA: Do you think I was wrong to support the national cause?

PADDY: You can do whatever you like with your money but this was money owed to me!

MURPHY: Gentlemen. Please. Mr. Kinsella.

KINSELLA: I raised that money through the sale of livestock.

PADDY: You still could have paid me something.

KINSELLA: That money went to secure the future of this country. What sort of an Irishman are you not to see that?

PADDY: I'm as good an Irishman as the next but I have to live too.

JOSEPH: How long would this country last if there were more people like you who refuse to pay their bills?

Some clapping, noises of approval.

KINSELLA: This has nothing to do with you Barry!

MURPHY: *(Banging the table)* Quiet! I'll remind you all again that this is a courtroom not a public house. *(To Joseph)* And sir, this is none of your concern.

JOSEPH: I came here to speak on behalf of Paddy Dooley.

Scene 5 - Road

The sound of marching footsteps which stop.

HUGHES: Ok, there is the hall. Curran, Perry, you go around the sides.

PERRY/CURRAN: Sir!

Running feet.

HUGHES: Stiff, with me and for God's sake, look a little less scared. Now, slowly…come in.

Sound of careful footsteps.

Scene 6 - Court

JOSEPH: I have known Paddy … Mr. Dooley here for over 20 years and a more honest man you couldn't find. It seems to me that Kinsella here is hiding behind the Republican movement as a way to avoid paying his lawful debts.

MURPHY: That's not for you to decide Mr. Barry.

KINSELLA: That's slander Barry.

JOSEPH: Well, I've had my say.

KINSELLA: I am not a wealthy man. God knows I've seen hard times like everyone. *(Muted laughter)* Neither am I a young man that can take an active role in building this nation. When I saw the call for the National Loan, I knew this was my way of supporting the cause so I sold some of my livestock.

PADDY: It sounds like you just gave the money away! *(To Murphy)* That National Loan is just that .. a loan and the money will be repaid in full with

44

5% interest on top. Where's the hardship in that? And here he is making himself look like a bloody patriot.

KINSELLA: What have you done for your country?

MURPHY: I've heard enough. Mr. Kinsella, do you deny that you owe the sum of £100 to Mr. Dooley?

KINSELLA: No .. but I'm trying to explain why I can't pay it.

MURPHY: The money is owed and must be repaid and frankly, I find it difficult to believe your reasons for not paying. You had the money at your disposal and your priority should have been to pay your debts. The National Loan is indeed a worthy cause but it's main target was towards people who could well afford to give money and not as an excuse for avoiding debt payment. Using it for this purpose shows contempt for the Republican movement.

KINSELLA: That's not what..

MURPHY: As I see it, you have two options. I can make an order to recover the money from the National Loan to repay the full debt. Or, you can pay £10 a month for ten months plus £5 in lieu of accumulated interest.

KINSELLA: That's not fair.

MURPHY: The choice is yours. *(Pause)* Mr. Kinsella?

KINSELLA: *(Hesitantly)* I'll withdraw the loan.

PADDY: Spoken like a true patriot

Laughter.

MURPHY: Very well. I'll ask you to remain in the Court until the proceedings are complete. I'll need to get further details of the loan. Sit down. Mr. Kinsella.

Kinsella, unhappy sits down.

MURPHY: Case number three involves the theft of a bicycle …

The main door bursts open, people yelp in fright.

HUGHES: These proceedings must cease immediately. This is an illegal assembly.

MURPHY: This is a court of arbitration sanctioned by Dail Eireann.

HUGHES: I have orders to close this down. I ask everyone to vacate the premises in a peaceful manner.

MURPHY: Where's your commanding officer?

HUGHES: These are his direct orders.

Sean moves forward.

SEAN: Who are you?

HUGHES: You know who I am.

SEAN: I know what you are. I'm just wondering who you are.

JOSEPH: Sean.

SEAN: He hasn't answered my question.

HUGHES: I don't want to resort to force.

SEAN: Are you one of the new lads from Cork?

HUGHES: I have more men outside and -

SEAN: Driven out of there with yer tail ….

HUGHES: Watch it!

SEAN: Or what?

HUGHES: I will use force.

MURPHY: Sean, leave it.

SEAN: Are you an Irish man?

HUGHES: Are you going to vacate this building?

SEAN: You'll have to drag us out.

MURPHY: *(Intervening)* Sean, that's enough. *(To Hughes)* It has been declared in the House of Commons that these arbitration courts are legal.

HUGHES: I know nothing about that, I have my orders.

SEAN: Orders from the empire!

HUGHES: I'll ask ye to leave one last time. Then I will have no option but to clear this room by force.

MURPHY: There's no need. Give me a few minutes.

HUGHES: We'll be outside. And you, Sean, is it? I'll be keeping an eye on you.

Hughes exits. Door closes

SEAN: We can't just stand by and let this happen.

JOSEPH: Come on Sean. We'll go before there's more trouble.

MURPHY: Listen to your father Sean. Now is not the time.

JOSEPH: Come on. *(As he passes Anne)* You better come with us Anne.

The sound of shuffling feet as people start to move out.

MURPHY: I would ask you all to leave these premises quietly and return to your homes. Give no provocation to the police. This Court will not be closing down. We will reconvene at another time. Mr. Kinsella, you will remain. The decision of the Court in your case still remains.

Scene 7 - Outside court

Footsteps, mumbling as people leave the Court.

STIFF: Go on than, move your arses.

SEAN: I'll move your face around for you, you English feck.

HUGHES: Constable Stiff! *(To Sean)* Keep moving…Sean.

SEAN: This isn't over.

END OF EPISODE

EPISODE 6 – RAILWAY STRIKE, JULY 1920

Scene 1 – Radio

UNION MAN: *(Crackle of radio)* The North Wall Railwaymen, Dublin, rather than assist in providing the army of occupation with munitions for the war against Ireland have already sacrificed over 1,600 pounds per week and it is probable that all Irish railwaymen will be affected within a short time. This is not a railwayman's fight alone, or a trade unionists, - it is a NATION'S fight. It is your fight. It is - *(Fade out to)*

VOICEOVER: Fractured – a family, a nation, a dream. Maynooth Railway Station July 1920.

Scene 2 - Maynooth Railway Station

Railway station sounds. The squeak of a bike. O'Reilly rides up.

SEAN: Just the man. Give us a cigarette there, would you, O'Reilly?

O'REILLY: Haw many is that you've smoked on me now?

SEAN: I can hardly go buy some, can I, in case I miss Doran?

O'REILLY: That'd be shocking altogether. We'd be a laughing stock in Dublin.

SEAN: *(Lighting up)* Aye, as if losing the bloody match to them wasn't bad enough, huh? Kildare were desperate.

O'REILLY: Desperate. *(Beat. They smoke)* Were you talking to Colgan since?

SEAN: I was. There's a boy not in good form.

OREILLY: He always has a flutter on Kildare, he probably lost a packet.

SEAN: 'Twasn't that that was bothering him. GHQ told him we're not doing enough for the cause down here.

O'REILLY: Fecking nerve - I'd like to see those boyos take action with the whole of the British army living in their county.

SEAN: And walking their streets.

O'REILLY: And stealing their women.

SEAN: Did one of them steal your woman?

O'REILLY: No, but they stole our land so they wouldn't be above it, would they?

SEAN: *(Laughing)* True for you.

Tomas hurries towards them, breathless.

SEAN: Jesus. What does he want? What is it you want, Tomas?

TOMAS: Oh, I didn't realise…I…eh…

SEAN: What?

TOMAS: No, sure it's grand. I see you're busy and all.

SEAN: Is something wrong?

TOMAS: No. Not at all. Well…it's just…Mammy

SEAN: Mammy? Is she alright?

TOMAS: She sent me looking for you.

SEAN: What's she looking for me for? I told her I was off out searching for a bit of work this morning.

O'REILLY: And she believed that? Jesus.

TOMAS: She believed it alright. Then didn't Poor Brid come in and tell her that Mattie Sullivan died of a heart attack last night and Mammy thought sure maybe you could go after his job.

SEAN: Go after a dead man's job and him not cold? You tell Mammy I will not.

O'REILLY: God rest his soul.

TOMAS: I told Mammy that but sure she said Mattie wouldn't mind at all. She said that he admired what yez were doing on the railway strike and it'd be his way of helping out.

SEAN: I don't want Mattie's help, you can tell her.

TOMAS: I told her I'd relay the message, nothing more. What are you doing here anyway? *(Beat)* Is this Volunteer work?

O'REILLY: Those sharp observations are what makes you an average soldier, Tomas.

TOMAS: Shut up.

SEAN: Tomas! *(To O'Reilly)* Leave him alone.

TOMAS: Yes, leave me alone. So? What's happening?

SEAN: Nothing. Just having a bit of a chat, is all.

TOMAS: About?

SEAN: The British stealing our women.

O'REILLY: And Sean stealing my cigarettes.

They laugh.

TOMAS: *(Not convinced)* Are ye on a job?

SEAN / O'REILLY: No / yes *(Tomas is confused)* Yes/No

SEAN: Alright. Yes. We are. Now, get out of here.

TOMAS: Why wasn't I asked? I'm never asked. Am I being left out in the cold?

O'REILLY: There's a fair few icicles hanging off you alright.

TOMAS: Shut up, you.

SEAN: For God's sake, Tomas, will you just go.

TOMAS: No. As a member of the Volunteers, I have a right to know what's happening.

O'REILLY: You have as much right as my arse. Now go or I'll report you to Colgan.

TOMAS: And I'll tell Colgan that -

SEAN: There he is.

BOTH: Colgan?

SEAN: Doran! The boyo with the brown bag, that's him. Gets off here every Sunday, goes to the toilet, gets back on the train and drives her to Dublin.

O'REILLY: Who's that he's talking to?

SEAN: I'm not right sure.

TOMAS: Mossie Kinsella.

They turn to look at him

O'REILLY: Are you still here?

TOMAS: Who's Doran?

O'REILLY: None of your business, junior.

TOMAS: I'm almost nineteen. I was there when Celbridge barracks got blown up during the -

O'REILLY: I'll blow you up in a minute if you don't feck off.

SEAN: Will you both just stop! *(They do)* Grand. *(To Tomas, thinking)* Right - just keep quiet and ...watch and learn, alright?

TOMAS: *(Thrilled)* I will.

O'REILLY: His presence has not been sanctioned by GHQ.

SEAN: He's my brother so any flack that's coming, I'll deal with it. I'm warning you, Tomas -

TOMAS: I'll just stand here, I'll do nothing.

O'REILLY: This is a mistake.

SEAN: Yes, well, we don't have time to sort it because here they come. It is Mossie.

TOMAS: Told you. *(They both look at him)* Sorry. *(Beat)* You'd both want to mind because Mossie's not the nicest.

O'REILLY: *(Losing patience)* It's not Mossie we're interested in.

SEAN: Focus, O'Reilly.

O'REILLY: If he'd stop yabbering, I could focus.

TOMAS: I'm not yabber- *(A look from Sean)* Sorry.

Doran and Mossie get nearer. They are laughing.

MOSSIE: ..one hundred yards from the finish line, doesn't Tyrrell's fecking donkey come to a halt and won't budge.

PADRAIG: That donkey sounds like my wife.

MOSSIE: I was shouting and screaming at it to move.

PADRAIG: That sounds like me.

They both laugh

MOSSIE: You're a terrible man. Anyways, I lost about -

Sean and O'Reilly come to stand in front of the two men.

O'REILLY: Gentleman.

MOSSIE: If it isn't the Barry boys and their little friend.

O'REILLY: The name's O'Reilly, Mr. Kinsella. And we'll thank you to move on.

MOSSIE: It's a sad day in Maynooth when I let myself be bossed about by the likes of you.

O'REILLY: A sad day indeed. Even sadder if I have to use this.

We hear the click of a gun. Tomas gasps but tries to cover it up.

O'REILLY: You wouldn't want to be shot, ey? On your way now, there's a good man.

SEAN: And we'll trust you'll keep this between ourselves because we know where you live, Mr. Kinsella.

MOSSIE: Right…right…

Mossie runs off.

SEAN: A quiet word, if you will, Mr. Doran

PADRAIG: About?

O'REILLY: I think you know.

PADRAIG: I'm…not right sure..

SEAN: I'll give you a clue. The railway men have to stick together, Mr. Doran.

O'REILLY: If we don't stick together, what happens Mr. Doran?

PADRAIG: The railway strike was never sanctioned officially.

O'REILLY: I asked you what happens if strikers don't stick together Mr. Doran?

PADRAIG: The strike fails, I suppose.

O'REILLY: No suppose about it. And we'd hate for this un-official strike to fail, Mr. Doran.

SEAN: That would be a terrible tragedy, so it would.

PADRAIG: I have three -

SEAN: See, at the moment, there is this policy in force -

PADRAIG: I know lads but -

SEAN: I don't think you do know, so me and this fella here, we are going to explain it to you. Would that be alright with you, now?

PADRAIG: What I meant was -

SEAN: I asked you a question? Would it be alright if we explained this policy to you?

PADRAIG: Yes.

SEAN: That's great altogether. *(To O'Reilly)* Off you go O'Reilly and get it through this boy's head just exactly what a strike is. Word from Dublin is that he's just not getting it.

O'REILLY: Not everyone gets things the first time around.

SEAN: That's true.

PADRAIG: I do get -

O'REILLY: There is a railway strike on, Mr. Doran. Now, you as a train driver are part of this strike.

PADRAIG: I know but look -

SEAN: Stop there now. Stop right there and let us explain a few things to you. You just have to shut-up.

Long beat as Doran shuts up, intimidated by Sean's tone.

O'REILLY: Now you're getting it. Right, so we have this strike on the railways at the moment where all the railway men, well, most of them, are refusing to carry forces of the Crown on the trains.

SEAN: They're also refusing to carry ammunition.

O'REILLY: And tans and auxies, all that sort of thing. Have you got me, Mr. Doran?

PADRAIG: Yes.

O'REILLY: Now, there has been a few reports of train drivers and guards breaking this strike.

SEAN: Which is not a good idea.

O'REILLY: Not if they want to stay alive anyway.

They laugh

SEAN: There's been reports of them ferrying soldiers all about the country.

O'REILLY: And if them soldiers shoot people well, who do you think is responsible for that person's death? *(Beat)* Well?

PADRAIG: You're not seriously suggesting that -

O'REILLY: The train driver that brought him down, that's who.

SEAN: The train driver that broke a strike.

O'REILLY: Killing their own countrymen.

SEAN: Fecking traitors.

PADRAIG: You don't understand, I have three children.

SEAN: No, you don't understand, you will do what you're told or -

PADRAIG: Or what? You'll shoot me is it? If I lose my job on the railway, I might as well be dead.

O'REILLY: You'll be paid for your strike action.

PADRAIG: Do you know how much money they're giving to the strikers? Not enough to feed a mouse.

SEAN: They're giving as much as they're able.

PADRAIG: A bit of mercy boys. I support what yez are doing but I have three children, one of them sick with TB. My wife won't cope if I lose this job. Please -

SEAN: Your wife won't cope if you end up on a hillside with a bullet through your head and the word 'traitor' carved out on your chest.

PADRAIG: I am a proud Irishman

O'REILLY: Then act like it. Now, be a good man, tell the Stationmaster that you won't be driving that train back to Dublin until all the soldiers are off it.

SEAN: And if you run, we've boys at the station exits.

O'REILLY: Who'll march you back down.

SEAN: Are we clear?

PADRAIG: The soldiers will just travel by road instead.

SEAN: Then let them travel by road. Let them take their chances with the ambushes.

O'REILLY: I thought we were understanding each other? You are going to go to the Stationmaster -

PADRAIG: They'll just take the road down and get there anyway. This strike is a waste of time -

SEAN: *(Losing patience)* I will sanction you to be shot through the head if you don't turn around and do what we say.

PADRAIG: You're asking me to sacrifice my family -

SEAN: I'm asking you to think of your country.

PADRAIG: I'm asking you to have a bit of compassion.

SEAN: I have compassion for all the boys being shot because the likes of you are supporting the Empire. Now turn around and go back to the Stationmaster or so help me God, I'll put a bullet in you myself.

Long beat as they eyeball each other. Finally, Padraig turns around and starts to walk away.

O'REILLY: BANG!

Doran jumps.

PADRAIG: *(In fright)* Jesus!

The boys laugh.

O'REILLY: Don't go getting yourself killed there now, Mr. Doran.

SEAN: That'd be an awful shame. The country needs the likes of you.

More laughter. Beat.

O'REILLY: Good job, Sean. I'll be away, so. Always a pleasure.

O'Reilly hops on a bike and leaves.

SEAN: *(Starting to walk)* There's a grand man, Tomas, you'd do well to remember it.

TOMAS: Aye.

SEAN: That operation went well.

TOMAS: Aye.

SEAN: Are you alright?

TOMAS: I'm grand.

SEAN: You don't look grand.

TOMAS: Well I am.

SEAN: Don't take me head off. What's the matter with you?

TOMAS: Nothing. Now I'd best -

SEAN: Me and O'Reilly, we did the right thing just there, you know that, don't you? Because if you don't, then maybe you need to have a think about what being a Volunteer means.

TOMAS: I know what it means. It's just…well, you said yourself the railway strike wouldn't work.

SEAN: As a strike, no, but this is civil disobedience…a sort of mass political protest but peaceful.

TOMAS: It's not peaceful if you'd shoot someone through the head for it.

SEAN: Are you questioning me?

TOMAS: Would you have shot him if he had refused to go back?

SEAN: *(Half laughing, bitter)* Well, not here, no, in full view of the street, but he'd have been shot, eventually.

TOMAS: For trying to feed his children.

SEAN: You'd want to shut your mouth with that sort of talk, Tomas.

TOMAS: I'm only asking questions.

SEAN: If you said that in front of O'Reilly or Colgan, you wouldn't last long.

TOMAS: You have to question things, Sean, you can't just go -

SEAN: The only question you need to ask yourself is, do you want a free Ireland?

TOMAS: You know I do.

SEAN: Well, how do you think it's going to come about? It's not just all smashing buildings and playing soldiers. *(Beat)* Sometimes you actually have to shoot someone.

TOMAS: Even your own?

SEAN: Yes, if they are traitors. Don't question me for doing my duty. *(Beat)* I thought you wanted this.

TOMAS: I do. But the man had three children and -

SEAN: You can't listen to them.

TOMAS: - one of them had TB.

SEAN: *(Frustrated)* That's why you haven't gone on to the big stuff yet.

TOMAS: What?

SEAN: That's why they keep you in the dark!

TOMAS: What?

SEAN: They think you're too soft, Colgan and them.

TOMAS: That's not fair. I'm always the first to Volunteer for drills and I'm the best shot in the company, you know that.

SEAN: It counts for nothing unless you believe in it.

TOMAS: I do believe in it.

SEAN: You could have fooled me. That man, that you feel sorry for, he is in our union, he pays his dues, he has to do what everyone else does.

TOMAS: I know but -

SEAN: Other workers have children, he's not the only one.

TOMAS: I know but -

SEAN: But nothing. We are in a fight here, Tomas. There can only be one winner.

TOMAS: But that man, he's not the enemy.

SEAN: As Daddy says, If he's not with us, he's against us.

TOMAS: Mammy's not with us.

SEAN: We wouldn't have Mammy, she'd be too much trouble, Jaysus.

They laugh slightly. Uneasy truce.

TOMAS: They really think I'm too soft?

SEAN: They do.

TOMAS: And you just let them say that?

SEAN: Oh no, like an eejit I told them to give you a couple more months and you'd be ready for ambushes and that.

TOMAS: Oh…right. Thanks Sean.

SEAN: But after today -

TOMAS: I will be ready.

SEAN: Are you sure, because what you were saying just there, it didn't sound like a soldier.

TOMAS: I'll be ready.

SEAN: A soldier that's not ready, he gets people killed.

TOMAS: *(With conviction)* I won't get anyone killed.

SEAN: Good. Because I put my neck out for you.

TOMAS: I'll never let you down, Sean

SEAN: Then no more questioning. A soldier always obeys orders.

TOMAS: I know that, sure.

SEAN: You're certain?

TOMAS: Cross me heart and hope to die.

SEAN: Right, well, go and tell Mammy that she can stuff her job, that I won't be working while my friends are striking.

TOMAS: Ah, now, I can't just - Is that an order, like?

SEAN: It's an order.

TOMAS: Right, so. And you're certain you want me to say - go stuff your job, Mammy.

SEAN: I do.

TOMAS: Grand so.

SEAN: Off you go. *(Tomas walks off, calling after him)* And just so you know, I'll deny I said it when she asks.

TOMAS: It's great to know you have my back, Sean.

SEAN: *(With affection)* Always, Tomas.

END OF EPISODE

EPISODE 7 – PLANNING KILL RAID, AUG. 1920

Scene 1 - Maynooth Street

The sound of church bells, people coming from mass.

COLGAN: Sean, a word.

SEAN: Sir…eh, yes, Mr. Colgan, Patrick sir.

COLGAN: Patrick will do off duty. I've been talking to Domhnall UaBuachalla, he's recommending you for a job. Would it be all right if I call around to the pub in a while?

SEAN: *(Thrilled)* Yes sir.

COLGAN: And not a word…

SEAN: Understood.

VOICEOVER: Fractured – a family, a nation, a dream – August 1920

Scene 2 - Barry's kitchen

Mary enters from the street. We hear the church bells clearly for a brief second, until the door is closed by her best friend, Cissy Boland.

CISSY: God. that feckin' Fr. Moran would give you a pain in the backside with the length of his masses. That was a hour and a half!

MARY: It was long enough alright.

CISSY: *(Pulling out a chair and plonking herself down)* I hate when they let those College priests have a go at a mass. *(Imitating the priest in a boring Cavan accent)* "And now part four of my series of sermons on the Ten Commandments: Numbers Seven and Eight - Thou shalt not Steal, and Thou shalt not bear False Witness. Commandments Six and Nine have been postponed to a later date, when I can pluck up the courage to talk about women and how I shouldn't be looking at them."

MARY: *(Laughing)* Cissy, stop! If anyone heard you…

CISSY: The way they drone on… I swear to God, Mary, that's what they're teaching them up in the college – speechifying! It's not the goodness of God, that's for sure… Here, I'm starving, have you any food? That host was no breakfast.

MARY: Will bread and butter do you? I'll make up a few rounds.

CISSY: Grand. Keep the wolf from the door. *(Pause)* I'm sure I've caught Fr. Moran eyeing my arse a few times up in the College.

MARY: Cissy!

CISSY: First time was in the refectory. I was picking up a fork off the floor in front of him. I'd swear he put it there so he could watch me bending over.

MARY: *(Laughing, shocked)* Ah now, Cissy!

CISSY: Just sitting on its own in the middle of the floor, right there in front of him… Ah I don't mind it, Mary. Reminds you they're human like the rest of us. Every man and woman has their urges - it's only natural.

MARY: *(She drops a plate of bread and butter on the counter for her)* Don't you know "urges" are a mortal sin, Cissy Boland! Eat that up now.

CISSY: Thanks. *(Pulling the plate towards her)* Well, it'll take more than an Our Father and three Hail Marys for me to get rid of my urges, that's for certain sure.

MARY: You will burn in hell, Cissy Boland.

CISSY: I wouldn't care if there were a few nice fellows there. I'd say Fr. Moran would be handsome now… if he wasn't blessed with the personality of a wet mop. And then there's the shy little red-haired fella from Mayo, he gets fierce quiet around you, so he does. But then, someone else has their eye on you, Mary, isn't that right?

MARY: What's that?

CISSY: You know fine well. All them times I have to lie for you, pretending that I'm going to Dublin with you. I'm not stupid - who is he?

MARY: *(Flustered)* I can't say, not yet.

CISSY: He's not taken?

MARY: No!

CISSY: That's all right then, apparently that's a big sin. Go on, tell me something. I need a bit of news to go with the bread and butter here.

MARY: *(Gives in to her excitement. Secretly)* We meet whenever we can, but if it's more than a few days, he writes to me in between. *(She unfolds a letter she has in her pocket)* Look, here's one of the letters.

CISSY: Give it here.

MARY: No, it's private.

CISSY: Sure I tell you what I hear at the side of the confessionals – go on, show me!

MARY: All right.

Nervous but excited, Mary hands it to Cissy

CISSY: God, his handwriting's very fancy.

MARY: I know, sure isn't he well-educated?

CISSY: Only the best for our Mary… "I thoroughly enjoyed our walk in St. Stephen's Green last Sunday. The flowers were lovely but not as lovely as you"! Oh, he's a charmer!

MARY: That he is!

CISSY: And look how he starts it – A Stor Mo Chroi. He must be a Sinn Feiner, using the Irish.

MARY: I'm not saying.

CISSY: Was he at mass this morning?

MARY: He might have been.

CISSY: Did ye receive communion together? At the railing, side by side, almost touching – in front of the priest, with your tongues out!

MARY: Jesus, stop it, Cissy! *(They laugh giddily, naughtily)* God, imagine… What would the stuffed frocks up in the college think if I was going with a fella right in front of them at Mass?

CISSY: *(Imitating a priest in confession)* A hundred Hail Marys and ten decades of the rosary! The Sorrowful Mysteries! *(They laugh)* They'd be jealous, that's what!

Footsteps as Tomas enters from the hall.

MARY: I thought you were supposed to be at early Mass, Tomas.

TOMAS: I'll be at the next.

MARY: Well, you've missed Fr. Moran droning on, so that's a blessing anyway!

CISSY: Morning, Tomas!

TOMAS: Are you eating us out of house and home again?

CISSY: *(Teasing)* I am. God, you look terrible. I heard that Lizzie O'Neill's a desperate one for keeping her fellas out late.

TOMAS: *(Embarrassed)* No, she isn't- wasn't- I wasn't out with her!

CISSY: Not for the want of trying. She'll be about fifty by the time you get around to holding her hand, I bet.

Mary laughs.

TOMAS: Yeah, well… how's Donnacha Kilbride?

CISSY: *(Drawing a blank)* I don't know. Why?

MARY: Never mind him, Cissy, come on, I've to run up to Mrs. O'Donoghue. I'll walk you out.

CISSY: *(Still confused)* What does he mean by that? I don't fancy him, Tomas, if that's what you're on about! Jesus, the thought…

60

MARY: *(Opening door, street sounds float in)* Come on, She needs the rashers for the Father, he does be ravenous on a Sunday morning after all the praying.

CISSY: But, what – Tomas!

She continues to protest all the way out.

TOMAS: Bye now, Cissy! It's been a pleasure.

He closes the door on her laughing to himself.

PADDY: *(Distant – from bar)* Hello! Anyone around?

TOMAS: I'll be with you now.

Fade

Scene 3 – Barry's bar

Footsteps as he emerges into the bar.

TOMAS: Good morning, Paddy. Mr. UaBuachalla. Is it me father you want?

UABUACHALLA: It is. We're catching the early train up to the match today.

TOMAS: I'll give him a shout. *(Shouts)* Daddy. Mr. UaBuachalla and Paddy are here for you. Daddy!

JOSEPH: *(Distant)* I'm coming now.

TOMAS: He's coming now. Ye should see Westmeath off handy enough today.

PADDY: We should. You have an interest in the football yourself, Tomas?

TOMAS: Oh yes, Mr. Dooley! A true Kildare man, me! Sure when they won the All-Ireland last year, I was out at the parade! All the white flags waving…

UABUACHALLA: You weren't at the match yourself?

TOMAS: No… I was working.

PADDY: I'll talk your father into letting you come one of these days, you're not a Kildare man until you've been to a match, ey? *(Footsteps as Joseph enters)* Here's Joseph now.

Joseph enters flustered, a bit unkempt and just about dressed.

JOSEPH: Sorry lads, I was just out with the, eh… there was a few bits of things to do with the…

UABUACHALLA: *(Seeing through the excuse)* No bother, Joseph! We better get a move on for the train, though.

JOSEPH: *(Already pouring three whiskeys)* Sure, ye'll have a quick one before we go, or what kind of a host would I be at all? A toast to the Lilywhites, yeah?

UABUACHALLA: *(As Paddy goes straight for a whiskey)* Ah, it's a bit early, Joseph. There'll be plenty to toast after, though.

PADDY: I'll join you, Joseph. To the Short Grass in the Big Smoke!

Paddy and Joseph clink glasses, drink. Slam the glasses back on the counter.

JOSEPH: Let's be off so.

Door opens to admit Colgan. The men exchange greetings with him, calling him by name so we know who he is.

COLGAN: Good morning, gentlemen.

UABUACHALLA: I see you were busy in Celbridge during the week.

COLGAN: *(Smiling)* We got a few things done.

UABUACHALLA: All the council members resigning as Justices of the Peace? And the stationery changed over to Irish? That's progress surely!

COLGAN: *(Half laughing)* Well, slowly but surely. Headed to the match are ye?

UABUACHALLA: We are. Paddy, you and Joseph go ahead, I just need a quick word with Colgan here.

PADDY: Right so, see you at the station, come on Joseph.

The two men leave, muttering, we hear the door open and close during this exchange.

UABUACHALLA: Tomas, run on inside there now and get me a sup of milk. I'm short in the shop.

TOMAS: *(Eager)* I will, of course. Hello Commandant Colgan.

He runs off.

UABUACHALLA: *(Low voice, aside to Colgan)* Always eager, that young fellow. Anyway, did you get them?

COLGAN: Aye.

UABUACHALLA: Maith an fear. I'll leave you to fill the lads in about Saturday so.

COLGAN: Are you sure about this, there's a lot involved already.

UABUACHALLA: Sean and O'Reilly are two of the best. I've been watching them.

COLGAN: Grand so, enjoy the match.

UABUACHALLA: Cill Dara abú! Slán!

Footsteps as he leaves, the door opens. O'Reilly enters as he leaves.

UABUACHALLA: O'Reilly, there you are, Colgan is waiting. I'll be off.

O'REILLY: Bye, Domhnall. *(Door closes)* Hello, Colgan.

Footsteps as Tomas arrives out with the milk.

TOMAS: Is Domhnall gone? I had his bread here and -

COLGAN: He had to run. Is Sean about?

SEAN: *(Distant)* I'm in the kitchen, Sir. Come on in, it's empty. Tomas, will you bring us in a few cold drinks?

TOMAS: Can I not join in?

ALL: No.

SEAN: *(Distant)* Just get the drinks, Tomas.

Footsteps as the others leave for the kitchen.

TOMAS: *(Beat. Slamming glasses down)* I'm not a servant.

Scene 4 – Barry's kitchen

The scrape of chairs as O'Reilly and Colgan settle themselves in.

O'REILLY: So… what do you need us for, sir?

COLGAN: I'll get straight to the point, Have either of you heard any whispers about Kill at the weekend?

SEAN / O'REILLY: No, sir.

COLGAN: Lads, what I'm about to tell you… I need to know I can trust you.

O'REILLY: Absolutely, sir.

SEAN: You can always trust us, sir.

COLGAN: I need you both to swear to me that you won't breathe a word of what I'm about to say, do you hear me?

SEAN: Of course!

O'REILLY: Absolutely, sir.

COLGAN: Swear to me now. Swear on the life of your mothers, swear to Mother Ireland .

O'REILLY: I swear.

SEAN: I swear it!

COLGAN: Right, on Saturday –

Tomas bursts in with the bottles.

TOMAS: There were no bottles in the back room, although I swore there were plenty there last night. I had to go down to the cold house and get them for you. *(Delighted with himself)* Mr. Colgan, sir. This is the coldest one – that's for you.

Lays bottle down.

SEAN: *(Mortified)* Will you feck off out back?

COLGAN: *(Sympathetic)* Thanks Tomas. Good lad. *(Waits for a non-existent penny to drop)* I'm teetotal though – keep it behind the bar.

TOMAS: *(Feeling stupid)* Sorry, sir… I forgot.

COLGAN: Maybe, eh… keep a look out front and let us know if anyone… unusual is coming over, will you?

TOMAS: Right away, sir! Sorry, sir.

Collects the bottle, leaves, door closes.

SEAN: Sorry, Sir, he's just…

COLGAN: Young…yes, I remember. I don't want him anywhere near this, have you got me?

SEAN: Yes.

COLGAN: All right. Well… *(Leans in)* For the last few months, after a certain… incident, County Inspector Supple in Naas has been a bit nervous in his house at night. So, he has a rota of RIC men come over every evening to stand guard outside and make sure he's tucked in nice and snug for the night.

O'REILLY: Isn't it well for him!

COLGAN: Every second night, four men from the Kill barracks cycle into Naas for guard duty at about half eleven. This Saturday, the lads from Kill Company are going to stop the RIC men on their way in from Kill, take their guns and bicycles.

SEAN: *(Excited)* An ambush!

COLGAN: An ambush, Sean. Taking their guns and bicycles and leaving them high and dry with a bit of a chill in their bones.

SEAN: Mighty!

COLGAN: Now, a lot of our men are watched, and might be stopped and searched if they were seen travelling far outside their own parish. But you two –

SEAN: *(Gets it)* They're not watching us.

COLGAN: Exactly. Now, here's what I want you to do.

He unfolds a bit of paper.

TOMAS: *(Distant)* Sean! Sean!

SEAN: It's fine. Go on, Sir.

COLGAN: I've got two boxes of cartridges I need to get over to the lads in Kill for Saturday night. Will you carry them for me?

O'REILLY: Yes, sir!

SEAN: Absolutely, sir - of course!

TOMAS: *(Distant, with growing urgency)* Sean!

COLGAN: You better see what he wants before he comes in.

SEAN: Sorry about this, Sir. I'll be as quick as I can.

Footsteps off.

Scene 5 – Barry's bar

Sean approaching Tomas

SEAN: What are you playing at? Can't you see I'm busy?

TOMAS: Mammy is just up the street with Mary. Look!

SEAN: Christ. When she comes in, you keep her talking and I'll get the lads out the back way.

He runs back to the kitchen.

TOMAS: Jesus.

Scene 6 – Barry's kitchen

Sean arrives back.

COLGAN: All good, Sean?

SEAN: *(Over enthusiastic)* Oh, ceart go leor! Right, I suppose we better be finishing up so-

COLGAN: *(Cuts him off, remembering the request)* Oh yes - one more thing. There's going to be a lot of men around for this but if you could stay on after delivering the boxes and maybe lend a hand, that help would be duly noted.

TOMAS: *(Distant)* That delivery won't be long now, Sean.

SEAN: *(Distracted by Tomas)* That's great. Now if we could –

COLGAN: We need extras just in case they don't co-operate. But you won't have guns because there aren't enough for everyone just yet.

O'REILLY: But we'll have another four after this Saturday.

TOMAS: *(Distant, panicked)* And the delivery is just being delivered.

SEAN: *(Trying to pass as calm)* I was just thinking sir, it might be good for you to get used to the back way out, just in case-

COLGAN: *(Cuts him off)* Oh, and Sean? Not a word to Tomas, right?

SEAN: Fair enough. Now if you could just -

COLGAN: There'll be plenty for him to do in due course.

TOMAS: *(Distant)* Sean!

COLGAN: *(Stops)* I'll be honest lads. This is… a bit of a test for you. You'll be on your own travelling over, with nobody else to think for you… Just act normally, go about your business as usual, and stay calm.

Quick footsteps approach. Tomas runs into the room.

TOMAS: The Tans, boys. Run.

COLGAN / O'REILLY: Jesus!

A stampede as Colgan and O'Reilly make a dash for the door. The door slams. Silence. Beat. The boys start to laugh with relief.

END OF EPISODE

EPISODE 8 – NIGHT OF KILL RAID, AUG. 1920

Scene 1 – Night time, outdoors

Night time sounds. Men shifting and shushing each other. We hear the faint sound of bicycles, which grows louder.

VOLUNTEER: Stop!

Indistinct shouting.   Sounds of gunfire rings out. All becomes mayhem. Fade to.

VOICEOVER: Fractured – a family, a nation, a dream.   Evening of 28th August 2020.

Scene 2 – Barry's Pub

The low murmur of voices. Tapping the counter.

BRIGID: Joseph, will you serve those gentlemen please.

We hear the door opening, street noises which fade. Mary enters.

BRIGID: Oh Mary, you got your new hat! Isn't it only gorgeous! Here, let me have a look at it.

MARY: *(Showing it to her mother)* There you are, mammy.

BRIGID: Isn't it beautifully made! Where did you get it?

MARY: I went to Switzers on Grafton St in the end. It'll be another few years before Clerys is open again, I heard them saying.

BRIGID: And the green ribbon, look! Did Cissy help you pick it out?

MARY: Cissy? Oh yes! *(Smiles)* And a nice gentleman there said I looked very pretty in it too.

BRIGID: Oh, you'll turn the head of some handsome young fellow with that, I'm sure!

MARY: What makes you think I haven't already?

The door opens again. Sean and O'Reilly arrive, in high spirits, both singing. This isn't their first pub tonight.

SEAN / O'REILLY: "… and Ireland long a province be, a nation once again"!

They cheer themselves.

BRIGID: Well, somebody's in good form!

SEAN: Ah Mammy, will you have a dance with me!

BRIGID: I will not – would you stop! Where were you till this hour? You barely had the dinner swallowed when you were gone out.

SEAN: Ah… *(Looks to O'Reilly)* me and O'Reilly, we had a bit of a party, I suppose.

O'REILLY: A great party. How's the lovely, Mary?

MARY: *(Abrupt, not wanting to encourage him)* I'll be in the kitchen if you want me, Mammy.

Mary moves off.

SEAN: You'll have to try a bit harder than that with her, O'Reilly. 'Twas a great party, Mammy.

BRIGID: And where did you get the money? You're still on strike. *(A thought strikes her)* Did you get a new job? Oh that'd be great news!

SEAN: Mammy, I'm on strike. You don't get jobs when you're striking.

BRIGID: You don't anyway! *(Warning)* You better not be up to any mischief, Sean, do you hear me?

SEAN: I wasn't Mammy, honest.

BRIGID: You promised me.

SEAN: It was just a bit of a get-together with the lads. We were having a few pints. They looked after me. They're good lads – it's alright.

O'Reilly sniggers.

BRIGID: *(Just about convinced)* I don't know what you're sniggering about, Joe O'Reilly, and the buttons on your trousers wide open. Looks like you need to get some food into you, a bit of soakage.

SEAN: That's probably not a bad idea.

BRIGID: Sit down the two of you, I'll give Mary a shout to get you some food. *(Calling)* Mary! Get your brother and his friend some sandwiches, there.

The scrape of chairs as Sean and O'Reilly sit down. O'Reilly initially speaks surreptitiously low, but his voice rises as he forgets where he is.

O'REILLY: Ah, but it was a glorious night, all the same! The brave IRA against the cowardly RIC - an ambush worthy of a song!

SEAN: Well, don't start singing, whatever you do! You haven't a note in your head.

O'REILLY: We'll have the words by the end of the night. *(Thinks)* "One moonlit night on the road from Kill…"

They are interrupted by Tomas, who plonks down beside them.

TOMAS: Mary said you were back, where did you get to?

O'REILLY: You've interrupted me flow, Tomas. "…the boys of the IRA stood still…"

TOMAS: What?

SEAN: He's writing a song, the eejit.

O'REILLY: About Kill. Now…'One moonlit night on the road from Kill

TOMAS: Were you at Kill?

SEAN / O'REILLY: No / Yes

Beat

O'REILLY: Sure, it doesn't matter now Sean. Sit in here Tomas and learn. Might help the big boys notice you.

SEAN: Don't tease him, O'Reilly.

TOMAS: I want to learn.

O'REILLY: So.. one moonlit night from the road to Kill, the boys of the IRA stood still…

SEAN: *(Conceding)* You might have something there…

O'REILLY: "…when through the air of the cold still night…"

TOMAS: You've used "still" twice. *(Sean shushes him)*

O'REILLY: "…four black uniforms came into sight!" *(Delighted with himself)*

SEAN: Oh, ye boyo! That's not bad, that's not bad!

O'REILLY: We'll have to write it down before we forget it. Have you a pencil?

SEAN: *(Checking his jacket)* I do. I've no paper though.

TOMAS: I'll get some in the kitchen

Scene 3 – Barry's Kitchen

Mary is buttering bread for the sandwiches.

TOMAS: The boys are in great from Mary. You'd want to hurry with those sandwiches. Is there paper here?

We hear him rifling in a drawer.

MARY: *(After a long beat)* I don't like that O'Reilly fellow.

TOMAS: *(Surprised at the change)* He's grand.

MARY: They say he was at Kill. Two RIC men died at Kill.

TOMAS: Yea, after they fired on our lads.

MARY: I heard the IRA lads just shot the RIC lads in cold blood, that there was no warning.

TOMAS: That's…I didn't hear that…our boys wouldn't do that. Sean wouldn't…

MARY: But O'Reilly would and Sean is very tight with him.

Long beat. Tomas is unsure what is expected of him.

TOMAS: I..eh…I've got the paper…so I'll eh…go.

MARY: *(With bite)* Yes, off you run.

Tomas leaves.

Scene 4 – Pub

SEAN: We can't just say what happened. That's not… poetic enough.

O'REILLY: True. We need to tell a good story, make people feel what it was like to be there.

Tomas returns.

TOMAS: One sheet of paper.

SEAN: Yeah, make the hairs on the backs of their necks rise up! The cracks of the bullets and the smell of the gunpowder!

TOMAS: So ye were definitely there then?

O'REILLY: Twenty against one! The lone Irishman against the might of the British Empire!

SEAN: Jaysus, that's powerful!

O'REILLY: You see, that's how you get people on your side - tell them what they want to hear. Then make them sing it! Romantic Ireland, eh!

SEAN: Right then. Try for another verse there. You getting this down, Tomas?

TOMAS: Aye.

O'REILLY: "The twenty polis hove into view…!"

TOMAS: I thought there was only four.

SEAN: *(Annoyed)* There was. But sure, that doesn't matter. This is a song… Will be a song… Or a poem maybe… We haven't finished it yet.

O'REILLY: "Tom Harris stood like Cú Chulainn of old…"

SEAN: Should we mention his name, do you think?

O'REILLY: You're right. Not right now anyway. If any of the RIC were to hear it…

SEAN: That would be the end of him alright.

O'REILLY: *(They pause, considering)* They're lifting a lot of IRA. Another one in Cork the other day.

Mary approaches with the sandwich.

SEAN: Bloody RIC. Betraying their own people and their own country.

MARY: *(Slamming the sandwich down)* And you went to school with half of them, Sean. There's your sandwich.

SEAN: Given with love as usual, Mary. Stay out of what's not your business.

MARY: So were you not friends with them? Did you not play football with them? Play chasing with them?

SEAN: It's not the same. They're different now.

MARY: And how are they different from you or me?

SEAN: *(Bitter)* They swore loyalty to the crown. They may as well have sold their soul to the devil.

MARY: *(Finding this ridiculous)* Ah here! The RIC are good men, doing their job to keep the peace for all the people of Ireland.

O'REILLY: You're pretty Mary, but you haven't a clue.

MARY: Don't patronise me, Mr. O'Reilly,

O'REILLY: The RIC are in bed with the Tans. Did you not hear what's after happening in Kill and Naas?

MARY: I know what happened in Kill. Two RIC men shot by the IRA and-

O'REILLY: I meant after that. And in Naas. Last night.

MARY: *(Concerned, not knowing the full story)* Well, I heard there was a bit of trouble, but…

SEAN: *(Mocking)* A bit of trouble? Oh, there was a bit of trouble, alright. *(Sarcasm)* Yes, last weekend was unfortunate.

O'REILLY: *(Sarcasm)* Terrible unfortunate.

SEAN: The polis opened fire on our lads and they were forced to shoot back to defend themselves.

MARY: I heard it differently.

O'REILLY: Well, you obviously didn't hear it all. The other night, the Black and Tans burst into Broughall's in Kill, the Old House, started firing into the ceiling then stole a rake of drink for themselves. The best of whiskey. Shot a man's horse on the way out! And the boys in the RIC barracks directly opposite did nothing, holed up nice and cosy, looking right out across the street at them doing it.

MARY: Well, the Tans are bad alright, but you can't blame the RIC-

O'REILLY: *(Getting aggressive)* That's not all. Didn't they barrel into Naas in a lorry then, loaded up on drink, firing shots all up and down the Main Street. Then they smashed the windows of Boushell's boot shop - right beside the RIC barracks - and set the whole building ablaze. Three children nearly killed.

MARY: The fellows in the RIC aren't like the Black and Tans. They wouldn't do anything like that.

SEAN: No Mary, they'll do nothing instead. Keepers of the peace, my arse!

BRIGID: *(Firm, calling across)* I think that's enough politics for one night. Let's leave it at that.

O'REILLY: *(Still riled up, angry with drink)* You think this is politics, Mrs. Barry? This is a war. A war against British oppression, and the RIC are part of that war, just like-

BRIGID: That's enough now.

O'REILLY: -the Black and Tans, just like the British Army...

SEAN: *(Playing friendly)* Ah come on Joe, let's leave it for now, alright?

O'REILLY: They all have to be wiped out, starting with the British Army, then-

BRIGID: *(Strong)* Mr. O'Reilly, I need you to leave! Sean, take him out.

SEAN: *(Knowing O'Reilly has gone too far)* Come on, Joe, you've had enough. I'm taking you home.

O'REILLY: *(Protesting, but clearly drunk)* Ah now Sean, I'm fine! Sure, I haven't finished that bottle yet.

SEAN: No. You're going home.

Sean bundles O'Reilly out the door, who protests weakly in his inebriated state.

BRIGID: Mary! You'll do well to stay out of all that talk.

MARY: But Sean is allowed, I don't think -

BRIGID: Will you go tidy up out back. Tomas, get some stock ready for tomorrow. Where the hell is your father when you need him?

The leave. Brigid begins tidying up. She picks up the paper Tomas has been scribbling on.

BRIGID: What on earth- ? Oh Jesus, Mary and Joseph.

Scene 5 – Barry's yard.

The clatter of bottles. A crunch of approaching footsteps. Sean enters through the gate into the yard.

SEAN: *(Laughing)* He was fairly buckled - the air hit him and the legs went to jelly!

Beat

TOMAS: Why wasn't I included for Kill?

SEAN: *(Evasive)* Well… there was a lot of men mobilised already. Wouldn't want to have it too crowded. Sure you were working here anyway so you wouldn't have been able to come.

TOMAS: And what happened exactly? I heard our lads shouted "hands up" and they started shooting at us. But Mary says -

SEAN: What does Mary know? The Sergeant went for his gun and we all fired…

TOMAS: All twenty of ye.

SEAN: Yes. Well no, I was at the back. I didn't see too closely what happened.

TOMAS: *(Trying to understand)* So did we fire first?

SEAN: What are you trying to say? *(Long beat)* These orders came from Mick Collins himself, to Colgan, to Harris. Eliminate the RIC. Take their guns. Job number one. Simple. The RIC's loyalty is to the King of England. Where do your loyalties lie?

TOMAS: Ah stop it! My loyalties lie with our men, of course they do. I know there'll need to be sacrifices, but-

SEAN: Sacrifice? What do you know about sacrifice? You're just a child. *(Beat)* Like I said before, soft.

Sean goes inside.

TOMAS: That's unfair and you know it!

He slams down a crate in frustration.

Scene 6 – Barry's bar

Sean enters.

SEAN: I'm going to bed, Mammy.

BRIGID: *(Holding up paper)* I'm after finding this, Sean. Can you explain it?

SEAN: 'Tis a bit of paper. It means nothing.

BRIGID: Nothing! It's a song celebrating the death of RIC men? How could you? Your own father!

SEAN: *(Angrily)* Oh, I am sick of hearing about a man I don't remember. He's dead, mammy. Get over it.

BRIGID: Don't you dare say -

SEAN: Don't you dare ever again make a holy show of me in front of the boys like you did at the election. You had no right. I'm telling you, I'm telling ye all, if I want to write songs about traitors getting killed, then I will. If I want to fight for my country, then I will. *(Calling)* And Tomas, if I want to shoot someone who I think is a threat, then I will. So ye better all pick your sides.

He stomps out, slamming door. Brigid sobs.

END OF EPISODE

EPISODE 9 – BRIGID AND JOSEPH, SEP. 1920

Scene 1 - Bedroom.

Brigid screams. Breaks down. Running footsteps. Joseph enters.

JOSEPH: Brigid?

BRIGID: He's gone. Joseph Junior is…he's gone. Gone.

JOSEPH: *(Embracing her)* Oh love….

VOICEOVER: Fractured…a family, a nation…a dream. 24th September 1920.

Scene 2 - Brigid and Joseph's bedroom

Sound of a clock ticking. Footsteps crossing the floor, a sigh, the sound of bedsprings as Brigid climbs into bed beside Joseph. The blowing out of an oil lamp.

BRIGID: Night, Joseph.

JOSEPH: Night. *(Sounds as they settle down)* Long pause. I was thinking maybe of changing the bread supplier.

BRIGID: Huh?

JOSEPH: The bread supplier. We're had two complaints this week about stale bread.

BRIGID: Oh?

JOSEPH: And Paddy said he heard Mrs. O'Sullivan say she was getting all her bread in Murphy's from now on, on account of ours not being up to standard.

BRIGID: Oh well, if Paddy Dooley says it then it must be true.

Pause. Joseph decides to let that go.

JOSEPH: The delivery man isn't to be trusted anyway.

BRIGID: No?

JOSEPH: Terrible smell of whiskey from his breath.

BRIGID: Takes one to know one I suppose. *(Long pause)* I'm sorry Joseph. That was….

JOSEPH: True

BRIGID: Unkind.

JOSEPH: The truth is rarely kind.

BRIGID: Still…

Long pause. They are lying with their backs to each other. Between them there is a chasm of space that we sense neither one ever crosses.

BRIGID: D'ye know today's date?

Silence

JOSEPH: I do.

BRIGID: I was filling out the order forms for Nolans today and I had to write it out three times. 24th of March 1921; 24th of March 1921; 24th of March..

JOSEPH: 1904. Twenty three minutes past five in the morning. I know Brigid. I remember.

BRIGID: No one else seems to. Mary is walking around with her head in the clouds. She dropped half a dozen bottles of stout all over the floor when that RIC patrol passed by this morning.

JOSEPH: Aye.

BRIGID: And Sean won't talk to me since that night after Kill. That boy, he'll break my heart with all his carry on. And as for Tomas. Ye'd think he of all of them...

JOSEPH: Tomas picked a bunch of wild flowers from the back meadow and left them on the kitchen table.

BRIGID: He was the one did that?

JOSEPH: He did. And Poor Brid left in a fruit cake and some scones while you were out. They're in the pantry.

BRIGID: Oh. I didn't know.

JOSEPH: Paddy offered to come in and help with the stocktaking tomorrow. Christ, even Mossie Kinsella was civil.

BRIGID: That took some effort alright.

JOSEPH: To be sure.

They laugh. Brigid turns to face the ceiling.

BRIGID: I've been really cross with ye Joseph.

JOSEPH: I've noticed.

BRIGID: I've been blaming you for the boys joining the Volunteers.

JOSEPH: I never..

BRIGID: I know. I just...losing another child would finish me altogether.

JOSEPH: They're grown men now Brigid. We have to allow them to make their own decisions.

BRIGID: I know Tomas signed up to please Sean, but I had meself convinced that Sean signed up to please you.

JOSEPH: He never told me he was thinking of joining up. I guessed alright, but…

BRIGID: He looks up to you Joseph – and I'm glad that's the case, I really am. But in looking up to you, he's rejecting his real father and everything he stood for.

JOSEPH: Sean knows your Seamus was a good man.

BRIGID: He was a good man.

JOSEPH: I didn't know him too well, what with him being a good bit younger than me – and away fighting in the army since he came of age. But there's one story about him stands out, he came into the pub one time – I think it was his last leave before…ye lost him. He had a few messages to get he said. He was carrying a shopping bag – that one ye keep in the kitchen – flowers all over it – and Mossie Kinsella was having a field day.

BRIGID: What was he saying?

JOSEPH: Ye know Mossie. 'Is this what the British Crown is reduced to Seamus?', says he. "Hiring horse-whipped men with fancy bags to fight their battles?" Seamus, God be good to him, paid no heed. Sat himself down at the bar with his pint and was asking after my mother, God rest her – this was a month or two before she passed. Then in comes Paddy and sure Mossie started up again. Asked Paddy if he liked Seamus's shopping bag. Said he was sure Seamus would lend it to him some time and the pair of them could go shopping together. Or that maybe Paddy should give up the farming and join the British Army, because it seemed that's where all the … well, a certain type of man would feel at home.

BRIGID: What kind of…

JOSEPH: Then he started in on me. There was no stopping him. Would I like Seamus' shopping bag? It seemed he was in the wrong place altogether – he thought he had come into a men's-only bar, but here he was at a branch meeting of the Irish Countrywomen's Association.

BRIGID: The man talks nothing but rage and bile.

JOSEPH: I'm telling you, Paddy was on the verge of throwing a punch – just what Mossie wanted of course. I wasn't far behind. Your Seamus though – he just sat there and laughed. "Mossie", says he. "I've been three hours walking through Maynooth with my very attractive little shopping bag. In that time not a single comment – good nor bad – have I received on its appearance. Seems to me Mossie you're more attracted to my little bag than you might have us believe." *(Brigid laughs softly)* Shut Mossie up for an entire week. That was the last time in this world I ever saw Seamus O'Rourke.

Brigid is lost in this story of her late husband. We can see how much she loved him.

BRIGID: I never heard that story before.

JOSEPH: Well, I only told it because that's Sean through and through. Easy going nature. A joke over a punch any day. He's taken more from your Seamus than he'll ever know.

BRIGID: *(Thoughtful, surprised at Joseph's insight)* Maybe.

JOSEPH: Different politics aye, but two good men nonetheless, prepared to stand up for what they believe in.

BRIGID: Standing up for what he believed in didn't get Seamus too far, God knows.

JOSEPH: *(Pause)* It must have been rough on you at the time. I never asked or thought or -

BRIGID: It was. If you hadn't come along..

JOSEPH: Ah stop would ye.

BRIGID: It's true though. Two small children and a pittance of a pension. *(Pause. This is difficult for her to say)* I never properly thanked you for that. I was so angry I think at the time, that the only options open to me were marriage or the poorhouse.

JOSEPH: Not great options right enough!

BRIGID: I was good in school ye know. Better than most others at maths and English.

JOSEPH: You're better at the bookkeeping that me anyways.

BRIGID: I would have loved to go to secondary school, if we'd have had the money. I might have been able to support my children meself then, without the humiliation of relying on the charity of strangers.

JOSEPH: Ye never had to rely on charity?

BRIGID: I did ye know. Father Dempsey used to come up to me every week with contributions from the collection. I've made sure to pay him back twenty times over in the years since.

JOSEPH: A good man, Father Dempsey.

BRIGID: He is right enough. He used to drive me mad though telling me I needed to get married again – and me only widowed a few short months. And then you came calling.

JOSEPH: Aye.

BRIGID: Why though?

JOSEPH: *(Evasive)* You seemed a grand woman.

BRIGID: You could have had the pick of Maynooth girls in your day. I was a widow with two children. Why me?

JOSEPH: Alright, 'twas Father Dempsey.

BRIGID: Christ almighty I hope you didn't think I sent him to you? Oh that's mortifying. Why in the name of God would he tell you to marry me?

JOSEPH: It wasn't quite like that.

BRIGID: What was it like then?

JOSEPH: Ah..there was…talk.

BRIGID: Talk?

JOSEPH: Yeah. Around the place. About me. Still being single at my age and that sort of thing.

BRIGID: Mossie Kinsella kind of talk?

JOSEPH: Something like that. There was no grounds to it now, or anything like that. No reason for it.

BRIGID: Sure who'd pay heed to anything that man had to say?

JOSEPH: It wasn't just Mossie, it was…others too.

BRIGID: What business was it of anyone's if you weren't married?

JOSEPH: Ah…talk like that can be harmful – I don't mind so much for myself, but I've the business to think about. Anne was upset about it too. She was soon to marry Denis Kilbride and said it would upset his career if she had a brother that.. Anyway, Mammy had recently passed away, God rest her, and Father Dempsey thought it might be a good time to bring another woman into the place. Put a stop to the talk, as it were.

BRIGID: And he said to ask me. God help us!

JOSESPH: Well, he wasn't quite so blunt about it.

BRIGID: No?

JOSEPH: No. He did give me a choice.

BRIGID: A choice? Of how many, can I ask?

JOSEPH: Two.

BRIGID: Two. Me and who else?

JOSEPH: You and…Mrs. O'Donoghue.

BRIGID: Maggie?

JOSEPH: Yes. Didn't Jack O'Donoghue die around the same time? Fell off the roof of Mossie Kinsella's barn.

BRIGID: So what was the arrangement then? You choose one of us to marry and the other one gets to be the Father's housekeeper?

JOSEPH: Yes – if he couldn't find another man to take her on. I think he had Paddy in mind for that.

BRIGID: Did you know Maggie at all?

JOSEPH: Not really, no.

BRIGID: How did I get to be so lucky, may I ask.

JOSEPH: Well….I told the Father I'd think about it. And I did. Then Paddy and myself had a talk about it.

BRIGID: *(A little bitter)* God forbid that Paddy would be deprived of his say.

JOSEPH: He was very helpful actually.

BRIGID: Was he.

JOSEPH: Yes. He said that the Lord Almighty himself would never in ten lifetimes persuade Paddy Dooley into a marriage with any woman of any description, but if I felt the want of a bit of company sometimes, now that my mother had passed, then maybe I should think on it for a while.

BRIGID: And did you?

JOSEPH: What?

BRIGID: Feel the want of company?

JOSEPH: Not really, no.

BRIGID: Right. Did Paddy have any advice on what woman you should choose?

JOSEPH: He did. He was very helpful there too. He said that it was much of a muchness really.

BRIGID: Much of a muchness?

JOSEPH: That's right.

BRIGID: *(Brigid is at a bit of a loss)* So why me?

JOSEPH: I thought about it for a week or two, and couldn't make up my mind so on the Tuesday at early morning mass, I asked the man above for a bit of guidance on the matter.

BRIGID: Did he have much to say?

JOSEPH: Not a lot, no. But then I walked straight from the Church to Mrs. O'Donoghue's house.

BRIGID: Maggie? You went to Maggie first?

JOSEPH: Well, her house is a lot closer to the Church than yours was at the time. You lived a good bit out if you remember. You were a mile or two beyond the crossroads.

BRIGID: And she turned you down? I can't believe she kept that quiet all these years.

JOSEPH: No. She wasn't there. I took it a sign that it wasn't to be and came on over to you.

BRIGID: I remember it well. 'Good afternoon Mrs. O'Rourke. Would you like to get married?'

JOSEPH: Well, I'm not much of a man for the romancing. You should know that by now. And anyway, I knew I wasn't what you wanted, so…. (*Long beat as both think that this is the life neither of them really wanted*) I hope…I've fulfilled my part of the bargain? I've tried to be as good a father to Sean and Mary as a man of my little experience could.

BRIGID: Ye have Joseph. The pair of them are lucky to have you.

JOSEPH: And I'm lucky to have them and you've given me Tomas. And little Moll.

BRIGID: And Joseph Junior.

JOSEPH: And Joseph Junior, the Lord have mercy on him.

There is a shout from another room. It is Moll, feeling unwell.

MOLL: (*Distant*) Mammy! Mammy!

Brigid immediately jumps out of bed and rushes to put on her dressing gown.

BRIGID: I'm coming love.

JOSEPH: Would ye leave her be. It's probably just a bad dream. She'll go back to sleep in no time.

Brigid ignores him and rushes out. We hear Joseph open the bottle of whiskey and pour himself a glass and drink it.

MOLL: (*Distant*) I feel hot, and sick.

BRIGID: (*Distant*) Were you down by the river today?

MOLL: (*Distant*) Only for a tiny bit. Judy was there and -

BRIGID: (*Distant*) The next time you are there, I will drag you home. (*Moll protests*) I mean it. Now, I'll open the window and it'll cool you down and we'll see how you are tomorrow.

The distant sound of a window opening, Brigid wishing Moll 'goodnight' and Brigid returning to the room.

JOSEPH: All ok?

BRIGID: She has a very high temperature again. Playing down by the river today. I warned her not to go near it. The smell coming out of it. It can't be good. I might take her to Doctor Grogan in the morning.

JOSEPH: Ye have a path worn to that man's house.

BRIGID: Yes, and I'll wear ten more if that's what it takes to keep another child of mine from the cemetery.

JOSEPH: Nobody is going to the cemetery, Brigid.

BRIGID: And what would you know about it Joseph Barry? Last time I checked it was whiskey in that bottle ye have hidden under the bed, and not the remnants of the bloody salmon of knowledge.

There is a pause as Joseph absorbs this latest criticism, and Brigid returns to bed.

JOSEPH: Moll is a strong child.

BRIGID: That's what we said about our Joseph.

JOSEPH: We did everything we could for him.

BRIGID: It wasn't enough though. It was never enough.

There is a long pause.

BRIGID: Nobody really understands.

JOSEPH: No. And we can't expect them to.

Long pause.

BRIGID: Are you…happy Joseph?

JOSEPH: Happy?

BRIGID: Yes. Do you think you're happy? In your life?

JOSEPH: *(He considers this question)* I've no complaints.

BRIGID: No complaints.

JOSEPH: I like you well enough, Brigid. I think we've made the best of it.

BRIGID: *(Sadly)* Yes.

She moves closer to him in the bed. He freezes.

BRIGID: *(Attempt to get close to him)* I like you well enough too Joseph.

JOSEPH: *(Deflect, uncomfortable)* Ye know Paddy is coming in early in the morning?

BRIGID: *(Off balance)* Paddy?

JOSEPH: To help with the stocktaking. He said he'd be in before opening.

BRIGID: Right.

JOSEPH: We'd better get some sleep so. Early start.

BRIGID: Early start. That's right.

They move apart. Joseph moves as far away in the bed as possible and turns his back. Long pause

BRIGID: Goodnight Joseph

JOSEPH: Goodnight Brigid. God Bless.

BRIGID: God Bless.

Silence for a while.

BRIGID: It's probably a good idea to change the bread supplier alright.

JOSEPH: What?

BRIGID: The bread supplier? You're probably right. We should change.

JOSEPH: Okay then.

BRIGID: Okay.

END OF EPISODE

EPISODE 10 – RIC STATION RAID, OCT. 1920

Scene 1 - Outdoor

Night time sounds.

SEAN: *(Whisper)* Have you got your gun, O'Toole?

ALAN: I do. Thanks for asking me along. I –

The sudden sound of squeaky bicycles

SEAN: Shussh. *(The bicycle sounds fade)* Come on.

They run, footsteps fading.

VOICEOVER: Fractured – a family, a nation, a dream. By late 1920, the IRA were raiding for arms…

Scene 2 - Indoor – RIC station.

DWYER: *(Calling after a member of the public)* I'll send someone up to take a statement tomorrow, Mr. O'Carroll. Bye now. *(To the others)* That man refuses to believe his son is stealing those cows. Stiff? *(He calls)* Stiff!

STIFF: Sir?

DWYER: How's the sandwiches for Blake's party coming along?

STIFF: I didn't sign up to make sandwiches for someone who's retiring.

HUGHES: You lazy little feck. Go stand at the door then, give us a whistle when Blakes comes.

STIFF: I ain't taking no orders from you, you ain't been promoted yet, you know.

HUGHES: So, you want Blake to come in and surprise us instead of us surprising him, is that it?

STIFF: It's just… I don't like going out there, I get abused by all and sundry.

DWYER: The lad has a point. I went into Caulfields's pub the other day and you'd swear I was carrying the black plague.

STIFF: It was probably the way you smelled, Sarge.

DWYER: You're a fierce funny chap, so you are. You weren't laughing a few weeks ago when we sent you to Buckleys for the butter.

STIFF: I wouldn't give 'em the business now. When they're all locked up, I'll be the one laughing.

HUGHES: I can't help thinking it's not right, though, to be locking up our own.

DWYER: I'll tell you what's not right. My wife will hardly go out the door these days, she says people she's known all her life cross the other side of the street to avoid her. If it goes on much longer, I'll have to retire meself.

HUGHES: And give into them? No chance.

DWYER: It's easier for the likes of you, when you don't have family or a sweetheart.

STIFF: Hughes does 'ave a sweet 'eart.

HUGHES: I do not.

STIFF: Course ya do. Wot's that red face for?

HUGHES: I have a red face naturally.

STIFF: A Stor mo Chroi.*(He makes a mess of pronouncing it)*

HUGHES: Where did…? You looked at my letter, you little English fec -

STIFF: Ya wrote it in work, I thought it was a report. *(To Dwyer who is laughing)* I wouldn't have thought nothing of it, Sarge, only there was this like, kiss beside it. Wot does it mean then A Stor mo Chroi?

The two men laugh.

DWYER: It means 'love of my heart..'

STIFF: Jesus.

HUGHES: It was to my mother. *(They laugh harder)* I'm fond of her.

DWYER: Even though you told us she's dead two years now?

More laughter.

HUGHES: Reading my private correspondence, that's an offense, Stiff.

DWYER: Who is this girl?

HUGHES: None of your business.

DWYER: So, there is someone!

HUGHES: I didn't say that, I just said it's not your business.

STIFF: Is she from your home place?

HUGHES: I'm saying nothing.

STIFF: She's not from Maynooth, there's just a load of old dogs here.

DWYER: There's many fine women in Maynooth, including my wife.

HUGHES: It's not your wife, Dwyer.

They laugh. Beat

DWYER: But she's a local lass, I bet.

HUGHES: I'm not saying, I've told her to lie low until all this trouble is over.

STIFF: Lie low. I'll bet you have.

More laughter.

HUGHES: Stop that now, she's a respectable girl.

STIFF: Respectable women are over-rated. That Cissy one, d'you know her, works in the College, she's got a gamey eye.

DWYER: Curb that talk now. You're an officer of the law.

STIFF: I'm not a priest, am I? Though by all accounts they're as bad as/

DWYER: Stiff!

HUGHES: That's terrible talk. *(To Dwyer)* But that's the English for you. *(Beat. Goes to door, peers out)* Where is this fella?

DWYER: He left about an hour ago, something about a broken window.

HUGHES: It must be a rake of broken windows, he's that long away.

STIFF: I couldn't believe he was retiring.

DWYER: Aw, he's getting on.

STIFF: He told me when I came over 'ere, like two months ago, that in Ireland, policing was a noble job and they'd have to carry him out of the station in a box.

DWYER: Aye, then it became a possibility and he didn't fancy it at all.

They laugh.

HUGHES: Kildare is not as bad as some of the places. I know a chap in Cork, he says it's savage for the RIC down there.

DWYER: Aye and it won't get any easier when McSwiney starves himself to death.

STIFF: Who's that?

DWYER: Lord Mayor of Cork, currently on hunger strike.

STIFF: They won't let him starve.

DWYER: And what would you have them do? If they release McSwiney, they have to release all the prisoners. That'll undermine the police force. Whatever way you look at it, it's a terrible business.

STIFF: It's a fuckin' terrible country, that's why.

HUGHES/DWYER: Shut up.

HUGHES: And I can see the hunger striker's point. A lot of them are untried and uncharged. It's not right keeping untried men in prison. That undermines us too.

DWYER: Would you retire yourself, Hughes, if it got worse up here?

HUGHES: I would not. It's all I ever wanted in my whole life.

STIFF: I'd be gone 'ome in the morning if I had enough money. I 'ate the job.

HUGHES: I love it.

STIFF: Why, for bleeding sake?

HUGHES: Aw, it's a stupid story but when I was, I don't know, a lad of about five or six, one of the neighbours, that Mammy got on well with, robbed her.

STIFF: Bet she didn't get on too well with her after that.

HUGHES: She did not. Anyway, two whole shillings was taken from her. Daddy was dead so Michael, my eldest brother, took Mammy off to the RIC station. And after a bit of a court case, they got the money back for her.

DWYER: Can't beat the RIC!

HUGHES: That's it. I thought, there's a job I want for meself.

DWYER: Jaysus, Stiff, did you know we're working with a saint here.

HUGHES: I'm not saying I'm a saint. Just that it's a good job and no IRA or Volunteer or Tan is going to put me off it.

Door opening, Teresa enters.

HUGHES: Hello there…Mrs?

THERESA: Miss. Teresa.

HUGHES: Miss. What can I do for you today?

THERESA: I've lost my cat.

HUGHES: Have you tried looking for it?

TERESA: Isn't that your job?

HUGHES: Not really no. We are -

TERESA: I was told by the Volunteers that they don't look for cats so I thought I'd try you lot. I must say, I'm very disappointed and -

DWYER: Hello there, Teresa. How's everything? You've lost your cat, have you?

TERESA: I have. White with a black patch on its eye. It looks like a fugitive.

DWYER: I think I know the one. I tell you what, I'll keep a special eye out for it.

TERESA: I'll be in tomorrow to see if there's any news.

DWYER: You do that. Good day, Teresa

TERESA: Write it down in the book.

DWYER: Stiff's going to do it for you now. Stiff?

Stiff, not at all happy, takes out the book, and turns some pages.

STIFF: Black and white cat, is it?

TERESA: That implies fifty percent white and fifty percent black. This cat is more eighty-three percent white and seventeen percent black. On his eye. Have you got that?

STIFF: I do.

TERESA: He answers to the name Bartholomew. Not B-A-R-T-O-L-M-U. which is how some eejit spelt it the last time he went wandering. *(Stiff dutifully writes it down)* Right. Good. I'll be on my way.

Footsteps as she leaves. The sound of the door opening, closing.

DWYER: There's a woman who could make you regret joining the RIC.

STIFF: Are we really going looking for her cat?

DWYER: If you're ever thinking of promotion, you need to know how to handle the locals. That's Teresa, just tell her you'll do whatever she asks.

STIFF: She seems like a hard nut, alright.

HUGHES: A conversation that's due to take place tomorrow, she'd kill it stone dead today.

DWYER: One of the local eccentrics, is Teresa.

HUGHES: Every place has them. Sure, Wolfhill, where I grew up, was full of them.

STIFF: Wot a name, Wolfhill, ey?

HUGHES: It doesn't live up to it. Small place on the border of Kildare and Carlow, nothing in it, really. We have -

Door opens. Teresa arrives back in. Running. She a bit flustered.

TERESA: This is a fine pickle.

HUGHES: What is Miss…eh, Teresa.

TERESA: Them outside, they'll probably shoot me for talking to ye.

DWYER: Who?

TERESA: The two fellows with guns and masks I'm after seeing with Sergeant Blake.

ALL: What?

The door bursts open. Sean and Alan O'Toole wearing scarves, enter with Blake at gunpoint.

SEAN: Hands up! No one move or we shoot Blake.

TERESA: I have to go looking for my cat.

SEAN: There'll be no searching for cats until we get what we want.

TERESA: I hate to tell ye, but a free Ireland's a bit of a way off right now.

O'TOOLE: Shut up.

BLAKE: *(Trying to calm things)* What is it ye want, boys?

SEAN: Guns. Everything you have here. Hand them over.

BLAKE: Do not men. *(To Sean)* Youse are nothing but thugs.

SEAN: I'll blow your brains out, that'll be some retirement present for you, won't it?

BLAKE: This is madness.

SEAN: Guns. Now.

BLAKE: I know your voice.

SEAN: You won't get a conviction on a voice. *(To Dwyer, Hughes and Stiff)* Hand over all your guns, all your bullets, everything you have here or this fella gets it.

ALAN: I'll go in the back, see what's out there.

SEAN: Good man.

Alan runs off.

TERESA: Excuse me, please.

SEAN: Where do you think you're going?

TERESA: Home.

SEAN: Didn't I just say -

TERESA: You did. I was up with your lot earlier asking ye to look for my cat and youse couldn't be bothered. Now, excuse me -

SEAN: Don't bloody move.

Long pause.

HUGHES: Aw now, boys, she's just a mad woman from the town you should -

TERESA: That's lovely.

HUGHES: Just let her go, boys. You can keep the rest of us.

SEAN: You all stay.

TERESA: For how long?

SEAN: For as long as it takes.

ALAN: *(Distant)* There's ham sandwiches in here. And drink.

SEAN: Forget about the sandwiches and drink. Any guns?

ALAN: *(Sounding as if he's eating)* I'm looking.

SEAN: Hurry up, will you.

A muffled bang from inside the room.

DWYER: Mind that press in there, we only got it replaced a month ago.

BLAKE: What are sandwiches and drink doing out back?

DWYER: Surprise party for you. On your retirement. *(With irony)* Surprise! *(Another bang)* Mind the fecking counter!

SEAN: He'll do what has to be done.

BLAKE: A surprise party. That was a nice thought.

DWYER: Aye, we invited all your old friends. They'll be waiting for you in the pub in an hour and -

BLAKE: That was thoughtful.

SEAN: Stop yabbering. *(Calling)* And will you hurry up back there.

Alan arrives out chewing a sandwich under his scarf. He tries to talk.

ALAN: Some guns, bullets and that. I took the drink as well. Nice sandwiches.

SEAN: Load them up. Take that fecking sandwich out of your mouth. Jesus!

The sound of guns being thrown into bags.

HUGHES: Just calm down, don't lose it, alright.

SEAN: Throw your gun into the bag. *(Long pause. Sound of gun being put in bag)* And ye other two. *(To Stiff)* Oh, look at the little Tan boy, shaking like a leaf. Are you scared.?

A click of a gun.

HUGHES: He was in the war, leave him be.

ALAN: *(Full of bravado, leaning in)* If we want to point a gun at a Tan, we will.

In one sudden swift movement, Hughes pulls the scarf down from Alan's face. Commotion.

ALAN: You bloody pulled my scarf down. I'll have you for that.

HUGHES: Alan O'Toole. I know you.

SEAN: Let's go. Let's go.

ALAN: I'll get you for that. I'll get you.

DWYER: We'll get you first, mark my words. I know you, Alan O'Toole.

Sean and Alan, guns clanking in the bag, run out.

BLAKE: Stiff, get yourself together man. Stop that shaking.

STIFF: Sorry. Sarge. It's just -

BLAKE: I don't want to hear it. Dwyer, get on your bike and off with you to O'Toole's. Tell his father that if we find out that his son is in the place, it'll be the worse for them.

DWYER: I will.

HUGHES: He's got a sweetheart in Kilcock, so I'll get on to the station there to keep an eye on her. We'll catch up with him sir.

BLAKE: He'll sing like a canary, I've known that lad since he was in nappies. He'll tell us what we want to know. Hughes?

HUGHES: Sir?

BLAKE: That was a reckless thing to do but... well done, it'll go down on your record.

HUGHES: Thanks sir. I'll get on out to Kilcock now.

DWYER: Stiff, go with him. Do you good to get to know the land.

STIFF: *(Shaking)* I thought I might write up the report, Sarge. I – I – I

Dwyer is about to say something but Blake notes how the young man is shaking

BLAKE: Good, idea, stay here. Write up the report.

TERESA: Which one of ye will be out looking for my cat?

HUGHES: I'd best be off to Kilcock. I'll be with the O'Tooles.

STIFF: I've a report to write.

They all leave.

DWYER: And Sergeant Blake is retiring, Teresa and going to the pub with his friends. I can safely say your cat is not top of our priority list. Boys, go get O'Toole. Make him sing.

END OF EPISODE

EPISODE 11 – SEAN GOES ON THE RUN, OCT. 1920

Scene 1 - Park

Park noises, outdoor. The girls are lying on the grass, trying to guess Cissy's new boyfriend.

MARY: It's never that smelly, black-toothed fellow with the limp?

CISSY: That's a fine way to talk about your father, Mary.

The girls laugh.

CATHERINE LONG: Is it the lad with the red hair and the skin rashes?

CISSY: Alan O'Toole? I wouldn't be seen dead with him, Catherine Long.

CATHERINE LONG: Just as well because the RIC picked him up yesterday evening and by all accounts he's half dead himself.

LIZZIE: What did he do?

CATHERINE LONG: Well, apparently him and this other fellow –

Fade

VOICEOVER: Fractured – a family…a nation…a dream

Scene 2 - Barry's parlour

Sounds of people preparing to eat, the clatter of dishes, drink being poured, chairs being pulled out.

JOSEPH: Six policemen killed ye say Father? Sit in there now.

FATHER DEMPSEY: Thanks, Joseph. That's right, Milltown Malbay. Only about ten days ago. That smells delicious Mrs. Barry.

BRIGID: Oh now, it's nothing Father. Sure aren't we only delighted to have ye. *(Moving back to kitchen, calling)* Help yourself now

FATHER DEMPSEY: I always look forward to your Sunday roasts, Mrs. Barry.

JOSEPH: Six dead, begod, that's a shocking state of affairs.

FATHER DEMPSEY: It is right enough. And Father O'Brien, my friend in Galway, tells me that people are being dragged out of their beds in the middle of the night and flogged in the street. *(Food being served)* That's enough, thanks.

JOSEPH: No!

SEAN: It's true Joseph. Happening in Cork too.

BRIGID: *(Coming from kitchen, another bowl is laid on the table)* Careful now, it's hot.

SEAN: And two Sinn Fein men just shot for no reason in Tipperary last week.

FATHER DEMPSEY: Happening all over the country, it seems.

Light footsteps as Moll enters, carefully carrying a jug of water.

BRIGID: *(From the kitchen)* Careful now Moll. Don't spill that water.

JOSEPH: It seems we've been spared the worst of it in these parts, thank God.

TOMAS: I don't know Daddy. They're saying there's at least ten people killed every week in Dublin.

JOSEPH: Ah well now…Dublin is a different kettle of fish.

FATHER DEMPSEY: And don't forget that nasty business in Kill. That poor man.

MOLL: What poor man Daddy?

TOMAS: Nothing for you to worry about Milly Molly! You go on in there and help Mammy. She's not able to manage without you.

MOLL: Is it the man who's starving himself to death beyond in Brixton Prison? *(There is an awkward silence)* We say prayers for him every day in school so we do. Do you think will he die Daddy?

TOMAS: Sure you don't need to be worrying about that Milly Molly.

JOSEPH: You go help Mammy, Moll. Good girl.

MOLL: Mary O'Brien says he must be like a skeleton now. She says he's definitely going to be turned into a saint. Are you going to make him into a saint Father?

FATHER DEMPSEY: Well now, that wouldn't be my job Molly. That would be a job for the Holy Father himself. Do what your daddy says and run in now and help your Mammy!

MOLL: I'd love to be a saint. I wouldn't like to have to starve meself though.

JOSEPH: Moll! Help your mother. *(She goes)* What are they teaching them in schools these days at all. Sure she's only a child.

FATHER DEMPSEY: Hard to shield them from it Joseph. They're going to hear about these things. Sure, wasn't the police barracks raided only the other day? Very fortunate that somebody wasn't murdered, so I've heard.

SEAN: I don't think it was that bad Father.

FATHER DEMPSEY: They stole guns son. Guns and ammunition. What do you think they're going to do with them? More senseless death and destruction.

Mary enters with more food.

MARY: You're right Father. Those Officers in the station could have been killed. I think it's a disgrace so I do.

SEAN: How can it be a disgrace Mary, when the Church itself has come down on our side?

FATHER DEMPSEY: Ah well now Sean, I don't think...

SEAN: 'Inhuman oppression' – that's what they called it. Amn't I right Father?

MARY: Ye are not right.

Brigid enters and sits down.

BRIGID: Now now. The Father is only here for his Sunday dinner. Let's leave politics out of it. Why the whole world can't just live in peace is beyond me.

MARY: A bit hard to live in peace when a man only trying to do a day's work has his life threatened by gurriers in masks.

SEAN: The only gurriers in this country are the ones supposed to be running it.

BRIGID: Sean..

MARY: You've no idea what you're talking about Sean Barry.

SEAN: Oh my sincere apologies Mary. I wasn't aware that being a world expert on fashion and hair curlers qualifies a person to be a political commentator.

BRIGID: That's enough!

MARY: Ye think ye know it all Sean.

SEAN: I think I know more than you.

MARY: Ye might be surprised the things I know.

BRIGID: *(Interrupting)* Father, will you lead us in grace, please?

FATHER DEMPSEY: I'd be delighted Mrs. Barry. In the name of the Father, and of the Son, and of the Holy...

There is a furious banging on the kitchen door.

JOSEPH: Who would that be, knocking at this hour? *(More banging on the door)* Why in God's name don't they come around the front?

There is shouting from behind the door, a young girl's voice.

GIRL 1: *(Distant)* Sean Barry! Sean Barry! Urgent message for Sean Barry!

SEAN: I better get that.

He walks out to the back door.

Scene 3 – Back door

SEAN: For God's sake, keep your voice down. What is it?

GIRL 2: Are you Sean Barry?

SEAN: I am.

GIRL 1: Urgent message from Paddy Colgan. Here. He says you've got 20 minutes – only about 15 now by my reckoning. It took me a good five minutes to get here.

The girls leave.

Scene 4 – Barry's parlour

Sean comes back into the kitchen.

BRIGID: What is it son?

MARY: Top secret mission for the Volunteers? Sure I don't know how they manage without you.

TOMAS: Sean?

MARY: Probably has to go and lick the arse of Paddy Colgan. I believe he has a team of Volunteers set up to do just that.

BRIGID: Father I'm so sorry. Mary! That's no language for a young lady. And with Father Dempsey here as our guest!

MARY: Sorry Mammy. I'm really sorry Father. I forgot meself for a minute.

TOMAS: What's wrong Sean.

FATHER DEMPSEY: Ah sure don't be worrying about me. I've heard worse in my time.

JOSEPH: Sean? Talk to us. What's happening?

SEAN: I have to go.

BRIGID: Ah for God's sake. Do ye have to be at their beck and call at all times of the day and night. Can ye not have a bit of dinner first?

SEAN: I can't Mammy no, I'm sorry.

BRIGID: What's wrong Sean? You're gone terrible white.

MOLL: I'd go white too if I had to lick Paddy Colgan's arse.

JOSEPH/BRIGID: Moll!

JOSEPH: Does it say where you have to go?

SEAN: On the back. Here.

He hands his father the note.

JOSEPH: Ye better get going. *(Standing)* What do you need?

BRIGID: Will someone please tell me what's going on?

JOSEPH: The RIC want to question him, Brigid.

BRIGID: The RIC? Jesus Christ, begging your pardon Father. What have you done?

SEAN: It's a misunderstanding.

BRIGID: What's a misunderstanding? Out with it. Now.

JOSEPH: Brigid, he really has to go.

SEAN: I can't talk about it Mammy. I'm sorry. But if they find me here..

BRIGID: What of it? Answer their questions. If you run now son they'll only think you're guilty. *(Silence)* Ah no. Ah son. Sean. What have you done?

SEAN: Nothing Mammy. Nothing. Honest to God, you know what they're like. They just want to question me. That's all it says. I'm not being arrested or anything. But…once they have me Mammy, they won't let go. You know that.

MOLL: Will they make you starve yourself like that fella in Brixton Prison?

SEAN: No Milly Molly. Don't you worry about that. There's nobody in the wide world could make me starve meself!

BRIGID: Where do you have to go?

SEAN: Dublin. There's a safe house.

BRIGID: How will ye get to Dublin on a Sunday evening? Sure there'll be no trains running.

SEAN: I don't know. I'll just leave here for the moment and figure it out. I'll take the bicycle. Maybe I can catch a lift on the road.

MARY: Don't be doing that Sean. It's not safe. You never know who's going to pick you up.

BRIGID: I'll pack a bag for you.

JOSEPH: He can't bring a bag with him Brigid. Sure it'll be clear to everyone he's a man on the run.

SEAN: I don't have time anyway. Look they'll be here in ten minutes. Do ye think maybe I could hide out in Poor Brid's for the night?

BRIGID: No you cannot. Poor Brid has enough on her plate, what with the little lad not settling. The poor child would lose his life if the RIC came banging on their door.

JOSEPH: I think you'd just better go now Sean. Ye can't get caught.

MARY: You can't just go outside like that either. Sure everybody knows who you are. They'll pick you up in no time.

JOSEPH: I've a big coat you could wear. It might disguise you a bit.

MOLL: You could wear my new scarf if you like? The one that Mammy knitted for me?

FATHER DEMPSEY: I have an idea that might work. *(He begins to remove his cassock)* Sean, quickly. Put on my cassock.

BRIGID: Father – no. That's not necessary at all.

JOSEPH: Yes it is Brigid. Here Father, let me help. Just put your hands up, there, I've got it.

The Father is left standing in his ordinary clothes.

MOLL: You look funny Father!

FATHER DEMPSEY: I do, don't I? I feel funny too Moll. Take the biretta too, Sean. I left it over there on the sideboard. The RIC tend not to question priests I find. Now make your way to the College. Ask for Father Hipwell. He's a good man. Tell him I sent you. They have visitors from Dublin all the time. One more priest in the car on the way back won't make too much difference.

BRIGID: Oh Father. Thank you.

JOSEPH: Don't go just yet, Sean. I've something you might need. Hang on there now.

He leaves the room.

SEAN: You're a good man Father Dempsey. I won't forget this.

FATHER DEMPSEY: I'll pray for you Sean.

BRIGID: Will you give him your blessing Father, before he goes? Keep him safe on the road.

FATHER DEMPSEY: I will of course. *(Murmur)* Go in peace and safety.

SEAN: I'll be seeing you, little brother.

TOMAS: Stay safe Sean.

SEAN: Bye Molly. See you soon!

MOLLY: Don't be starving yourself Sean.

SEAN: I won't. I promise.

SEAN: I'll be lonely without ye Mary. No one to fight with me. Friends?

MARY: Friends. Give me a hug. *(She hugs him)* Please be careful Sean. I don't want anything to happen to you.

SEAN: Course I will. The ladies of Maynooth would be distraught if anything was to happen to Sean Barry, now wouldn't they?

MARY: *(Laughs, tearful)* How will they manage without you?

SEAN: God knows!

Joseph returns with a wad of banknotes, which he hands to Sean.

JOSEPH: Here. A bit of money. You'll need it.

SEAN: You're a good man Joseph Barry. *(To Brigid)* I'm so sorry Mam. I know you're disappointed in me.

BRIGID: I'm not disappointed in ye son. I could never be disappointed in ye. Sure look at the cut of you! You make a very handsome priest. What mother wouldn't be bursting with pride!

SEAN: Bye Mam.

They hug.

BRIGID: Look after yourself Sean. Come back to me in one piece.

SEAN: I will Mammy. I promise. *(He looks at the Father)* Father Hipwell, right Father?

FATHER DEMPSEY: Father Hipwell. He'll get you sorted.

SEAN: Right. I'll send word as soon as I'm safe. See ye all soon!

He leaves. There is a long pause, as the family adjust.

FATHER DEMPSEY: I'd better be going too. Wouldn't do for the RIC to find me here in this garb. They'd know immediately where to look for Sean.

BRIGID: Oh Father. I don't know where we'd be without you. And you didn't even get a bite to eat, God knows. Let me just get a plate together for you to take home.

FATHER DEMPSEY: Not at all. Not at all. The RIC will be here before you know it. You've enough to be doing.

JOSEPH: Thank you Father. For everything. I..

FATHER DEMPSEY: Goodnight Joseph. Goodnight all.

BRIGID / JOSEPH: Goodnight Father.

He leaves in a hurry. Door closes.

BRIGID: God, what a mess. What are we going to do at all?

MOLL: I'm starving. Can we eat now?

BRIGID: Oh for God's sake Moll. Can you think of nothing but your belly?

JOSEPH: I think Moll might have the right idea.

BRIGID: What? Joseph, the RIC..

JOSEPH: Mary, will ye please take away the Father's plate, and Sean's too. Wash them up. *(The clatter of tidying up)* Move up now everyone. Put food on your plates and start eating. *(To Brigid)* Everyone. When the RIC arrive, we're having a bit of dinner. We don't know where Sean is.

MOLL: Do we have to say Grace again, or can we just eat?

JOSEPH: I'd say we can just eat Molly. The roast looks..

There is another loud banging on the front door.

MOLL: Ah no! I was just getting started.

JOSEPH: We don't know where Sean is.

He gets up to open the door.

Scene 5 - Front Door.

We follow Joseph out to the door. Hear him opening it. Sounds from outside as the men talk.

DWYER: Joseph

JOSEPH: Sergeant Tom Dwyer. To what do I owe the pleasure?

DWYER: I'm sorry about this. I'm here in an official capacity.

JOSEPH: I see.

DWYER: This is Officer Stiff and Officer Hughes. We're here to bring your Sean in for questioning.

JOSEPH: Sean you say?

DWYER: That's right Joseph. We need to question Sean.

JOSEPH: About what, can I ask?

DWYER: We'd eh…we'd rather not reveal that for the moment, if you don't mind. It's a confidential matter. I'm sure ye understand.

JOSEPH: Sean's not here.

DWYER: Not here?

JOSEPH: No.

There's an awkward moment.

DWYER: Would ye mind if we came in to have a look for ourselves, like?

JOSEPH: Is it that ye don't believe me Tom Dwyer?

DWYER: Not at all Joseph. Not at all. It's just – we need to confirm these things. All above board, you know?

JOSEPH: I don't actually. Time was a man would take his neighbour at his word.

STIFF: Yes well, changing times old timer. We're got a warrant to search the property, and Sergeant Dwyer here don't need your permission.

DWYER: Officer Stiff! (*Beat*) Can we come in, Joseph?

We hear the door opening wider and the tramp of feet as the men enter.

Scene 6 - Barry's parlour

DWYER: We're disturbing your dinner. Very sorry Mrs. Barry.

BRIGID: Yes Mr. Dwyer.

DWYER: We were looking for Sean?

BRIGID: I think Mr. Barry has already told you he's not here?

DWYER: That's right. Have ye any idea where he might be?

BRIGID: None at all, Mr. Dwyer. Will that be all?

DWYER: We..eh…we'd like to search the house, if that's alright.

BRIGID: And if it's not?

DWYER: I have a warrant, very sorry Mrs. Barry. Officer Stiff, will you please search the bar and the cellar?

JOSEPH: Nobody is going near my cellar without me to supervise.

DWYER: Fine. Officer Hughes, please take the rest of the ground floor. I'll take the upper floor.

Joseph and Stiff leave the room

BRIGID: Nobody's rooting through my bedrooms without me there either.

TOMAS: I'll go with you, Mammy. Just in case. Come on, Moll, you come too.

They leave. Mary and Hughes are left alone

MARY: A fine spectacle you're after making of me altogether! Is this how you treat all your girlfriends Joseph Hughes?

HUGHES: Mary love, I'm so sorry. I didn't know the suspect was your brother. I..

MARY: Oh – so it's 'the suspect' now is it? And what am I to you then? Huh? The suspect's sister?

HUGHES: I swear I had no idea. I thought we were picking up a customer in the pub.

MARY: On a Sunday afternoon? When every God-fearin' place in the village is closed? Have ye no sense Joseph Hughes?

HUGHES: I didn't think! I'm just doing my job Mary – same as any man.

MARY: Except it's not the same, is it?

Moll shouts from upstairs.

MOLL: *(Distant)* Don't go in my room Mr. Dwyer. It's private! No! Mammy, tell him to get out of my room.

MARY: It's not the same at all.

We hear the sound of Moll crying, and Brigid trying to comfort her.

HUGHES: Mary, please. I love you with all my heart. You know what I do for a living, sweetheart. You've always known. I've never made a secret of it.

MARY: And you're proud of it?

HUGHES: I can't tell a lie Mary. I believe I'm doing the right thing. This is who I am love. I can't change who I am. I love you Mary. I can't change that either.

He goes to embrace her. Tomas enters suddenly. **TOMAS:** What's going on?

HUGHES: Just finishing up in here. *(Calling)* Nothing on this level Sergeant Dwyer.

MARY: Nothing is right!

Tomas is still suspicions. There is the sound of voices outside as the Officers leave.

TOMAS: The rest of the RIC traitors are leaving now. Bye bye!

HUGHES: Goodbye Miss Barry.

MARY: *(With grit)* Yes, goodbye. I hope we don't see you around here again.

Enter Dwyer, Joseph, Brigid and Moll.

DWYER: Apologies for the intrusion Mrs. Barry.

BRIGID: Goodbye Mr. Dwyer.

MOLL: They went into my room Daddy.

DWYER: If ye hear anything from Sean ye might let us know.

JOSEPH: I don't think so.

DWYER: I'm sorry Joseph.

JOSEPH: I don't want you near my pub or my shop again.

Door closes.

Scene 7 - Bedroom – some hours later.

Mary sobs quietly.

TOMAS: *(Distant. Growing closer)* Mary? Mammy's wondering if you can put Moll to bed. *(He enters pause)* Are you all right? *(He feels awkward)* Sean'll be grand, you know.

MARY: Leave me alone. I'll be down in a minute.

Long beat

TOMAS: That RIC man you were talking to today, he was the same one as was in the pub on the day of the rally, wasn't he?

MARY: I wasn't talking to him.

TOMAS: We're living in dangerous times, Mary.

MARY: What are you saying?

TOMAS: You should be careful. *(Beat)* I'll send Moll up.

His footsteps retreat. Mary starts to sob again.

END OF EPISODE

EPISODE 12 – WOMEN'S FIRST AID, OCT. 1920

Scene 1 - The Dwyer's home

BETTY DWYER: I don't think I can go. Brigid must hate me.

DWYER: Betty love. She's been your best friend for years.

BETTY: Tom! You arrested her son last week.

DWYER: That's not your fault.

BETTY: I can't face her.

DWYER: Just go. If you don't leave now you'll be late.

VOICEOVER: Fractured – a family, a nation, a dream.

Scene 2 – Parish Hall

Sounds of people talking quietly and walking into the hall, taking seats etc.

POOR BRID: There ye are Mrs. Barry. I thought I'd come in a few minutes early and give you a hand setting up.

BRIGID: Ah you're very good Mrs. O'Sullivan. There's not much to do. And we've a good crowd in already.

POOR BRID: Very exciting for our women's group isn't it? Our first public meeting. I think it was a great idea to focus on first aid. I've loads of questions! *(To attendee)* How'ye Mr. O'Brien! Hope your mammy is feeling a bit better? *(To Brigid)* Death's door, the Lord have mercy on her. Shocking pain. I knew when I saw her last month, and the bloodshot eyes of her and the terrible blue tinge to her skin that she wasn't long for this world. How many chairs will we need do you think?

BRIGID: There should be enough there, I'd say. Madge O'Doherty gave me some notes to copy out – basic first aid – so we can give them to people at the end. I did 20 copies. I hope that's enough.

POOR BRID: Ah Mrs. Barry. You copied all these by yourself? Why didn't you ask me to help? God knows you've enough on your plate, what with Sean and everything.

BRIGID: Ah. Good to have something else to focus on. Takes my mind off it all.

POOR BRID: Has there been any word?

BRIGID: We got word he was safe – whatever that means. To my mind though, if you're not safe enough to be able to sleep in your own bed, then you're not safe at all. But sure, what do I know?

POOR BRID: The RIC don't have him anyway, and that's something I suppose. I couldn't believe they sent Tom Dwyer to your house to pick him up.

BRIGID: I know.

POOR BRID: And you friends with Betty this long time.

BRIGID: Twenty years.

POOR BRID: She was always in and out of the place when I lived with you. 'No sugar Brid. I'm sweet enough'!

BRIGID: In fairness, she was very good to me when I married Joseph. There were plenty who weren't.

POOR BRID: Have you seen her since?

BRIGID: Hard to avoid, and she only living across the street.

POOR BRID: Have ye spoken?

BRIGID: What do you say? She looks the other way and so do I.

POOR BRID: God.

BRIGID: I know. And Joseph is refusing to serve them in the shop.

POOR BRID: I suppose you can't blame him.

BRIGID: No. And in one way I'm glad because of Sean, but then I feel terrible mean because didn't I used to be in exactly the same position as Betty? I should know what it's like. It's just…when it comes to your own door…

POOR BRID: And your own son.

BRIGID: And my own son. I'm really feeling for poor Kevin Barry's mother, I'll tell ye. He's only a child, God love him – same age as Tomas.

POOR BRID: It breaks my heart Mrs. Barry. I can't believe they're going to hang him.

Enter Maggie.

MAGGIE: What? Oh Brigid no. They're never going to hang him? They couldn't.

POOR BRID: They are Mrs. O'Donoghue. November 1st. Did you not hear?

MAGGIE: Nobody told me. How come nobody told me?

POOR BRID: Sure it was in all the papers.

MAGGIE: In the papers? How? When did this happen?

POOR BRID: They court martialed him. It was so unfair. It wasn't his bullet at all that killed the soldier.

MAGGIE: There was a soldier killed?

BRIGID: Yes Mrs. O'Donoghue – do you not remember? I felt very sorry for him – only a young lad too.

MAGGIE: You felt sorry for him?

BRIGID: Well of course I did.

MAGGIE: God you're very forgiving altogether.

BRIGID: What?

POOR BRID: They say hanging is a terrible death. If the rope doesn't break your neck quick enough you can be there for hours. Shivering and shaking…

MAGGIE: Mrs. O'Sullivan…

POOR BRID: The breath being slowly squeezed out of ye. And your eyes bulging and your face turning blue. And your limbs hanging off ye

MAGGIE: STOP will ye! God I'm very sorry Mrs. Barry. That's terrible insensitive of Mrs. O'Sullivan to be saying things like that.

POOR BRID: Insensitive? I only…

MAGGIE: Talking about hanging like that and her poor Sean facing the gallows himself in less than a week.

BRIGID: What? No Mrs. O'Donoghue…/

POOR BRID: Sean isn't…/

Enter Anne.

ANNE: Sean is going to the gallows? Brigid! Why didn't you call me? Compos mentis! I'll organise an injunction immediately. Erratum!

MAGGIE: The poor lad! I never even knew the British had him.

BRIGID: No. Anne. He's not..!

ANNE: I might need Donnacha's help. *(To an attendee)* My son. He's in UCD you know. Studying Law.

POOR BRID: *(Shouts)* It's Kevin Barry who's going to be hanged. Kevin Barry. Not Sean Barry.

MAGGIE: Kevin Barry? Kevin Barry? Oh bless us and save us. And there was me thinking it was young Sean ye were talking about.

ANNE: Kevin Barry? Kevin Barry above in Mounjoy Prison? Sure we know that. That's not news. How is that news?

BRIGID: It's not news. Nobody said it was news. We just said it was terrible sad.

MAGGIE: Aye it is. Terrible sad indeed.

POOR BRID: And poor Terrence McSwiney, God rest him.

MAGGIE: Ah don't be talking. Sure hasn't the Father been praying for him night and day. I can't get the man off his knees at all.

POOR BRID: What it must be like to starve yourself to death.

ANNE: I believe there's huge crowds in London paying their respects.

POOR BRID: 74 days. The pain he must have endured, and his body slowly weakening and shrinking, and him losing all his faculties...

ANNE: A very well educated man. Didn't make it to UCD mind, but he did attend the Royal University in Cork, which is almost as good, I believe.

MAGGIE: The funeral will be only huge.

POOR BRID: And him going blind, I heard, and falling into unconsciousness from the hunger.

Teresa enters.

TERESA: I'm late. Our last meeting started nine minutes after it was supposed to, so I left the shop four minutes later than I should have.

BRIGID: That's fine Teresa. We're still waiting on...

TERESA: I was further delayed by a large group of school children on their way to the church to pray for Terrence McSwiney.

POOR BRID: Oh the children! Did you see my Colm there with all his friends?

TERESA: I saw Colm, yes. No friends.

ANNE: *(Under her breath, to Brigid)* Now, there's a surprise.

BRIGID: Sure they were all probably separated from their friends going to the church. They'd have to be on their best behaviour. Isn't that right Mrs. O'Donoghue?

MAGGIE: Of course that's right. The Father always says that teacher of theirs must have been selected from the demons of hell, with the cane never out of her hand, and a mouth on her sharper than a butcher's knife.

POOR BRID: What?

BRIGID: Ah he's only joking I'm sure.

MAGGIE: No, he actually said...

Enter Madge the Midwife. Late 50s, nervous, traditional, not a great believer in modern medicine.

BRIGID: Mrs. O'Doherty! Great to see you. It's very good of you to come. Thanks for doing this. Come on over here. I've organised this desk for you, I hope that's alright.

MADGE: That's lovely thanks Mrs. Barry. I've never done this before. I don't really know what to do.

BRIGID: Ah you'll be grand. I've made copies of those notes you gave me, they're over here. So you can just work from them if you want, and answer any questions that people have. You'll be great, don't worry.

MADGE: I'll do my best.

BRIGID: Look, we've got a great crowd. They're all interested in what you have to say. I'll just introduce you and then you can start.

MADGE: Righty oh!

BRIGID: Hello everyone. *(Sound of people dies down)* Thanks for coming. We're delighted to see you all here. This is our Maynooth Women's Group, as you know. It's about women helping women – all women, regardless of politics or whatever.

ANNE: Ahem!

BRIGID: We're very lucky today to have Mrs. Madge O'Doherty here. She has delivered many of our children – and even some of us over the years! *(Sound of laughter)* She's here to talk to us about first aid, and how we can help ourselves – and each other – in case of any emergency.

Audience claps.

ANNE: Ahem!

BRIGID: Anne, we might have questions after we're heard what Mrs. O'Doherty has to say.

ANNE: Oh I'm not here to ask a question. No, No. Good Lord no. I'm not staying.

BRIGID: No?

ANNE: No of course not. I'm just here to make a little announcement about my Legal Advice Clinic.

BRIGID: Your Legal Advice Clinic?

ANNE: That's right. Many of you may know that my son, Donnacha is studying Law in UCD. Therefore I myself am in a position to provide ex gratia legal advice to any person requiring it. I've gained valuable experience in the Volunteer Courts, so rest assured it will all take place in loco parentis. Please contact me for further information. Good day to you all. Prima facie.

Sound of her leaving, door opening and closing.

BRIGID: Em. Thank you Anne. Mrs. O'Doherty?

MADGE: Right, well, first of all..

TERESA: Excuse me.

MADGE: Em, yes?

TERESA: I'd be grateful if you could outline your proposed content for this meeting. I'm quite familiar with most aspects of first aid, and don't want to waste my time.

MADGE: Oh.

BRIGID: I don't think you can ever go over this important topic too many times – isn't that right Mrs. O'Doherty? Don't we always have something new to learn?

MADGE: Yes, that's right.

TERESA: Will you be covering the new innovations being discovered on the continent for the treatment of previously incurable diseases? I believe we're very close to a cure for syphilis.

MAGGIE: Oh bless us! Anyone with syphilis deserves everything they get. The Father has no time for anything like that. I mean when Dermot O'Brien...

BRIGID: *(Interrupting)* You were saying Mrs. O'Doherty?

MADGE: I was saying?

TERESA: You were about to outline your proposed content for this session. I need to know if it is worth my while to stay.

MADGE: That's right. Well, em...

TERESA: Do you think, for example, you could cover gunshot wounds? I believe there are tremendous innovations in antiseptics and anaesthesia since the end of the war. Perhaps you could outline some of these for us.

MADGE: Well...

TERESA: The Carrel-Dakin method has proven particularly effective. What is your opinion on it?

MADGE: Carrel..?

TERESA: The Carrel-Dakin method. Using a solution of sodium hypochlorite as an antiseptic in the treatment of infected wounds, thus dramatically reducing the need to amputate.

POOR BRID: Have you ever had to do an amputation Mrs. O'Doherty? I'd say the blood loss must be horrific.

MADGE: No. I've never had to perform an amputation. I'm a midwife.

POOR BRID: Just say now one of the little babies was born with a terrible infected injury? Would you have to amputate then?

MADGE: Babies aren't ever really born with infected injuries.

POOR BRID: Yes, but just imagine one was. Would you have to amputate, and how would you do it?

MADGE: Well, if a baby was born with an infected injury..

POOR BRID: Yes..a really bad one.

MAGGIE: Ah the poor pet.

MADGE: I would try to treat the infection first.

POOR BRID: How would you do that?

TERESA: Would you use the Carrel-Dakin method?

MADGE: I would first of all, clean out the wound.

TERESA: Excellent. With a solution of sodium hypochlorite.

MADGE: Well, no. I don't have any of that. I would use some clean salty water.

TERESA: Water?

POOR BRID: And if that didn't work? Would you amputate then?

MADGE: No. I would apply a bread poultice.

TERESA: A bread poultice?

MADGE: Yes, you heat up some milk in a pan and put in some bread...

TERESA: I know what a bread poultice is. My grandmother used to use them for goodness sake. Medicine has moved on since then.

POOR BRID: And if that didn't work? If it was still really badly infected, with pus coming out of it and all smelly and starting to turn a funny colour? Would you amputate then?

MADGE: Well, no.

POOR BRID: No?

MADGE: No. I..I don't know how to amputate. I'd have to call the doctor. *(Silence)* Sorry.

There is an awkward silence for a moment, as everyone including Madge realises her deficiencies.

TERESA: Right, well I already know all about bread poultices and salty water. I can see there's not much for me to learn here. I'm going to go now.

Sound of Teresa exiting. Some disappointed murmurs from the audience.

BRIGID: Mrs. O'Doherty has gone to the trouble of doing up this great information note for us all on basic first aid practices. Would you like to tell us about that Mrs. O'Doherty?

MADGE: Em..

BRIGID: Look it says all about how to treat nasty cuts… with… (*She consults the leaflet*) …clean salty water and a bread poultice. Fantastic. And it deals with infection too.. very interesting. Bread poultice. High temperature – now that's a tough one. Doesn't Moll get terrible high fevers. I'm always trying new ways of bring it down. What do you recommend Mrs. O'Doherty?

MADGE: Em..I think it says it there. A cold compress.

BRIGID: Ah thank you– a cold compress. Just what she needs. I never thought of that. That'll do the trick.

MADGE: And…a bread poultice.

BRIGID: A bread poultice – great.

MAGGIE: I might try a bread poultice for the Father's constipation next time. He gets terrible bunged up.

POOR BRID: Maybe you could use it for an amputated limb too. I'd say those fellas Teresa was talking about have never even heard of a bread poultice.

MAGGIE: You'll have to let us have your recipe Mrs. O'Doherty. Mine doesn't seem to be as good as yours.

MADGE: Well, I just…

Sound of the door opening, heavy breathing, footsteps. Two young girls run in

GIRL 1: Mrs. O'Doherty! Mrs. O'Doherty! Quick – you're needed.

BRIGID: We're having a First Aid Class at the moment. Mrs. O'Doherty is a bit busy.

GIRL 2: It's an emergency. Quick!

MADGE: What is it? Who needs me?

GIRL 2: It's Larry Brophy. He's in the bookies. He's after taking a really bad turn.

GIRL 1: He turned a really funny shade of green and grabbed his chest and just fell down on the ground like a sack of spuds.

Sound of people gasping in horror. Some people leaving.

GIRL 1: Quick Mrs. O'Doherty – you're needed.

MADGE: But…Doctor Grogan? Surely he must…

GIRL 2: Doctor Grogan's at a funeral mass over in Kilcock. He'll not be back before four o'clock. Mr. D'Arcy in the bookies said to send for you.

MADGE: I'm not really experienced in ..

GIRL 1: He looks bad Mrs. O'Doherty. You could be his only chance. There's no one else.

BRIGID: You'd better go Mrs. O'Doherty.

MADGE: I'm terrible sorry Mrs. Barry.

BRIGID: Not at all, not at all. You're needed. We can do this again later. You were fantastic, you really were.

MADGE: Was I? I thought I was making a mess of it all.

BRIGID: No, you were brilliant. Go on, quick. Sounds like poor Larry Brophy needs you more than we do.

Sounds of consternation. Chairs pushed back. People rushing out.

BRIGID: Sorry about that everyone. We'll have to do this another time.

POOR BRID: Not at all Mrs. Barry. Sure poor Larry Brophy needs her more than we do. I'll just run out and see if I can help.

MAGGIE: Good idea Mrs. O'Sullivan. I'll make a bread poultice and follow behind you.

Sounds of them leaving. Door closes. Brigid sighs and begins to stack the chairs. Door opens. Betty enters.

BETTY: Oh. Hello Brigid.

There is a silence as the two women look at each other.

BRIGID: Betty.

BETTY: I thought I would come a bit late and sneak in at the back where no one could see me. It's already over?

BRIGID: It is.

BETTY: I missed it so.

BRIGID: You did.

Again, a strained silence. Betty turns to leave, thinks better of it, then turns to face Brigid.

BETTY: Oh Brigid I'm so sorry. I never thought…

BRIGID: What? That your husband would be sent to arrest your best friend's son?

BETTY: He didn't want to do it. He hates himself.

BRIGID: He could leave if he wanted.

BETTY: And do what Brigid? He can no more leave the RIC that your Seamus - God rest him - could have left the British Army. There's bills to pay. I thought you of all people would understand that.

Betty turns to leave. Brigid softens.

BRIGID: Ah I do Betty. I do understand. I really do. And I know it's not your fault. It's not even your Tom's fault. It's just…Sean.

BETTY: It's different when it comes to your own door. I know Brigid. I'd be the same. Anybody would.

BRIGID: I miss him.

BETTY: If you never want to speak to me again I'll understand.

BRIGID: I've no idea if he's safe, or in danger, or God knows what.

BETTY: You're the only one who's stood by me and Tom these past couple of years. You managed to keep Joseph on our side too.

BRIGID: Not any more Betty. He can't be persuaded.

BETTY: I know. I went in for a pint of milk last week and he refused to serve me.

BRIGID: He's upset.

BETTY: I know. He's a good man.

BRIGID: Your Tom is a good man too. I know that.

BETTY: Two good men. Two different sides. Do we have to be on different sides? *(Pause)* D'ya fancy a cup of tea?

BRIGID: I do. Why not? Let me just tidy up here and we'll go back to my house.

Sound of the women stacking chairs

BETTY: What about Joseph?

BRIGID: What about him? It's my home too and I can bring my friends in if I want to. If I can separate you and Sean then so can he. Sean's my son after all.

BETTY: How is he? Have you heard from him at all? *(Stacking chair sound ends)* Oh. I didn't mean…I would never…I was just asking after him. Brigid…I wouldn't ever. You know I wouldn't.

There's silence for a while.

BRIGID: Maybe it's best if we don't talk about Sean.

BETTY: Yes. Probably for the best.

BRIGID: Look. Maybe we'll have tea some other time. I've a good bit to do here.

BETTY: Oh. Right. Some other time – yes. *(Pause.)* Friends?

BRIGID: *(Nods slowly, but doesn't meet her eye)* Aye, friends.

END OF EPISODE

EPISODE 13 – PLANNING THE MATCH, NOV. 1920

Scene 1 –Barry's Pub, the girls

Sounds of girls raucous laughter.

CISSY: Jesus, Mary and Joseph! I wouldn't be seen dead with him. Sure he's half my size.

LIZZIE: And twice your age!

CISSY: You're right there Lizzie.

CATHERINE: You're the only one of us with a fella Cissy. Would ye just tell us who he is? Why does it have to be such a bloody secret?

LIZZIE: Oh my God Catherine. Bet he's RIC!

Sounds of horrified gasps from the girls. Fade

VOICEOVER: It's Sunday, November 7th 1920. Fractured – a family, a nation, a dream.

Scene 2 - Barry's Pub, Brigid and Maggie

The door opens. We hear wind outside. Footsteps of Brigid entering. Door closes. Sounds of the chattering of the girls in the background.

BRIGID: That's a cold one. Mary! What are the girls doing in here?

MARY: *(Annoyed)* It's my day off Mammy, as ye know. I was to meet up with the girls but Tomas is off God knows where and I'm stuck here looking after Mr. Dooley! No offense Mr. Dooley.

PADDY: Oh, none taken Mary. None taken. Just another small one while you're there. *(Sound of whiskey being poured into a glass)* Slainte.

MARY: We'll be gone as soon as Tomas comes home.

Door opens. Wind. Door closes.

MAGGIE: Yoohoo! I just saw you come in Mrs. Barry and I thought I'd get those elbow patches you promised me – oh Holy Mother of God!

BRIGID: Are you alright Mrs. O'Donoghue?

MAGGIE: What is a coffin doing in the middle of the pub? Please tell me it's empty.

BRIGID: No. It's poor Larry Brophy. May he rest in peace.

MAGGIE: I'm not the better of that. In God's name, what's he doing here?

BRIGID: There was nowhere else. He lived on his own and by all accounts, the place he lived in was in a bad way.

MAGGIE: That wouldn't surprise me. And are you happy with him being here?

BRIGID: Twas my idea. It'll only be for a short while ... just to give people a chance to pay their last respects.

MAGGIE: Well at least the lid is on. It was hard enough to look at him when he was alive.

BRIGID: Ah now Mrs. O'Donoghue.

MAGGIE: Not meaning to speak ill of the dead but he was a strange man. I never really liked him.

BRIGID: Sure, you hardly knew him. *(Silence)* Come on. Pay your respects before we go upstairs. Hello Mr. Dooley

PADDY: Morning ma'am. Mrs. O'Donoghue.

MAGGIE: Morning Mr. Dooley. We've just been to the memorial mass for Kevin Barry.

PADDY: Oh, was there many there?

MAGGIE: The church was packed. I'm surprised you weren't there yourself. You being a big republican and all.

PADDY: *(Indignantly)* I was outside Mountjoy jail last Monday when they hung him. I went to the mass that they had after that. One mass a week is more than enough for me.

MAGGIE: *(Almost aside)* Not even one mass a week from what I've seen. And as for that fella in the coffin, I don't think I ever seen him there.

PADDY: We can't all be as saintly as you Mrs. O'Donoghue.

Scene 3 – Other part of the pub, the girls

CISSY: For the last time...he's not RIC! Do ye think I'm mad or what?

LIZZIE: I don't know Cissy...wouldn't put it past you. Some of them are fine things.

CATHERINE: Ughhhhhhh! Are you blind or what Lizzie?

MARY: She must be – she fancies Tomas!

Loud laughter.

CISSY: Mary! Don't be so mean about your brother. I think he looks very grown up in his Volunteer uniform. If I wasn't so in love with my mystery man I might even take my chances there!

ALL GIRLS: Woohoo!/Cissy! / Watch out Lizzie / Tomas!!

Scene 4 - Other part of the pub, Brigid and Maggie

Chatter from the girls in the background.

MAGGIE: Tomas looked very smart in his uniform at Kevin Barry's Mass. Terrible pity Sean couldn't be there.

Brigid and Paddy exchange a look.

BRIGID: Sean is in England for a few weeks.

MAGGIE: England? I didn't think he'd be seen dead there!

BRIGID: Just visiting his Aunt Nora.

PADDY: I didn't think either of you ladies would go along to the mass. I wouldn't have thought ye were supporters of the cause.

BRIGID: You know my feelings on that Mr. Dooley. But that young lad had a mother too. I went along to pray for her.

MAGGIE: And Father Dempsey went to great trouble in preparing a sermon. Sure I had to go to support him.

PADDY: *(Sarcastically)* I'm sure he appreciates that Mrs. O'Donoghue.

MAGGIE: *(Not getting it)* Oh, he does. He relies on me more than people think. I must say, I thought it was a great sermon.

BRIGID: But what was that foolish young lad doing? Breaking his poor mother's heart and him only eighteen years old.

PADDY: He was fighting for his country.

BRIGID: The way things are going, there won't be much of a country left to fight for. I'm sure his mother would rather have her son than the country!

PADDY: Well, I met his mother last Monday and she was proud of her son. Her only regret was that she couldn't bury him in her family grave. They wouldn't even release him after they hung him. The bastards stuck him in a grave inside the jail. Pardon my language!

BRIGID: I still think it's a waste of a young life. What good will come of it?

PADDY: Kevin Barry was a true martyr for his country. In the week since his death, more people have joined the Volunteers than had joined in the last two months. The country is answering his call.

BRIGID: Ah, will you listen to yourself. Just another crowd of innocent young men queuing up to be shot at!

Scene 5 - Other part of the pub, the girls

CATHERINE: He must be one of the Volunteers so.

LIZZIE: *(To laughs and hoots from the others)* Tom Farrell; Joe O'Reilly; Peadar Mullanney; Tim Tyrrell; Daniel Joyce; Peader White..

CISSY: I'm not tellin ye.

CATHERINE: I bet it's yer man O'Reilly.

LIZZIE: Seamus O'Rourke; Jim Fitzsimons; Mick Dwyer; Con Lavelle.

CISSY: It's none of them. My man's got class.

CATHERINE: Donal Og Murphy.

CISSY: Jesus! I said class not gas. That fella can fart for Ireland.

More laughter. The door opens. Tomas enters. Door closes.

Scene 6 - Other part of the pub, Brigid and Maggie

Sound of the girls chat can be heard in the background.

MAGGIE: Tomas. There ye are now. I was just telling your mother that you looked very smart in your uniform.

BRIGID: Go straight up and change out of that.

TOMAS: Hello Mrs. O'Donoghue. Mammy I…

BRIGID: I don't want you seen wearing that in the pub. People will be in fear of their lives coming in here.

TOMAS: But..

BRIGID: For God's sake, will you just do as you're told.

TOMAS: *(Producing an envelope from his pocket)* It's just that Father Dempsey gave me this letter for you.

MAGGIE: Oh! the Father never mentioned anything to me about that.

BRIGID: *(Thinking fast)* Oh yes …. He asked me the other day about supplying refreshments …. For some event in the college. I asked him to draw up a list.

MAGGIE: I wonder what event that would be?

BRIGID: When you've changed Tomas, come straight back down. There's work to be done. We'll go up Mrs. O'Donoghue. I'll see if I can put my hands on those elbow patches.

MAGGIE: Right ye are Mrs. Barry. And you can tell me all about this event of yours.

PADDY: Oh, Mrs. Barry. If Joseph is above, will you ask him to drop down? I want a word.

BRIGID: I will.

They exit to the back room. After a few beats, Mary picks up a bottle of whiskey and comes around the counter to Paddy.

MARY: Will you have another drop Mr. Dooley?

PADDY: Well now Mary, have you ever known me to refuse? Especially when it's going free!

MARY: Indeed'n I haven't *(Tops up his glass)* The girls and I were noticing sparks flying between you and Mrs. O'Donoghue!

PADDY: She'd try the patience of Job so she would. She must drive that poor priest mad.

MARY: She'd be a good match for you Paddy. A well off widow woman.

PADDY: Will you stop? God forgive me but I don't think her late husband fell off Mossie Kinsella's barn roof at all. I'd say he jumped.

MARY: God forgive you is right Paddy!

PADDY: She's best avoided.

Joseph and Tomas enter.

JOSEPH: Tomas, you can start clearing the tables and sweep the back. Then you can ….

TOMAS: Daddy, I think I know what needs to be done.

JOSEPH: Right you be. *(Tomas sets about his work. Joseph goes to Paddy)* Young lads! They know it all.

PADDY: Weren't we the same ourselves?

JOSEPH: I suppose. You were looking for me?

PADDY: I was wondering if you wanted to go to Croke Park the Sunday after next?

JOSEPH: Dublin and Tipperary?

PADDY: That's the one. Domhnall got two tickets but you know yourself, if Kildare aren't playing, he's not interested so he gave them to me.

JOSEPH: Should be a good one.

PADDY: I'd say so. The Jackeens will be out for blood after losing the all Ireland

JOSEPH: I don't know Paddy. I think I might leave it.

PADDY: We'll have a few drinks afterwards.

JOSEPH: That's the problem. I got an awful time from herself after the last one.

PADDY: The joys of married life!

JOSEPH: You wouldn't know much about that Paddy.

PADDY: No, thank God!

Both men laugh.

JOSEPH: What about Tomas? He's never been to Croke Park.

PADDY: Would he be interested?

JOSEPH: I'd say he would.

PADDY: Would you give him the day off?

JOSEPH: Of course. He's a hard worker, never takes much time for himself.

PADDY: How would Brigid feel about that?

JOSEPH: Sure what's it got to do with Brigid? The lad is nineteen. He can do whatever he likes. *(Calling)* Tomas. Come here. *(Tomas approaches)* Paddy wants to ask you something.

PADDY: I have a spare ticket to the Dublin Tipperary match the Sunday after next if you'd like to come along?

TOMAS: In Croke Park? Well … I don't know …

JOSEPH: You can have the day off.

TOMAS: I will so. Thanks Paddy.

JOSEPH: That's settled. Give Paddy a top up there Tomas.

Tomas goes to get the bottle.

PADDY: Good man. You're very good to do this for Larry.

JOSEPH: It's not much. Poor Larry! Sure he has no one else to do it for him.

PADDY: Ah but still. There's them that wouldn't bother.

JOSEPH: He was a good customer over the years. It's the least we could do.

PADDY: Did you lay him out yourself?

JOSEPH: I did. It wasn't a nice job. I couldn't leave the lid off. You know he was three days before he was found?

PADDY: I heard that.

JOSEPH: Poor Larry kept himself to himself when he was alive. I don't think he'd want people gawping at him when he's dead.

PADDY: No. You're right there.

JOSEPH: Anyway, I need to finish off that job in the back. I might see you before you go Paddy.

PADDY: Righto. *(Joseph goes off, Tomas returns with the bottle and tops up Paddy's glass)* Fill her up there Tomas! *(Sound of the glass being filled)* So, I don't imagine there will be many in to see Larry off?

TOMAS: You're probably the first.

PADDY: He was a quiet aul divil. A decent skin. Sure there was no harm in him at all.

TOMAS: Did you know him well Paddy?

PADDY: As well as anyone I suppose. He did a few jobs for me over the years. I'll tell you something. He was a great worker ... I mean ... for his size. I've never seen a man plaster a wall so quickly.

TOMAS: He was a small man alright.

PADDY: Sure you could pick him up and put him under your arm.

Laugh.

TOMAS: Poor Larry.

Pause.

PADDY: Do you know who I met at the Robertstown match down in Clane last week? Mattie Doyle.

TOMAS: Mattie Doyle?

PADDY: Ah, you're probably a bit too young to remember. He moved to Robertstown to take on his brothers farm. Mary would remember. *(Calls to Mary who is behind the bar)* Mary, do you remember Mattie Doyle? You were friendly with his daughter ... was it Nora?

MARY: *(Moving nearer)* Maura.

PADDY: That's it, Maura.

PADDY: *(To Tomas)* He told me a story about a young girl, one of his neighbour's daughters. She had all her hair cut off by the volunteers. Mattie said it was in the papers.

TOMAS: The volunteers?

PADDY: Aye.

MARY: But why would they do that?

PADDY: Well, the story that Mattie had was that she was carrying on with a British soldier.

TOMAS: Oh. Do ye hear that Mary?

He catches Mary's eye. She looks away.

PADDY: Mattie was telling me that the same thing has happened in a good few places around the country. What gets into these young ones? Are there not enough decent Irish làds that they could be chasin?

MARY: There must be more to it than that.

PADDY: Sure, what more can there be? She shouldn't have gotten involved with a British soldier in the first place. They're the enemy.

Scene 7 - Other part of the pub, the girls

LIZZIE: Seamus Muldoon, Padraig Smullen, Jimmy McPherson, Tony McCluskey

Girls laughter.

CISSY: He's married for Christ's sake!

LIZZIE: Yeah…and that's why you're keeping him such a secret. It's Tony McCluskey! Oh my God!

CISSY: Would ye stop.

MARY: We can go now girls if ye like. Tomas can take care of things.

LIZZIE: Tomas! Come over here and answer a question for us!

TOMAS: What can I do for ye ladies?

LIZZIE: Who do you think is Cissy's secret boyfriend.

TOMAS: *(Teasing)* Cissy has a secret boyfriend? Well, if I was a betting man…

LIZZIE: Which ye are. Amn't I always seeing ye hiding from your mammy in the bookies of a Saturday?

MARY: Only because you're looking out for him especially, isn't that right Lizzie?

'OOOHHHs' from the girls

LIZZIE: Shut up Mary I've better things to be doing with my time.

TOMAS: I'd put my money on….Donnacha Kilbride.

Silent pause. Then raucous laughter.

MARY: Donnacha Kilbride? Auntie Anne's Donnacha?

LIZZIE: Donnacha up above in UCD?

MARY: Cousin Donnacha?

LIZZIE: Studying Law?

MARY: Are ye mad Tomas?

CISSY: What's so mad about that?

LIZZIE: Ah no offence Cissy, but Donnacha Kilbride has his sights set far higher than you. Donnacha Kilbride. Jesus. I won't be taking any tips from ye for the Grand National Tomas.

MARY: Men! Ye haven't a clue. Cissy wouldn't look twice at him anyway, sure ye wouldn't Cissy?

CISSY: *(Pause)* No, of course not.

Scene 8 - Other part of the pub, Paddy

TOMAS: Will you have another one Paddy?

PADDY: I will. One for the road. I'll go after this one. The father will be wondering what's keeping me.

TOMAS: How is your father?

PADDY: Alive! *(Laughter)* Here's to Larry. May he rest in peace wherever he is.

TOMAS: God rest him.

Pause.

PADDY: I've been wondering since I came in ….. I didn't want to say anything to your father …

TOMAS: What is it Paddy?

PADDY: Could he not have gotten a smaller coffin?

TOMAS: What?

PADDY: Look at it.

TOMAS: That's the usual size.

PADDY: If you didn't know Larry, it wouldn't look so bad. But you could fit Larry twice into that. Surely there was something smaller.

TOMAS: He'd have to get it in specially and he couldn't wait long seeing as Larry wasn't found … for a while … ye know?

PADDY: I suppose.

Pause.

TOMAS: Well, I'd better get back to work

PADDY: Don't mind me. I wonder where he is though.

TOMAS: Who?

PADDY: Larry.

TOMAS: I'd hope he's up above. In heaven.

PADDY: No, I mean which end?

TOMAS: What?

PADDY: Which end of the coffin. Unless he's in the middle.

TOMAS: God forgive you Paddy!

PADDY: What?

TOMAS: You'll go straight to hell for talk like that and us with you for listening to you.

PADDY: Sure what harm? I'm sure Larry would have no objections.

TOMAS: It's not right Paddy.

PADDY: We could always tilt the coffin and if we heard him sliding, we'd know.

TOMAS: *(Trying not to laugh)* Ah, will you stop Paddy.

PADDY: Sure I'm only having a bit of a laugh.

Sounds of the girls leaving. Excited chatter.

MARY: We're leaving now Tomas. Can you tell Mammy I'll be home by 10.

LIZZIE: Bye Tomas!

PADDY: I'd better be off too. We'll have to make a plan for our visit to Croke Park. We might slip in early and have a drink or two before the match. Say nothing to your mother and father.

TOMAS: Only if you're buying Paddy.

PADDY: Of course. It'll be your first time there. We have to celebrate.

LIZZIE: I don't know Tomas. He might lead you astray.

Laughter.

PADDY: Don't mind her Tomas. She's only jealous that she's not coming along.

LIZZIE: I am of course Mr. Dooley! A day in your company is every young girl's dream!

PADDY: Would ye go on outta that now. I'm going home now Tomas before I get myself into trouble!

TOMAS: *(Laughing)* Bye Paddy.

MARY: Lizzie! Get out, go on!

LIZZIE: I'm going. I'm going.

Sound of her leaving.

TOMAS: Mary?

MARY: What is it Tomas. The girls are waiting.

TOMAS: Did you hear what Paddy was saying earlier? About the young girl getting her hair cut off.

MARY: *(Trying to be nonchalant)* I heard bits of it. Sure I wasn't paying much attention.

TOMAS: Mary. I hope you know what you're doing.

MARY: What do you mean?

TOMAS: I know Mary.

MARY: What are you talking about?

TOMAS: Please. Just be careful.

Pause. Footsteps as Mary leaves the pub. Door opens, and closes.

END OF EPISODE

EPISODE 14 – BLOODY SUNDAY, NOV. 1920

Scene 1 - Barry Kitchen

Tomas is wrapping sandwiches. Paddy enters

PADDY: All set?

TOMAS: I am. I got early mass so I'd have plenty of time to make us a bit of lunch. Ham sandwiches.

PADDY: And I hope you put in a bit of the strong stuff too, Tomas?

TOMAS: Taken care of!

PADDY: A man after my own heart! Off with us so. It'll be a great day.

VOICEOVER: Fractured – a family, a nation, a dream… November 21st 1920. Sunday.

Scene 2 - Barry's pub

Music in pub. As the music fades, polite applause.

JOSEPH: Well done Con O'Sullivan. Ye get better every time.

CON: Thanks Joseph

MARY: Do you know "The Coulin" Mr. O' Sullivan?

CON: Begod, that's a hard one Mary. I'm learning it at the moment but I'll need a bit more practice before I play it in public.

MARY: I'm sure Mrs. O' Sullivan must be delighted to have such great music in the house.

CON: Brid is tone deaf. She wouldn't know whether it's good or bad. *(Laughter)* Mind you, it suits me. She thinks it's all marvellous.

More laughter.

BRIGID: I hear you're teaching the tin whistle it to young Colm.

CON: Aye. I think he likes it. Sure you know yourself, the poor divil doesn't say much.

JOSEPH: Give us another tune there, Con.

CON: How about a song from the man of the house!

JOSEPH: Ah now!

CON: Come on Joseph.

Cajoling from the others.

JOSEPH: I'd need a few more whiskeys before I could do that!

BRIGID: And he's had more than enough already!

Laughter.

CON: That's telling him Mrs. Barry

BRIGID: I'm serious.

Beat.

MARY: Sing "the parting glass" Daddy

CON: Aye, that's the one. Come on Joseph. I've heard you sing it lots of times.

JOSEPH: Well, ye asked for it. Don't blame me.

CON: A bit of hush now.

Joseph steadies himself and begins to sing.

JOSEPH: Of all the money that e'er I had / I spent it in good company. And all the harm I've ever done / Alas, it was to none but me.

And all I've done for want of wit / To memory now I can't recall.

So fill to me the parting glass / Good night and joy be to you all.

Of all the comrades that e'er I had / They're sorry for my going away. And all the sweethearts that e'er I had / They'd wish me one more day to stay.

But since it fell into my lot / That I should rise and you should not. I'll gently rise and softly call / "Good night and joy be to you all"

As he sings, his voice fades out to play under the next scene.

Scene 3 - Croke Park, same time

Tomas and Paddy are in the middle of the crowd. They are eating the sandwiches.

PADDY: *(Shouting over noise, and music)* They are grand sandwiches, Tomas. They go well with the whiskey. Now, if the Jackeens lose, we'll have to have a pint to celebrate.

TOMAS: And if they win, we'll go for a pint to drown our sorrows.

PADDY: You're your father's son and no mistake. I'll tell you where's a good –

The sound of firing, screaming, mayhem. The music grows louder. Fade out.

Scene 4 - Barry's pub, later

Mary, Brigid and Joseph are tidying up. Sounds of glasses and sweeping.

JOSEPH: Begod, that was a grand day. It's nice to have a sing-song, raises the spirits.

BRIGID: There was more spirits drunk than raised, I'm thinking and it a Sunday too. Moll, will you bring in those glasses to be washed, there's a good girl.

As Brigid talks, the door to the pub opens. Hughes comes in.

JOSEPH: A bit of whiskey warms the throat. And God knows, it's cold enough out there -

MARY: *(Quietly)* Daddy *(No response, louder)* Daddy!

Joseph then spots Hughes. There is an awkward silence.

HUGHES: Hello, Mr. Barry. I was wondering -

JOSEPH: Sean isn't here if that's what you're about.

HUGHES: I'm not here in an official capacity.

JOSEPH: While you wear that uniform, you'll always be in an official capacity. What do you want?

HUGHES: Your younger son got the train to Dublin this morning – is that right? Was he off to Croke park?

BRIGID: Is that a crime now?

HUGHES: I'm sorry to be telling ye this but shots were fired in Croke Park about an hour ago. People were killed, I thought ye needed to be told.

BRIGID: Shots fired? At the match?

HUGHES: Yes. Anyway, I'll be on my way.

BRIGID: You must know more?

HUGHES: I'm sorry, I don't.

Brigid moans, collapsing. Mary rushes to her.

MARY: Mammy!

HUGHES: I – I hope he'll be alright. *(Beat)* I'll get going.

JOSEPH: Aye, do.

As he leaves, Brigid continues to cry and Mary comforts her. Poor Brid and Maggie hurry in before the door closes.

POOR BRID: We saw that RIC man coming in. Mrs. O'Donoghue said to me, it's never good news when RIC men come in anywhere.

MAGGIE: What happened? Is it Sean?

MARY: No, trouble in Croke Park. Shots fired. He knew Tomas was there …

MAGGIE: Shots fired! Oh my God. But that explains the trains.

BRIGID: What?

MAGGIE: Some of the trains from Dublin have been cancelled. The father was expecting one of his priest friends. I went to the station to meet him but the train never showed up. To be honest, I was glad. That Fr. Kenny is a bad influence. God knows what kind of state Fr. Dempsey would be in for tomorrow morning's mass.

BRIGID: *(Interrupting Maggie's speech somewhere in the middle)* Joseph, we have to find out what happened. If the trains were cancelled –

JOSEPH: If the trains were cancelled, Tomas probably can't get home because of the delays. Let's not panic yet.

POOR BRID: There could have been one of those bombs on the train. I heard about a bomb on one in Cork and they were finding bits of arms and legs for miles around.

JOSEPH: Brid!

MAGGIE: I'm sure he'll be fine Mrs. Barry although God knows it's dangerous in Dublin these days. A cousin of mine was in there last week and was jumped on by a gang of thugs for no reason at all. He was walking along minding …

BRIGID: *(To Joseph)* You should have known better than to let him off with Paddy Dooley. That fella would find trouble where there's none.

MAGGIE: God knows, that's true.

POOR BRID: Ah no, Mr. Dooley is not like that at all …although I did hear …

JOSEPH: No offence Mrs. O'Sullivan and Mrs. O'Donoghue, but can ye just leave?

POOR BRID: We're only trying to offer comfort.

JOSEPH: Just…please…just go. *(Beat)* Now.

They leave, a bit miffed, bidding goodbye to Brigid and expressing hope for Tomas.

JOSEPH: God helps us if they decided to offer despair.

BRIGID: *(To Joseph)* I'll never forgive you if anything happens to Tomas.

MARY: That's not fair, mammy, Daddy didn't go shooting into the crowds did he?

BRIGID: You should have known better than to let him go with Paddy.

JOSEPH: It was just a match! *(Beat. They lapse into silence)* I can't stay here. I'll go down to Father Dempsey, he has a telephone, he might know more.

As Joseph goes to the door, it opens. Paddy and Tomas enter. Tomas is limping slightly and is being helped / supported by Paddy. He is wearing Paddy's jacket. Both men look shook and exhausted.

PADDY: That's it Tomas. Take it easy. Sit in there now. *(Tomas sits)*

BRIGID: We heard there was trouble in Croke Park. Jesus, is that blood on his shirt?

TOMAS: It's not mine, Mammy, there was…a…man

He can't continue.

PADDY: A little whiskey might help him Joseph. It would certainly help me.

BRIGID: As if ye didn't have enough already. He probably fell because he was drunk. I should never have …

JOSEPH: Brigid! This is not the time.

BRIGID: And you're worse. Encouraging him.

PADDY: Please. The lad has had a terrible shock.

JOSEPH: Mary, will you get two glasses of whiskey.

Mary goes behind counter – we hear her dispensing the whiskey.

JOSEPH: *(To Paddy)* – What happened?

PADDY: I hardly know Joseph, it was absolutely terrible.

BRIGID: Isn't it obvious what happened? He walked our son into a dangerous situation.

PADDY: I brought him to a football match. Do you think I would have gone if I thought there was going to be trouble?

BRIGID: All I know is that my son has come home injured and covered in blood and you are responsible.

JOSEPH: Brigid!

TOMAS: Mammy!

JOSEPH: That's not fair, Brigid!

BRIGID: *(Ignoring them)* That shirt'll have to be thrown out, Tomas. Go straight up and get it off you …

PADDY: Leave the young lad.

BRIGID: I'll deal with you in a minute. Tomas, go straight up and get changed. Mary, help him upstairs.

Reluctantly he goes with Mary

PADDY: I wouldn't do anything to harm Tomas, I was trying to protect him.

BRIGID: He's covered in blood! Why don't you get your own family and stop trying to take over mine. I want you out of here now!

PADDY: Ah Brigid.

BRIGID: Don't you Brigid me! I want you out of here now.

PADDY: But …

BRIGID: Now!

JOSEPH: Brigid!

PADDY: It's alright Joseph.

JOSEPH: Will you be okay?

PADDY: I'll be grand.

Paddy leaves, closing the door behind him. Silence for a moment. During the following Tomas and Mary return, Tomas having changed his shirt.

JOSEPH: *(Tentative)* I know you're a bit upset but -

BRIGID: Upset is not the word for how I feel. Your friend, or whatever he is, almost killed my son.

JOSEPH: *(Anger)* He's my son too and Paddy is a good man, a long time friend and you had no right to send him packing.

TOMAS: You sent Paddy packing?

MARY: Aw Mammy!

BRIGID: Don't 'aw Mammy' me. Sit here, Tomas. Mary get him a bite to eat.

TOMAS: I wouldn't be standing here if it wasn't for Paddy.

BRIGID: You wouldn't have gone to the match if it wasn't for him and your father.

TOMAS: *(Emotional, annoyed)* Listen to me for once. I wouldn't be alive if it wasn't for Paddy. You didn't see what they did. You didn't see what he did.

JOSEPH: Mary, another drop of whiskey along with some food for him.

MARY: All right, Daddy.

Mary moves to get the bottle

TOMAS: I'm not hungry…I…couldn't eat anything. It was horrible. They just…

JOSEPH: It's all right, son, you don't have to tell us what -

He becomes more emotional as his tale goes on.

TOMAS: I do. It's important. The match was on…there was an aeroplane… then shooting. Tans all around the park… shooting at everyone... everywhere... Jesus! Paddy... he pushed me down. The man behind me was hit...he was pumping blood... I'd only been talking to him...chatting about the Dubs...blood was everywhere... I put my jacket over him... what else... started to say act of contrition. *(Accepting the whiskey)* Thanks, Mary. *(He takes a shaky sip)* It seemed to last for ages but....I suppose it couldn't have. Soldiers were everywhere. I had Paddy's jacket. And after, we just walked and walked, trying to get home. They searched us... looking for guns. *(With grit)* By Jesus, if I had one, I would have shot them stone dead.

BRIGID: Aw son...

TOMAS: You weren't there. You didn't see what they were doing.

BRIGID: But why would the soldiers just...shoot people.

TOMAS: Because they don't care about us, Mammy. We don't matter to them. The just shoot innocent people.

BRIGID: Thank God, you're home safe.

TOMAS: Only for Paddy, Mammy. *(She doesn't respond. Beat.)* I think I'll go to bed. Don't throw that shirt out, Mammy. It'll be a reminder.

BRIGID: Oh what, for God's sake?

TOMAS: Of how important it is to fight for our freedom. *(Brigid is shocked)* Will you give me a hand up the stairs Mary?

MARY: I will, lean on me there.

They move off. Long beat.

JOSEPH: You surpassed yourself tonight.

BRIGID: Don't.

Brigid remains still with her back to Joseph

JOSEPH: God knows, I don't ask much from you but you will apologise to Paddy. He saved our son's life and he didn't deserve to be treated like that. *(He waits. Nothing)* Good night so.

He exits. Brigid doubles over in sorrow at Tomas' words, realising she has lost another son to the cause.

BRIGID: No! – I won't lose another one.

END OF EPISODE

EPISODE 15 - CHRISTMAS EVE, DEC. 1920

Scene 1 - Father Dempsey's house.

FATHER DEMPSEY: Goodnight, Mrs. O'Sullivan. See you at Christmas mass tomorrow. *(Closes the door with a sigh of relief)* Thank God.

We hear him humming 'Silent Night' to himself as he potters around. A loud knocking on his door. He answers expecting it to be Mrs. O'Donoghue.

FATHER DEMPSEY: Mrs. O'Donoghue, really there is no need - *(Opening door)* - well, well, well, and a very happy Christmas to you. Come on in.

We hear Sean laugh.

VOICEOVER: Fractured – a family, a nation, a dream....Christmas 1920.

Scene 2 - Outside church

Sound of church bells as people pour out of the church.

FATHER DEMPSEY: Happy Christmas, Mrs. O' Sullivan, Happy Christmas Mrs. Kilbride. ...Ah, Mrs. Barry, a favour if I may?

BRIGID: Of course, Father.

FATHER DEMPSEY: It's a little tricky, I've an Italian priest staying with me since last night. Unexpectedly. I've nothing in the house for him and I know that he'd love a proper cooked Irish Christmas dinner and aren't you just the woman to give it to him.

BRIGID: Me? But I -

ANNE: I couldn't help overhearing, Father. Sure why don't you just ask me. We're doing turkey this year and no offence, Brigid, but the Barry's tend to have goose and -

BRIGID: *(Taking offence)* I'd be delighted Father. Tell him to come around three. *(Spotting Paddy Dooley)* Oh, Mr. Dooley, a word, please?

She catches up with him.

PADDY: *(Wary)* Hello, Mrs. Barry.

BRIGID: *(Not used to this)* Hello. I've been waiting to speak to you since...well...anyway...I didn't see you and anyway, I feel I should apologise -

PADDY: No need. Let bygones be bygones and all that. How's the young lad? Joseph says he's gone very quiet in himself.

BRIGID: Yes…he's angry too over it, as he should be, I suppose. Anyway…I'm sorry. I should never have…Happy Christmas, Mr. Dooley.

PADDY: And to you, Mrs. Barry.

She walks away. Fades.

Scene 3 – Outside church

ANNE: Mary, Donnacha came home from his studies in UCD last night. He wondered if Cissy might be about?

MARY: Cissy?

ANNE: Yes, he was saying there was something he wanted to give her.

TOMAS: *(Under his breath to Mary)* I know what he'd like to give her.

Mary giggles.

ANNE: Do you, Tomas? I think he's just probably passing on something he got from someone else.

TOMAS: *(Trying not to laugh)* Most likely Auntie Anne.

Mary explodes in giggles.

JOSEPH: *(Calling)* Brigid, Brigid, over here!

ANNE: I hope she's not going to talk to Tom and Betty Dwyer, Joseph. Oh good, she's avoided them. I don't know how they have the nerve to show their faces at mass.

TOMAS: I don't know how they do it either, Auntie Anne.

JOSEPH: Let's leave the politics for today. Mary, Tomas, let's drag your mother away from Mrs. O'Sullivan or there'll be no dinner made.

ANNE: You'll have to put on a fine show today, what with your Italian visitor.

JOSEPH / MARY / TOMAS: What?

ANNE: I'll let Brigid fill you in. I hope he likes goose. Excuse me. *(She goes, voice fading)* Hello, hello, happy Christmas!

Scene 4 - Barry's parlour – some hours later.

TOMAS: *(Off)* Alright, alright! I was only seeing if they were done yet.

BRIGID: *(Off)* I'll tell you what's done – you're done, the both of ye. We've a priest coming, so out of my kitchen.

JOSEPH: *(Off)* I don't know why you agreed to -

BRIGID: *(Off)* Because I wasn't having your sister and her turkey lording it over us, that's why. Out!

Joseph and Tomas enter the parlour.

JOSEPH: Did you get anything?

TOMAS: Got the taste of a carrot, is all. You?

JOSEPH: I sneaked a spoon into the stuffing.

TOMAS: I love Mammy's stuffing. I think that's probably my favourite bit of Christmas dinner.

JOSEPH: *(A bit put out)* What about the goose?

TOMAS: Oh, the goose is lovely… but the stuffing…! *(Beat)* Sean loved the stuffing.

JOSEPH: Aye. I hope wherever he is that he's a nice dinner to go to.

TOMAS: They look after the lads in the safe houses. He'll be grand, Daddy.

JOSEPH: Aye and God is good. Would you like a drop of whiskey, Tomas? The good stuff. To toast him.

TOMAS: I don't know…Mammy -

JOSEPH: For the day that's in it.

He takes two glasses, we hear him pour.

TOMAS: Careful now, not too much. That costs a fair penny!

JOSEPH: Sure it's grand! Here, take that now. To Sean and 1921 and -

BRIGID: *(Distant)* Tomas?

TOMAS: *(Guilty)* Eh….yes…yes…Mammy?

BRIGID: *(Distant)* Make sure all the plates are the same. Use the ones on the top shelf.

TOMAS: Aye. Aye.

JOSEPH: *(Toasting again)* To the new year of 1921. May it be the year we get our freedom and peace at last and -

BRIGID: Joseph!

JOSEPH: *(Guiltier)* eh…yes…Brigid

BRIGID: Put away that drink!

Tomas laughs.

JOSEPH: Down the hatch, quick Tomas. *(They clink. Drink)* God, that's powerful stuff!

TOMAS: Woah, that's mighty!

There's a sudden loud knocking at the door. Brigid and Mary and Moll bustle out from the kitchen.

BRIGID: That's him. Tomas, tuck your shirt in, for God's sake. Were you born in a barn? Mary, take that lipstick off.

MARY: Aw Mammy!

BRIGID: He's a priest. He doesn't need you flaunting your lips in front of him. *(More knocking)* Moll, you look lovely. Joseph, get the door.

JOSEPH: A minute Father, I'm coming.

Joseph gets the door.

MAGGIE: Hello! Hello! I just called to wish ye all a very happy Christmas. *(Beat as she registers their faces)* What's the matter? Ye all look like mannequins.

BRIGID: We were expecting someone else, Mrs. O'Donoghue. An Italian priest. A friend of Father Dempsey.

MAGGIE: A friend of Father Dempsey? Oh, you must have that wrong. Sure the Father would have told me. There's not a thing he doesn't tell me and if he was having a priest friend to stay -

BRIGID: It might have been last minute, now if you wouldn't mind-

MAGGIE: Did he say what this priest's name was? I never heard of an Italian friend. There was one chap now, a French chap. I caught him swigging back the alter wine like there was no tomorrow. They drink an awful lot of wine in Europe you know, Mrs. Barry. Savages, but not as savage as here. How is your ankle Tomas-?

TOMAS: Well, it's not too bad now-

MAGGIE: -after they riddling everyone with bullets up in Croke Park? Did you ever think you'd hear the likes of it, Joseph? And the men shot all over the place, and the blood everywhere. Running in the gutters.

JOSEPH: It's a terrible state of affairs alright Mrs. O'Donoghue-

MAGGIE: There was one big huge fella - seven foot tall he was, I heard – and didn't he get shot clean through the neck I heard, so that his veins were burst and the blood pumping out all over the place. Oh, shocking altogether-

JOSEPH: Yes, eh-

MAGGIE: And didn't he fall with the loss of blood on top of this little fella from Nenagh, Jimmy something, and he only five foot tall himself. Clean broke his neck so he did, and he drove straight into the ground like a nail under a hammer. They had to dig him out, he'd gone in so far.

JOSEPH: Mary, bring Moll into the kitchen, would you? *(Mary and Moll leave)* Now, Mrs. O'Donoghue -

134

MAGGIE: Sure he was only four foot six after. It's true, I heard it! Another fella – big bullets, the soldiers were using, could rip through three men's guts and out the other side. Except this other fella now was a big lad, big thick skull on him, probably a boxer, and a bullet went through two men in front of him and got lodged in that same big thick skull.

BRIGID: I think maybe you shouldn't be talking about these things in front of the children -

MAGGIE: No, but that's the thing - he's alright now. A miracle! They had to leave the bullet in him, but it didn't do him any harm. Except he can't blink his left eye now, so everyone thinks he's winking at them and they don't believe a word he says anymore.

BRIGID: Right so, -

MAGGIE: Isn't that shocking? The British army taking away a man's good standing in the community.

JOSEPH: We're expecting this priest anytime now so -

MAGGIE: I'd love to meet him, Joseph but sure I have to get the dinner on for the Father. I could have cooked for the Italian but sure maybe the Father didn't want to put me to the trouble. So, happy Christmas to you all! Happy Christmas.

She leaves. Joseph locks the door. They half-laugh at Maggie except Tomas.

BRIGID: Are you alright, son? She shouldn't have gone on like that about the shootings.

TOMAS: *(Sombre but strong)* I'm grand.

BRIGID: Are you sure?

TOMAS: *(Sharp)* I'm alright, Mammy.

BRIGID: All the same, it's- *(More knocking on the door)* Mary. Moll. He's here. Joseph, door.

We hear Mary and Moll coming from the kitchen.

JOSEPH: Coming father.

SEAN: *(Distant in a put on Italian accent)* A-please, before you open! Will you allow me an old Italian custom? A-please bow your heads before I enter and a-bless this house.

JOSEPH: Eh... right so!

Laugher from Mary and Tomas.

BRIGID: Tomas! Behave yourself. It's a man of God.

Joseph opens the door.

SEAN: I a-bless this house in the name of the Father… *(Moll looks up at him)* …and of the prodigal son…

MOLL: Sean!

There are cries of joy as the family is re-united. Hugs and tears.

BRIGID: Oh Sean, Sean, my darling boy! It is you!

SEAN: Hello, Mammy.

MOLL: Are you a priest now, Sean? *(The others laugh)*

SEAN: Nearly, Molly! I'm just pretending at the moment.

MOLL: You look funny.

SEAN: And so do you! You're getting big since I last saw you.

BRIGID: Are you alright, Sean? Have they been feeding you at all?

SEAN: *(As she fusses over him, getting him to sit down)* I'm grand, Mammy. Yes, they've been feeding me. I'm well able to feed myself too.

BRIGID: Well, I don't know but you look awful thin under those vestments. Wait till we get a big dinner into you.

Rushes off to get it ready.

SEAN: That must be why the priests and the nuns wear black. They say it's very slimming, isn't that right Mary?

MARY: Tell that to Father O'Rourke above. Can barely fit through the door!

They laugh. Tomas has been a bit quiet.

SEAN: How are you, Tomas.

TOMAS: It's really good to see you, Sean.

JOSEPH: Right so! This calls for a celebration! Tomas, get down that dusty bottle of expensive whiskey and we'll have ourselves a toast!

TOMAS: *(Buying into mood)* The one nobody's touched in years?

JOSEPH: That's the one!

Tomas takes down the bottle and sets up a row of three glasses.

MARY: What about me?

SEAN: *(Joking)* What about ye?

JOSEPH: Tomas, a port for Mary. And one for your mother.

Tomas pours.

JOSEPH: A toast. To Sean!

ALL: To Sean!

Fade.

Scene 5 - Barry's yard

Sound of gate cautiously opening and closing. It is Joseph Hughes. We hear voices from inside.

TOMAS: I'll get the bin for you, Mammy!

HUGHES: Shit. Shit. Shit.

The door to the house opens. Hughes trips over a cat who miaows. A clatter of bins.

HUGHES: *(Hissed)* Christ.

TOMAS: *(Stepping into yard)* Hello? Anyone here? *(Beat. Sounds of the cat hissing)* Bloody cat. Out. *(To himself)* Christ.

He picks up the bin. Footsteps as Sean arrives out. Beat

SEAN: I know Mammy has banned politics for today, Tomas, but how are you after...

TOMAS: The massacre? Because that's what it was. *(Beat)* I'm how you would expect, I suppose. Bastards.

SEAN: Must have been tough. *(Tomas doesn't answer)* You'll get your chance for payback, don't worry about that.

TOMAS: Good. *(After a beat)* There's been loads of arrests since you were gone, Sean. The day after Croke Park they picked up Tom Harris, and a few others from Naas.

SEAN: I know. And Colgan too.

TOMAS: Yeah, that was a blow. You stay safe, d'you hear?

SEAN: No better man! *(Beat)* Right. Let's get back or Mammy will send out a search party. *(Loudly)* So – where is the sweetsa for the priesta!

Sean and Tomas go on in, closing the door after them.

HUGHES: Sean Barry, home for Christmas.

Scene 6 - Barry's parlour

The family have just finished eating.

BRIGID: Are you planning on hiding out in Father Dempsey's for a few more days, Sean?

SEAN: No Mammy. It'd be too risky. *(Standing up)* In fact, I better leave now. The Father has arranged for me to go back to Dublin with a friend of his.

BRIGID: Stay another while, it's only been a few hours.

SEAN: I wish I could but it's not safe.

MARY: *(Lightening the mood)* Well, promise you won't use that awful Italian accent when you're talking to the Tans? That'll get you found out, so it will!

SEAN: *(Playing along)* Sure, they wouldn't know an Italian any better than we would! Tell ye what I do, I pretend I'm up from Kerry, looking for the parochial house, and sure they can't understand me at all then, and let me on my way!

They laugh.

SEAN: *(In a Kerry accent)* I'm terribly sorry officer but is there any way you could show me the way to the residence of the Archbishop or the Monsignor himself blessings of God on you and all his holy saints!

TOMAS: *(Laughing)* You sound like one of those machine guns they have!

SEAN: *(Joking)* As long as they don't use one to answer me, I'll be grand. *(More laugher)* I really have to go. Come here, Mammy. *(Hug)* That was the nicest dinner I ever had.

BRIGID: And you were the nicest present I ever had, son.

There's a noise in the yard, off.

SEAN: Check that out, Tomas.

There is instant, wary silence in the room. We hear Tomas opening the back door into the yard.

TOMAS: *(Calling back into them)* It's just Dwyer's cat in around the crates.

SEAN: You never know. Need to keep on your toes. I really better go. Bye, Mary.

MARY: Promise you'll keep safe. Promise.

SEAN: I will. Sure, who'd you have to fight with if I was gone. *(To Tomas)* Tomas.

TOMAS: Make sure you keep that promise to Mary.

SEAN: I will. See you soon, Molly Mae. I'll bring a present from Dublin next time.

MOLL: I love you, Sean

SEAN: And I love you too cute face. Daddy, thanks for the whiskey.

JOSEPH: Anytime, Sean. Just keep in touch.

SEAN: Mammy.

BRIGID: *(Emotional)* Go. Go before I try to stop you.

SEAN: All right. Arrivederci!

He leaves.

BRIGID: *(Loud, upset)* What the hell does that mean?

TOMAS: What?

BRIGID: That thing he said?

TOMAS: Oh. Goodbye, I think. In Italian.

MARY: *(Explaining quietly)* "Until we meet again."

BRIGID: *(Wistful)* Until we meet again… *(Beat)* I hope he's not Italian the next time we see him. *(Composed again)* Right, let's tidy this all away.

TOMAS: Ah, can we not have a break first?

BRIGID: If you're a volunteer, volunteer for a bit of washing up. Mary, take the bin out to the yard. Joseph, come with me. Moll, run up and get ready for bed.

The clatter of activity. Moll running upstairs. Fade.

Scene 7 – Barry's yard

Mary is putting out the bin.

HUGHES: *(Whisper)* Mary! *(Louder)* Mary!

MARY: Jesus, you put the heart crossways in me. *(Annoyed)* What are you doing here?

HUGHES: Freezing myself mainly. And that fecking cat from next door -

MARY: I asked you what you're doing here.

HUGHES: I came to talk, Mary. I do see you down the town and you won't look at me ever since -

MARY: Ever since the time you came to arrest my brother.

HUGHES: That was my job. I told you that. I had no idea who he was.

MARY: *(Silent for a while, then)* He's not a bad lad, Joe.

HUGHES: And neither am I.

MARY: If you say so. What is it you want?

HUGHES: You, Mary. *(Beat. Her silence gives him courage)* There's a lad in the barracks, Stiff, he was a soldier in the war, and he was saying that the trenches were always quiet on Christmas Day. There was a truce between the English and the Germans. Can we have a truce?

MARY: *(Softening)* For Christmas Day?

HUGHES: For always? I have a present for you. *(He hands it to her)* Open it.

Mary is unsure, then quietly opens the paper to reveal a book.

HUGHES: It's a book of old Irish legends. I know you love them.

MARY: *(Moved)* Aye, I do.

HUGHES: These are about Ireland, in a simpler time, with simpler ways. It's about where we all come from, no matter what we believe in now.

MARY: *(Teasing)* You old romantic.

HUGHES: Just pretend I'm Diarmuid and you're Grainne.

MARY: Eh, I don't think that ends very well for them…

HUGHES: Maybe. But they loved each other and that's all that matters.

MARY: *(With affection)* How long were you practising that speech?

HUGHES: About two days. *(They laugh)*

MARY: I've missed you.

HUGHES: I've missed you. *(They kiss)* I saw you had a priest over.

MARY: *(Unsure)* Aye. A friend of Father Dempsey's.

HUGHES: There's a few rogue ones going around, I've heard. But then, it is Christmas, and no family should be apart on Christmas Day.

MARY: *(Soft)* No.

TOMAS: *(From off)* Mary, have you emptied the bin? We need it in here.

MARY: Hide, quick. *(Shouting back to Tomas)* Just coming.

Hughes moves back to his hiding place. Tomas enters.

TOMAS: I thought I heard voices.

MARY: No. Now, here's the -

She moves to go by him.

TOMAS: Where did you get the book?

MARY: Oh this…sorry, when you said voices…I didn't think you meant Cissy. She..gave me this?

TOMAS: *(Suspicious)* Not like Cissy to be into books?

MARY: It's Irish Myths and Legends. Full of people getting into all sorts of mischief. *(She laughs. She moves to walk by him)* Excuse me.

TOMAS: I meant to say earlier, Mary, your hair is lovely like that. Please don't do anything that might ruin it.

He moves in. Mary breathes out.

END OF EPISODE

EPISODE 16 – THE DWYER'S HOME, JAN. 1921

Scene 1 – Street

Sounds of running footsteps, heavy breathing and laughter.

REBEL 1: We got him good, so we did. Did ye hear him scream? I got him right in the face.

REBEL 2: That was me! You got his jacket. Mud running all down his precious uniform. Serves him right.

REBEL 3: Well done lads. Now we need to go back and get his wife.

REBELS 1/2: His wife?/ What for?

REBEL 3: She's an RIC bitch. She has to pay the price.

REBEL 1: But she's…a woman.

REBEL 3: What's your point?

REBEL 1: Well..eh..I just -

REBEL 3: She's married to an RIC man. We don't need her like in this town. She's lucky she's not dead already.

REBEL 2: *(Sings)* Dead, dead, with a bullet through the head.

REBEL 1: *(Terrified)* RIC bitch! RIC bitch!

REBEL 2/3: Whoohoo!/ RIC bitch/ Let's get her!

VOICEOVER: Fractured – a family, a nation, a dream.

Scene 2 – Dwyer Home.

DWYER: *(From upstairs)* Gurriers, the lot of them. Honest to God Betty, they couldn't have been any more than twelve years of age.

BETTY: That's terrible Tom.

DWYER: Bloody cheek of them. My jacket is destroyed. I have to wear this tomorrow.

BETTY: Throw it down here love. I'll give it a scrub and dry it front of the fire this evening. It'll be grand.

DWYER: If I had done something like that at their age – Jesus! I wouldn't have lived to tell the tale.

BETTY: I know.

DWYER: Disrespecting an officer of the State.

BETTY: Dreadful.

Comes down the stairs. Voice becomes clearer.

DWYER: I should have run after them. Given them a fright. Taught them a lesson.

BETTY: No Tom. You did the right thing. It could have been an ambush. God knows what could have happened to you.

DWYER: It's not in my blood to walk away.

BETTY: No. *(Pause)* But sometimes we have to. Here, let me see that. Just a bit of mud. It'll be good as new in the morning. Sit down and have your dinner before it goes cold. I'll get you a nice cup of tea.

Her footsteps exit.

DWYER: Could you bring in some butter for the spuds?

BETTY: *(From the kitchen)* Sorry, we're out. *(Footsteps come in again)* I'll go into Kilcock tomorrow.

DWYER: For Christ's sake. You shouldn't have to walk three miles to get a pat of butter.

BETTY: I don't mind. I'll take the bike.

DWYER: Nothing but Sinn Feiners in this place. It'd make ye sick.

BETTY: Tea?

TOM: Aye. It's no wonder their children are the way they are.

Sound of tea pouring. Also the sound of Tom eating his dinner, knife scraping of plates etc.

BETTY: Milk is in the jug.

DWYER: Well they can keep their bloody butter. And I'll keep my hard-earned wages and spend them somewhere else. This place won't see a shilling of it. *(Silence for a moment)* Sorry Betty love.

BETTY: It's okay Tom. Hard day?

DWYER: Ah, the usual.

BETTY: Short staffed again?

DWYER: Three down. Noel Roberts hasn't shown up for two weeks.

BETTY: Poor man.

DWYER: What?

BETTY: He must be finding it tough.

DWYER: We're all finding it tough Betty.

BETTY: I know, it's just…

DWYER: Some of us are just more willing than others to do what it takes to keep law and order in this country. *(Betty starts to clear the table)* It'll probably get worse before it gets better. Young Hughes – Joseph Hughes – you know him?

BETTY: I think you mentioned him – the Cork lad?

DWYER: That's him. Good lad. Nice fella. Just made sergeant. He heard this morning. No doubt he'll be posted elsewhere before we know it.

BETTY: That'll be lonely for him.

DWYER: Ah I think there's a girlfriend somewhere.

BETTY: Brave girl.

DWYER: What?

BETTY: Well, you hear stories, don't you? What happens to those poor girls who go out with RIC men. Is she local I wonder? She'd want to watch out for herself.

DWYER: There was a time when nothing in the world would stop you from going out with an RIC man.

BETTY: Different times Tom *(Pause)* I was so proud to be walking beside you in your fancy uniform.

DWYER: Was?

BETY: Well – don't get much of an opportunity these days do we? I'd say if we walked down this street together and you in your uniform it'd be more than a bit of mud that'd be thrown at us.

DWYER: Anyone lays a finger on you they'll have every RIC officer in Maynooth on their backs. *(Pause)* It'll get better love. It's bad now I know, but it'll pass. We'll get through it.

BETTY: Try telling that to Domhnall UaBuachalla. His shop is destroyed. 'God Save the King' painted all over it.

DWYER: I know. Bloody Tans. Give us all a bad name.

BETTY: The Tans did it?

DWYER: Aye. Left a message to say if he didn't stop calling himself UaBuachalla, the shop would be torched next time.

BETTY: It's no wonder everyone hates us.

DWYER: Nobody hates..

BETTY: I can't leave the house Tom. Nobody speaks to me. Nobody smiles at me. Nobody looks at me. I can't get served in a shop. Nobody sits with me in Mass. Nobody calls to my door. If I fell down and died in the street I don't think a single solitary soul would care enough to spit on me.

DWYER: Ah I would sweetheart. I'd spit on you. A good big gob of it right in the face.

BETTY: *(Laughing)* Ah go on. Ye make a joke out of everything. I'm serious Tom. It's awful.

DWYER: It'll get better love. I promise.

BETTY: When?

DWYER: Soon. And we'll get through it together. We always have.

Pause. Betty considers this.

BETTY: I...heard from Mammy today.

DWYER: Oh yes? How is she?

BETTY: Fine. You know Mammy. News about everyone from home. I think she writes it all down as it happens and waits until she has at least five pages filled before posting.

DWYER: How many deaths?

BETTY: Only two.

DWYER: That was disappointing for her. Any suspicious circumstances?

BETTY: None. Two peaceful passings.

DWYER: *(Joking)* She should join the RIC.

BETTY: She...was hoping I might go and visit her for a while.

DWYER: Sorry love. I can't be taking leave. We're flat out. There's enough slackers in there as it is.

BETTY: I could go on my own.

DWYER: I have to set an example for the lads. What?

BETTY: I'm happy to go on my own. Sure Mammy and me have loads to be doing. She's fierce lonely since Daddy died.

DWYER: He died over five years ago.

BETTY: Seven years next month, the Lord have mercy on him. And she needs help on the farm.

DWYER: She has your brothers.

BETTY: Somebody to get a few messages for her.

DWYER: Can they not...

BETTY: Do a few jobs around the house.

DWYER: I might be able to take a week in later on in the year. August maybe. We can go then.

BETTY: She's worried about me.

Silence

DWYER: She thinks I can't look after you?

BETTY: She's heard the stories. She doesn't think it's safe for me anymore.

DWYER: I think I might be a better judge of what's safe for my own wife, thank you very much.

BETTY: I want to go. I hate it here Tom. I want to go home.

DWYER: This is your home. Has been for 20 years for God's sake. *(Pause)* How long for?

BETTY: Just until things settle down. You said yourself it wouldn't be long.

DWYER: Please don't go. It's hard enough with .. *(There is a sharp knock at the door)* Who's that at this hour?

Tom walks to the door and opens it.

DWYER: Hughes. Come in.

HUGHES: Very sorry to disturb you Sergeant Dwyer, Mrs. Dwyer. We're three men short for this evening's patrol and Head Constable Byrne said you might be able to help out. *(He senses the awkwardness in the room)* I'm on the beat here for another hour and then…I can see that you're busy. I'll tell him..

BETTY: No, no it's fine. You go Tom. You're needed.

DWYER: Are you sure? If you want..

BETTY: Not at all. *(She brushes the dirt off his jacket)* Here you are – good as new. We'll talk later love. Give us both time to think. Stay safe.

Sound of the front door opening again, and Mary practically falling through.

DWYER: Mary! What are you doing here? Come in girl. It's freezing out there.

MARY: Oh, sorry Mr. Dwyer. I wasn't expecting..I came to talk to…Mrs. Dwyer.

DWYER: To Betty? And here she was only just this evening saying that nobody ever called into her any more. Come on inside, she'll be delighted to see you.

Mary is in a bit of a panic. She stares at Joseph, who shrugs and grins.

HUGHES: Evening Miss.

MARY: Constable.

DWYER: Sergeant to you Mary! This young lad is going places.

Mary's eyes widen in surprise. Joseph nods and winks.

MARY: Oh! I didn't know!

DWYER: Sure how would you? This young lad is going places.

BETTY: Mary. How lovely to see you. What..Come in…come in. Will you have tea?

MARY: Em…thanks Mrs. Dwyer.

DWYER: We'll leave you to it then. *(He smiles at Betty)* Bye love! I shouldn't be too late.

HUGHES: *(Trying to communicate with Mary.)* Hopefully I won't be too late either. I just have to finish my beat. Another hour should do it.

BETTY: That's lovely.

HUGHES: Em…goodbye then.

He leaves.

DWYER: Be home as soon as I can.

He exits. Door closes.

BETTY: Sit down Mary. I haven't seen you in a long time. Is your mammy keeping well?

MARY: She is Mrs. Dwyer.

BETTY: Joseph?

MARY: Fine too. *(Awkward pause)* I'm terrible sorry Mrs. Dwyer about you not getting served in the shop. I don't think it's very fair. It's not your fault that Mr. Dwyer is…

BETTY: Don't worry about it Mary. Joseph is upset about Sean and that's very understandable. Was that what you came to see me about?

MARY: Yes, it was.

BETTY: Well you're a very kind girl to think of me. Take after your mammy so ye do.

MARY: I can get your messages for you if you want. Just give me a list. No one will know.

BETTY: Ah thank you Mary, but I wouldn't want you going against Joseph's wishes. He's just supporting his family, that's all.

MARY: The RIC officers are just doing the same. I think they're very brave so I do.

BETTY: Don't let too many people hear you say that.

MARY: What's it like to be married to a Sergeant Mrs. Dwyer?

BETTY: Same as any other man I suppose.

MARY: Oh but it's not the same – it can't be. He's so important and brave and clever and

BETTY: Are we talking about Mr. Dwyer here?

MARY: Mr. Dwyer? Yes.

BETTY: I married Mr. Dwyer over 20 years ago Mary. Even then it wasn't easy.

MARY: Did your family disown you?

BETTY: No, nothing like that. They were delighted for me. The RIC was a very respectable job – is – is a very respectable job.

MARY: Of course it is. They're the only people willing to do what it takes to protect law and order in this country.

BETTY: Mary, when an RIC man wants to get married, he has to get permission from his superiors.

MARY: Permission?

BETTY: To make sure his wife is suitable. It wouldn't do, for example if an RIC Officer was to marry a woman with connections to the Volunteers.

MARY: *(Pause)* Even if that woman had nothing to do with the Volunteers herself?

BETTY: They can't take any chances.

MARY: Just as well you don't have any connections to the Volunteers so Mrs. Dwyer!

BETTY: It is, isn't it? *(Pause)* Because if Mr. Dwyer really wanted to marry me, he would have had to leave the RIC.

MARY: But he loves it so much. He really believes in what he's doing. He's so dedicated.

BETTY: He is. And that's one of the reasons you want to marry him in the first place, isn't it?

Pause

MARY: *(Desperately)* What am I going to do?

BETTY: Being married to an RIC man is hard, Mary.

MARY: I'm strong.

BETTY: You have to live far away from your family and friends. Nobody talking to you. Nobody serving you in the shops.

MARY: We always said it would be the two of us against the world.

BETTY: When the whole world is against you love, two is a very small number.

Faint sounds comes from outside the window, so is heard distantly at first. A rebel song is heard from the front of the house, sung by a group of rowdy young men. It gets louder as it goes on, with shouts of 'RIC Scum', 'RIC

Bitch' and 'Traitors'. It continues through the following scene, growing more and more violent.

MARY: It's only for a short time. It'll get better.

BETTY: Then wait until it gets better. For your own sake – and his.

MARY: You won't tell anyone, will ye Mrs. Dwyer?

BETTY: Sure who would I tell?

A stone is thrown against the window.

MARY: What in the name of God…

The chanting gets louder. There is a banging on the front door.

BETTY: Get down Mary. Don't let anyone see you.

MARY: Who is it?

BETTY: I don't know. Two or three big lads. Their faces are covered.

MARY: Cowards. I probably know them. Let me have a look.

The window smashes in. The women scream.

BETTY: No! Get down!

MARY: I'm not afraid of them.

BETTY: Well you should be.

The song is getting more and more aggressive, as are the chants. 'Death to the RIC'; 'Retire or die'; Leave the RIC or have your house blown up!' there is lots of laughter as the chants get more violent.

MARY: Are they threatening to blow your house up?   Now?

BETTY: I don't know!

MARY: We have to get out of here.

BETTY: You can't be seen.

MARY: The back. Come on.

BETTY: You go. Jump over the wall into Murphys and around by the side entrance.

MARY: What about you?

BATTY: It doesn't mattter about me.

MARY: Of course it matters about you. We need to get you to safety.

BETTY: I've nowhere to go Mary.   There's nobody who'll have me.

A piercing RIC whistle sounds from outside.

HUGHES: Blagards! Get on there with ye. Upsetting respectable people like that.

REBEL 3: Nothing respectable about the RIC or anyone related to them!

REBEL 2: Traitors to the cause, the whole lot of them.

REBEL 3: RIC bitch! Up the Rebels!

ALL: RIC bitch! Up the Rebels!

REBEL 3: We know you're in there Betty Dwyer.

REBEL 2: Get your traitor husband to resign or face the consequences.

REBEL 1: Up the Republic!

ALL: Up the Republic!

Sound of whistle again.

HUGHES: Move on there now immediately or you'll have consequences of your own to face.

He starts to take out his baton.

REBEL 3: Beat your own people would you?

HUGHES: No people of mine would threaten an innocent woman alone in her own home. Ye should be ashamed of yourselves.

REBEL 3: It's the like of you who should be ashamed. Come on lads. I think we've made our point.

They leave. Joseph runs to the front door. The front door opens.

JOSEPH H: Mrs. Dwyer! Mary! Are ye alright?

MARY: Joseph!

HUGHES: Oh thank God! *(They hug. Joseph pulls away)* Mary – em...

MARY: It's okay. Mrs. Dwyer knows our secret. I was so worried about you. Those lads could have done anything.

HUGHES: Ah they're just young fellas. All talk. Are ye alright Mrs. Dwyer? That was a terrible experience for you.

BETTY: I'm fine Constable, thank you. That was very brave of you.

MARY: They said they were going to blow the house up.

HUGHES: Anyone lays a finger on you they'll have every RIC officer in Maynooth on their backs.

BETTY: There weren't too many of them here when they were needed.

HUGHES: Well – we're short staffed this evening.

BETTY: Let's hope everyone reports for duty the night those lads come back to set fire to our house.

HUGHES: You probably shouldn't stay here this evening Mrs. Dwyer. Can I escort you to a safe place?

BETTY: There aren't any safe places for RIC wives.

HUGHES: A friend's house?

BETTY: We don't have any friends Constable.

HUGHES: At least let me take you to the station. I'll appraise Sergeant Dwyer of the situation and he'll…

BETTY: He'll what? Retire from the constabulary? I don't think so. Would you retire Constable Hughes?

HUGHES: No of course not. Not for anything. Who else is going to defend law and order in this country?

BETTY: I'd appreciate it if you could tell Sergeant Dwyer what's happened and ask him to come home as soon as he can.

MARY: I'll wait with you Mrs. Dwyer.

BETTY: Thanks Mary, but you've been put in enough danger this evening. I'd much prefer to know that you're safe.

HUGHES: I'll bring you home a stor mo chroi.

BETTY: She might be safer going on her own.

MARY: *(Hesitates, afraid)* I'll be fine. It's more important to get Mr. Dwyer home. Go. Quickly. *(She kisses him briefly and he exits)* I might go out the back way.

BETTY: Mary?

MARY: Yes?

BETTY: Two is a very small number…

END OF EPISODE

EPISODE 17 – PLANNING THE AMBUSH, FEB. 1921

Scene 1 - UaBuachalla's house

UABUACHALLA: *(Furtive)* The Long brothers are under surveillance, they think. But Catherine Long got this to me. *(He unfolds some notepaper, hands it to Mullaney)* Here.

MULLANEY: *(Reading)* Routes and times. This is fantastic, Domhnall.

UABUACHALLA: And I know just the boys to carry it out. Listen up. *Fade.*

VOOIVEOVER: Fractured – a family, a nation, a dream. January 1921

Scene 2 - Barry's pub

Mary humming 'Tabhair Dom do Lamh.' Tomas is busy putting a Boycott Belfast Goods poster up.

TOMAS: You're fierce happy there.

MARY: Is a girl not allowed be happy these days?

TOMAS: Don't ate me, I'm just commenting. Hand me the tape there.

MARY: Here, *(Handing it to him – reading)* 'Boycott Belfast Goods' Jesus, Tomas, do you want Mammy to skin you alive? You can't be putting up posters like that. You're running a bar.

TOMAS: It's a public information notice, so it is.

MARY: It doesn't matter what it is, she'll flay you.

TOMAS: I'll take my chances.

MARY: *(Pulling on her coat)* I'm off out. It's been very nice knowing you, Tomas.

TOMAS: *(Laugh)* Where are you off to? I hope you're not – I hope you're not going into Dublin, it's bad there these days.

MARY: I'm off out with Cissy, Catherine, and Lizzie.

TOMAS: Lizzie O'Neill, is it?

MARY: Aye.

TOMAS: How is she? I haven't clapped eyes on her in an age.

MARY: She's working in Carton now. *(Teasing)* I might bring her back after.

TOMAS: Do. Aye. It'd be grand to see her.

MARY: Will you talk to her this time?

TOMAS: *(Defensive)* I talked to her last time.

MARY: You opened your mouth but nothing came out.

TOMAS: Look, I don't care if you bring her back or not. I was just saying I hadn't seen her.

MARY: If you like her you should court her. *(Tomas doesn't reply)* Girls like fellows who take the lead. *(Mossie Kinsella enters. Mary's demeanour changes)* Mr. Kinsella.

MOSSIE: There she is, the bauld Mary. Wouldn't serve me the Sunday of the rally. How are you?

TOMAS: She's off out, Mossie. What can I do for you?

MOSSIE: *(To Mary)* Bye now. You're looking lovely, so you are.

MARY: I'll see you later, Tomas.

She leaves.

MOSSIE: That's a right cheeky rip of a sister you have.

TOMAS: What is it you want? A pint, is it?

MOSSIE: I was in UaBuachalla's, that slimy little fecker, told me to be off with myself when I asked for a bit of Irish D.

TOMAS: See my poster. You're out of luck here too.

MOSSIE: Since when?

TOMAS: Since the last while. Me father hasn't had any Belfast goods sold in the place and he's sick of people asking for them.

MOSSIE: And where am I to get some quality snuff? You tell me that?

TOMAS: I'll tell you, you won't get it in any proper Irishman's establishment.

MOSSIE: Proper Irishman. Would you look at yourself? A jumped up child, that's all you are.

TOMAS: Is there anything else I can get you?

UaBuachalla and Pat Mullaney enter. Tomas snaps to attention.

TOMAS: Mr. UaBuachalla and Mr. Mullaney, sirs. Can I help ye?

UABUACHALLA: I hope so, Tomas. We were -

MOSSIE: Following me, are you? Watching me? Can a man not walk around in his own town without being followed.

UABUACHALLA: We've more important stuff to be doing than watching you.

MOSSIE: Aye, like refusing to serve a man a decent bit of tobacco. This country has gone to the dogs. A pint, there, Tomas. *(Tomas pulls him a pint. Lays it on the counter)* It'll be the last pint I drink in here.

He shuffles down to his seat. Beat as the men make sure he is out of the way.

UABUACHALLA: *(Low, urgent)* Is your mother in, Tomas?

TOMAS: She's upstairs, will I -

UABUACHALLA: It's you we want. Is she likely to come down?

TOMAS: She's with Poor Brid so they'll be at it for hours.

UABUACHALLA: Grand. Get a bottle or two of stout there for us, We've a bit of business we'd like to discuss with you.

Tomas places some bottles on the counter, the men take them.

MULLANEY: Always good to know a fellow who runs a pub.

Tomas laughs a bit too much.

TOMAS: Sorry. I'm a bit… well…anyway, what do ye want?

MULLANEY: Join us at the table and we'll talk.

TOMAS: I've to stay behind the bar, if Mammy came down and – *(He stops as the two men look at him)* Right. Well, I'll just get myself a drink, hang on a second there now.

The men retire to the table. Tomas pours himself a drink and follows the men down.

TOMAS: What can I do for ye?

UABUACHALLA: I'll let Mullany fill you in, Tomas. We've a bit of a job planned.

TOMAS: Oh, aye?

MULLANEY: Your brother talked very highly of you.

TOMAS: Have you heard from him? Me mother is going out of her mind.

MULLANEY: I haven't, no, Tomas. But no news is good news.

TOMAS: Mammy wouldn't agree.

UABUACHALLA: Brigid Barry is a fearsome woman, Mullaney. If she was behind us, we'd have won the war already.

TOMAS: That's what me father says.

MULLANEY: Is she not a supporter?

TOMAS: She's, well, she's a bit lukewarm but since Sean…well, she's not for the RIC anymore, that's for sure.

MULLANEY: Because we can't take a risk that -

TOMAS: Hasn't she hung that bill banning Belfast Goods over the bar? Mammy's not for the British.

UABUACHALLA: Tell the lad about the job.

153

MULLANEY: We're a bit short for men since the arrest of the two lads the other evening.

TOMAS: What lads?

MULLANEY: Conway and Blake.

TOMAS: Conway, the schoolteacher?

UABUACHALLA: And Blake the butcher's apprentice, as fine a soldier as ever there was.

TOMAS: That's a blow.

MULLANEY: On top of Harris and Colgan it's a disaster.

UABUACHALLA: Which is why we've come.

TOMAS: What'll I have to do.

MULLANEY: What you're told, for starters.

UaBuachalla laughs. Tomas doesn't.

TOMAS: Which will be?

MULLANEY: We're planning an ambush for the Maynooth RIC.

TOMAS: The local lads? Dwyer and them?

MULLANEY: Have you got a problem with that?

TOMAS: They came for Sean, so no, I've got no problem.

MULLANEY: Because if you have -

TOMAS: I said I don't.

MULLANEY: There's no room for old sentiments.

TOMAS: I know that.

UABUACHALLA: This lad was there at Croke Park last November, he saw what they were capable of.

TOMAS: I did.

MULLANEY: Alright. For this ambush we need men we can trust.

TOMAS: You can trust me.

MULLANEY: Have you ever had to fire a gun at someone?

TOMAS: No.

MULLANEY: And do you think you might like to?

TOMAS: Only if it wears a British uniform.

UABUACHALLA: That's the spirit.

MULLANEY: This is to go no further than across this table, have you got me?

TOMAS: Cross my heart.

MULLANEY: Hope to die, ey? Good man. Right, for the past few weeks, we've had a few boys keeping an eye on the RIC routine.

UABUACHALLA: The Long brothers, you know them up the Moyglare Road.

TOMAS: John and Patrick, is it?

UABUACHALLA: The very men. They've been keeping tabs on their RIC neighbours, looking to see what times they change shifts, what times they do their rounds at, what routes they take, all that.

MULLANEY: We now know that they start their nightly patrol dead on ten o'clock, they go in single file, about six of them, down the Moyglare Road, past the church and on into the town. The plan is to catch them at the church.

UABUACHALLA: The low wall opposite it is where it'll take place.

MULLANEY: Once the first shot goes off, all hell will break loose. That first shot has to be a good one, it has to fell someone.

UABUACHALLA: Fell them all, hopefully.

TOMAS: And where do I come in?

MULLANEY: I've been told you do well in training.

UABUACHALLA: He's a great man with a rifle.

MULLANEY: Is that true?

TOMAS: Aye. I'm used to it as the College get me in to shoot the rabbits in Spring.

MAULLAY: It's not rabbits you'll be shooting now, boy.

UABUACHALLA: It'll be fish in a barrel.

They laugh a little.

MULLANEY: We're asking you to take part, Tomas. We need good shooters.

Beat as Tomas hesitates.

UABUACHALLA: I said it in sixteen, I'll say it again, if you want to walk away, walk away. But if you say yes, you say yes.

TOMAS: I don't want to walk away, this is my fight. It's just…

UABUACHALLA: You know these men, some of them anyway?

TOMAS: I do.

UABUACHALLA: It's not an easy thing we're asking, we know that.

MULLANEY: Ask yourself this, if they caught you with a gun, defending your country, what would they do to you? What would Sergeant Dwyer, your neighbour do?

UABUACHALLA: I'll tell you what he'd do, Tomas, he'd come hunting you down, like he did your brother, wouldn't he?

TOMAS: He would, I suppose.

MULLANEY: No suppose about it. Those men may say they're Irish, but in their hearts they're English.

UABUACHALLA: Didn't the DMP and the RIC beat the arse of people in the lockout, didn't they do it during the land wars. We can't let them keep doing it.

MULLANEY: Didn't the British send our men off to the front? Kept them poor at home so they'd go off and die for the king's shilling?

UABUACHALLA: Didn't they try to kill all in front of them last November.

MULLANEY: Isn't Hannah Skeffington a widow now because they killed her husband and him a pacifist?

TOMAS: Aye and I saw a man killed standing right beside me at Croke Park in November. One minute he was laughing and then next...gone.

MULLANEY: And it's the likes of the RIC that are propping them up.

UABUACHALLA: Are you with us, Tomas?

TOMAS: I am.

UABUACHALLA: Good boy, your brother will be proud.

MULLANEY: We'll be in touch with the details.

They clink glasses. Off we hear Brigid.

BRIGID: *(Distant)* Brid, hang on and I'll open the back door. It's shorter than going around the front. Bye, bye Colm, take care now love.

The back door slams, we hear Brigid enter the bar.

BRIGID: *(Calling from bar)* Tomas, have you not work to be going on with?

TOMAS: I'm just chatting to the customers, Mammy, being sociable.

BRIGID: And drinking our profits too by the looks of it. Mr. Buckly, I'm sure you'll excuse Tomas, he has work to be going on with.

TOMAS: And I'll work when I'm finished talking, Mammy.

BRIGID: You're finished talking now. Go and tidy up the back yard.

TOMAS: I just -

BRIGID: It won't tidy itself.

Tomas reluctantly gets up and moves away.

BRIGID: Mr. Buckley and Mr. -

UABUACHALLA: It's Mr. UaBuachalla, Mrs. Barry and this is Mr. Mullaney.

BRIGID: The niceties of your name don't concern me, Mr. Buckley. But what does concern me is my son. I have lost one lad to the cause and I won't lose another one.

UANUACHALLA: With all due respect, Mrs. Barry, Tomas is a grown man now, he can make his own decisions.

BRIGID: Tomas has head his head filled with rubbish from your Gaelic League and your Volunteers and your -

UABUACALLA: Tomas is no fool, he understands what's needed and what's not.

BRIGID: I'm no fool either. If one hair on his head is disturbed, then I will -

MULLANEY: You'll what, Mrs. Barry? You'd hardly side with the RIC now, would you after what they did on your Sean?

BRIGID: Forgive me but I've forgotten your name, probably because it's not important. Did I ask for your opinion?

MULLANEY: It's Paddy Mullaney, Mrs. Barry. I'm a schoolteacher from Leixlip.

BRIGID: Is it a medal you want for that? I know there's no good going on when the likes of you are talking to my son. I'm telling ye to stop it.

MOSSIE: *(Calling across)* He has him hanging up the Belfast Boycott posters Mrs. Barry. I couldn't get my snuff this morning.

BRIGID: That's an entirely different matter, Mr. Kinsella.

MOSSIE: I don't think it is. I couldn't get -

BRIGID: The Catholics are treated like animals up the north. Fired from their jobs, burned out of their houses. Why would we help the likes of those people stay in business?

UABUACHALLA: Well said, Mrs. Barry.

MOSSIE: All I want is a bit of snuff and -

BERIGID: Well. You won't get it here.

MOSSIE: Then I'll take my business elsewhere.

BRIGID: I'm sure the loss of two shillings a year will ruin us entirely, Mr. Kinsella.

The men laugh at that.

MOSSIE: You're above yourself, Brigid Barry. Nothing but a jumped up jezebel who married a man who -

UABUACHALLA: I'd leave it there, Mossie, now.

MULLANEY: A bit of respect for the woman.

BRIGID: I'll thank you to leave, Mr. Kinsella.

MOSSIE: I'm leaving. But you'll rue the day you treated Mossie Kinsella like that, so you will. You'll rue it.

He slams his glass down and storms out.

UABUACHALLA: You handled that well, Mrs. Barry.

BRIGID: You leave Tomas out of your plans. Or you'll rue the day. *(She exits to the back of the bar calling)* Tomas!

Beat

MULLANEY: Charming lady.

UABUACHALLA: You heard what she said about the Boycott. She's with us whether she knows it or not.

MULLANEY: I'd rather she knew it. Are you sure that young lad is as good as his brother?

UABUACHALLA: I think there's a lot of potential there. Give the lad a proper chance.

MULLANEY: Only because I trust you, Domhnall.

As they down the last of their drinks, Tomas arrives back out and we hear him sheepishly take down the Boycott poster.

UABUACHALLA: What are you taking the poster down for?

TOMAS: Because -

Brigid arrives out.

BRIGID: Because politics has no place in a pub, isn't that right Tomas?

UABUACHALLA: I thought you'd hung that, Mrs. Barry.

TOMAS: We still won't be selling the goods, Mr. UaBuachalla, it's just like…the poster…

BRIGID: Is not welcome. Hand the poster back, Tomas.

TOMAS: Mammy!

BRIGID: Hand it back.

TOMAS: I will not.

BRIGID: Fine so. *(She takes the poster and rips it)* There now. Gone. I'll be out back if you need me Tomas.

She nods to all three and leaves.

TOMAS: I am sorry about that, just ignore her. She's upset over Sean and doesn't know who to blame and -

MULLANEY: For her own good, she shouldn't go shouting her mouth off like that.

TOMAS: She means no harm.

MULLANEY: It's dangerous talk in these times.

TOMAS: I know, but she's for the boycott and hasn't she set up her women's group, a sort of peaceful Cumann na mBan, but -

MULLANEY: Are you on board for the ambush?

TOMAS: I am.

MULLANEY: Then I'll be in touch. Slan, Tomas.

They move to leave, Mary arrives back in. They greet her as Miss Barry and leave.

MARY: *(Amused)* She tore it up! I told you she'd hate it.

TOMAS: I hate her. She made a show of me. *(Beat)* I thought you were out for the day.

MARY: Cissy is sick, vomiting all morning and I don't want to be catching anything.

TOMAS: And...Lizzie?

MARY: Ooohh.

TOMAS: You said you were off out with Lizzie, that's why I'm asking.

MARY: She was called into work. She said she thought she saw you in Carton yourself last week.

TOMAS: No.

MARY: She said there was a few of you. Drilling and that.

TOMAS: No.

MARY: Because if it was you and Mammy found out -

TOMAS: I can't live my life for Mammy. And so what if I was drilling in Carton, would that be such a great wrong?

MARY: Do you think I want another brother on the run?

TOMAS: Do you think I want to sit by and let the British kill us all?

MARY: You sound like Sean.

TOMAS: Good.

MARY: I thought you'd more sense.

TOMAS: I thought you had more. Do you not believe in freedom, Mary?

MARY: And what freedom would I gain in an Irish Ireland?

TOMAS: Whatever freedom you wanted, we'd be in charge of ourselves. No more British run RIC and no -

MARY: I'm not talking politics. I'm only saying, Lizzie said she saw you and I said to her, well, if it was Tomas, isn't he fecking stupid to be running around like an eejit for Ireland when he should be running around like an eejit for Mammy.

TOMAS: You did not.

MARY: And she laughed so she did.

TOMAS: *(Hurt)* Thank you for that.

MARY: You are very welcome.

She floats off, laughing.

TOMAS: And I hate you too!

END OF EPISODE

EPISODE 18 – RIC AMBUSH, FEB. 1921

Scene 1 - Outside Barry's Pub

Evening street sounds

MARY: I'd like to report a missing person Sergeant Hughes.

HUGHES: Certainly Miss Barry. And who is it that's missing?

MARY: My boyfriend. At least, I think he's my boyfriend. He hasn't been very attentive lately.

HUGHES: Now that's terrible altogether Miss Barry. When did you last see this reprobate?

MARY: Last night. 10:30. He walked past my house and blew me a kiss.

HUGHES: Blew you a kiss did he? Cheek! If you were my girl you'd get the real thing. Like this. *(Sound of a kiss. Mary laughs)* And this. *(Longer kiss)* And maybe even..

MARY: I love you Joseph Hughes!

HUGHES: I love you too Mary Barry.

VOICEOVER: Fractured – a family, a nation, a dream.

Scene 2 - Outside RIC Barracks

Feet shuffling/movement of guns/checking of ammunition.

MULLANEY: Here ye are, get down, for God's sake, do ye want to be seen. O'Reilly did you brief these lads at all? Larkin has all his boys in place.

O'REILLY: I haven't had the chance yet.

MULLANEY: And when do you suppose you might have the chance? When they get their heads blown off, is it? Mick Flynn said the men need to be briefed now.

O'REILLY: It's only a quarter to yet.

MULLANEY: Your point being?

O'REILLY: The officers in the station don't move out until the hour strikes so, I thought I'd brief the boys now, before it all kicks off.

MALLANEY: Bloody excuses. Farrell - take over.

FARRELL: Yes sir. Our target tonight is the RIC officers stationed in that building across the way. They will commence their nightly round in fifteen minutes, Head Sergeant Dwyer usually leads the column with five officers falling in behind. They move in single file. They will not be expecting trouble so it should be easy to get a shot off.

MULLANEY: I have positioned men all along the roads leading in and out of Maynooth, any sign of the Auxies or the Tans and we will have prior warning.

FARRELL: Once the first shot goes off, all hell will break loose. The aim is to get their guns. Keep firing your weapons until you are given the order to retreat.

MULLANEY: Once you are given the order to retreat, hand your weapons over to Lizzie or Ellen here. They will dispose of them.

FARRELL: Any questions?

TOMAS: Where do we go when we retreat?

MULLANEY: You go home Tomas Barry. You say nothing and you wait and see what happens. Do not, anyone, under any circumstances, bring your weapon with you.

FARRELL: Make no mistake, when this ends, the Tans will be crawling all over this town. They will come in and knock on your doors and destroy your houses and if you are caught with a weapon, then you will be arrested. Maybe shot.

MULLANEY: And we have too many of our boys out of action in Ballykinlar to want to lose anymore.

TOMAS: Rumour has it that this new camp in the Curragh will be filled in weeks, that the Tans will go around arresting everyone now.

MULLANEY: Thank you for those inspiring words, Tomas Barry.

TOMAS: I just meant -

MULLANEY: Keep your noses clean, your weapons out of sight and you need not fear the Tans.

Scene 3 - RIC Barracks

Sound of a drawer opening. A whiskey bottle is taken out of it, opened, and poured into a cup. It is gulped in one go, and Dwyer breathes out in relief.

HUGHES: Oh! Sorry to disturb you Sergeant Dwyer. I'll er give the boys a shout now, will I?

DWYER: What? Right...yes. Thank you Hughes.

HUGHES: Stiff! Curran! Perry! Moving out in ten minutes. *(To Dwyer)* It's a cold one out there now. *(Dwyer doesn't respond)* You'd want to be well wrapped up, so you would. Perry's mother sent him another parcel, a red scarf in it this time, you could hang a man with it. *(Dwyer still doesn't respond)* Then you could use it as his shroud, it's that big. *(Nothing)* I was thinking of raiding a few houses on patrol tonight, what'd you think?

Curran suggested the house of God, but I thought, Jesus. *(He laughs a bit at his own joke)* Sarge! Sarge?

DWYER: Sorry…what?

HUGHES: Is everything alright there?

DWYER: Everything's grand…have you called the boys for patrol?

HUGHES: I have.

DWYER: Grand.

Beat. Silence.

HUGHES: It'll all be grand, Sarge.

DWYER: What?

HUGHES: With…well…your wife. She'll come back.

DWYER: I don't think that's any of your business, Hughes.

HUGHES: No. Sorry.

DWYER: *(After a couple of beats)* No, it's me. Sorry.

HUGHES: It wasn't my business

DWYER: No but still…you were only trying….

HUGHES: To help…yes.

DWYER: I appreciate it.

HUGHES: She had a shock.

DWYER: Yes.

HUGHES: She'll come back.

DWYER: Does the whole station know she left?

HUGHES: No…I don't think so.

DWYER: No matter, they'll find out soon enough.

HUGHES: I'm sure she'll -

DWYER: She won't. Why would she?

HUGHES: Because this is her home.

DWYER: Not anymore it's not. This place is as lawless as the rest of the country and I hate it. I didn't take good enough care of her, Hughes.

HUGHES: You did your best.

DWYER: I kept telling her things would be alright. What a fool I was.

HUGHES: They will be alright. Those boys, they were just thugs, looking for a bit of trouble, so they were.

DWYER: I keep asking myself if the job is worth it.

HUGHES: You know it is.

DWYER: That's what I used to think. But I've lost friends and neighbours and now my wife because of it.

HUGHES: We've all lost people. I can't even visit home anymore.

DWYER: And you're happy with that?

HUGHES: I was never that fond of me brother anyways. *(Dwyer laughs)* But yes, I think in the end, it'll be worth it. I like the job.

Sound of Curran coming in.

DWYER: What is it, Curran?

CURRAN: Sarge, Stiff says his leg is fierce sore so can he be excused patrol duty this evening.

HUGHES: Tell him he'll have a fierce sore arse if he doesn't get a move on. Five minutes.

CURRAN: He won't like that.

Exit.

DWYER: That young fellow, Stiff, is getting worse. He'll barely work the counter now.

HUGHES: And he's drinking on the job. Oh, sorry sir – I didn't mean...

Scene 4 - Outside The Barracks.

Sounds of breathing, bodies moving, possibly birdsong / wind.

MULANNEY: Ms O'Neill – any final instructions?

LIZZIE: The weapons have to be handed to me quick. Also, if any of you boys are injured, come with me too.

MULANNEY: Miss O'Neill knows a safe house where a doctor can be found. Do not attempt to make it home or go on the run with an injury

TOMAS: What if it's only a minor injury, like a nick or something?

O'REILLY: Are you planning on having a wet shave while you're waiting for this ambush?

TOMAS: No.

O'REILLY: Because you don't generally tend to get relatively minor nicks from bullets.

TOMAS: I know you don't get nicks from bullets, I'm not stupid.

LIZZIE: 'Course you're not. Don't mind him, Tomas, he's just a grumpy arse.

O'REILLY: Miss O'Neill, I'll thank you to know who's in charge here.

LIZZIE: I'll thank you to know who's hiding your guns for you.

O'REILLY: A favour we'll never hear the end of, I'm sure.

MULLANEY: A favour we appreciate. O'Reilly I don't want to have to speak to you again. Go and see who we have and sort the men into position.

Scene 5 – RIC Barracks.

Sound of the men getting ready for patrol. Low chat, footsteps.

HUGHES: Stay where you are Sergeant Dwyer. Have a rest this evening. The four of us can handle the patrol.

DWYER: Are you sure?

HUGHES: Yes. Stiff?

STIFF: Sarge.

HUGHES: Give the Chief a dram of that drink you have hidden up your sleeve, will you?

STIFF: I don't have drink hidden up my sleeve, Sarge.

HUGHES: Are you inviting me to do a body search?

Curran and Perry snigger.

STIFF: If I have drink, it's purely by accident. Hang on till I see. It's just a small bit.

HUGHES: That's all the Chief needs. Pour away. *(Sound of the drink being opened and poured)* A bit more, there's the man.

More pouring

DWYER: That's pure gorgeous, so it is. I needed that.

CURRAN: You wouldn't want to be getting too fond of it now, Chief. When my mother left my father, he became a fierce man for the bottle.

HUGHES: Right lads, single formation.

DWYER: Did she tell you she had left me?

CURRAN: Ah now, Chief as if…

DWYER: Then when I say she has gone to visit her mother, she has. Understood?

CURRAN: Understood.

STIFF: Right you are.

DWYER: I do not want my wife and me to be talked about by anyone. Now get out on patrol.

Scene 6 – Outside RIC Station

LIZZIE: Is this your first ambush?

TOMAS: Is it that obvious?

LIZZIE: Yes.

TOMAS: You must think I'm an awful eejit.

LIZZIE: No such thing.

TOMAS: I've trenched roads and wrecked railway lines and that. I'm not a complete beginner.

LIZZIE: That's how all of them started off too. O'Reilly was afraid of his own shadow his first ambush.

TOMAS: Was he?

LIZZIE: Cross my heart. It was at Kill -

TOMAS: That's only a few months back.

LIZZIE: Isn't that what I'm telling you? A few months back. Now look at him, full of swagger.

TOMAS: My brother was at Kill.

LIZZIE: Sean. Isn't he on the run now?

TOMAS: Aye.

LIZZIE: He was good, Mullaney liked him. Cool under fire, that's what he said about Sean. Big boots to fill.

TOMAS: I think they might be a few sizes too big.

LIZZIE: You'll be grand, so you will. The rules for ambush - point, press and pray.

TOMAS: *(Laughs)* You're a brave woman.

LIZZIE: Divil a bit. I love the excitement.

TOMAS: Stop would ya.

LIZZIE: What would I be doing at home only polishing shoes for me brothers?

TOMAS: Mary does that for us.

LIZZIE: Shame on you. Haven't you two arms?

TOMAS: I do but -

LIZZIE: Then you should polish your own shoes. I hope a new Ireland has a law that gives women the freedom not to polish the boots of boys.

TOMAS: When I become leader, I'll make that law.

LIZZIE: When I become leader, I'll make it meself. *(Tomas cracks up)* What?

TOMAS: You're a gas ticket, so you are. A woman leader.

O'REILLY: Miss O'Neill, Barry, what are you two gaustering about? Come over here.

LIZZIE: Hasn't he the sweet tongue on him all the same? Don't let him boss you about.

TOMAS: I won't so. Thanks Lizzie.

They move over to O'Reilly

O'REILLY: Tomas Barry, you take up position here. Hang on, that can't be right…Mullaney, over here, please?

MULLANEY: *(Crossing)* What is it?

O'REILLY: You have the young Barry boy in front here.

MULLANEY: Aye?

O'REILLY: It's his first real action.

MULLANEY: I know that.

O'REILLY: Should he not be hanging back? Observing. Getting a bit of a shot off, fine, but up front…

MULLANEY: Are you doubting my plan?

O'REILLY: I'm just asking if it's right to put an inexperienced -

MALLANEY: So? You are doubting it?

LIZZIE: It sounds like doubt to me.

O'REILLY: Who asked you? Look, Mullaney, Tomas is eager, I'll give him that and -

MULLANEY: And he's also the best shot in the company or so I've heard, is that right Barry?

TOMAS: I suppose I -

MULLANEY: This is no time for modestly. You either are or you aren't?

TOMAS: Then I am, so.

MULLANEY: *(To O'Reilly)* Up the front with him. Take the first shot Tomas, make it a good one.

Scene 7 – RIC Station

HUGHES: Right lads – into formation. Currran, behind me. Stiff, stay with Perry at the back.

STIFF: Aw Sarge. Do I have to? It's just, I'm not comfortable with that red scarf.

PERRY: What's not to be comfortable about? It's not your scarf.

STIFF: It's too bright. In the war you'd be shot easy wearing a fing like that.

PERRY: I'll take my chance.

STIFF: It's like a target on your neck.

HUGHES: He has a point. Take it off.

PERRY: But it's warm, Sarge.

HUGHES: It's too bright. No point in inviting trouble.

PERRY: My mother spent two months knitting that for me.

STIFF: She wasted her time then.

He and Curran laugh

PERRY: You little English feck.

HUGHES: Boys. Come on. Perry, take off the scarf. See you when we get back Sergeant Dwyer.

Scene 8 – Outside RIC Station

Sounds of marching footsteps as the patrol emerge from the station.

MULLANEY: Here they come. This is our chance. Ready boys.

FARRELL: Go on Tomas Barry, would you? Shoot. Jesus, are you waiting on an invitation?

TOMAS: I'm waiting until I get a clear shot.

FARRELL: The lad in the front, he's in charge, that's who you need to -

TOMAS: *(Suddenly doubtful)* But, but that's not…Dwyer.

MULLANEY: Shoot. Jesus! Shoot!

One single shot fires, followed by gasps of anguish from the patrol. More shots follow. Shouts of 'Run', 'It's an ambush', 'Get out of here'.

O'REILLY: Yes! One of them is down! Yes!

MULLANEY: That's it boys, we have them on the run. Keep firing until you can't see them anymore.

More panicked shouting from the patrol.

MULLANEY: Right, boys. Hand over your guns. Go home. Good work.

The voices of Curran and Dwyer are some distance away. Panicked voices run throughout this scene in the background.

CURRAN: Shot bad, sir. Jesus. We need an ambulance. We couldn't see a thing, just the shine on the rifles. Aw Chief. Somebody get an ambulance. Jesus. He's bleeding bad.

TOMAS: I killed him.

LIZZIE: Stone dead, now if you're caught with that rifle you'll be stone dead yourself. Come on.

DWYER: Bring him into the nearest house. I don't care what they say. Raid it if ye have to.

LIZZIE: It's a shock the first time. But it gets easier crossing that barrier. I seen it happen.

TOMAS: Was it Dwyer I shot?

LIZZIE: I don't know who it was. Come on, you've got to go now. Ellen Kenny will help you. D'you know Ellen Kenny?

TOMAS: Aye.

LIZZIE: She'll get you home. She's waiting down the road there. Go, now, for heaven's sake.

TOMAS: There's blood all over him.

LIZZIE: Yes, you done well Tomas Barry. Now get out of here. Go!

DWYER: Whoever you are, we are coming for you! Get out of your homes. We will find every last one of ye! Every last one of ye! We are coming!

MULLANEY: Run!!!

END OF EPISODE

EPISODE 19 – AFTER THE AMBUSH, FEB. 1921

Scene 1 – Streets of Maynooth

Tomas is running from the ambush, climbing walls, landing heavily. We hear his footsteps and his heavy breathing. He is panicked. Lines from the previous episode are going through his head in an echoey way, all running over and through one another, including the sound of the shot.

LINES: I KILLED HIM/WAS IT DWYER I SHOT?/ STONE DEAD/ IT'S A SHOCK THE FIRST TIME/I DON'T KNOW WHO IT WAS/EXCELLENT SHOT/KEEP FIRING UNTIL YOU CAN'T SEE THEM ANYMORE/SHOOT/JESUS ARE YOU WAITING FOR AN INVITATION/WAS IT DWYER I SHOT/BUT THAT'S NOT DWYER/BUT THAT'S NOT DWYER/BUT THAT'S NOT DWYER...ETC

TOMAS: Oh Jesus Mary. I'm sorry. I'm so sorry.

VOICEOVER: Fractured – a family, a nation, a dream.

Scene 2 – Barry's Pub.

Sound of glasses being washed / put away.

BRIGID: I can't get her down at all.

MARY: Does she still have the headache Mammy?

BRIGID: Yes Mary. And the bad chest. She says she can't sleep until Tomas tells her a bedtime story.

MARY: That'll be some story. Out after curfew again – what'll his excuse be this time?

BRIGID: It's hard for a young lad like himself to be in every evening before 10 o'clock.

MARY: Hard for us all Mammy.

BRIGID: I've noticed – and you staring out that window like you were waiting for the second coming!

MARY: I am not.

BRIGID: It's hard on ye love, I know. You should be out there with your friends, enjoying yourself in safety. In my day..

MARY: *(Imitating her in a old woman voice)* 'In my day...'

BRIGID: G'wan outta that! It's not that long ago you know. Sure I was almost married at your age.

MARY: How did you know Mammy?

BRIGID: How did I know what?

MARY: How did you know that my daddy was The One.

BRIGID: The One? Is that what they're calling it these days?

MARY: Seriously Mammy, did your heart not thump really fast whenever you saw him?

BRIGID: I suppose it did.

MARY: Did you get butterflies in your tummy when he held your hand?

BRIGID: Your daddy wasn't much of a one for hand-holding.

MARY: Did you spend all your time just thinking about him and wondering what he was doing?

BRIGID: Yes – and staring out windows hoping he'd walk past some evening after curfew! *(Beat. Quietly, gently)* Tell me about him. Is he a nice lad?

MARY: Oh, Mammy I…

Sound of the back door being opened and footsteps coming in.

BRIGID: Tomas? Is that you? What time do you call this?

TOMAS: Sorry Mammy. I…got delayed. *(He enters the room. Sees Mary. Looks stricken)* Sorry Mary.

MARY: You can be as sorry as you like. You won't get away with it though.

TOMAS: *(Horrified)* What?

MARY: That's the second time this week I've had to close up. It's not fair Tomas.

BRIGID: Where were you, for God's sake? I was worried.

MARY: Probably out with Busy Lizzie. Giving her some kissy kissies!

BRIGID: She was in looking for you earlier alright. I thought that girl had her eye on Sean.

MARY: She's not called Busy Lizzie for nothing!

TOMAS: Would ye stop.

MARY: Ah, are we embarrassing you Tommy Wommy?

BRIGID: Leave the lad alone, would ye.

MARY: Like he left me alone to close up twice this week?

TOMAS: I'm sorry Mary. I'm really sorry.

MARY: *(Surprised at his sincerity)* Yeah, well. You can cover for me tomorrow.

BRIGID: Are you all right son? You're very pale.

TOMAS: I'm fine.

BRIGID: I hope you're not coming down with whatever Moll has.

Sound of Moll entering.

MOLL: Tomas – you're home!

BRIGID: Moll! You'll catch your death. Get back up to bed.

MOLL: I want Tomas to tell me a story.

BRIGID: Ah it's very late Moll, and Tomas is tired.

MOLL: Just a short one.

TOMAS: Maybe tomorrow Moll.

MOLL: I can't sleep without my story.

TOMAS: I have to help Mary tidy up in here.

MARY: Oh that's right, blame me.

MOLL: Please Tomas? I've been feeling sick all day. You tell the best stories.

TOMAS: I really can't Moll.

MOLL: Awwwww.

TOMAS: Oh alright. Just a short one then.

MOLL: Hurray! I think I'll feel much better afterwards. Can you tell me the one about the dragon and the princess and the grumpy troll?

They exit.

BRIGID: I'll help you with the clean up. I'll just go check on Joseph. See if he needs anything.

Sound of Mary walking to the door, opening it.

MARY: *(To herself)* Where are you Joseph Hughes? Not like you to be late for patrol.

Scene 3 – Maynooth Main Street.

Tom Dwyer's voice comes from afar at first, getting closer before he arrives at the pub and enters.

TOM: Bastards! We're coming for you! Do ye hear me? Ye may well get out of your beds now because you'll have no peace tonight. Murdering cowards! You're finished the whole lot of ye! You'll be sorry!

MARY: Mr. Dwyer! What's going on?

DWYER: Mary! I'm finished with ye all. *(Shouts to the street)* Do ye hear that everyone? I'm finished with ye all. Shower of betrayin', cheatin', thievin' murderin' bastards! Well justice is coming and I hope ye all burn alive in this stinkin' pile of shit that ye call a town!

MARY: What's wrong Mr. Dwyer? Who's coming? Has something happened?

DWYER: Has something happened? Has something happened? Don't play the innocent with me girl. You knew. You led that poor lad a merry dance. Are ye happy now? Are ye?

MARY: What are you talking about?

DWYER: You know well what I'm talking about. I'm talking about Joseph.

MARY: Joseph is above in bed sick. Do you want me to get him?

DWYER: Ah for Christ's sake will you cop yourself on. I'm talking about Sergeant Hughes. Your Sergeant Hughes

MARY: My…

DWYER: I know all about it Mary. Mrs. Dwyer told me before she left.

MARY: Please don't tell anyone Mr. Dwyer. She said she wouldn't tell anyone.

DWYER: She was worried about you. Can you believe that? Wanted me to look out for you. Was it me that the shot was intended for, was it?

MARY: What are you talking about?

DWYER: He's gone.

MARY: Gone?

DWYER: Are you happy now? Done your bit for your country have you?

MARY: Who's gone?

DWYER: We sent for Doctor Grogan but it was too late.

MARY: Where is he gone?

DWYER: He took a bullet. It was an ambush.

MARY: Doctor Grogan took a bullet in an ambush?

Sound of Brigid running in.

BRIGID: Mr. Dwyer! What's going on?

DWYER: *(Antagonistically)* Mrs. Barry.

BRIGID: Sean is not here, if that's what you want.

DWYER: Tomas?

BRIGID: Upstairs, reading a bedtime story to his sister. Joseph is in bed sick, Mary as you can see is trying to close up the pub and - after helping her - I plan to visit the lavatory. Is there anything else you'd like to know?

DWYER: I'd like to know why you've spent the past six months ignoring my wife.

MARY: Mr. Dwyer..

DWYER: I like to know why you feel it's perfectly alright to turn your back on a woman who has never shown you anything but kindness.

BRIGID: I really don't think…

DWYER: I'd like to know why you think you're so bloody superior to everyone else.

BRIGID: What are you..

DWYER: I'd like to know why you think it's perfectly fine to protect your criminal son from justice.

Joseph enters in pyjamas.

JOSEPH: What in the name of God? Tom? What are you doing here? I told you before – your lot…

DWYER: My lot Joseph? My lot? My lot that you were quite happy to use for many a year to get rid of trouble makers from your pub.

JOSEPH: What are you…

DWYER: Your best customers these days aren't they? Blowing up half the town so they are – your sons among them – and threatening my wife.

JOSEPH: My sons had nothing to do with that.

DWYER: Are you sure Joseph? *(Sound of Tomas and Moll, coming down the stairs)* Ah there's the hero himself. Where were you tonight Tomas? Huh? Where were you and your cowardly friends when a decent man was killed in the street?

BRIGID: Good God, who was killed?

DWYER: Shot through the head like a wild animal.

MARY: I think he said it was Doctor Grogan.

DWYER: His body riddled with bullets.

BRIGID: Oh the poor man.

DWYER: Were they meant for me Tomas, were they? Well here I am, ye little fuckin' bastard. Kill me now why don't ye

Sounds of a scuffle, fists, yelling. Moll screaming.

BRIGID: Joseph!

MARY: Mr. Dwyer!

DWYER: He was a good man. A good man doing a good job.

JOSEPH: Get out of my house! Coming in here accusing my son of murder. I'm going to report you.

DWYER: He has a family. Do you want to send the telegram Tomas? Do you want to write the letter of condolence?

BRIGID: Holy Mother of God. Tomas had nothing to do with this. Why would Tomas kill Doctor Grogan?

DWYER: It's not Doctor Grogan who's dead. It's Joseph Hughes. Sergeant Joseph Hughes. *(Mary screams. Silence)* Dependable, reliable, honest, hard-working, kind, decent. Dead.

Mary sobs.

BRIGID: One of your men? I don't think I knew him.

DWYER: He had a girl. *(To Mary. Accusingly)* He was going to do whatever it took to marry her. He spoke to Mrs. Dwyer about it.

BRIGID: God love her. It'll be a terrible shock.

JOSEPH: Still and all – I'm sorry you've lost one of your men Tom, but that's no excuse to come barging in here making accusations against my family. And scaring the life out of Moll and Mary.

DWYER: No. *(He is almost broken)* He was a good man. He deserved better.

BRIGID: You should probably go home Mr. Dwyer. You've had a terrible shock.

Dwyer goes to exit, pauses at the door.

DWYER: The Tans are on the way. I hope they burn this shithole town to the ground.

Scene 4 – Barry's Pub.

TOMAS: It wasn't me. I was with Lizzie.

MARY: I can't believe it.

TOMAS: *(Defensively)* I was. Ask her if you don't believe me.

MARY: I can't believe he's dead.

BRIGID: Did you know him love?

MARY: *(In a daze)* Yes. No. I don't know.

MOLL: Don't be sad Mary. At least it's not Doctor Grogan. We're going to see him tomorrow. Aren't we Mammy?

BRIGID: I don't know about that Moll. How long before the Tans arrive?

JOSEPH: God knows. Could be here any minute. We'll take what we can. Fill the cart and get out of here.

BRIGID: Where'll we go?

JOSEPH: Out towards Paddy's place. They're unlikely to come that far. Tomas – go out now and warn everyone. Wake them up if you have to. Don't be seen.

BRIGID: Make sure Poor Brid knows. Tell her she can come with us if she wants. Poor little Colm will lose his life if the Tans come near him.

TOMAS: I'll be as quick as I can.

Front door opens and closes.

JOSEPH: We'll board up the windows. I have some pallets in the cellar. Tell Tomas to come and help me when he gets back.

Footsteps exiting.

MOLL: I don't want to go anywhere Mammy. I feel sick.

BRIGID: I know love. It's just for a little while.

MOLL: Will I lose my life if the Tans come near me?

BRIGID: No love, of course not. I won't let them near you anyway.

MOLL: I'm scared Mammy.

BRIGID: No need to be scared. I'm much scarier than they are.

Brigid makes a scary face and roars. Moll laughs.

MOLL: Yes. Even Daddy is scared of you.

BRIGID: Is he now?

MOLL: He is. I heard him telling Paddy Dooley the other day. Can I bring my dolly?

BRIGID: Of course you can. But we have to hurry.

MOLL: Do I have to go to school?

BRIGID: No. Not for a few days.

MOLL: Hurray! No school! No school Mary! *(Tomas enters)* No school Tomas!

TOMAS: That's great Moll.

BRIGID: That was quick.

TOMAS: I went to Poor Brid first. Con sent me back to help Daddy. He's going to spread the word.

BRIGID: Your Daddy's in the cellar. He wants help blocking up the windows. Come on Moll. Mary, get packing.

MOLL: *(As she walks away)* Why was Mr. Dwyer so angry?

MARY: He knew Sean was here, ye know?

TOMAS: What?

MARY: At Christmas. He saw Sean.

TOMAS: Oh.

MARY: Could have arrested him. Could have been a hero at work.

TOMAS: But he didn't?

MARY: He said everyone deserves a happy Christmas.

TOMAS: I'm sorry Mary.

MARY: He saved Mrs. Dwyer when she was being threatened.

TOMAS: He did.

MARY: I was waiting for him to walk past the window. 10.30. Tuesdays, Thursdays and Saturdays. He's always there. Second in line. He blows a kiss as he walks by, every time. Just a small one. Fingers to his lips, like that. *(Silence)* He was going to do whatever it took to marry me. That's what Mr. Dwyer said. He did say that didn't he?

TOMAS: He did.

MARY: *(Panicking)* He must have known that I was a little bit afraid. Oh God Tomas, do you think he knew I was afraid? He might have thought I didn't want to marry him. Imagine if he thought that. Imagine if he died thinking that I didn't love him enough. I love him Tomas. I love him so much. *(She becomes distraught)* I love him more than anything. How am I going to get by without him? I can't. I just can't.

Tomas is devastated. He goes to Mary and touches her gently on the shoulder. She turns to him and sobs into his shoulder.

MARY: How could somebody just kill him? How could they do that? He's such a good person. I love him Tomas. I love him so much.

TOMAS: I'm sorry Mary. I'm so sorry.

END OF EPISODE

EPISODE 20 – SEARCH FOR MCCULLAGH, MAR. 1921

Scene 1 – RIC Station

DWYER: All right, boys, we're off to the Long's house up the Moyglare Road today. Rumour has it they know more than they're letting on about the ambush last week. We'll turn the place inside out and upside down if we have to. Got that? Stiff?

STIFF: What?

DWYER: Are you listening?

STIFF: Yes Sarge. Inside out, upside down.

DWYER: They have a playwright staying with them. He's a sympathiser. I want him arrested on sight. You got that, Stiff?

STIFF: Yes. Yes, I have.

DWYER: Are you sure?

STIFF: Inside out, upside down. Yes, yes, I have it.

DWYER: Right. Let's go boys.

Sound of marching footsteps out of the station.

VOICEOVER: Fractured – Early March 1921

Scene 2 - Barry's pub.

JOSEPH: I thought you were going to make a start on the tables.

MARY: I was just about to.

JOSEPH: Then there's the crates to be brought up.

MARY: I'll do it!

JOSEPH: I know you're worried about Sean, Mary, we all are, but no news is good news, ey?

MARY: Yes…Oh Daddy, when will all this fighting end?

JOSEPH: I don't know, a stor, but if we want to keep a roof over our heads, we have to just get on with it.

The front door opens and Cissy enters

JOSEPH: Hello Cissy. It's early for you. Are you taking to the drink now?

CISSY: *(A bit upset)* Hello Mr. Barry. I just want to have a quick chat with Mary.

JOSEPH: Don't keep her too long though she could do with some cheering up.

Joseph wanders off out of earshot but remains in the bar.

CISSY: What's wrong?

MARY: Everything. Sean…everything..

CISSY: Sean will be fine. Just think of your fancy man and you'll cheer right up. *(Mary starts to cry)* Ah God, Mary, I'm sorry. Tell me.

MARY: I can't.

CISSY: Did you finish with him?

Mary straightens herself.

MARY: I don't want to talk about it. I…I can't. *(Pause)* What did you want?

CISSY: Can we go upstairs?

MARY: I'm supposed to be working.

CISSY: Please?

MARY: Joseph is way over there, he won't hear a thing. What is it?

CISSY: I want you to swear on your life that you won't breathe a word.

MARY: What's ails you?

CISSY: Swear!

MARY: I swear.

CISSY: Not a word to anyone.

MARY: My lips are sealed.

CISSY: I'm in a terrible…

Just as Cissy is about to reveal, the front door opens, street sounds, door closes and Con O'Sullivan enters with Seamus McCullagh, the playwright.

CISSY: Shussshh.

CON: Come on in Seamus. The best pub in Maynooth.

MCCULLAGH: Very nice indeed Mr. O' Sullivan.

CON: You're to call me Con.

MCCULLAGH: Indeed … Con.

CON: Hello ladies. Seamus, here we have two for the price of one! We came in specially to see you Mary but Cissy being here is an added bonus. Girls, I'd like you to meet Mr. Seamus McCullagh, the well known playwright.

CISSY: I've never heard of him.

CON: You girls are hardly mixing in the same circles. Anyhow, Seamus, this is Mary Barry, whose stepfather owns the pub and this is Cissy Boland.

MCCULLAGH: Charmed, I'm sure. It's a pleasure, ladies. *(He takes their hands)* Miss Barry.

Sound of Mary's hand being kissed.

MARY: Mr. McCullagh.

MCCULLOUGH: Miss Boland.

Sound of Cissy's hand being kissed.

CISSY: Pleased to meet you, Mr. McCullagh.

MCCULLAGH: Let's dispense with the formalities. You can address me as Seamus.

MARY: *(Sarcastically)* That's most kind of you.

MCCULLAGH: *(Not noticing)* I declare Con that in the few days I've spent in Maynooth, I am constantly amazed at the natural beauty of the female population!

CON: Oh aye. Some say we have the best in Ireland.

MCCULLAGH: And the present company far exceeds any expectations I might have had. *(The girls are not impressed. No response)* I have travelled the length and breadth of the country. I speak from experience. *(Pause)* Truly, there must be something in the air out here.

CISSY: The only thing in the air at the moment is the smell off the river! It's rotten.

MCCULLAGH: I did notice an unusual odour along the main street but one would become oblivious to such things in the presence of great beauty.

MARY: *(Not impressed)* What can I do for you Mr. O' Sullivan?

CON: Oh yes. As you know, I'm a member of the Gaelic League.

MARY: I don't think we're allowed forget it, are we?

Cissy makes as if to go.

CISSY: Mary, I might leave and come back another -

CON: A minute of your time, Cissy. We won't keep ye long. The League is thinking of setting up a drama class with a view to staging some plays of Irish interest and we're looking to recruit members. We've had a lot of interest already.

MARY: You're looking for us to join?

CON: I remember seeing you recite some poetry a few years back and I thought you were very good.

CISSY: I don't think Mary's poems would suit the Gaelic League!

MARY: I have better things to be doing than reciting poems.

CON: Oh…right so. Cissy, you were also on my list and you might be able to recruit some of the students from the college.

CISSY: I don't know. I only called in to talk to Mary and -

CON: I'm sure you can use your charms! *(Calling Joseph)* Joseph, come here.

Footsteps, Joseph arrives over.

JOSEPH: Yes, is there a problem?

CON: Meet Seamus McCullagh, the playwright. This is Joseph Barry, owner of the pub and a great supporter of the Gaelic League.

MCCULLAGH: Pleased to meet you Mr. Barry

JOSEPH: McCullagh? Didn't you do a concert in Dublin last year to support the striking railway workers?

MCCULLAGH: It was actually a play that I wrote. I am delighted to hear that my reputation has preceded me as far as Maynooth

JOSEPH: My stepson Sean worked on the railways. It was appreciated.

CON: Seamus here is going to help the League set up a drama class and we're recruiting members.

JOSEPH: Cavorting around on stage? I've heard stories about these actors … and the women! It's said that they are just a step up from …. Well you know?

MCCULLAGH: I can assure you, this is merely to further the Irish tradition of storytelling. We'll be performing wholesome Irish plays which celebrate our rich culture and highlight events from our history.

JOSEPH: If it's for the League, I suppose it's alright as long as it doesn't put notions in their heads.

CISSY: *(Interested despite herself)* You had a play performed in Dublin?

MCCULLAGH: Indeed I did, called "Self-Reliance". I directed it also. It was based on the struggle during the great strike in 1913. The Evening Telegraph described the prison scene as "striking".

CON: Which is apt seeing as it was about strikers ey? *(A little laugh at his own joke)* And it's going to be done in the Abbey Theatre.

MCCULLAGH: Con is slightly previous in his remarks. I have submitted it to the Abbey for consideration. Mr. Yeats himself was quite impressed with the script. He did suggest that it needed some re-writing which I am currently doing.

CISSY: Who is Yeats?

MCCULLAGH: *(Amazed at her lack of knowledge)* William Butler Yeats is a world-renowned Irish poet and founder of the Abbey Theatre in Dublin! I would propose that the Gaelic League here would make their debut performance with one of his short plays.

CON: And Seamus here will direct it!

MCCULLAGH: My services are at your disposal.

JOSEPH: What brings you to Maynooth?

MCCULLAGH: I have a friend, Patrick Long, who lives in Moyglare. I'm on what you might call an extended holiday. Since the performance of my play, the authorities have been more than a little interested in my movements so I felt it best to remove myself from Dublin.

JOSEPH: *(Slightly panicky)* You mean you're on the run?

CON: Not at all. He was just advised to …..

JOSEPH: We've had some trouble here lately. I don't want to bring more to my door. An RIC man was shot here a few weeks back.

MARY: Murdered you mean!

The front door opens and Catherine Long, Patrick Long's daughter bursts in, breathless.

CATHERINE: There you are Seamus, you have to go quick.

CON: What's wrong, Catherine?

CATHERINE: A lorry full of soldiers and RIC have raided our house. They arrived about an hour ago. They ordered my brothers outside. Wouldn't even let them put their coats on. They've been shivering in their vests for ages. They're turning the house upside down. Then the RIC man, the Tan, you know that English one?

CON: Stiff?

CATHERINE: Yes, he was acting funny. He asked me did I know anything about the Hughes murder and then he asked about you!

MARY: Do you know something about that murder?

MCCULLAGH: I never murdered anyone in my life.

CATHERINE: He was asking everyone the same question, Mary, but he was acting really funny, going on about losing the battle. And then they started on the presses and drawers, throwing everything about. The house is destroyed.

JOSEPH: Were they looking for guns?

CATHERINE: I don't know. I managed to slip away.

MCCULLAGH: How did they hear I was in Maynooth?

CON: You weren't exactly lying low.

MCCULLAGH: I didn't think I had to.

CON: There's talk in the village that we have an informer among our own. Seems like it might be true. Where are they now, Catherine?

CATHERINE: They're still there. I knew you'd probably be in a pub. You'd better go.

MCCULLAGH: *(Panicking)* She's right Con.

Runs towards front door.

CON: Not through the front door, Seamus. Joseph, can you bring us out the back way?

JOSEPH: Alright but quickly and if he's caught, don't say ye were here. I'm in enough trouble with the RIC as it is. Come on.

Hasty footsteps.

CON: You better come with us Catherine. If you're spotted coming out, they'll suspect something. Go back the long way.

CATHERINE: I'm coming. Bye Mary, Cissy.

Sound of her footsteps.

MCCULLAGH: *(Distant)* What did I do? I only wrote a play!

CISSY: It must have been some play!

MARY: Maybe Mr. Yeats is looking for him to help run the Abbey Theatre!

The girls laugh a little, sound of Joseph arriving back.

MARY: So, what was it you wanted to tell me?

CISSY: Oh, Mary, you can't breathe a word. I –

Joseph approaches the girls.

JOSEPH: I'm not the better of that. Go on with you Cissy, we've had enough distractions for today.

CISSY: I won't keep her long.

JOSEPH: You have ten minutes.

He starts stacking glasses.

MARY: Hurry up Cissy, I think he means it.

CISSY: Are you sure we can't go upstairs.

MARY: My mother is up there. Just tell me.

The front door opens and Harold Stiff, a young RIC man enters. His behaviour is erratic.

CISSY: Not again.

Footsteps crossing over.

STIFF: Is he here?

JOSEPH: Your sort is not welcome.

STIFF: My sort?

JOSEPH: You know what I mean.

STIFF: The sort of person just trying to do their job? Is that what you mean?

JOSEPH: You can do your job somewhere else.

STIFF: Do you people really think I want to be here? That I like it?

JOSEPH: I don't care ....

STIFF: I came in here with a simple question. I didn't threaten anyone. Now would you please answer the bleedin' question! Is he here?

It's becoming obvious that there is something not right about Stiff.

JOSEPH: Who is it you're looking for?

STIFF: McCullagh.

JOSEPH: Never heard of him. What does he look like?

STIFF: I don't know but I have to find him.

JOSEPH: Why do you want him?

STIFF: *(Pitifully)* I'm following orders ... I'll be in trouble if I ... if I don't find him. Please help me. We're losing here you know? *(Erratic)* Oh, oh, did you hear that? Can you hear him?

JOSEPH: Are you alright?

STIFF: Someone is calling me. Are you sure you haven't seen him.

JOSEPH: He's not here.

STIFF: What am I going to do?

JOSEPH: I promise you, he is not here. Mary, get the lad a glass of whiskey.

CISSY/MARY: But Mr. Barry ../Daddy!

JOSEPH: Get it, Mary. *(We hear Mary prepare the drink. Joseph hurries her)* Come on.

MARY: Here Daddy. *(Handing him the drink)*

JOSEPH: Now son, get that into you. It'll help you.

STIFF: *(Changing)* Are you trying to bribe me? Have you got something to hide?

JOSEPH: I just want to help, that's all. Take a drink. It'll warm you up on a cold day like today. *(Reluctantly, Stiff accepts the glass and takes a drink)* Aye, that's it.

STIFF: I should go.

JOSEPH: Will you be alright?

STIFF: I have to keep looking.

JOSEPH: Maybe you should go back to the barracks.

STIFF: The barracks?

JOSEPH: It sounds like you've had a busy day.

STIFF: I have. People calling me. I'm…I'm tired.

JOSEPH: I have to go down the street anyway. I'll walk with you. *(No response)* It's only a short distance. Come on.

STIFF: I can search again tomorrow.

JOSEPH: Of course you can. I won't be long Mary. *(He guides Stiff to the door)* Steady now, son. Steady now.

The door opens, street noises, and closes.

CISSY: If he wasn't an RIC man, you could almost feel sorry for him.

MARY: *(Sharp, emotional)* He has a mother and father like the rest of us. *(Pause)* What did you want to tell me? Another romance?

CISSY: Gone sour! Oh Mary…I'm pregnant.

MARY: *(Blesses herself)* What!

CISSY: Nearly four months.

MARY: But how ….

CISSY: Ah God Mary, I didn't think you were that innocent.

MARY: I mean, how did you let it … are you sure?

CISSY: I haven't had my friend in months and I feel sick every morning so yes, I am sure.

MARY: Whose is it?

CISSY: It doesn't matter.

MARY: Is it one of the students from the College?

CISSY: I don't make a habit of this!

MARY: I'm sorry *(Slight pause)* It's not the fella with the broken nose?

CISSY: I wouldn't be seen dead with him!

MARY: The smelly fella, Timmy, that works on O'Connors farm?

CISSY: No.

MARY: What about ..

CISSY: I'm not telling you. Isn't it enough that I'm pregnant.

MARY: It's never the lad with the black nails, the gardener from the College.

CISSY: For God's sake, are you going to list every man in Maynooth? If you must know and you're not to repeat this to anyone … but … it was Donnacha.

MARY: My cousin Donnacha! Auntie Anne's Donnacha? Oh God…Have you told him?

CISSY: You're the first to know.

MARY: What will Auntie Anne say?

CISSY: I'm not telling her.

MARY: You have to tell Donnacha.

CISSY: He might want to do the gallant thing and marry me. I'm not sure I'd like that.

MARY: But what's the alternative? Go into a home?

CISSY: I might go stay with my aunt in Dublin for a while to have the baby.

MARY: Adoption.

CISSY: Yes. No. I can't think about it being taken away by strangers.

MARY: Then tell Donnacha.

CISSY: What if he doesn't believe me?

MARY: You can't do it on your own. *((Sound of door opening, footsteps)* Shussh. *(Raising voice)* How did it go, Daddy?

JOSEPH: He's back in the barracks. The other lads brought him to his room.

MARY: What did they say?

JOSEPH: Not much but I got the feeling that this wasn't the first time. *(Pause)* This place has been like the train station all day. Cissy, you'll excuse Mary. There's work to be done.

CISSY: I'm going, Mr. Barry. See you, Mary. *(Quietly to Mary)* Not a word, remember.

MARY: Lips are sealed.

Footsteps, door opening, street sounds. Door closing.

JOSEPH: What was that about?

MARY: Ah, you know Cissy.

JOSEPH: I do, more's the pity. A wild young wan. Go on, get started with the cleaning. I'll bring up the crates.

Sound of him lifting crates.

MARY: You were very good for looking after that RIC lad.

JOSEPH: It's hard to see someone in that state and him only a young fellow, especially after what happened with the other RIC man.

Footsteps, rattling crates.

MARY: Daddy…was it local lads killed him, do you think?

JOSEPH: Sure, how would I know, Mary. Better off not thinking about it.

Footsteps, moving off. Door opening and closing.

MARY: How can I ever not think about it? How can I ever not think about it. *(She sobs)* Oh, Joseph.

END OF EPISODE

EPISODE 21 – BALLYKINLAR CAMP, FEB. 1921

Scene 1 - Ballykinlar camp, outdoors.

Sound of marching.

WILLIAMS: Left. Right. Left. Right. Turn. Attention. Go and find him for me. Examine every face in Ballykinlar if you have to.

Running footsteps.

VOICES: Calls of 'Not here, Not here, Not here'.

WILLIAMS: *(To himself)* Bloody hell. *(Aloud)* Dismissed.

Sounds fade.

VOICEOVER: Fractured – Feb 1921. Between 1920 and 1921, many Irishmen were interred in British run camps. These men were held without trial and with no idea when or if they might be released. The most notorious camp was Ballykinlar in County Down.

Scene 2 - Inside hut

Footsteps, men talking as Prisoners stream into the hut from outside. They are tired and dishevelled. Pat Colgan enters towards the front of the group and Sean Barry follows in near the rear.

SEAN: Commandant Colgan, sir!

COLGAN: Sean! They caught you too.

SEAN: *(Goes over to him, now a private conversation)* A month back. I heard you were here only yesterday. What was all that about?

COLGAN: The parade?

SEAN: Yeah.

COLGAN: They're looking for Aidan Corri again. You know that boy that was part of Collin's squad on Bloody Sunday.

SEAN: But we have a decoy.   They don't even know what Corri looks like.

COLGAN: They had eyes on him.

SEAN: They did? Where?

COLGAN: Remember they took over Hut 31 as a Post Office a few days ago?

SEAN: Yeah.

COLGAN: Well did you notice the windows as we passed?

SEAN: They've painted them white.

COLGAN: They did. But they left a few gaps here and there. About the width of a pair of eyes…

SEAN: *(Understands)* Had they men in there?

COLGAN: I believe so. British Intelligence, travelled up from Dublin, I heard. Apparently, they have a photograph of Corri.

SEAN: *(Pause)* Damn.

COLGAN: *(Solemnly)* I won't let what happened to Whelan happen to Corri. That's for sure.

SEAN: I know you won't, Sir. I can't stop thinking of that poor bugger. He was so sure he was being released.

COLGAN: I tried to tell him it was a trap…at least we know now.

SEAN: Yeah. Do you think they identified Corri today?

COLGAN: I wouldn't think so, they would have taken him if they had.

SEAN: That's true. Where was he in the line, anyway?

COLGAN: *(Smiles)* Right before me.

SEAN: What!

COLGAN: They know I'm the Camp Commandant, so they know that I've a responsibility to hide him. Once they saw me, they looked everywhere else but where I was standing.

SEAN: *(Laughs)* Ha! Hiding in plain sight.

COLGAN: That's it.

SEAN: You're a cute hoor alright!

COLGAN: That's Commandant Cute Hoor to you, Barry!

Laughter. Door opens, sounds from outside. Footsteps in. Sgt. Major Williams and Sergeant Love enter. Williams is English, pretends to be affable and pleasant, but can't be trusted. Williams' interaction with Colgan is always full of gentle smiles from both of them.

WILLIAMS: *(Beaming)* Good morning, all.

COLGAN: Sergeant Major Williams. Sergeant Love. And how are you both, this fine morning?

WILLIAMS: We are very well indeed, Colgan, very well.

LOVE: We are very well indeed.

COLGAN: I presume you had your breakfast or would you care for some of our culinary delights?

WILLIAMS: Oh, no thanks! I had a wonderful breakfast already, one of your "Ulster Frys" I believe they're called. Very delicious. You're rather fond of your pigs, aren't you?

COLGAN: Well I suppose we are if we can afford it, but in general we're not too fond of anything that squeals.

Laughter.

WILLIAMS: *(Smiles)* Quite. Speaking of squealing, we're still looking for your fellow Corri. You haven't seen him this morning, have you?

COLGAN: What does he look like?

WILLIAMS: *(Smiles again)* Alright, I know you don't exactly trust me, and I can understand that, what with you in your position and me in my position, but I can assure you he will be treated with the utmost respect. We have the papers directly from the Phoenix Park in Dublin. He's due for release. I really don't understand why he's hiding here.

COLGAN: Due for release?

WILLIAMS: Yes, immediately.

COLGAN: Same as Whelan?

WILLIAMS: Yes. Whelan was released from here.

COLGAN: Released from here alright, but into the bloody hands of an execution party.

WILLIAMS: I really don't think that's true. I'm certainly not aware of anything like that happening.

SEAN: No, of course you're not. Your hands are clean, right?

WILLIAMS: *(Sighs)* I wasn't talking to you, Barry. Look, Colgan, I know you've had some japes with us over the last few weeks, swapping some other fellows in for Corri, but it really doesn't make any sense. The real Corri doesn't get his long-overdue freedom, and the shams you sent out in his place are just going back to another camp. *(Addressing all the prisoners in the hut)* I really wish you'd all see sense on this. We want to send him home to his family. Don't you wish you could be back home with your families? Well, he's one of the lucky ones. We want to send him home.

SEAN: Yes, in a coffin.

Laughter.

COLGAN: Anyone here believe this man? *(Muttering of 'no')* There is your answer, Sir.

WILLIAMS: *(Nods sadly)* I see. *(Pause)* I'm sorry about this, Colgan, I really am. I am now forced to take further action.

Footsteps as Williams leaves. Love hangs back, then approaches Colgan.

COLGAN: *(Hastily whispered)* Sergeant Love, I've a dispatch for you.

LOVE: All right, hurry up with it.

Colgan takes letters from his jacket.

COLGAN: That one is for Mick Collins in GHQ. About the G-men from Dublin hunting Corri. The other is your usual cover, a lovely letter from one of the men about his fun time in here. Sean might write one next time, ey?

SEAN: Be honoured, Sir. I haven't so far as my mother has a tendency to…overreact.

COLGAN: Just keep it all very nice with a minor complaint here and there. Love, you all right with that?

LOVE: I'll sort it out for ye.

COLGAN: Aw, thanks Love.

LOVE: *(For the millionth time…)* Stop it.

SEAN: Sergeant Love. Did you ever think of changing your name? Doesn't sound very menacing for the Army.

LOVE: *(Smiles)* Would you prefer if I was called Churchill?

They laugh. Footsteps exiting. Door closes.

SEAN: He's some fella! Fair play to him. That's a dangerous game, being a courier like that.

COLGAN: He's a good lad alright. Never accepted so much as a penny for all he's done for us. He's a good heart.

SEAN: Tell us though, how does he get the dispatches out of the camp?

COLGAN: The man is a genius, he's been held up by the RIC a few times on his way home to Castlewellan, and twice he was taken to the barracks and stripped. Never a thing found.

SEAN: So how does he do it?

COLGAN: D'you know Jack Fitzgerald?

SEAN: From Newbridge? Over in the workshop?

COLGAN: That's him. Well, Love has two pairs of boots, and when he leaves one in to be "repaired", Jack sews the dispatches under the sole of the boot so they won't be found.

SEAN: Sews them in!

COLGAN: He swaps the boots when he gets home and a local IRA man in Castlewellan takes out the dispatch and sews it back up again.

SEAN: Brilliant!

COLGAN: He'd be court-martialled and shot if he was caught.

SEAN: Fair play to him is all I can say!

COLGAN: A true Irishman, down to his "sole"!

Footsteps growing louder.

SEAN: Ha! Maybe Love is a good name for him, after all! *(They laugh. Footsteps louder)* Oh, here's the heavies. Williams is back with Got-Me. And Little is with them. And some high ranked officer. They mean business, Colgan.

Door bangs open. Banging footsteps of a lot of soldiers entering.

COLGAN: Willimas, we meet again. And Little, how are you. I don't believe I've had the pleasure of -

GOT-ME: *(To Colgan)* On your feet, Paddy.

COLGAN: I think you mean to say: On your feet, Commandant Colgan.

GOT-ME: I'll say what I want to say, got me? And anyway, that's your name, innit? Colgan, Patrick. So, I'll say it again. On your feet! Paddy!

He places his baton under Colgan's chin. Colgan stands.

COLGAN: I'd really rather you didn't push a baton up under my chin, Mr. Got-Me.

Scraping sounds as he stands.

GOT-ME: You watch it, sonny boy, got me? You play the game with me, and I'll play the game with you, got me? *(To the room)* The rest of you, hop it. Go on, get out. On the double!

Footsteps as men leave the room.

SEAN: I'm not leaving. Commandant Colgan needs a witness. *(He is struck with a baton)* You better -

GOT-ME: I better what? I better what, Paddy. I better -

CAMERON: Stop that this instant. I am Major-General Cameron. Out with you.

SEAN: I will not. I -

COLGAN: I'll be all right, Sean. Wait outside.

SEAN: I will, Sir. *(With bite)* Right outside, sir.

Footsteps as he leaves. Door opens, closes.

CAMERON: That's better. Now, I understand from my men, Mr. Colgan, that you are responsible for hiding the fugitive Corri from us?

GOT-ME: That's right, he is, Major-General Cameron, sir.

CAMERON: Little!

LITTLE: Yes, Sir.

CAMERON: How long has this been going on?

LITTLE: Well sir, it's probably… a few months.

CAMERON: *(Disbelief)* A few months?

LITTLE: Yes, sir.

CAMERON: Damn it, man, you've a thousand men held prisoner here and you haven't been able to find one of them in all that time?

LITTLE: *(Uncomfortably annoyed)* Well sir, Commandant Colgan here hasn't exactly trusted us to give safe passage to Corri.

CAMERON: You call him Commandant? You recognise his rank as IRA?

LITTLE: No, Sir, not at all. It's just the organisation of the camp prisoners, sir. It's easier for them, and for us, if they have a hierarchy. That way, we know who to go to when we need something done.

CAMERON: But you haven't got something done, have you, Williams? Have you Little? You haven't got Corri.

LITTLE: No, sir.

CAMERON: Sounds like you've been here too long. Going soft on the prisoners. I did well to replace you, Little.

COLGAN: If I may, sir, Lt. Col. Little has always been-

GOT-ME: *(Shouts in Colgan's face)* Do not speak unless you are spoken to, Paddy! Got me? You got me, Paddy?

CAMERON: *(Annoyed by Got-Me's vulgarity)* Stand down.

GOT-ME: Yes Sir.

CAMERON: So, Colgan, Little here calls you the Commandant, does he?

COLGAN: The prisoners here elected me to be their Commandant, sir. To represent them. And Lt. Col. Little here, respected their decision, and it allows us to work together so my men are well looked after.

CAMERON: Commandant to Commandant, eh?

COLGAN: If you wish, sir.

CAMERON: *(To Little)* Equal to equal?

LITTLE: Well I wouldn't exactly say-

CAMERON: I see you've a cosy little arrangement here… *(To Colgan)* Your men, you say? I thought all prisoners were our men, are they not, Little?

LITTLE: Yes sir.

CAMERON: To do with as we wish.

LITTLE: *(Not comfortable with this)* Well… within reason of course.

CAMERON: *(Temper rising)* Within reason? This is war, man, God damn it! Is it reasonable to ask for a little cooperation when we're at war with these insurgents?

LITTLE: Of course, sir.

CAMERON: Have you interrogated this man?

LITTLE: We've questioned him several times and-

CAMERON: Have you "interrogated" him?

LITTLE: He was kept in solitary for about a month... *(Reads Cameron's growing temper)* ...no sir, we haven't "interrogated" him.

CAMERON: Well then, I think we know where to start, don't we?

Colgan's usually calm exterior shows his nervousness now. This situation is more dangerous than he imagined. Got-Me is almost straining at his leash.

CAMERON: Sergeant Williams.

WILLIAMS: Yes sir.

CAMERON: Can you summarise the various attempts this man has made to conceal the whereabouts of the Corri fellow we're after?

WILLIAMS: Yes sir, of course sir. I believe the first time I requested the whereabouts of this Aidan Corri, he asked me why I wanted him. I explained to him that he was to be released, and gave him my "word of honour" on this.

CAMERON: *(Chuckles)* Released? Lucky fellow.

WILLIAMS: *(Smiles)* Indeed sir. He took my word, and gave Corri up to us. Unfortunately for this fellow, he was not Corri, but rather some unfortunate by the name of Slowey from Drogheda. Of course, it took the Auxiliaries quite a lot of time and eh... "effort" in the bowels of Dublin Castle to find that out.

CAMERON: Yes, I've heard about their "effort".

WILLIAMS: He swore he was Corri the whole time, and it was only because an RIC man from Drogheda recognised him that we knew it was Slowey. Could have saved him from a lot of beatings and water torture if we'd known earlier... So we asked again, and another man was given up, but eventually he turned out to be a Fahy from Galway. After some more "persuasion", of course... And then another, and another...

CAMERON: *(Standing in front of Colgan)* Rather noble of them, don't you think?

COLGAN: Yes sir, I do think that. *(Beat)* And now I also understand the worth of a British Army officer's "word".

Cameron bristles, but keeps his cool. Got-Me wants an order to attack Colgan but holds his ground.

COLGAN: I'm not sure if you're aware, sir, but I think you'll find that news of what happens in here has a way of getting to the press in England. I would imagine it wouldn't be pleasant for all of your high and mighty friends and families to read about how noble your present tactics are, and what you just confirmed to me happens in Dublin Castle.

GOT ME: Just say the word, Sir. Say the word.

COLGAN: And before you set your rabid dog on me and "release" me too, it's also worth knowing that there are nine hundred and ninety other Corris in this camp, and every one of them is loyal to a man.

Cameron takes this in, keeps face, changes tack.

CAMERON: I see… Right, well, we've tried threatening you – and they were just threats, you understand, and what Williams said about the Castle was just a ruse, not at all true… but I can see now that you are a man of honour. I respect that. A lot more than I respect some of the other cretins here. *(Indicates Williams, Little, Got-Me)* Look here, I see no reason to hide the truth from you. The thing is, I'm being made a damned fool of in the eyes of my superiors. I have a thousand men here in Ballykinlar. And I can identify every bloody one of them but Prisoner Corri. *(Seriously, standing directly before Colgan)* I promise you now, sir, and I give you my word of absolute honour as a senior officer in the British Army, if you produce Corri, I guarantee he will not be taken away and harmed.

Colgan looks coolly to Williams, then back to Cameron.

COLGAN: I do know which one is truly Corri, sir…

CAMERON: Excellent!

COLGAN: But I will not find him for you. I am a man of honour, sir. But how can I trust the word of any British officer anymore, when I'd already heard from outside what happened to those poor men who went as Corri? You just confirmed it.

CAMERON: *(In a blustering rage, turns on Williams)* Damn you!

GOT-ME: If you want, sir, I can-

CAMERON: Don't touch him!! *(Deliberates)* Lock him in solitary for the rest of the week. Standard terms. *(Warning)* Nothing else! You understand?

GOT-ME: Yes, sir. Got you, sir.

Sounds of Colgan being taken. Dragged. Door opens.Outside.

Scene 3 - Outside hut

COLGAN: There's no need to be so bloody rough. Get -

SEAN: Get your hands off him. Commandant Colgan, Sir, what -

COLGAN: It's ok, Sean. I'm off to solitary. Tell the lads where I am and why.

SEAN: I will.

COLGAN: And write to your poor mother, for God's sake. And –

A thump.

SEAN: Get your hands off him. Get your hands off him.

CAMERON: And take that savage down too.

Sean is grabbed. Dragging sounds.

SEAN: I'll be proud to go. Proud.

He continues to shout this out.

CAMERON: We'll see how proud you'll be after a fortnight. Take him away.

Sean still yelling how proud he is. Marching footsteps. Door closes.

END OF EPISODE

EPISODE 22 – SEAN'S LETTER, MAR. 1921

Scene 1 - RIC Station. Night

DWYER: I heard just now, boys that the Tans in Kells got one of the lads that shot Hughes last month. *(Cheers – he speaks over the cheers)* A Patrick McDonnell. He resisted arrest and was –

The sound of a shotgun.

DWYER: Curran, go check that out. That was from upstairs.

CURRAN: Yes Sarge.

His footsteps running.

DWYER: As I was saying, Patrick McDonnell resisted arrest and –

A shout from upstairs.

CURRAN: *(Distant)* Sarge, Sarge, up here quick. We need an ambulance.

VOICEOVER: Fractured – March 1921

Scene 2 - Barry's Pub. Day

Joseph whistles as he tidies. Internal door opening, footsteps. Tomas enters.

TOMAS: You started early, Daddy. Will I open up?

JOSEPH: Leave it for a bit, Tomas. They'll hardly be banging the doors in. Sit down there, I want a word.

Pulls out a seat for him.

TOMAS: Is everything alright?

JOSEPH: I was going to ask you the same question.

TOMAS: *(Defensive)* I'm fine, so I am.

JOSEPH: I get the feeling there's something you're not telling me. What are the volunteers up to nowadays?

TOMAS: I…I'm not sure. I'm not as involved as I was.

JOSEPH: You were out late the other night?

TOMAS: Just kicking a ball around with some of the boys. It got dark so we went back to John Joe's.

JOSEPH: Really?

TOMAS: If you don't believe me, you can ask him yourself.

JOSEPH: I heard that a gang of lads tried to blow up Louisa Bridge in Leixlip that night.

TOMAS: I know nothing about that. I never even heard about it.

JOSEPH: If you say you weren't there, I'll believe you but just be careful. This is not some game.

TOMAS: I know.

JOSEPH: You've not been yourself lately. Is it the whole Croke Park business?

TOMAS: That was months ago.

JOSEPH: I've heard tell of men coming back from war, men who'd seen terrible things. They wouldn't be right for years. *(Pause)* Think about that now.

TOMAS: It's not that Daddy. It's.. *(In a rush)* well, I've been wondering…well, are we doing the right thing by fighting?

JOSEPH: The Volunteers, you mean?

TOMAS: Aye. How can they think that they'll ever get the better of the British?

JOSEPH: To believe otherwise would be foolish for them, I suppose.

Hasty footsteps approach. Brigid enters.

TOMAS: Maybe there's a better way

BRIGID: Joseph, this letter has just come. I think it's Sean. Will you open it, I just can't.

Sound of paper being passed over.

JOSEPH: It's his writing alright. I'd recognise his scrawl anywhere.

BRIGID: For God's sake Joseph, just open it.

Sound of a letter being opened.

TOMAS: Hurry up, Daddy.

JOSEPH: It is from Sean.

BRIGID: Read it.

JOSEPH: Are you sure you ….

BRIGID: No, you read it.

JOSEPH: *(Clearing his throat)* Dear Mammy, I hope this letter finds you all well and I am sorry that I have not been able to write to you before now. You may have heard that I was *(Pause)* captured.

BRIGID: Captured!

JOSEPH: *(Continuing)* I was captured and am now imprisoned in Ballykinlar camp in County Down.

BRIGID: Dear God, he's a prisoner. Ballykinlar?

TOMAS: It's up north. I've heard it's a savage -

JOSEPH: *(Cutting him off)* Aye, that's where all the volunteers are being put. *(He continues)* I have been here a few weeks now but already it feels like a lifetime. No one here knows how long we can be kept. Some men are here since the place opened last December.

TOMAS: Patrick Colgan is there. I wonder is Sean with him?

JOSEPH: He might well be.

BRIGID: Will you keep reading!

JOSEPH: *(Reading)* There are two camps here. I am in camp two and sleep in a hut with twenty-five other men. There are forty huts.

TOMAS: That's a thousand people! They must be jammed in like sardines.

JOSEPH: *(With an edge – don't upset Brigid)* I'm sure it's fine, Tomas. *(Reading)* It is very cold here and is always raining. I don't sleep well, the beds are close to each other and it is very noisy. Maybe I will get used to it.

TOMAS: *(Laughing)* That's Sean! He always complained if I made the slightest noise in our room.

BRIGID: Have a bit of sympathy. I wonder how you'd feel if you were stuck there. Go on, Joseph.

JOSEPH: *(Reading)* The camps are surrounded by barbed wire so it feels like we are in a big cage but the volunteers are allowed run the camp although the British sentries are never far away.

TOMAS: *(Trying to soften it for Brigid)* So they're free to wander around as they like. It's not like a real prison.

BRIGID: It's worse than a real prison! Sure they never even know when they're getting out or anything. *(To Joseph)* Keep reading.

JOSEPH: Now...where was I...oh yes, *(Reading)* There is a chapel here and one of the prisoners is a priest. *(Commenting)* Fat lot of good that'll do him.

BRIGID: Joseph!

JOSEPH: Sorry, Brigid. *(Reading)* The volunteers run classes in the recreational building and I am improving my Irish.

TOMAS: It could only improve. He was never good at it.

BRIGID: Oh, for goodness sake! Will you stop criticising your brother.

TOMAS: Sorry.

JOSEPH: The food is not good nor is there enough of it. I close my eyes sometimes and try to taste that lovely Christmas dinner you put before me. I'm sorry now that I didn't have time to eat it all. *(Commenting)* There's no argument there! That was a great feed. *(Reading)* There's talk of another camp being built in the Curragh. We are hoping that the few Kildare lads that are here might be transferred. I hope you are all safe and well there. Give my best to Joseph, Mary and Tomas and give Moll a big hug from me. Tell Tomas to mind himself. *(Both Joseph and Brigid look at Tomas who looks away)* Please write back with all the news. I cannot say too much in the letter as they are censored twice, first by the volunteer line Captain and then the British. Send it to me in Camp 2, F Company, Hut 4, Ballykinlar, County Down. God bless you all. Your loving son. Sean. *(Long silence)* It doesn't sound too bad.

BRIGID: I pray that they keep him there until all this is over.

JOSEPH: Aw Brigid...

BRIGID: I know he's alive and I don't have to worry about him. I'll always know where he is which is more than I can say for you, Tomas.

TOMAS: You don't have to worry about me.

BRIGID: That's easy for you to say. When you have children of your own, you'll understand.

Front door opens, street sounds, door closes. Footsteps. It's Mary. She looks pale and shaken.

BRIGID: Ah Mary. We just got a letter from Sean. He's in Ballykinlar prison camp but he's OK.

MARY: He's alive?

BRIGID: Yes. Are you alright. You look upset.

MARY: I'm so glad Sean is alright, Mammy because everyone else is dying.

She is tearful.

BRIGID: What ails you child?

JOSEPH: *(Pulling out a chair)* Sit her down here.

BRIGID: What's wrong?

MARY: *(Sobbing)* I just ......

JOSEPH: Did someone do something to you?

MARY: No. It's just that ......

BRIGID: Take your time.

Mary settles herself and manages to speak through the sobs

MARY: Patrick McDonnell was shot last night.

JOSEPH: Who?

TOMAS: Patrick McDonnell, a student priest from the college. That's terrible.

BRIGID: *(To Tomas)* How do you know him?

TOMAS: He was in the Volunteers.

BRIGID: The bloody Volunteers, nothing but trouble.

JOSEPH: Was he shot in the college?

MARY: No. He was down at his home in Kells and the report is that the Tans raided the house. He ran across the fields and they shot him.

JOSEPH: God rest his soul.

MARY: They say he was involved in the ambush here in Maynooth but I can't -

TOMAS: No he wasn't!

All look at Tomas.

JOSEPH: How do you know?

TOMAS: I mean … I don't think he was … he couldn't have been.

JOSEPH: Why?

TOMAS: He went home for Christmas and hasn't been back to college since.

MARY: I knew Patrick. I knew he wouldn't do something like that. To murder a man in cold blood. That's the work of a savage.

TOMAS: It's a war, Mary.

BRIGID: At times like these, men are capable of anything. Whatever the cause, they're still just murdering thugs!

JOSEPH: They must have wanted him for something.

Knocking on the door. Footsteps as Joseph crosses to open it. It's Poor Brid.

JOSEPH: Mrs. O'Sullivan, what brings you here?

POOR BRID: Have you not heard about the shooting?

JOSEPH: Mary's just telling us. The poor young fellow. And him studying for the priesthood.

POOR BRID: Not that shooting. That was tragic. This is the one happened last night, below in the RIC station. A young Tan there blew his head off.

BRIGID: *(Blessing herself)* Holy Mother of God!

JOSEPH: One of Dwyer's men?

POOR BRID: Yes. The young fellow I seen you with last week Joseph. The one you brought back to the barracks. There's many in the village didn't like to see you do that.

JOSEPH: He was a young lad too with a family. I'd want a heart of stone not to help him.

POOR BRID: By all accounts, he did it in his room last night. There wasn't a piece left of him. Brains everywhere.

JOSEPH: He wasn't right in the head. The nerves, I suppose. He was like a lost child when he came in here.

BRIGID: You could have got in trouble involving yourself like that.

JOSEPH: You would have done exactly the same thing, and I know it. He was only a few years older than our Tomas here. They told me down the station that day that he hasn't been great since the ambush. Hughes, the boy that was killed, died in his arms.

At the mention of Hughes name, Mary breaks down again and Tomas is very uncomfortable.

BRIGID: Ah Mary. It's ok. *(To Joseph)* She's very upset.

JOSEPH: She saw the state that the young Tan was in that day … and hearing so soon after the news of her friend in the college ……

BRIGID: All young men! Even if they are Tans. *(To Mary)* Mary, you should go for a lie down. It's all been a shock. You'll feel better for it.

MARY: I will.

She stands up.

BRIGID: I'll go up with you.

MARY: I'll be alright. I will. You might give me Sean's letter. I'll read it upstairs.

BRIGID: There you are.

Sound of letter being handed over. Footsteps as Mary moves off.

BRIGID: I'll bring you up a cup of tea later.

MARY: *(Distant)* Thanks Mammy.

Footsteps fade.

BRIGID: She took that very badly. *(To Tomas)* Was she sweet on him?

TOMAS: *(Nervously)* Who?

BRIGID: The lad in the college, Patrick McDonnell?

TOMAS: No, sure he was to be a priest.

BRIGID: What you are never matters where love is concerned. I'll talk to her when she calms down and see if there's more to it. *(A change, turning to Tomas)* It looks like the brave Volunteers saved themselves a bullet.

TOMAS: What do you mean?

BRIGID: They got two RIC men for the price of one. What sort of crowd are you involved with at all Tomas?

JOSEPH: Tomas had nothing to do …

BRIGID: The Volunteers may well have pulled the trigger when that poor unfortunate man put the gun to his head!

POOR BRID: Put the barrel in his mouth, Brigid. And he was a Tan.

TOMAS: Can you both just stop! *(They react)* I'm going out, I'll be back soon.

Hasty footsteps. Door opens.

BRIGID: What about your coat?

Door slams closed.

BRIGID: I'm sorry about him, Brid. That was rude. What's happening to them all?

POOR BRID: You're grand. We all have bad days. I'll get going now, I haven't told Mrs. O'Donoghue the news yet. Bye now.

They bid their goodbyes. Footsteps, door opens, street sounds, door closes.

JOSEPH: You should ease off Tomas, Brigid. He's not responsible for everything the Volunteers do.

BRIGID: The sooner he gives them up the better.

JOSEPH: I don't think it's something you can just give up.

BRIGID: It might be no harm if he was locked up with Sean until all this is over.

JOSEPH: Ah Brigid!

BRIGID: I'm serious. I wish I could lock all my children away and keep them safe. If I could get Tomas into that prison, I -

JOSEPH: You think it's safe in there? If Sean told us everything that goes on we'd never get the letter!

BRIGID: It can't be any worse than here.

JOSEPH: You said it yourself. It's a prison. I've heard stories about sick men being left to die. Lads being shot for no reason at all. *(He's said too much. Pause)* Look, Sean is a strong lad. He'll be fine but don't be wishing Tomas into that place.

BRIGID: So, it's all right when my son is in it but not when yours is?

JOSEPH: Tomas is your son too.

BRIGID: I know, I know. I'm sorry…it's just…the constant worry of not knowing where they are, what they're up to, what they're thinking. I'm going mad, Joseph, I think I'm going mad.

JOSEPH: Come here. *(He wraps arms about her)* Tomas told me earlier that he thinks the Volunteers have it wrong with all this killing. He's looking for a better way. And given time, he'll find it, so go easy on him.

BRIGID: Please God Sean will find it too.

JOSEPH: Aye. Please God.

Beat

BRIGID: Joseph?

JOSEPH: Aye?

BRIGID: You did well to help out that Tan lad. I know you're not fond of them.

JOSEPH: I hate them, Brigid, but he was someone's Sean.

BRIGID: He was. God help his poor mother and Patrick McDonnell's poor mother.

JOSEPH: God help us all, Brigid.

END OF EPISODE

EPISODE 23 – ANDREW'S VISIT, APR. 1921

Scene 1 - Judge

Court sounds, shuffling.

JUDGE: The court, having carefully considered the evidence brought before it is of the opinion that Sergeant Joseph Hughes, RIC, Maynooth was wounded at Maynooth on 21stFebruary 1921 in an ambush by armed rebels whilst on duty and that he died at Stephen's Hospital Dublin on 22nd February 1921 from shock and haemorrhage following gunshot wounds. It was wilful murder by person or persons unknown.

Gavel banging. Sounds of crowds shuffling out.

VOICEOVER: Fractured – April 1921

Scene 2 - Barry's Pub

Joseph walks into the pub whistling jauntily. His whistling peters out as he surveys the glum scene.

JOSEPH: No wonder the world and its mother are beating down the door of the place. Look at the happy smiles that greet them with their pint! Tomas and Mary, will ye cheer up. *(Pause)* Well...if ye won't...excuse me, please.

Sound of rummaging.

MARY: *(In slight irritation)* What are you looking for, Daddy?

JOSEPH: A pencil and a bit of paper. Now, Miss, your name?

MARY: *(Snapping out of it, confused)* What?

JOSEPH: What do you mean, "what"?

MARY: Sorry. I wasn't… what is it?

JOSEPH: Name?

MARY: My name?

JOSEPH: Yes.

MARY: *(Unsure but complying)* Mary. Daddy what -

JOSEPH: Surname?

MARY: You know what it is.

JOSEPH: Mary you know what it is. Unusual but fine.

Sounds of pencil scratching paper. Mary giggles a little.

JOSEPH: Relation to Head of Family?

MARY: *(No idea what's happening)* Step-daughter, I suppose.

JOSEPH: Religious Profession?

MARY: Roman Catholic.

JOSEPH: Education?

MARY: *(Again, no idea)* I can read and write, so that's-

JOSEPH: *(Writing)* Not Enough. *(Next question)* Alive or Dead?

MARY: Sorry?

JOSEPH: Are you alive or dead?

MARY: Tomas, what is he going on about?

JOSEPH: How about you, Tomas are you alive or dead?

TOMAS: Are you feeling alright, daddy?

JOSEPH: I'm feeling fine, son! It's you two I'm wondering about. Moping about the place these days with the long faces on ye, driving good customers away, making them feel like they've landed in purgatory or something!

TOMAS: Sorry, daddy.

MARY: Sorry.

JOSEPH: Well, "sorry" is no good if you don't pull up your socks around here. The pair of ye are about as cheerful as a mortuary chapel on a wet Saturday. Are ye alive or dead? I don't know what's been put in the water here lately...

MARY: *(Trying to lighten up a bit)* Maybe it's the smell of the river from the college.

JOSEPH: *(Not buying it)* Very funny. *(To Tomas)* Tomas get out the front door there and greet a few people on the street. Show them that it's not a mortuary chapel.

TOMAS: *(On his way from behind the counter)* It's not exactly a variety show either...

Door opens, street, door closes.

MARY: What was that about, daddy? All the questions?

JOSEPH: *(Smiles)* I was doing my own census, Mary. *(Slightly mocking)* I was reading in the paper earlier that the lads up in Dail Eireann have issued a solemn decree that no Irishman or Irishwoman was to give any information whatsoever to the British authorities! And that includes the census.

Door opening and closing as Tomas returns.

MARY: I don't understand what the point is of the Dail telling everyone not to fill in the census form? I mean, what does it matter?

JOSEPH: Just being awkward, I suppose.

TOMAS: That's not it. It's too much information.

JOSEPH: I thought you were supposed to be outside, drumming up business?

TOMAS: Sure there's nobody there to drum on.

MARY: What do you mean, "too much information"?

TOMAS: Think about it, the Tans and Auxies are hungry for informers, if everyone was to kindly tell the British census all the names and addresses of every man, woman, child and priest, do you think the authorities would just use that to decide where in Kildare to build another school?

JOSEPH: *(Considers this)* I never thought of that.

TOMAS: But they have. They're letting on it's just another census, same as the last time.

JOSEPH: *(Convinced)* You might be right there. They're sneaky like that.

TOMAS: It's the perfect opportunity for them.

JOSEPH: A crowd of gangsters is what the British are! In the paper this week, I read the English were saying that Irish cattle have foot and mouth disease, so they're putting an embargo on Irish beef.

MARY: But that's not true, is it? We would have heard.

JOSEPH: Of course not! The paper said there's been no evidence presented anywhere, that it was all made up. Again, being sneaky.

MARY: But how can Mr. O'Sullivan or Paddy Dooley make a living if they can't sell their cattle?

JOSEPH: They can't. They'll just have to try and sell them wherever they can, along with every other farmer, but for a pittance this time.

TOMAS: Maybe it won't be so bad - we'll have sirloin steaks for dinner instead of stewing beef for years to come! *(They all chuckle)*

JOSEPH: *(To Tomas)* Well that's the first bit of a joke I've heard from you in a long time.

TOMAS: Yes well... there's not been much to joke about lately.

JOSEPH: Maybe you're just getting older and a bit more sense.

TOMAS: I wouldn't be sure about that.

JOSEPH: *(Grinning ahead of himself)* Speaking of jokes, here's a good one I read in the paper. One of the fellas that does a turn at the Theatre Royal, Jimmy... something. What's this it was now...?

TOMAS: Was it about how all you do on a Saturday is read the paper?

MARY: *(Knows what to expect)* Don't do one of your bad impressions, whatever you do.

JOSEPH: Oh yes! *(Bursts into a bad Dublin accent)* I was in the Hodges and Figgis the other day with me mot, and she bought me a buke all about how ships are made. I wasn't sure about it meself, but as it turns out, it was riveting! *(They groan)* D'ye get it? Rivets. They use rivets – riveting - to build ships, to join all the-

TOMAS: We get it, Daddy. We get it.

JOSEPH: Then why aren't you laughing?

MARY: Let's just say, if I wanted someone to deliver a joke, I'd pick the post office rather than you.

TOMAS: *(Laughing)* She said that, daddy, not me!

JOSEPH: *(Mock indignant)* Well that's just grand, isn't it? Me trying to cheer you both up, and you treating me like that.

MARY: *(Gives Joseph a little hug)* Don't mind me, I'm only codding ye.

JOSEPH: *(Giving in)* As long as you don't wear a hole in that table polishing the same spot over and over again, I'll let you away with it this time.

MARY: Was I doing that? God, I was miles away. *(She smiles at Joseph)* Sorry.

JOSEPH: *(To Tomas)* And you can stop sniggering too! Come on, let's get the rest of that stock in.

Joseph heads out the back, Mary tidies up behind the bar. Door opens, Andrew enters.

MARY: How are you doing? Grand day, isn't it?

ANDREW: Not too bad now.

MARY: I haven't seen you around here before. What can I get for you?

ANDREW: I'll have a pint.

MARY: *(Cheerily, as she goes to get him a pint)* Sure why else would you be here! You look…familiar. Do I know you?

ANDREW: No, I don't think so. I'm just…passing through. Having a look around.

MARY: Are you here to see the College?

ANDREW: No, no…

MARY: You're hardly here to see the sights, are you? Maynooth isn't bad, but it's no London or Paris, I'll have you know!

ANDREW: *(Smiles)* No! But sure there must be something good about it, I suppose, for people to live here.

MARY: Oh there is… There's the College, as I said… and the castle… and the Fitzgeralds of Carton! But they might not interest you… *(Running out of things, then an idea)* And here, of course! Best pub in Maynooth.

ANDREW: I'm sure it is.

MARY: Are you going to be living here?

ANDREW: No, I'm just on my way home. I thought I might stop here and see what it's like.

MARY: *(Seems a bit odd)* Right so…

ANDREW: *(After a pause)* Do you see much of the present troubles here?

MARY: *(A beat)* Not much until recently. *(Beat)* Getting worse though.

ANDREW: *(Nods)* Yes. Getting worse.

MARY: I don't know how it's got to be so nasty. *(Places pint on table)* There's your pint.

ANDREW: Thank you. *(Drinks)* It's tough alright. I'm Andrew, by the way.

MARY: Pleased to meet you, Andrew. I'm Mary.

ANDREW: It's hard to know who to trust.

MARY: *(Cautious)* Everyone is so suspicious now. You have to be careful who you smile at or say hello to, in case they're the "wrong type".

ANDREW: Yes.

MARY: *(Considers what to say, then)* Something tells me you're not here to see the sights.

ANDREW: I'm not, Mary. The people mainly, I suppose.

MARY: The people?

ANDREW: See what people are like here, what kind of people they are.

MARY: *(Wary, thinking he might be a spy)* Which side they're on, you mean?

ANDREW: *(Annoyed)* No, not which side. *(Beat)* Why does there always have to be a side?

MARY: *(Thoughtfully)* Why indeed.

ANDREW: I stopped here because my brother lived here.

MARY: Oh?

ANDREW: And I wanted to see, hoped to see… if he was happy here.

MARY: Was he one of the ones arrested?

ANDREW: *(Hesitating, but feels safe)* I'm Andrew… Hughes. My brother was Joseph Hughes.

Mary lets out a tiny gasp and is frozen with the shock of hearing his name again.

ANDREW: He was shot dead about six weeks ago here, in February. *(Beat)* He was an RIC man.

MARY: Yes. I…heard.

ANDREW: Did you know him?

MARY: *(Considers her reply)* Not too much. He seemed a good man though.

ANDREW: *(Reflective)* He was that. A good man. And a good brother.

MARY: Was there much between you?

ANDREW: Just shy of three years. Perfect for an older brother to beat up anyone picking on me in school.

MARY: He looked after you.

ANDREW: He did. He always had that kind streak in him. A sense of justice. Took care of me when I started in the mines too.

MARY: A miner? I didn't know…

ANDREW: Oh, there's a fair few mines around that part of the world. We were in the mine at home in Wolfhill - Queen's County, near The Swan. Joe followed the eldest brother Michael and became a miner like Daddy, and then I followed suit. He used to show me how to follow the lodes, put an extra prop beside you in the tunnel you're working on, and how best to pick out the coal.

MARY: *(Little smile)* You called him Joe.

ANDREW: Joe and Andy. That was us. A pair of messers. *(Laughs)* A pair of gurriers at times, truth be told.

MARY: *(Interest piqued)* Oh? What did ye get up to?

ANDREW: Any sort of mischief really. Robbing apples from the nuns' orchard, covering the handle of the chapel door with coal dust…

MARY: *(Smiling)* I thought he had a sense of justice?

ANDREW: *(Chuckling)* He liked a bit of fun too.

MARY: Are there many others in the family?

ANDREW: Mam and Dad are gone. Two sisters and three brothers. Well… two brothers now… I look after Willie, he's… simple, God love him. I don't think he understands yet. Joe always had a soft spot for him.

MARY: I think I do remember him a bit now. He came in here the odd time *(Smiles, remembering)*

ANDREW: Was he welcome?

MARY: *(Unsure how to answer)* Well, it was difficult…

ANDREW: There's a lot of people want nothing to do with the RIC now, want rid of them. I don't blame you. These are difficult times, dangerous times.

MARY: *(Toe in the water)* He was very fair. He helped me here one time when Moss- a customer got a bit angry. He stepped in and… He was my knight in shining armour.

ANDREW: *(Laughs)* He would have loved to have heard that!

MARY: And I think it's fair to say, he was a handsome man too.

ANDREW: He would have definitely loved to hear that!

MARY: Your smile is very like his. And the way you throw back your head when you laugh.

ANDREW: *(Struck by this observation)* God, you really had a good read of him while he was here.

MARY: *(Smiling shyly)* He was nice to look at.

ANDREW: *(Thinking, reassured)* And he must have been happy enough here so, if you saw him laughing and smiling so much…

Footsteps as Tomas comes back in. He starts to make a lot of noise stocking bottles.

ANDREW: *(Jokes)* Or maybe he was just smiling at you, eh?

MARY: *(Irritated by Tomas making noise)* What are you doing, Tomas?

TOMAS: I'm just bringing in some stock for Daddy. *(To Andrew)* Hello, I haven't seen you about before?

MARY: Andrew, this is Tomas, my brother.

TOMAS: Pleased to meet you. Passing through our wonderful village, ey? Don't let the smell of the river put you off.

ANDREW: No…no, I won't. Nice to meet you. I was telling your sister that I just came to see what kind of a place this is. My brother was shot here last month. Joseph Hughes?

Tomas is caught off guard. He doesn't know what to say.

TOMAS: Oh…I see. I mean, yes, it's a terrible tragedy, sir. It's, eh… I'm sorry for your loss.

ANDREW: Thank you. I just wanted to see the place and meet a few of his friends… or people he knew.

TOMAS: Right… *(Trying to keep things light)* Well, I suppose we didn't really know him that much, being a policeman and all. But it's a busy little town, so I'm sure he had his hands full. Plenty of… disputes and arguments, a few fists thrown the odd time…

ANDREW: *(Smiles)* A few in here maybe?

TOMAS: The odd one or two. We can calm that down ourselves.

MARY: *(With a bit of bite)* Tomas is a law onto himself.

ANDREW: Joe was like that too. Could handle himself. He was stationed in Naas for years, before he came here, and he always seemed to be pulling lads apart outside the pubs, or the courthouse. He was well liked there though, I believe and everybody knew him, so if there was ever a bit of a row on the street and he was spotted rounding the corner, someone would shout "Ah lads, stop. Here's Hughes!" and they'd break it up and all be friends again, and have a chat with him and a smoke together when he came up. He liked that. That he could stop a row by his presence alone.

MARY: He was respected.

ANDREW: He was. Less so here, I felt… *(Slightly apologetic)* If you'll excuse me talking about… your town like that.

TOMAS: *(Awkward)* No, it's fine! It can be a bit rough alright. And sure, he wasn't here too long really. To get to know him, like. Anyway, I better -

Tomas feels awkward. Andrew speaks detachedly, numb.

ANDREW: I was the one that had to identify him. In Steevens Hospital. Such an odd train journey up there… It's strange, but you grow up in the country seeing animals live and die, or even working in the mines, so you're kind of used to seeing death. It's not something that gets in at you normally. But seeing your brother, seeing Joe… and the back of his head gone… and his lovely shiny hair matted with blood… I'll never forget the look on his face… *(Mary, unseen cries silently)* And the inquest was so… well, it wasn't a normal inquest, now that there's martial law. It's a "court of inquiry". Captains and Major Generals and all very… clinical. Cold. Technical. Entry wound, two inches in front of the left ear. Severe laceration of the brain. Killed in an ambush by persons unknown was the verdict. As if that helped. *(Mary starts to cry audibly)* I'm sorry, Mary. I didn't mean to upset you. It's horrible to hear, I know. I forgot. I'm very sorry.

MARY: No…no…I'm so sorry for you. So sorry for your brother.

TOMAS: I'd better… *(Considers, then extends his hand)* Very sorry for your trouble. I wish… *(Pause)* I need to get back to…

Footsteps as Tomas leaves. Mary is recovered but quiet. Andrew feels awkward.

ANDREW: Sorry.

MARY: Don't apologise. It's not your fault.

ANDREW: I wasn't meaning to upset you or your brother.

MARY: *(Looking towards the back room, thinking)* Don't worry about him.

ANDREW: Would you know if he had a sweetheart?

MARY: What makes you think he did?

ANDREW: *(Shrugs)* It seemed like he did, in one of the letters he sent me. Not that he gave too much away in case the rebels got hold of the post. I think she was a Grainne. Do you know a Grainne?

MARY: *(Pauses, then shakes her head)* No. Maybe it was a different name?

ANDREW: It was definitely Grainne. *(Pause)* I would have liked to meet her. Get to know her a bit, find out what she's like. Though God knows, it probably would have been a sad meeting at first…

MARY: Did he say much about her? In his letters?

ANDREW: *(Smiles)* "A stór mo chroí", he called her in one of them. That'd be him alright - he'd love showing off his Irish! *(Pause)* I think he meant it though.

MARY: *(Smiling, she repeats in a low voice)* A stór mo chroí…

ANDREW: *(Standing)* Well, if you'll excuse me Mary, I'd better be going. Nice and all as it is talking with you, the air around here - Maynooth… it feels heavy with him. I think it'd might bring me down a bit if I stayed much longer…

MARY: *(Not wanting him to leave)* But surely you'd need something to eat before your journey home? I can get you something from the kitchen. There's some corned beef left over from-

ANDREW: No, no, please. I'm not hungry. The train is due soon anyway. You're very kind though, for offering. *(Smiles at Mary and nods to himself)* There are kind and good people in Maynooth. *(Steps away, then turns)* If he had time, I think he would have liked you, Mary.

Footsteps as he leaves. The door opens. Street noises.

MARY: I was-

ANDREW: Yes?

TOMAS: *(Distant)* Mary, can you bring out the crate I left behind?

MARY: I was… sorry, for your loss. *(Beat)* It was a terrible loss. Heartbreaking…

ANDREW: *(Nods again)* Goodbye Mary.

The door closes. Footsteps as Tomas comes in.

TOMAS: Did you hear me, I said…*(Feeling awkward)* You alright?

After a brief pause, Mary stands runs at Tomas, hitting and pounding on his chest and arms

MARY: Why did you let it happen? Why? You knew! About him. About me. About the ambush. You knew, didn't you? You and your… precious IRA… And you led him into that… dear God… His poor head… His beautiful face…

A swirl of rage and tears, she shoves Tomas into the table.

TOMAS: Jesus, Mary….

MARY: Answer me! Damn you, Tomas! Damn you to hell if you let him be killed and did nothing about it!

Mary storms out. A door slams.

TOMAS: *(Small)* I'm sorry, Mary…

END OF EPISODE

EPISODE 24 – TOMAS IMPRESSES MULLANEY, APR. 1921

Scene 1 - Tomas Barry's Bedroom

BRIGID: *(Distant but getting closer)* Tomas, I need you in the pub. Your father's not back yet and I've a women's meeting. *(Entering room, Shuffling from Tomas)* Will you - What's that behind your back?

TOMAS: Aw nothing, Mammy.

BRIGID: Nothing is it? Give it here. Now. *(Sound of book being passed over. Pages flipped.)* The Art of War. Lord save us. Have you learned nothing?

TOMAS: It's not that kind of a war book. It about using strategy and fooling your enemy.

BRIGID: Right, now I'm your enemy. Pub. Now. *(Tomas protests)* Now!

TOMAS: Can I get my book -

BRIGID: Now, I said! *(As she leaves, upset)* The Art of War. God.

VOICEOVER: Fractured – April 1921

Scene 2 - Barry's pub

Sounds of Tomas cleaning up the bar. Door opens, O'Reilly enters, looks around to see who's there. He's more serious and cautious than when we've seen him before. He comes up to Tomas at the counter.

O'REILLY: Are we good, Tomas?

TOMAS: Everyone's out, O'Reilly. Daddy as well.

O'REILLY: Where's your mother? She has a habit of throwing me out.

TOMAS: *(Smirks)* You have a habit of giving her good reason to. She's gone to one of her women's meetings. Teresa's giving a lecture on how to treat gunshot wounds.

O'REILLY: Jesus. Knowing her, that'll be pretty gory.

TOMAS: She certainly doesn't hold back. Not a bad skill to know these days though.

O'REILLY: Hmm.

The door opens . Pat Mullaney and Tom Farrell enter.

MULLANEY: *(Nods to both)* O'Reilly. Tomas.

TOMAS: Mr. Mullaney, sir.

MULLANEY: Good to see you again. This man here is Tom Farrell, he's my Vice Commandant for the Leixlip column.

They all shake hands.

TOMAS: Another Farrell from Leixlip? You must grow on trees over there.

FARRELL: Near enough. My brother Jim was with you on the ambush here in February, right? He said you were some shot. Got that RIC fella right in the head. Well, fair play to ya - we need snipers like you.

TOMAS: Let's sit down over here. It's more out of the way.

Scraping of chairs as they take a seat.

TOMAS: Can I get you some tea, boys?

O'REILLY: Jaysus, some pub... I dunno, are you old enough for tea yet, Tomas?

A guffaw from Farrell.

MULLANEY: Well, if tea is good enough for Pat Colgan, it's good enough for us. Thanks Tomas.

TOMAS: I'll be back in moment. The tea is made, sir.

Footsteps as Tomas moves away.

MULLANEY: So... this is it, eh? The only four lads left around here that we can trust. Sean arrested, Colgan and Harris lifted -

O'REILLY: I hear Colgan has put order on that camp in County Down.

MULLANEY: That he has. *(Tomas returns)* Thanks Tomas.

TOMAS: I'll just pour, sir.

Sound of tea being dispensed. Cups being lifted.

MULLANNEY: Here's to Sean, a good soldier and a good brother to Tomas here. Himself and Colgan will have those boys in Ballykinlar trained up like machines in no time. Slainte.

O'REILLY: You'd want to raise more than a cup of tea as a toast if it's Sean you're talking about!

They chuckle. Tomas gets down to business.

TOMAS: So, where are we at?

MULLANEY: Well as you know, I'm the only Commandant in the area left, which is far from ideal.

FARRELL: *(Smirking)* Ah you're not that bad.

MULLANEY: Thanks for that. There's a lot of good men gone, nearly half our active units, and there's more being arrested every day. Most of us on the run, lying low...and I'm supposed to be a teacher as well!

O'REILLY: *(Smirking)* What are you teaching them in school, how to take out a policeman from 30 yards?

MULLANEY: Most of the lads that haven't been arrested yet are running around now like headless chickens.

FARRELL: Yeah, there's a fair few of them are chickens alright.

MULLANEY: We need to put some order on these fellas.

TOMAS: What do you propose we do?

MULLANEY: Well, as I see it, we have three problems. We're missing good people in leadership, ambushes are getting more and more dangerous and worst of all, the men are terrified of getting involved in the first place for fear of reprisals from the Tans.

O'REILLY: We need to get these lads some target practice, toughen them up.

MULLANEY: We don't have enough ammo to go around to waste it firing on each other.

O'REILLY: Oh…right…yes, good point.

TOMAS: I've been thinking about women.

FARRELL: Jaysus, we've all been thinking about women!

TOMAS: No, I mean for… manoeuvres.

FARRELL: I know the kind of manoeuvres you're thinking of!

TOMAS: Operations, then! Ambushes.

O'REILLY: Is it Lizzie O'Neill you're thinking of for your manoeuvres?

TOMAS: Actually, yes, it is.

O'REILLY: I thought that!

TOMAS: Just not in the way you're thinking of.

FARRELL: Maybe that way too?

MULLANEY: Alright, leave the fella alone. *(To Tomas)* What are you thinking of?

TOMAS: Well, I was thinking about that RIC ambush up the road there…

FARRELL: Bullseye for Tomas – good man!

TOMAS: And how I hadn't realised Lizzie was involved.

MULLANEY: One of our best.

TOMAS: I never heard about Lizzie joining up. So it's fair to say, that if I didn't hear about her, then the RIC or the Tans didn't hear about her either.

MULLANEY: What are you getting at?

TOMAS: How many men are interned in Ballykinlar?

FARRELL: Two, three hundred? It keeps growing every day.

O'REILLY: Get to the point, Tomas.

TOMAS: Nearly two thousand.

FARRELL: Jaysus, that many?

TOMAS: And then there's all the new camps built because that one is full – Spike Island in Cork, Bere Island, Gormanstown, and now at Hare Camp in the Curragh.

FARRELL: There must be thousands upon thousands...

TOMAS: And how many women have been arrested and interned?

TOMAS: Barely a handful.

MULLANEY: Do you mean...?

TOMAS: Women aren't being arrested. The RIC can't search them, so they can't arrest them. Why not get more women involved?

FARRELL: But women are involved. They run the safe houses, run messages.

TOMAS: But they can do so much more. Act as spies. Handle munitions. Maybe get involved in an ambush or two if they want.

MULLANEY: De Valera won't let women get involved in any kind of combat duties – he stopped them from that after the Rising.

TOMAS: Yeah well, that's only because Connolly was dead. "Irishmen and Irishwomen", that's what he had in the proclamation. Cumann na mBan have been sent back to the kitchens thanks to Dev, but there's a lot of them would love to get in on the action.

MULLANEY: Lizzie's well up for it alright.

TOMAS: And I'm sure there'd be more willing to get involved. Ellen Kenny for instance. All the while the British are looking to pin something on the men, the women could be running about on operations undetected. Hiding in plain sight.

MULLANEY: There's something in that alright. It's against what GHQ would propose, but these are desperate times... and they don't need to know, so...

FARRELL: We'd have to be careful not to go with Cumann na mBan. They might be known, so they might be watched. Maybe... if they haven't been arresting them, it's because they're watching them go about their duties and following them to meetings or safe houses. Maybe that's how they're spoiling ambushes.

MULLANEY: It's a possibility. *(Thinks)* But none of the women were involved in any of the failed ambushes lately. Except Lizzie, of course. But sure she was in as much danger as any of us. *(Beat)* I'd say that's fairly unlikely. They've enough to be doing trying to catch us lot without following the Cumann as well.

TOMAS: We should get some outsiders as well though. Women they'd never expect.

O'REILLY: What, like your mother? *(They laugh)*

O'REILLY: There's more chance of Mossie Kinsella being made a saint than there is of getting her involved!

MULLANEY: Who are you thinking of?

TOMAS: Well, I hadn't really anyone in mind, to be honest.

O'REILLY: What about Mary?

MULLANEY: Who's Mary?

O'REILLY: His sister. She's always giving out to me about what we're doing, but she's got two brothers in the IRA now, one of them locked up…?

TOMAS: We don't exactly see eye to eye on that, and anyway, she's…

O'REILLY: She's what?

TOMAS: She wouldn't be up for it. I'm fairly certain she wouldn't do it.

O'REILLY: Jaysus, mother and daughter the same. *(Mocking)* So only the Barry men are brave enough?

TOMAS: *(Annoyed)* She's brave enough in her own way.

O'REILLY: *(After a pause)* How about Cissy? I haven't seen her around much lately… but she's fairly feisty. I'd say she'd be handy with a revolver - if you could control her!

TOMAS: Maybe… I haven't seen her much either, though…

MULLANEY: Well, who have you seen lately, then?

TOMAS: *(Thinking)* Em…

MULLANEY: Come on now, there's no point suggesting an idea and not having anyone to propose for it. Who else could there be around here, Tomas?

TOMAS: Well… *(Flustered, then gets an idea)* Maybe… but I don't know what her leanings are… or if she even has any leanings one way or the other…

MULLANEY: *(Impatient)* Who?

TOMAS: *(Looking to O'Reilly)* What about Teresa?

O'Reilly stares back blankly, then laughs loudly.

O'REILLY: Teresa! The mad one?

MULLANEY: Who's Teresa?

TOMAS: She's not that mad.

O'REILLY: She's fairly odd now, you'd have to admit.

TOMAS: She is… but I'd say she'd be pretty ruthless if it came down to it.

MULLANEY: *(To O'Reilly)* Would she be reliable?

O'REILLY: I don't know… She certainly has a very… clinical way of looking at things.

TOMAS: Very exact. By the book.

MULLANEY: *(To O'Reilly)* Would she take orders well?

O'REILLY: *(Conceding)* I suppose so.

TOMAS: And she's a memory like a photograph. I reckon she could relay coded messages without them written down, perfect to the letter. *(Remembering)* She's teaching that women's group right now how to treat gunshot wounds.

MULLANEY: She sounds perfect! Right, Tomas. Good man! You get her signed up and we'll find a good mission for her.

TOMAS: *(Alarmed at the quick decision)* I don't know if she'd do it, sir. I've no idea what she thinks about… the whole mess at the moment. I haven't talked to her about it. I suppose I haven't really talked to her at all…

MULLANEY: Well, talk to her then. Find out.

TOMAS: I will, but… give me some time. To scope her out. Make sure she doesn't lean the other way and give us up.

MULLANEY: Fine. That's a smart idea, Tomas.

TOMAS: Thank you, sir.

FARRELL: Well, before you get too far ahead of yourselves, there's also the small matter of what seems to be an informer giving our plans away to the RIC. That day a few weeks back when we lay in wait on the three roads between Leixlip, Celbridge and Maynooth and not one member of the RIC ventured out? They must have been tipped off.

TOMAS: Are we sure that was an informer though? I mean, it was lashing raining that day. Maybe they had no reason to go out in the rain?

MULLANEY: What about last Sunday in Lucan? We waited on the side of the river the police always go along, and what happens? They pass on the other side about 80 yards away, too far to land a shot. Emptied our revolvers for nothing.

O'REILLY: Well, I'm fairly sure Mossie Kinsella is an informer. He's a shifty character and always seems to be snooping around. His only loyalty is to himself.

FARRELL: That's for certain. I saw him over in Leixlip a couple of weeks ago and he laughing and chatting with the RIC sergeant there.

MULLANEY: *(Concerned)* What was he doing in Leixlip?

FARRELL: Up to no good, no doubt. Probably slipping messages about plans he might have heard about.

O'REILLY: It feels like all our plans are being sabotaged right now. We have to take action and strike back.

FARRELL: Exactly.

O'REILLY: We need to teach them a lesson. They can't inform on us, have us arrested or shot, and expect to get away with it.

TOMAS: Look, I don't like the man either. He's caused trouble here more than a few times, but did you actually see him passing information?

FARRELL: *(Avoids this)* Well, we don't have to shoot him. A punishment beating. That would sort him out.

TOMAS: But we shouldn't be going after informers to… get rid of them, just because we can.

O'REILLY: *(Warning)* Don't be getting soft on us again, Tomas…

TOMAS: I'm not, I'm just saying that there are other ways. I've been thinking a lot about this lately…

O'REILLY: Look. We have a system that works. We plan ambushes and we execute them. If an informer sabotages our plans and puts us in danger, we have to get rid of them. Simple as that.

TOMAS: But there are other ways where nobody need get hurt or feel they have to take a life. But still bring the Empire to its knees.

MULLANEY: *(Pause)* Like what?

TOMAS: Most of our plans these days involve ambushes of some kind. Shootings, bombings – dangerous things to do if you care about reprisals against you or your family, or if you care about having murder on your soul.

FARRELL: It's hardly murder! It's… shootings…

MULLANEY: Look, nobody wants to take a life. But we're in a war now, and sometimes killings are needed. You know that, Tomas.

TOMAS: How many million Britons are there? Do you really think that you killing a few ex-army Tans, or even Irishmen in the RIC, is "driving them out"? They'll come back with a thousand more, and a hundred thousand more.

FARRELL: Good riddance to them! They deserve to die, the lot of them!

O'REILLY: Well, I'll leave them all dead in a ditch, I don't care.

TOMAS: Lads, this has become a brutal war. After that bloody Sunday in Croke Park last November, the number of beatings and arrests has multiplied.

MULLANEY: Do you think we don't know that?

TOMAS: And as for shootings and bombings, we're killing them, so they kill us, so we kill them… round and round in a big vicious circle. It's getting out of hand.

O'REILLY: What do you expect us to do?

TOMAS: There are 500 people dead in the four months since the start of the year. *(They quieten)* For every RIC man or British army killed, they'll just bring in more Tans, more Auxiliaries. We can't just kill them all.

O'REILLY: *(Sarcastic)* So what's your "grand plan" then? What have you figured out that the lads in GHQ haven't?

TOMAS: Kildare is a garrison county. There's more soldiers and Army barracks in Kildare than in most counties. That's why we haven't been able to do much up to now – you can't move for soldiers or RIC. There's a hell of a lot more of them than there is us.

O'REILLY: I'm still not hearing a plan.

MULLANEY: Give him a chance.

TOMAS: Look, we can't beat them by the numbers. But we can beat them by disrupting how they function.

FARRELL: What do you mean, "how they function"?

TOMAS: How does an army work? Think about it.

FARRELL: They work on their stomach.

O'REILLY: That's what they march on, you eejit.

FARRELL: Oh right…

TOMAS: *(Ignoring this)* An army works as one unit. Information is gathered. It's passed up the chain of command to the top. A decision is then made by the top brass. That decision comes back down the chain as orders for the troops. They mobilise and carry out those orders.

FARRELL: That's a fair summary.

TOMAS: Based on the result of how those orders went, they send information back up the chain, etc, etc, until the next action. It only works because it's all connected. If you break those connections, it all falls apart.

MULLANEY: Break the connections?

TOMAS: "Disruption" is the plan. We throw as many spanners into the works as we can find.

O'REILLY: *(Scoffing)* Like what, exactly?

TOMAS: First thing - information. An army feeds on information. Without it, it can't make decisions. Every day, mail dispatches carry reports and maps and God knows what else up to Army Command in Parkgate Street and down to all the barracks.

MULLANEY: Raid the mail trains.

TOMAS: Raid the mail trains. Stop Army HQ getting the information in the first place.

MULLANEY: We've done it before. Alright. We can do that.

TOMAS: Second thing – orders. And urgent information. The post is no good if they need to make quick decisions or react to something immediately. So they use the telephones and the telegraph. If we cut the lines, they won't be able to contact each other quickly.

O'Reilly scoffs, seeing Mullaney's interest.

MULLANEY: That makes sense.

TOMAS: Third – mobilisation. If they can't telephone or send messages between the stations and barracks, they have to send men over with orders directly. Over the last while, we've been getting into gun battles with them in ambushes, but all we really need to do is just stop the orders getting through.

FARRELL: But that's what the ambush is for. Take out the man and you take out the message.

TOMAS: Why not just steal the police bicycles, or puncture or break the wheels on their cars and trucks? Blow a hole in a few bridges if you want. No one need get hurt, and the orders don't get through.

MULLANEY: It's the message that's important, not the man.

TOMAS: Exactly.

MULLANEY: *(Impressed)* That's good work, Tomas. Did you think of this all by yourself?

TOMAS: *(Smirks)* I think Mick Collins has a fair handle on it too, to be honest. I was just trying to think of what's best for us here in Kildare, what's simple but effective.

MULLANEY: *(Genuine respect)* I thought Sean was supposed to be the brains of the family. *(Looking at O'Reilly, teasing)* He certainly gives you a run for your money, O'Reilly

O'REILLY: *(Annoyed)* I'd say I could beat him in a sprint all the same.

FARRELL: But what about informers? It's all very well bringing down the might of the British Empire by cutting a few telephone wires and stealing a few bikes, but what if an informer gives us away and sets us up to be killed?

MULLANEY: Any informer that's identified as such is to be shot. That's the order.

O'REILLY: *(Engaged again)* Yeah, but the problem is that we don't know who the informer or informers are.

MULLANEY: They need to be caught in the act.

TOMAS: I did have an idea on this as well…

O'REILLY: Jaysus, you're full of ideas today…

MULLANEY: What are you thinking?

TOMAS: Why not… let informers go about their business?

Disbelief from all three. Splutters of laughter.

O'REILLY: What, just let them at it? Let us be caught?

TOMAS: Well no, not exactly. We've a few suspects, right? *(they agree)* How about we let each of them accidentally overhear a juicy bit of information and let them pass it on.

MULLANEY: But not real information, is that what you're saying?

TOMAS: Correct. A nice juicy bit of false information that an informer couldn't wait to pass on. Nothing involving us, naturally. Just something that we heard.

FARRELL: *(Laughing)* A wild goose chase!

TOMAS: But the best bit is that we give each suspect a different juicy bit of false information. *(Beat)* And then we wait and see what one gets acted on. And that's your informer.

MULLANEY: By God, that's a great plan! We can tell one of them where there's supposed to be a stash of rifles, and see if it's raided!

FARRELL: We can tell another one where and when an ambush is supposed to happen and see if they bring reinforcements!

MULLANEY: Oh, whoever this fella is… he's in for a big surprise!

FARRELL: Fair play, Tomas. That thinking is… beyond your years.

O'REILLY: *(Sarcasm)* Let's see if it works first.

TOMAS: *(With bite)* It will, O'Reilly.

MULLANEY: There's a serious lack of leadership in Maynooth at the moment, Tomas. That was some… very impressive thinking. *(Beat)* I'm going to make you Vice Captain for Maynooth Company until further notice, reporting to me.

O'REILLY: *(Protesting)* But I'm Vice Captain!

MULLANEY: And now Tomas is as well.

TOMAS: Thank you, sir!

MULLANEY: Alright, we'll be off so. *(A scraping of chairs as they move)* We'll get to work on some of those disruption techniques. I'll take Leixlip and Celbridge, if you can organise Maynooth and Kilcock.

TOMAS: Yes, sir.

MULLANEY: And I'd like you to put that plan to flush out any informers into effect as soon as you can.

TOMAS: Yes, sir… *(Thinks)* There was nothing planned for the next few weeks. Maybe if I work on getting some ideas together for operations down the line, I could set up the informer traps just before them. That way, we flush them out at just the right time before the British know they're caught.

MULLANEY: That's good thinking. Yes, do that. And Teresa, don't forget her.   Goodbye Tomas.

Footsteps as the men leave, calling out 'goodbye' Door opens, street, closes.

TOMAS: YES!

END OF EPISODE

EPISODE 25 – MAILBAG ROBBERY, MAY 1921

Scene 1 – Railway station

Sound of steam train, growing louder as it nears. Night sounds.

MULLANEY: Right, when I give the order, we go. Tomas, your duty is to -

TOMAS: Board the train at the station. Hold up the driver, keep him held up until O'Reilly gives me the signal to leave.

MULANNEY: O'Reilly?

O'REILLY: Board the train, grab the mailbags with you. Once we have secured them and taken them from the train, I give the signal to Tomas to leave.

MULANNEY: And then?

TOMAS: We meet the Cumann na mBan contact who will take the bag for safe keeping.

MULANNEY: Good. Right, get ready boys, here we go.

The train screeches into the station, running footsteps.

VOICEOVER: Fractured – May 1921.

Scene 2 - Lizzie O'Neill's house.

Poorly furnished. Bare and dirty looking. Lizzie herself is clean and appears to have put some effort into her appearance. She takes a pair of boots belonging to her brother and starts polishing them.

LIZZIE: Why can't they polish their own boots, that's what I want to know. Are they crippled? Are they paralysed? Are they – *(A coded knock on the door)* Just a minute. *(Door opens)* Tomas. Hello.

TOMAS: Where is everyone?

LIZZIE: That's a fine greeting so it is.

TOMAS: Sorry… sorry now, Miss O'Neill. I was told to report here, I only have an hour or so.

LIZZIE: The others won't be long. Would you like a glass of milk, Tomas?

TOMAS: No, thank you. It's one thing you're never short of in the pub is a drink.

LIZZIE: Aye. Well, sit won't you?

TOMAS: Grand. Thanks. *(He sits. Beat)* 'Tis a grand comfortable seat, anyway.

LIZZIE: God, but you're a fierce liar, Tomas Barry. You'd want an arse of lead to be comfortable on that.

TOMAS: I had the procedure done there, not twelve months ago.

LIZZIE: *(Laughs)* God, but you're funny. Like your brother.

TOMAS: *(A bit put out at the mention of Sean)* Aye, he's a clown, alright.

LIZZIE: I heard he's in Ballykinlar, that's a horrible place.

TOMAS: It is and the food isn't up to much, which is causing Sean the most hardship.

LIZZIE: But he's in good spirits?

TOMAS: He says he is, which is all we can go on.

LIZZIE: If you write him, tell him I said 'hello'.

TOMAS: Are your brothers not about?

LIZZIE: In all likelihood, they're in your father's pub, we won't see them for hours. I'll get the mailbag, it was dropped off last night.

Footsteps. A press being opened. Dragging of mailbag across floor.

TOMAS: They can put away their drink alright.

LIZZIE: And you admire that do you?

TOMAS: I'm just saying -

LIZZIE: Well don't just say! Since the cholera took Mammy and Daddy, I've been left to clean and wash and tidy after them while they go about spending all our money in your pub. *(Thump as bag is laid down)* There's the bag.

TOMAS: I can't be held responsible for how they spend their money.

LIZZIE: Just think on it next time you serve one of them a pint.

TOMAS: But sure…that's what men do.

LIZZIE: And isn't it fine for them? Getting out all day and then drinking all night and the women are left with the…the house.

TOMAS: And a fine job you're doing.

LIZZIE: More lies. Have you had another operation that has made you blind?

TOMAS: No, I have not.

LIZZIE: This is a horrible house and you know it. Sure, there's been nothing nice in it since Daddy brought home the tablecloth in 1916 when he went looting up in Dublin.

TOMAS: Isn't it a roof over your head?

LIZZIE: It's a stone around my ankle, is what it is.

TOMAS: I thought…well, I thought girls liked being in charge of a house.

LIZZIE: Tell me, Tomas Barry, would you like to be cleaning up after your mother and Mary and them swanning off up to the pub? Would you like to be making their beds and washing their underclothes with your hands -

TOMAS: I wouldn't but -

LIZZIE: But what? I'm no different to you.

TOMAS: You're a woman.

LIZZIE: It doesn't automatically make me want to wash my brother's underclothes. Are you stupid in the head?

TOMAS: I am not! And I'm sorry if whatever I said offended you. *(Beat)* I am.

LIZZIE: No, I'm sorry. It's not your fault. Sure, didn't you recommend me and the other women for the ambushes and that? You're a lovely boy, Tomas and -

TOMAS: Am I?

LIZZIE: You are. It's my brothers, they just…and, Tomas, did you ever just want to escape? Just leave everything behind?

TOMAS: Go on the run, like?

LIZZIE: No. Just…walk away and leave your life and start a new one.

TOMAS: Not really, no.

LIZZIE: You're lucky so because I would. I'd go in a heartbeat.

TOMAS: Go where?

LIZZIE: Anywhere.

TOMAS: But sure…what would you do?

LIZZIE: I don't know, do I?

TOMAS: You'd want some sort of a plan of what you'd do otherwise, sure you'd fall on hard times and -

LIZZIE: You are a tonic for my soul, Tomas.

TOMAS: I'm just explaining -

LIZZIE: There was time you hardly spoke to me and now when you do, it's a big disappointment.

TOMAS: That's not very nice.

LIZZIE: It's not very nice telling me I can't run away.

TOMAS: I didn't say that. I said you'd need a plan and money and that.

LIZZIE: I'll get money and I'll get a plan.

TOMAS: Great. *(Silence)* If you went though -

LIZZIE: What?

TOMAS: - well, I'd probably miss you.

LIZZIE: Would you?

TOMAS: Probably.

LIZZIE: The girls were right so.

TOMAS: What girls?

LIZZIE: All the girls, Cissy and them. They kept saying, Tomas Barry is mad for you so he is, only I didn't believe them.

TOMAS: I'm not mad for you.

LIZZIE: Right! *(Another coded rap on the door)* Coming. *(Door opens)* It's O'Reilly and Mullaney.

They all exchange greetings.

O'REILLY: Glass of milk there, Miss O'Neill.

LIZZIE: It's not the Shelbourne you're in, O'Reilly. I was told to stay with you at all times by my command.

O'REILLY: And I was told that there'd be a glass of milk waiting for me when we finally got to where we're going.

MULLANEY: Tomas, get us a glass of milk, would you? There's a good lad.

TOMAS: *(With no enthusiasm)* Yes, sir.

He goes to get it.

O'REILLY: Right, let's get cracking on the mailbag. *(Sound of the mailbag being opened)* Orders from GHQ are that any money found is to be confiscated, recorded and spent on arms or sent to the dependant's fund. Any interesting correspondence is to be sent directly to Mick Collins. *(To Lizzie)* And that doesn't mean correspondence about the latest fashions, Miss O'Neill.

LIZZIE: And it doesn't mean pictures of women in their underclothes either.

O'Reilly laughs. Tomas returns.

TOMAS: Here's the milk, boys.

MULLANEY: Thanks Tomas. *(Setting milk down)* Here's the plan. We read all the letters we can and -.

TOMAS: The lads in Carlow brigade say they spend their time crossing out random sentences and writing on the top 'Passed by the IRA' before enveloping it again

MULLANEY: That's a good one so it is. We'll do that. Pencils, Miss O'Neill.

LIZZIE: I have some at the ready.

The sound of letters being torn open will underpin this scene.

O'REILLY: I heard you were in Celbridge the other night, Tomas.

TOMAS: Aye. There was about six of us. Jesus, one of the lads took apart a plate glass window that was advertising the cigarettes from Belfast. Smashed it to smithereens all over the road.

MULLANEY: Good enough for them.

O'REILLY: How many shops did ye raid?

TOMAS: *(Wary)* Four.

MULLANEY: Was there not five on the list?

TOMAS: Aye, there was.

MULLANEY: What happened?

TOMAS: We - I - saw little point in terrorising a woman who was ninety if she was a day.

MULLANEY: That's not your call, Barry.

O'REILLY: Getting above yourself there, Barry.

TOMAS: She was deaf as a post. She wouldn't have known what we were about. I handed her a note, explaining that it wouldn't be in her interests to have Belfast goods in her shop.

O'REILLY: Excuse me, isn't that very civilised now? Maybe we should just hand the British Empire a note explaining that it's not in their interests to have British soldiers in our country.

TOMAS: Shut up.

MULLANEY: If it says five shops, you raid five shops.

O'REILLY: He's gone soft since he killed the RIC chap.

TOMAS: Fuck off.

MULLANEY: Boys. Stop. *(To Tomas)* And don't you be using such language in front of a lady.

LIZZIE: I hear worse from my brothers when they've been drinking. If you want to tell O'Reilly to 'fuck off' in my house, then you can, Tomas.

TOMAS: Thanks. Fu -

MULLANEY: I won't have it! D'you hear? If you two can't get on, then ye can go right now. *(Mumbles of 'sorry sir')* Good. Remember what rank ye are for God's sake. Now you, Tomas. If it says five shops, then you raid five shops. I don't care if the old woman keels over and dies, she's a traitor to the Republic and what do we do to traitors?

TOMAS: Warn them off then if they don't listen, execute them.

MULLANEY: Exactly. Next month, you go back to that old woman and you make sure she has obeyed orders, right?

TOMAS: Yes, Sir.

MULLANEY: And you, O'Reilly, you can stop baiting Tomas and trying to rise rows.

O'REILLY: I wasn't trying to -

MULLANEY: Don't take me for a fool. I know exactly what you were about. Now, let's get to business.

The sound of them sorting through mail again.

TOMAS: Here's a card someone posted from Dublin. *(Reads)* Having a great time in the city despite the shootings. Had dinner in Jammet's Oyster Bar. See you soon.'

MULLANEY: That's doing no harm.

TOMAS: Even with the picture of the RIC Depot in Dublin in it?

ALL THREE: Tear it up.

We hear Tomas tearing it up. Laughter.

O'REILLY: Here's a ten shilling note someone is being sent for their birthday. Write that down in the book, Miss O'Neill.

They work in silence for a while.

MULLANEY: What do you think of Lloyd George's offer for talks to Dev?

O'REILLY: Would you trust him?

MULLANEY: Not as far as I could spit him.

TOMAS: I think it's worth having a look at it. There's no obligation to accept anything.

MULLANEY: He's only making it because the Yanks have him under pressure. He's embarrassed because England is looking fierce bad in the eyes of the world.

TOMAS: He's still making it though. We need to capitalise on it.

O'REILLY: For Dev to talk to him, he'd need to guarantee to treat us, north and south as one unit.

TOMAS: Aye, and to acknowledge that we have the right to decide how we want to be governed in our own country.

LIZZIE: Our own country! Doesn't that sound grand.

They take a moment to think about this.

MULLANEY: Aye. Any progress on recruiting that woman you were telling us about, Tomas?

TOMAS: Teresa? Not yet. She's hard to pin down. Herself and the women are in a play that Con O'Sullivan is doing with the Gaelic League or something and sure, it's all they can really talk about.

O'REILLY: Teresa in a play, *(Laughs)* Jesus, that'd be worth seeing.

MULLANEY: Next time you get a chance, have a chat with her. If she's as clever as you've said, we could do with her.

TOMAS: I will.

O'REILLY: Any news on the informer?

LIZZIE: Informer?

Beat.

MULLANEY: Good one, O'Reilly. Nicely done.

LIZZIE: There's an informer?

MULLANEY: We think there's an informer. We're not sure.

LIZZIE: What will you do if there is?

O'REILLY: What we do to all informers, Miss O'Neill. Arrest them, let them say their act of contrition and then shoot them in the head.

TOMAS: She doesn't need to hear that.

LIZZIE: I'll decide what I want to hear. Have you shot many in the head?

O'REILLY: Depends. Sometimes, we give them a warning to leave. This fella though…

TOMAS: He's scuppered quite a few plans.

MULLANEY: He'll be pretty scuppered himself when we catch up with him.

LIZZIE: Have ye any suspects?

O'REILLY: Some.

LIZZIE: Anyone I know?

O'REILLY: We couldn't be telling you that now.

LIZZIE: Nice to feel part of the team, so it is.

TOMAS: They won't even tell me, so I wouldn't worry about it. *(Referencing envelope)* Here's a good one - some eejit has just written to a 'Bridie Doyle' in Athy thanking her for taking him in to her safe house. Jesus.

MULLANEY: Who the hell did that? I'd march him out of the Volunteers so I would.

O'REILLY: There's stupid eejits on all sides. Destroy that letter, Tomas.

TOMAS: Done.

MULLANEY: Oh. What have we here? Money for the Mission to China. Five pounds. What'll we do?

TOMAS: I'd say take it. What about the mission in Ireland?

LIZZIE: That's terrible, so it is. And all them priests converting them little Chinese people and all them rosaries being said for the holy souls. You couldn't take that, so you couldn't.

MULLANEY: I think the church has enough money and anyway, I hear Cardinal Logue has made a bit of a speech against us -

TOMAS: I heard that it's to be read at mass.

MULLANEY: So, I say, take it. O'Reilly?

O'REILLY: I don't mind stealing, but it's like we're taking it from the Holy Father himself. That can't be right now.

TOMAS: The Holy Father would give it to us if we asked him. Sure, isn't he always preaching about sharing and that.

LIZZIE: Your mother would skin you alive, Tomas Barry if she could hear you.

O'REILLY: It's pure thievery.

TOMAS: Right, I'll tell ye what. Have you change of five pounds, Mullaney?

MULANNEY: I have. *(Sound of clinking money being handed over)* There you go.

TOMAS: Thank you. So, let's put this back for the Mission and take the bit over for ourselves. *(Hands money to Lizzie)* That way we're all happy.

MULLANEY: You should be with Dev if he goes to them peace talks.

TOMAS: I hope he does. Wouldn't it be great all the same, no more fighting. Sean'd be home, me mother would be happy, we'd all go back to normal.

O'REILLY: This is my normal. *(A beat)* I love this, don't ye?

TOMAS: No. *(They look at him)* No, I don't.

O'REILLY: *(To Mullaney)* What about you?

MULLANEY: I want to win and when we do, it'll stop and…I'll probably miss it.

LIZZIE: Me too. It beats cleaning up after me brothers.

O'REILLY: You're outnumbered, Barry.

TOMAS: *(Ignoring him)* Any more letters there?

O'REILLY: Are you a real soldier at all, I wonder?

MULLANEY: I think we're about done, here. Let's put everything back. Good work, boys. There will be more over the coming weeks. Lizzie, will yourself and Ellen Kenny sort out putting them back into the post.

LIZZIE: No bother at all.

MULLANEY: Good girl.

A sudden furious hammering on the door. They freeze.

LIZZIE: Just a minute, can't you. Stall them while I hide this.

HAYES: *(From outside)* Is O'Reilly in there? Or Mullaney?

MULLANEY: It's all right. I know that voice. *(Lizzie lets a young Volunteer in)* Hayes, what is it?

HAYES: Sir, sir, they've taken over the Custom House. News from Dublin just now. One of the lads, he was delivering a message cycled up to Dublin today and sure he couldn't get down the quays. The Volunteers are after being sent to the Custom House. The place is blazing. The auxies are firing on them.

TOMAS: For God's sake, whose idea was that?

MULLANEY: An attack like that, it'll show the numbers in the Volunteers -

TOMAS: It's suicide.

HAYES: They say it's to force Lloyd George's hand. He can't afford America or any other country to see that.

TOMAS: But the boys -

MULLANEY: Are prepared to die for Ireland. Anything else, Hayes?

HAYES: Not yet.

MULLANEY: I might go up myself, have a look.

O'REILLY: I'll go with you. Tomas?

They look at Tomas

TOMAS: I can't, I've to get back to the pub, I promised me mother and there'll be questions asked otherwise.

MULLANEY: All right. Stay, help Miss O'Neill clear up. Come on O'Reilly. Hayes.

They leave. Tomas and Lizzie are left alone. Awkward silence.

BOTH: I - You go - No, you -

TOMAS: Right, so… thanks for giving me permission to say…fuck off to O'Reilly.

LIZZIE: No bother. If you hadn't I would have. He's an awful eejit.

TOMAS: Aye, he is. Here, let me help you with that bag. *(They finish concealing the bag)* I'd better -

LIZZIE: Go. Aye.

TOMAS: Sure, I might see you and Cissy with Mary one of the days.

LIZZIE: Me maybe. Cissy doesn't be well these days.

TOMAS: What's wrong with her?

LIZZIE: I'm not rightly sure.

TOMAS: Poor Cissy.

LIZZIE: So, it'll just be me calling in.

TOMAS: Then do. Anytime like.

LIZZIE: I will so.

Awkward silence.

TOMAS: Bye so.

He goes. Lizzie closes the door on him and smiles, enigmatically.

LIZZIE: Be seeing you, Tomas.

END OF EPISODE

EPISODE 26 – CISSY AND ANNE, JUNE 1921

Scene 1 - Outside the church.

Latin hymn from inside. Cissy and her father Frank are outside.

FRANK: *(Angry)* By God you will. We'll see what the Father has to say about this. Get in there now.

CISSY: Leave me alone. I will not.

FRANK: You'll do as I say ye little hussy or live to regret it.

CISSY: You can't make me do anything. You're just…

The sound of a slap. Cissy cries out.

VOICEOVER: Fractured – June 1921

Scene 2 - Inside Church

FATHER DEMPSEY: Thank you all for your attendance at Mass today. God Bless you all for the week ahead. *(Shuffling as people leave)* Just before you go…*(Shuffling eases off)* I've been asked to read a statement on behalf of Cardinal Logue. *(Audible sighs)* As you may know, we were honoured to welcome his Lordship to Maynooth College this week, when he presided over a full meeting of the Irish Bishops. The Cardinal begins by thanking His Holiness the Pope for his donation of 200,000 lira to assuage the sufferings of the Irish people. 'Last October we had to place before the world a picture of Ireland which, however horrifying in itself, was but an inadequate representation of the indignities and outrages to which our country has been subjected. Since then, every horror has been intensified, and we are now living with even darker doings, because our countrymen spurn, as they rightly do, the sham settlement devised by the British Government.'

During the above, we hear conversation between Lizzie and O'Reilly,

O'REILLY: 200,000 lira! Donate it to the Volunteers and we'll assuage some suffering I'll tell ye!

LIZZIE: Cause it more like!

O'REILLY: Only to those most deserving of course! Like your man Sergeant Tom Dwyer over there. How can he show his face in mass?

LIZZIE: I don't know. What's 200,000 lira in pounds and shillings do you think?

O'REILLY: A lot. *(They both snigger)*

ANNE: Can you both be quite, please.

FATHER DEMPSEY: 'In defiance of Ireland, a special Government has been given to one section of her people, remarkable at all times for intolerance, without the slightest provision to safeguard the victims of ever-recurring cruelty.'

O'REILLY: With God on our side, who can be against!

LIZZIE: I'd say a fair few Tans might have a go.

O'REILLY: Bloody bastards.

ANNE: Kindly refrain from blaspheming in the house of the Lord.

O'Reilly and Lizzie snigger.

FATHER DEMPSEY: The statement goes on to say that a fund has been set up to help alleviate the distress of so many of our citizens whose property and livelihoods *(The sound of a commotion at the door)* - have been destroyed by our current troubles. It's called the White Cross Association, and the Cardinal would be grateful for any donations.

CISSY: Mass isn't over! Mass is still on. Daddy!

The crowd murmurs. The priests voice fades out.

FRANK: Beggin' your pardon Father. We…I…

CISSY: I told ye Daddy. The sermons go on for bloody ages.

ANNE: Shameless.

FRANK: Come on, back out.

Frank drags Cissy out of the church, their voice receding.

FRANK: Making a holy show of me.

CISSY: It was your idea to come here. You're hurting me.

FRANK: Don't get sassy with me young lady. You're in no position to give cheek. Out. Get out.

CISSY: I'm going. I'm going.

FRANK: Ashamed of ye so I am. Bloody ashamed.

Church door slams closed. Murmurs.

JOSEPH: Brigid, Is that young Cissy?

BRIGID: It is, Joseph. I wonder what's wrong.

JOSEPH: I think we can guess what's wrong.

Cuts to

REILLY: BeGod – Cissy is looking fairly well fed.

LIZZIE: I think she's been eating for two!

Father Dempsey doesn't know what to do as the whispering continues.

FATHER DEMPSEY: Now, the Cardinal goes on to say…eh…where was I…I'll just…

POOR BRID: The poor girl. Ruined so she is. And she so small I'd say the birth might kill her altogether. You can be split in two with the force of a giant baby.

ANNE: Brazen little tramp. These women – all the same.

FATHER DEMPSEY: Ah yes – 'Meantime, let us place ourselves and our interests in the hands of God…'

ANNE: Taking advantage of good men.

FATHER DEMPSEY: '…and continue to beseech Him in public and in private to grant us the blessings of a just and lasting peace.'

ANNE: Lying…

FATHER DEMPSEY: That's it.

ANNE: Cheating…stealing the good name of a person.

POOR BRID: You're talking very loud there, Mrs. Kilbride.

FATHER DEMPSEY: I'll .. em look forward to chatting to you all on the way out. Peace be with you.

CROWD: And also with you.

Latin music starts up. Choir singing. Footsteps as people shuffle out.

POOR BRID: Are you all right there, Mrs. Kilbride?

ANNE: I'm grand. Father Dempsey. Please allow me the honour of being the first parishioner to donate to the White Cross Association.

FATHER DEMPSEY: How very generous of you, Mrs. Kilbride.

ANNE: Oh it's nothing Father. We all have to do our bit for the poor unfortunates. Do you think ten shillings would be an appropriate amount?

She takes out a ten shilling note and waves it around for everyone to see.

FATHER DEMPSEY: I'm sure the Cardinal would be very grateful Mrs. Kilbride – as he will be for any donation of any size.

POOR BRID: It's not the size of the collection that matters, it's the weight of the coin! Isn't that what you always say Father?

FATHER DEMPSEY: Well…I don't know if that's exactly what I say.

POOR BRID: Mrs. O'Donoghue, she says that it is. She says -

FATHER DEMPSEY: Ahem …just say goodbye to the people who are leaving. See you down there!

POOR BRID: What's his hurry…

Scene 3 - Outside Church.

FATHER DEMPSEY: Hello there – Joe O'Reilly, isn't it. Peace be with you.

O'REILLY: And you, Father. That was a very interesting statement from the Cardinal.

FATHER DEMPSEY: The Church has always supported the oppressed Mr. O'Reilly.

O'REILLY: Is that so? Good to have it on our side then.

FATHER DEMPSEY: I thought the King's speech in Belfast was also very positive.

O'REILLY: Ach. Just words Father. Meaningless. I wouldn't believe any of it.

FATHER DEMPSEY: That IRA statement was a little concerning though.

O'REILLY: What one was that Father?

FATHER DEMPSEY: The one where they said that they would destroy all the homes of I think what they called their 'active enemies'?

LIZZIE: That's right Father. For every house that the British destroy, another one in the same area is going to be destroyed by the IRA. It was in the paper.

FATHER DEMPSEY: That's not the way to peace, Miss O'Neill.

O'REILLY: And you think The Government of Ireland Act is?

FATHER DEMPSEY: Of course not. However…I'd be very unhappy if this IRA strategy was implemented in Maynooth.

O'REILLY: Nothing to do with me Father. I don't know anything about that. Ah here's the man! How are ya, Tomas.

TOMAS: Father. O'Reilly, Miss O'Neill.

FATHER DEMPSEY: Hello Tomas. I didn't see Mary with you this morning?

TOMAS: No – she's a bit under the weather.

FATHER DEMPSEY: I'm sorry to hear that.

O'REILLY: I hope it's not the same complaint that Cissy has!

He laughs loudly at his own joke.. There is an awkward pause.

TOMAS: Moll wasn't feeling too good either, so Mary stayed home to look after her.

FATHER DEMPSEY: Moll's been poorly for a while now.

TOMAS: She had a bad dose last year, and I think she's just a bit weakened from it. She'll be fine. How about you Father?

FATHER DEMPSEY: Me?

TOMAS: I hear you almost got caught up in that raid last week.

FATHER DEMPSEY: On the Kilcock Road – that's right. The poor man was very shaken. Three armed men stopped him and took almost three hundred pounds.

LIZZIE: If anyone gives any large donations to the White Cross Association, you know where it's coming from!

TOMAS: Auntie Anne!

O'REILLY/LIZZIE: Mrs. Kilbride!

O'REILLY: I can just see her in her black mask.

TOMAS: (*Posing as Anne with a gun*) Stand and deliver!

All laugh.

FATHER DEMPSEY: Stop would you. It's no laughing matter. Three hundred pounds stolen. They should be strung up.

O'REILLY: Oh, I don't know. Probably taken for a good cause.

FATHER DEMPSEY: They still should be ashamed of themselves .

LIZZIE: Are ye walking down towards the river, Tomas?

TOMAS: I might be.

LIZZIE: I might go with ye so.

TOMAS: Might ye now?

LIZZIE: If you're lucky.

TOMAS: Come on then so. See ye Father.

Footsteps as they leave. O'Reilly takes a pound note from his pocket.

O'REILLY: Here, father. A pound for the White Cross Association. (*Beat*) Don't bother thanking me.

Footsteps as he walks away. Footsteps approach.

FRANK: Can I have a word Father?

FATHER DEMPSEY: (*Distracted*) Sorry…Of course Frank. Hello, Cissy.

CISSY: (*Hangs her head*) Father.

FATHER DEMPSEY: Would you like to come into the parochial house? It might be a bit more private.

FRANK: This won't take long. You can see the situation she's in.

FATHER DEMPSEY: I can.

FRANK: Her mother is devastated. *(His voice breaks)* The shame. We didn't even know until two weeks ago. Walking around town like a tramp all this time. Can you help us? Please Father?

CISSY: I don't need help.

FRANK: There's places I know where they take women like this. Fallen women.

CISSY: I'm not going to one of those places.

FRANK: You'll go where I and the Father tell you.

CISSY: Sarah Maguire was sent to one of those places two years ago and she never came back.

FRANK: How could she come back, and she in disgrace?

CISSY: Please let me stay. I'll work hard, pay my own way. The baby'll be no trouble.

FRANK: Who'll have you?

CISSY: I'll do all the looking after.

FRANK: Nobody'll have you.

CISSY: You and Mammy?

FRANK: We won't be able to lift our heads in this place. You're going.

CISSY: *(Crying)* Daddy. Please. Don't do this.

FRANK: Father?

FATHER DEMPSEY: Frank – maybe we should think about this.

FRANK: We've made up our minds.

CISSY: I'll be good, I swear. I'll keep the house, do all the work. Please Daddy. I know Mammy doesn't want this.

FRANK: Let go my hand. Get off. *(He pushes her off. She cries out)* Don't you dare tell me what your mother wants – you've destroyed your mother – destroyed her! And she crying night and day.. *(His voice breaks)* Are there papers to sign Father?

Pause, as Father Dempsey assesses the situation. He sighs.

FATHER DEMPSEY: I have some in the house.

FRANK: *(Hands Cissy the carpet bag)* Hold that suitcase and stay there.

Footsteps as the men walk away. Cissy cries. Footsteps approach.

BRIGID: Are ye alright love? *(She falls, crying, into Brigid's arms, desperate)* There, there, now love.

ANNE: Oh for goodness sake!

CISSY: Mrs. Barry, Mrs. Kilbride, they're sending me away. I don't want to go. I don't want to go to one of those places.

BRIGID: Oh love.

ANNE: What did you expect?

CISSY: Please Mrs. Barry. Will you talk to him?

ANNE: Charlatan!

CISSY: Tell him it's a mistake. Tell him to let me stay. Those places are horrible. I can't go there. I just can't.

ANNE: Good enough for you.

BRIGID: Anne!

ANNE: The girl's nothing but a tramp.

JOSEPH: Ah now Anne...

ANNE: Cajoling some respectable man no doubt. Trying to nab herself a rich husband. Well it didn't work out so well for you did it, Cissy?

CISSY: I was not. I -

BRIGID: Anne that's enough!

ANNE: It's on the street you should be.

CISSY: On the street is it?

BRIGID: Now Cissy...

ANNE: That's right.

CISSY: And my innocent child?

ANNE: That child is no more innocent than you are. The product of a sinful, sordid, illicit relationship.

JOSEPH: We really should get going.

CISSY: And the man in this relationship. Is he sinful and sordid too?

JOSEPH: We have to open the pub in half an hour.

ANNE: You trapped him. Enticed him and trapped him. Told him a pack of lies no doubt.

CISSY: He told me a pack of lies!

ANNE: Encouraged him.

CISSY: He said he'd look after me. He said he'd support me. He said he loved me.

ANNE: Love? What would someone like you know about love.

CISSY: And then he left me!

ANNE: What did you expect? I've never met this fellow but he sounds like a very sensible chap indeed.

CISSY: Oh you've met him.

BRIGID: Now Cissy…

CISSY: In fact, I'd say you know him extremely well.

Maggie and Teresa, holding flowers exit the church and witness the next scene.

ANNE: How dare you.

JOSEPH: Let's all calm down. Here's Teresa coming over now. Didn't she do well with the flowers in –

CISSY: Was it living with you that turned him into a lying bastard, Mrs. Kilbride?

JOSEPH: Aw now -

ANNE: My husband wouldn't touch a dirty tramp the like of you.

CISSY: Your husband?

ANNE: And he never laid a finger on that other harlot Sarah Maguire either! She lied! Lied about it all. Every bit of it. That baby was never his and neither is this one.

CISSY: Sarah Maguire? Sarah that was sent away?

ANNE: She got what was coming to her – for all her tears and her pathetic wailing. And so will you, ye dirty little bitch!

CISSY: I wouldn't touch your husband with a twenty foot pole. It was your precious son did this to me. Donnacha.

There is a startled silence.

ANNE: Liar!

CISSY: Have you heard from him recently?

ANNE: He's busy.

CISSY: Oh that's right. He's studying law isn't he? In UCD?

ANNE: He wouldn't go near…

CISSY: Only he wasn't doing much studying that last time I saw him.

ANNE: He has a career.

CISSY: Failing his Christmas exams didn't help.

ANNE: A future.

CISSY: Didn't bother going in after that.

ANNE: His whole life ahead of him.

CISSY: He's a dropout, Mrs. Kilbride!

ANNE: He wouldn't waste all that on you.

CISSY: Oh, he promised to get a job. He was going to support me. Support us. We were going to go to London.

ANNE: A tramp.

CISSY: But he's gone. I went up to Dublin last week and he was gone. Do ye think he's gone to London without me? Where is he Mrs. Kilbride? Where is he? Where's Donnacha? Tell me where Donnacha is!

ANNE: *(Shouts)* Let me go! You're a liar. You're a liar. You're all liars! Every one of you. Liars. Liars. Liars!

CISSY: I'm no Sarah Maguire! Ye can't get rid of me that easy. I'm going nowhere. Where is he? Tell me!

Scuffle. Both women shouting.

JOSEPH: Take Cissy there, Brigid. *(He breaks the two women apart)* I'll look after my sister. Come on now, Anne, Time to go home. Come on now Anne. There's a good girl.

Footsteps as he leads her off.

BRIGID: Cissy, love, come on now.

ANNE: It's all lies. My Donnacha. He's in UCD. Studying Law. Lies.

CISSY: *(shouting after her)* I'm no Sarah Maguire! I'm going nowhere! I'm having this baby and I know exactly what I'm going to do with it! *(She sees people staring)* What are you all staring at? Am I entertaining you?

BRIGID: Come on now, love. No one is staring.

TERESA: That's not true. Everyone was. I was myself. Here. Flowers left over from the alter.

CISSY: What am I supposed to do with them, Teresa?

TERESA: Flowers make you feel better, it's not quite a scientific fact but it is documented.

CISSY: Oh

TERESA: Do you feel better?

CISSY: Not really.

TERESA: Okay then. I'll have them back. *(She takes flowers back)* It works for most people. *(Pause)* I assume you are in your third trimester?

CISSY: What?

TERESA: The child. It will be arriving soon.

CISSY: I suppose.

TERESA: There is a 4.4% infant mortality rate in this country. That means a lot of children die.

CISSY: Right.

TERESA: You should have a vaginal delivery if at all possible. Caesarean sections are problematic.

BRIGID: Teresa...

TERESA: And avoid taking Twilight Sleep. A new study has shown that it can increase the risk of haemorrhage.

CISSY: I don't think that's an option where I'm going.

TERESA: You're going then.

CISSY: I don't want to.

TERESA: I never do anything I don't want to. Some people do. I don't know why.

CISSY: I've nowhere else to go. *(Footsteps as Father Dempsey and Frank approach)* They're back. Oh no....

FRANK: The papers are signed. The Father will bring you. I wash my hands of you.

CISSY: Daddy. Please..

FRANK: Now!

He grabs her. She screams. Sound of her being dragged off.

CISSY: *(Fading)* I don't want to go! I don't want to go!

END OF EPISODE

EPISODE 27 – STACUMNY AMBUSH, JULY 1921

Scene 1 - Barry's pub

MULLANEY: GHQ have promised us enough gelignite to send the bloody train to mars. They're giving us ammunition and we'll have a lot of local help.

FARRELL: Grand. I'll get John, the brother, to block the roads in and out.

TOMAS: But there's a ceasefire coming.

MULLANEY: Your point being?

TOMAS: Why are we wasting our bullets? And we still haven't identified the informer. We'll need a lot of help and it's a bad plan anyway and -

MULLANEY: A bad plan? This order came from Mick Collins. Are you in or out?

TOMAS: In, I suppose. But -

MULLANEY: That's it, boys. See ye on the fifth.

General excitement.

VOICEOVER: Fractured, July 1921. A Few Days Before The Ceasefire.

Scene 2 - The side of Stacumny rail bridge. Afternoon.

FARRELL: All right boys, take up positions along here, do not be seen and - *(Running footsteps)* About time! *(Sees it's not Tomas)* Sorry, I thought you were Tomas. Is he not with you?

RYAN: *(Irritatingly eager)* I have no idea who Tomas is, Sir.

FARRELL: Never mind. You are?

RYAN: Proinsias Ryan, reporting for duty, Sir. What's happening?

FARRELL: No one briefed you?

RYAN: It was all hush, hush, Sir. They said you'd fill me in.

FARRELL: Right. We're at Stacumny bridge.

RYAN: Oh yes, I know it well. A grand bridge.

FARRELL: *(Impatience)* Indeed. Anyway, the Celbridge-Lucan road is back that way *(Points),* and in the other direction you have Ardclough *(Doubts himself)* or Newcastle, I think…Anyway, we need everyone we can get for this operation, which is big, so that's why you're here.

RYAN: And I'm delighted to be here, Sir. It's an honour. And may I say -

FARRELL: *(Snapping)* If you'll just stop…and let me speak.

RYAN: Absolutely. Sorry, Sir.

FARRELL: *(Heaving a sigh)* Now, I can't give you all the details – I don't know them myself – but let's just say that there's a train coming from Dublin soon with over a thousand troops newly arrived from England, and eh… this is their…last stop. *(Smiling)* Kaboom!

RYAN: Kaboom! Got you. Wow.

FARRELL: Now remember, if another train comes along while we're getting ready, you hide.

RYAN: I will. Where do you want me, Sir?

FARRELL: Go up on the bridge there. Keep out of sight. This is our only chance at this.

RYAN: Grand, Sir. I'll get on up.

Running footsteps as he leaves.

FARRELL: The rest of you boys, stay hidden in there for Christ's sake. *(Tomas comes running up)* Tomas! Where the hell were you?

TOMAS: *(Panting)* I know, I know! I'm here now, amn't I? Who was that boy I just passed? And the lads back there in the bushes. Who are they?

FARRELL: We need all the help we can get, right? You said so yourself.

TOMAS: I know. It's a big operation, but… *(Quietly to Farrell)* Who are they? Can you trust them?

FARRELL: They'll be fine. I'll take care of them.

TOMAS: Tom, there's an informer around here somewhere. You know that. What if…?

FARRELL: I know. And despite all your ideas we still haven't found him.

TOMAS: It's not my fault. I planted false information everywhere. Anyway, what's happening here? Are we nearly ready?

FARRELL: I think so…

TOMAS: We're running out of time, Tom.

FARRELL: Well, where were you till now? You were supposed to be here ages ago.

TOMAS: I couldn't get away from the pub.

FARRELL: *(Teasing)* Did Mammy not let you out to play?

TOMAS: *(Scowls back)* I was running the place on my own. I had to wait for Da- my father to come back to take over from me. I can't just leave.

FARRELL: Alright, take it easy. Mullaney said to wait here till he gets back. There's... been a bit of hitch.

TOMAS: What sort of hitch?

FARRELL: We don't have enough explosive for all the mines.

TOMAS: What? How much are we short?

FARRELL: I don't know. Mullaney wouldn't say. He's gone down to the tracks to try and figure it out. He's not happy.

TOMAS: Who's the engineer?

FARRELL: Cullen.

TOMAS: Well, where is he? I thought he requisitioned enough to blow up the entire Great Southern & Western Railway if he wanted to?

FARRELL: He did, but it hasn't come through.

TOMAS: But that was ordered ages ago.

FARRELL: It was.

TOMAS: From GHQ.

FARRELL: Yes.

TOMAS: So where is it?

FARRELL: How the hell am I supposed to know? Don't blame me. Talk to Cullen about it if you want.

TOMAS: Well, where is he?

FARRELL: Where do you think he is? He's out laying the mines under the tracks with Mullaney.

TOMAS: I'll speak to him.

FARRELL: Look, I know you got promoted recently, but you don't have to go around trying to fix everything.

TOMAS: I'm not. I'm just - I don't think this operation is a great idea.

FARRELL: And you already told us that.

TOMAS: Why try to kill people who'll be leaving the country anyway?

FARRELL: O'Reilly's right what he says. You have gone chicken.

TOMAS: O'Reilly talks a lot of nonsense. I don't believe in wasting bullets is all. Especially on bad plans. Where's Cullen?

FARRELL: Jesus, Tomas, are you deaf? Cullen's the lead engineer here, he's got 20 minutes tops, and he's out there trying to do the miracle of the loaves and fishes.

TOMAS: I can't just stand here and -

FARRELL: You might be a smart lad Tomas, but you don't understand what it takes to be a good soldier yet. You're given your orders and you carry them out. That's how these big operations work. We all have a job to do, right? Don't forget that.

TOMAS: I won't. Like you said, I'm smart.

FARRELL: Haven't you come out of your shell since Sean left, ey? I'm not sure I like it. *(Footsteps)* Aw, here's Mullaney, now.

Footsteps crossing to Tomas.

MULLANEY: Tomas! Where the hell were you?

TOMAS: Sorry sir, I got delayed.

MULLANEY: I needed you an hour ago. Could have done with you helping Cullen out on the tracks.

TOMAS: I know. Sorry.

MULLANEY: Have you got a rifle?

TOMAS: Eh… no. I didn't think -

MULLANEY: Jesus. We don't have one for you. And all the extra rifles and revolvers we got are already given out.

TOMAS: There's a shortage of rifles?

MULLANEY: We were told we'd have them, to pick them up with all the explosives and batteries last night in Dunboyne. And did we get them? No.

TOMAS: Sir, I have a bad feeling about all this. I -

MULLANEY: Really? That is insightful. Is it because we only have an eighth of the gelignite we need? Because we've no guns? I told them, we're not playing games here, for Christ's sake.

TOMAS: What happened the rest of it?

MULLANEY: That's all they had, apparently! *(Imitates person from HQ)* "Sorry, that's all we can afford to give you. Still, you can't back out of it now. Do the best with what you have."

TOMAS: Jesus…sir – I think we should -

MULLANEY: We were up all night trying to figure out how to make it work with less explosive. I'm not even sure if it will… *(Slumps down)* We're all exhausted. We even had to commandeer a car this morning to get the battery from it. There's about 25 civilians held in the farmhouse back there, including the postman…

FARRELL: *(Holds up a bag, grinning)* Minus his sack of post.

They laugh a little, strained.

TOMAS: Is there anything gone right?

MULLANEY: We do have a lad from Dublin, McGuinness, who has one of those Thompson machine guns. That's some weapon, I tell ya. Firing off rounds, one after the other… You'd run from that alright!

Laughter again.

TOMAS: What do you need me to do?

MULLANEY: Keep a lookout with Farrell in case any soldiers get out unhurt and come this way. If they do, take Farrell's rifle – you're a better shot than he is.

FARRELL: Ah here!

TOMAS: I'm not sure that -

MULLANEY: I am. Just follow your orders Tomas. Do what you did back in Maynooth in February.

TOMAS: *(Not happy)* I'm a bit out of practise and -

MULLANEY: You'll still be better than Farrell.

Farrell Protests. Two toots of a whistle sounds.

MULLANEY: That's the signal, boys. We've got about four or five minutes. Whatever happens, don't get distracted by the explosion. Keep your concentration so we can catch any stragglers off guard. Good luck lads!

A shuffling as men get into position.

FARRELL: Right so. Everyone get ready. *(Silence. The faint rumbling of a truck)* That doesn't sound like a train. *(The rumbling grows louder)* Jesus! What the hell is that?

And louder. And stops. English voices on the air.

TOMAS: It's a lorry of Tans. How did –

MULLANEY: Jesus, fall back! Fall back!

FARRELL: Where did those Tans come from?

MULLANEY: I've no idea. But you better start shooting.

TOMAS: Are you sure that's wise, Sir? They might not know we're here. *(A shot goes off)* Jesus, they know now.

The rifle shots increase in intensity.

MULLANEY: Hold the fort here. I'll see if I can get closer.

Mullaney runs off.

TOMAS: *(To Farrell)* Here's one of our boys coming right at us. Cover him for Christ's sake! *(Farrell struggles with the gun)* Cover him!

FARRELL: My aim's no good. Here, you take it.

He attempts to pass the gun to Tomas

TOMAS: I..I don't -

A shout of pain in distance. The man running towards them has been shot.

FARRELL: Damn it, he's been shot. He's a sitting duck for those Tans.

TOMAS: Cover me, Farrell. NOW. I'm going to go out there and help him.

FARRELL: But Mullaney said – *(Running)* Tomas! Get back.

We follow Tomas as he runs across the no man's land. He slides to a halt. It's Ryan, the soldier from earlier. He's in pain.

TOMAS: Can you stand?

RYAN: I don't think so, I've been shot in the leg.

TOMAS: Lean on me, there's a good lad. *(He lifts the man up. Ryan groans)* Now, quick as you can bear, let's get you back. *(Ryan yelps in pain. Shooting. Gunfire)* Almost there.

FARRELL: *(Calling, faint)* Hurry up, Tomas. There's too many of them.

A round of machine gun fire rings out.

TOMAS: Good man McGuinness! That Thompson is a great yoke! *(Ryan laughs a little)* Keep pushing, nearly there. Farrell, help me get this boy down.

Sounds of Ryan being helped. He yelps again.

FARRELL: Are you shot, son?

RYAN: I got one in the leg.

FARRELL: We need to get someone to look after him. Tomas, the woman you recruited, Teresa, she knows how to treat gunshot wounds, right?

TOMAS: Yes, but…

FARRELL: But what?

TOMAS: She's not… fully recruited yet…

FARRELL: For Christ's sake! What have you been doing, twiddling your thumbs all this time?

TOMAS: She's just… you don't know her, she's hard to pin down is all. I'll get on to her again…

RYAN: I think I need a doctor.

TOMAS: I'll bandage you for now. It'll help with the bleeding. *(Footsteps. Mullaney arrives)* Mullaney, how's it going over there?

MULLANEY: We can't keep this up. We have to retreat.

FARRELL: But we nearly have the soldiers at the top of the bridge. I might have got one of them.

MULLANEY: *(Resigned)* It's useless. Feckin' HQ and their stupid plans! I told them we couldn't do it without more supplies!

RYAN: Sorry, sir.

MULLANEY: What are you sorry for? Is it your fault?

RYAN: Well…no sir.

MULLANEY: Then shut up. Aw feck it anyway, I better let them know to get out of here.

Mullaney lets out three whistles which is passed on in distance.

MULLANEY: Where the hell did those Tans come from anyway? This was our chance, to do something big in Kildare! And now, we have to abandon it. Damn it to hell!

TOMAS: It's almost as if they wanted it to fail.

MULLANEY: What?

TOMAS: I'm not saying anything exactly, it's just… well, I thought the odds were against us from the start.

MULLANEY: Hmmm. Well, I have to go back out there. Try and get the men away through the farm to the side there. Cover me if those bastards start firing.

Scrabbling as Mullaney runs off.

TOMAS: Right, up you get Ryan. We better get out of – *(Sound of a bike. Lizzie appears, having come over the bridge)* Lizzie!

LIZZIE: Tomas, what are you doing here?

TOMAS: I was on observation this side of the bridge. You… came over the bridge. Where the soldiers are.

LIZZIE: Yeah. I know.

TOMAS: How did you get through?

LIZZIE: I just sneaked around the back.

TOMAS: *(Confused)* Around the -?

LIZZIE: *(Looking at the injured man)* What happened him? Is he shot?

FARRELL: Yes, we need to get him out of here. We've stopped the bleeding for now.

LIZZIE: Number Three house is nearby. I know where it is from here. We can bring him there and bring the doctor over to him.

FARRELL: Good idea.

LIZZIE: It's across the fields though so it's a bit of a haul.

FARRELL: I'll give you a hand.

TOMAS: Or maybe I could...?

Running steps as Mullaney arrives back, panting.

MULLANEY: What are ye still doing here?

FARRELL: We're just going, sir. I'm helping Lizzie bring this fella to one of the houses.

MULLANEY: Lizzie, you were to stay back in case we needed you.

LIZZIE: Well, it looks like you need me here, doesn't it! Don't worry, I'll take care of him.

She lifts a groaning Ryan to his feet.

MULLANEY: *(To Lizzie)* Before you go, there's another man after falling down the embankment trying to get away. I think his leg is broken.

LIZZIE: Get the men to bring him to Number Three house. That's where we're going now.

FARRELL: I know two women with us in Lucan with a horse and trap. I'll get them to bring the doctor and then they can take them home as well.

MULLANEY: Good stuff. *(Smiling)* Who had the great idea to get more women involved, and yet still hasn't recruited one himself?

TOMAS: I will recruit her, sir...

MULLANEY: This day isn't over yet, Tomas. I just had an idea... We're not going home with nothing. McGuinness is still with us, and has a full cartridge for his Thompson... I'm going to gather all the ammunition we've left, get about seven or eight men, and attack the barracks in Lucan tonight. I'm going to salvage something out of this day, God damn it! I'll be in touch with you, Tomas. Go on home now.

TOMAS: I might... catch up with Farrell and Lizzie, see if they need a hand. And make sure that lad's alright, of course...

MULLANEY: Of course, Tomas. Just be ready when I call you.

He runs off.

TOMAS: Damn. *(Beginning to run, calling and voice fading out)* Lizzie, wait for me. Wait for me.

END OF EPISODE

EPISODE 28 – TRUCE CELEBRATION, JULY 1921

Scene 1 – Outside

ANNOUNCER: In view of the conversations now being entered into by our government with the government of Great Britain, and in pursuance of mutual conversations, active operations by our forces will be suspended as from noon, Monday, 11 July.

Cheering

VOICEOVER: Fractured – July 1921 – a ceasefire was called, bonfires were lit and all over Ireland, people celebrated.

Scene 2 - Barry's pub

All the following scenes take place at various locations inside the pub. The excited sounds of people chatting and drinking and celebrating. As Con starts to speak, a certain amount of 'shushing' can be heard.

CON: Hello everyone, for those that don't know me, I'm Con O'Sullivan. I'll be your MC for this afternoon. On behalf of Joseph and Brigid Barry, I'd like to thank you all for coming along to celebrate the signing of the truce last Monday. *(Cheering etc)* We are delighted to have Domhnall UaBuachalla here who will say a few words on this momentous occasion.

Cheering

UABUACHALLA: Dia Dhuit go leir agus -

CON: I know I can speak for all here when I say that this truce gives us hope and the prospect of putting hundreds of years of history behind us and facing the future as a united Irish republic.

Cheering

UABUACHALLA: I have only a short -

CON: Just a minute Domhnall. *(To audience)* The simple pleasures of being able to go about your business without fear. Being able to enjoy these bright summer evenings without worrying about the curfew. I myself

UaBuachalla interrupts him.

UABUACHALLA: I can't stay too long so if you don't mind …

CON: Of course Domhnall. It's just that …

UABUACHALLA: I'll be going soon. *(Beat. Con reluctantly gives the stage to UaBuachalla)* Go raibh maith agat Con agus gabhaim buíochas le Conradhna Gaeilge as an ócáid seo a eagrú. Thank you Con and well done to the Gaelic League for organising this event for what is indeed a momentous occasion. Unfortunately, I will not be able to stay long with you today as I have been summoned to a meeting in Dublin but I've no doubt that you'll manage without me.

PADDY: Stand a round of drinks Domhnall. That'll soften our disappointment.

Laughter

UABUACHALLA: Now Paddy, I wouldn't want to be encouraging the consumption of alcohol so early in the day. *(Laughter)* If I can just be serious for a moment. I had a meeting with all the other TDs during the week and Mr. De Valera is keen the Irish people understand that the upcoming negotiations with the English government will be of worldwide interest. These negotiations are only the starting point of the journey and our representatives will do their best to secure a just and peaceful end to our struggle. *(Cheering)* It will be a long journey and while I have no wish to take away from today's celebrations, De Valera does issue a warning against having undue confidence of a successful outcome.

TERESA: Does that mean that the negotiations have fallen down already?

UABUACHALLA: Of course not.

TERESA: If the man leading the talks feels that way, it certainly doesn't give me any confidence, undue or otherwise.

UABUACHALLA: This is a complicated situation and no one can predict what will happen. And if, God forbid, these discussions fail, we must be ready to resume our struggle.

BRIGID: Some of our boys are still struggling. When will my son be released from that prison camp?

CON: Aw now, this is a celebration and not the time to be going into this sort of stuff.

UABUACHALLA: We did try and have that as part of the truce.

MARY: You mustn't have tried very hard.

CON: Ah now, Mary.

UABUACHALLA: The British wouldn't budge. They will be reviewing the situation throughout the negotiations.

CON: Right, we'll carry on …

BRIGID: You had no trouble "securing the release" of the volunteer leaders. I wonder how the men still locked up will feel about that. One rule for the leaders and another rule for them!

General murmurs of agreement. Con steps in.

CON: Come on people. We're here for a party.

UABUACHALLA: We just need to have patience. If we succeed in these negotiations, we'll see an Ireland like we never dreamed of.

Con steps in. Closing down discussion.

CON: Thank you for coming along, Domhnall.

UABUACHALLA: Na bac leis Con. Slan. *(The audience respond with goodbyes etc. He makes his way out stopping at Brigid)* And Brigid, I'll make a few enquiries about Sean. Bye now.

BRIGID: *(To his disappearing back)* Not just Sean! All of those poor boys.

We hear the door open and close under the chatter.

CON: I think we've all forgotten why we're here. I'll ask the boys to give us a few more tunes. Off ye go!

His voice fades out, music. Backdrop of music as the following scenes take place. Chatter underpins all these exchanges.

Scene 3

Mary and Brigid are working behind the bar.

BRIGID: Trying to make out we're all happy when some of us are missing our precious sons. It's a sham, Mary.

Beat, Mary plunges in.

MARY: Cissy had a baby girl there last week, Mammy.

BRIGID: I heard. I was talking to her mother. God love her, she's distraught. Orange juice on the top shelves Mary.

Bottles clink

MARY: Cissy knows her mother would have her back but her father won't allow it.

BRIGID: That's about the size of it.

MARY: I was wondering if Auntie Anne might like to know.

BRIGID: Your Auntie Anne would rather hear that she has lost every penny she has. On the top shelf, Mary. Are you here at all today?

Clinking of bottles.

MARY: Cissy hates it in Dublin. And now that she has the baby she just wants to come home and -

BRIGID: Your Auntie Anne will not take her in. You can forget about that.

MARY: But maybe when she sees that baby -

BRIGID: She doesn't want to see the baby.

MARY: But maybe -

BRIGID: Maybe nothing.

MARY: I think Auntie Anne is horrible, carrying on like that. We all know -

BRIGID: I won't have that, Mary. Your Auntie Anne is…she's not horrible or terrible. She's just unhappy. And seeing that baby will be a constant reminder that she has placed her faith in the wrong people and she'll have nothing left to cling to. Can you understand that?

MARY: She'll have Cissy and a lovely grandchild to cling to. Would you not take her in, Mammy?

BRIGID: No. Anne is Joseph's sister and there'd be hell to pay.

MARY: When have you ever been scared of creating trouble?

BRIGID: This subject is closed, Mary. I have enough to worry about between your father's drinking - look at him over there – not to mention Sean's imprisonment, Moll being sick again, you not being yourself and Tomas fraternising with all sorts of shady people – that Mullanney fella was in this morning already. I do not need the extra trouble of Cissy and her baby on my head. Now, finish that up, I'm going to check on Moll. That's where my concern lies.

Footsteps fading as she walks off. Mary gives an exasperated sigh.

MARY: *(Mutter)* And my concern lies with Cissy. And I promised I'd -

POOR BRID: Hello Mary. *(Mary jumps, startles, bottles rattle)* I don't mean to frighten you.

MARY: It's fine, Mrs. O'Sullivan. Are you looking for Mammy?

POOR BRID: I am.

MARY: Upstairs with Moll. You'd want to watch yourself with her.

POOR BRID: Did something happen?

MARY: Don't mind me. Go on up to her. Hello Colm. *(Beat)* Is he still not talking?

POOR BRID: No *(Upset, whisper)* but sure we have to keep hoping. Stay strong. Gods knows what horrors the poor little chap has seen.

MARY: He's lucky he has you and Con now.

POOR BRID: You said it, Mary. Every little kiddie needs a good family. Anyway, I'll run up to Brigid, I'll only be a minute. Con will be looking for me soon for his play.

MARY: We're all looking forward to that.

POOR BRID: It's very good, so it is. I've got the best part.

MARY: *(Teasing)* Is that because you're married to the director?

POOR BRID: *(Missing the joke)* No, it's because I'm the best. Teresa is terrible. Come on, Colm. *(Fading)* Come on pet. Come on. Good boy.

A rapping on the counter.

TOMAS: Give me a pint there, Mary, will you? And a lemonade.

MARY: Don't rap at me. You're supposed to be giving me a hand.

TOMAS: And I will in a minute. I'm just buying a drink for Lizzie, is all.

MARY: And who's paying?

TOMAS: Take it out of my wages. *(Mary lays drinks in front of him)* Thanks.

We follow him through the pub.

TOMAS: Hello, Mrs. O'Donoghue, yes a great day. Hello, Paddy. Con, you're doing a great job. *(Sound of him placing drinks on the table)* For the lady. Is there anyone sitting in this chair?

LIZZIE: Not unless they're invisible. *(Tomas is not sure what to do next)* Do you want to sit down Tomas?

TOMAS: Yes. I bought you a lemonade.

LIZZIE: Nothing stronger?

TOMAS: I didn't think…well…I didn't expect to see you here. I don't know what you drink.

LIZZIE: And why wouldn't I be here?

TOMAS: It's just that … I don't know … I was hoping …

LIZZIE: I couldn't pass up the chance to sit in a pub with all these men and see what us women are missing out on. Sit will you.

Scraping of a chair.

TOMAS: What do you think so far?

LIZZIE: We're not missing much.

TOMAS: *(Laughing)* You're not wrong there.

LIZZIE: I might try a pint though.

TOMAS: You will not!

LIZZIE: Now, Tomas Barry, are you telling me what I can or cannot do?

TOMAS: I wouldn't dream of doing that. I'd sooner go up against a squad of Tans.

LIZZIE: You'd have a better chance of winning against them. *(They laugh)* Aw, sure, I'll make do with the lemonade so. *(Drinks)* I heard your mother having a go at UaBuachalla. Is there no word on when Sean and the others are coming home?

TOMAS: We just had a letter last week. Nothing. And Mullaney was here this morning. Training and recruiting of men and women is ongoing, he says. So much for a ceasefire.

LIZZIE: Ah, that's just Mullaney. Sean'll be out before you know it. Sure, he's probably planning his escape already.

TOMAS: Aye and if he is, he'd hardly write home about it.

They share a laugh

LIZZIE: True enough.

TOMAS: Will you be happy to see Sean back?

LIZZIE: I'll be happy to see them all free.

TOMAS: But especially Sean? I heard that you and him were … ye know.

LIZZIE: Did he tell you that?

TOMAS: No, but …

LIZZIE: Your brother has a high opinion of himself.

TOMAS: Don't I know that only too well.

(Both laugh)

LIZZIE: I'm waiting for the right man. *(She smiles at Tomas)* Who might that be, I wonder? *(Tomas doesn't respond)* Do you want a clue?

TOMAS: All right

LIZZIE: He's an awful fecking slow eejit.

TOMAS: I am not!

LIZZIE: Did I say it was you?

TOMAS: No, but…well…look, the weather is nice at the moment … you might like to go for a walk some evening.

LIZZIE: *(Not making it easy)* Who with?

TOMAS: Me, I suppose.

LIZZIE: Tomorrow evening?

TOMAS: That'd be grand.

TOMAS: Right you be.

They clink glasses.

Scene 4

The sound of a glass being struck with a fork. The noise dies down a little.

CON: I have a very special act for you all now. It's been many a year since there was any drama put on in Maynooth but that will soon be remedied. *(Looking around)* I seem to have lost one of the cast. Has anyone seen Brid?

BRID: Here, I'm here. Colm stay with Mary there. *(Sound of running footsteps up the room)* Excuse me, excuse me, I have to get up onstage. Here I am, Con. Oh, Mrs. O'Donoghue, do you know what I heard last week? I heard -

CON: Brid! Will you and Teresa take your positions.

BRID: I will, Sorry.

CON: Mary, you said you'd keep an eye on the lines … if you wouldn't mind.

He gives Mary a copy of the script.

MARY: Of course.

CON: Picture the scene, everyone. It is just before dawn. The sun is beginning to make an appearance in the east and the birds are starting their morning song.

Con makes bird sounds to create the atmosphere. Teresa coughs impatiently.

CON: Let the play begin..

POOR BRID: *(Highly dramatic)* "I am thinking we are come to our journey's end, and that this should be the gate of the gaol"

TERESA: *(Like a machine gun)* "It is certain it could be no other place. There was surely never in the world such a terrible great height of a wall"

POOR BRID: *(Highly dramatic)* "He that was used to the mountain to be closed up inside of that! What call had he to go moonlighting or to bring himself into danger at all?"

TERESA: *(To Con)* Is she going to do it like that?

CON: Like what?

TERESA: Nobody speaks like that.

POOR BRID: I'm just saying the lines as they're written.

CON: The play is set in Galway Teresa. Maybe they speak like that over there. Carry on and maybe Brid, not so dramatic.

POOR BRID: I thought I was very good.

TERESA: *(Rapid delivery)* "It is no wonder a man to grow faint-hearted and he shut away from the light. I never would wonder at all at anything he might be driven to say"

POOR BRID: *(Copying Teresa now)* "There were good men were gaoled before him never gave in to anyone at all. It is what I am thinking" *(To Con)* …eh..what's my next line?

CON: Mary?

MARY: I was busy watching it. 'Tis fierce good. How do they …

CON: You were supposed to be following the lines

MARY: Wait now, it's here somewhere.

She starts rummaging through the script

POOR BRID: While Mary is looking, *(Dying to get her own back on Teresa)* I have a question. Why does Teresa never look at me when she's saying the lines?

TERESA: Because you're always standing behind me.

CON: *(Trying to stand up for Brid)* She doesn't always stand behind you. Sometimes you move ….

TERESA: *(Interrupting him)* I believe in theatre terms it's known as upstaging.

POOR BRID: What are you talking about? *(To Con)* What is she talking about?

CON: *(Hasn't a clue, starts to blab)* Upstaging is …. I remember Seamus talking about this … it happens when …

TERESA: It's when an actor moves towards the back of a stage to make another actor face away from the audience thereby placing the second actor in a poor position from the audience's point of view.

CON: *(Still flustered)* Oh yes, that's it. We'll have to look out for that in future.

POOR BRID: And another thing. Why am I playing the older woman?

TERESA: You look older.

CON: *(Cutting in before it develops)* I think we'll leave it at that for now. *(To the audience)* That was just a small sample. Ye get an idea of what's going on. Ye'll have to come along to see what happens when we put it on later in the year. Thank you ladies. *(He starts a round of applause)* And now for some more music from Maureen O'Leary and her music students.

More music starts up.

Scene 5

Paddy is sitting at one of the tables. Mossie approaches and stands slightly behind Paddy.

MOSSIE: Look what the cat dragged in, Mr. Paddy Dooley, Farmer (*Beat*) Debt Collector.

PADDY: It's a free country, Mossie.

MOSSIE: Not yet it isn't (*He laughs at his own joke*)

PADDY: Are you wanting something?

MOSSIE: No.

PADDY: Well, you can stand somewhere else, so.

MOSSIE: Last I heard you were barred from this pub.

PADDY: Ye heard wrong.

MOSSIE: Thrown out by the woman of the house no less. That's what I heard. (*No response from Paddy*) A woman. That's about all you'd be able for.

PADDY: I want no trouble.

MOSSIE: You keep well away from trouble don't you? Let others do your dirty work.

PADDY: What are you talking about?

MOSSIE: I had the Volunteers in to me every day pestering me for money.

PADDY: The money you owe. For over a year now.

MOSSIE: It's not my fault if your Volunteer friends can't find the record of my contribution to the fund.

Con arrives.

PADDY: You mean the loan! I doubt you ever gave it. Hello Con, I hope you can improve the conversation at the table.

CON: (*Unsure what's going on*) I'm just…well, reminding you, Paddy, that we're starting rehearsals for that other play next Wednesday.

PADDY: That's grand.

MOSSIE: Paddy Dooley is in a play? It'll suit him. He's been pretending to be something he's not all his life.

PADDY: None of your business, Mossie.

MOSSIE: It'll be everyone's business if we see you gallivanting up on a stage. Tell, me Con, does he have to wear a frock?

CON: Mr. Kinsella, this is serious theatre not one of those pantomimes.

MOSSIE: I'd pay to see Paddy in a frock. *(Laughs)*

Footsteps as Poor Brid rushes over.

POOR BRID: Con! Con! Come and see. Look. Look at Colm. Up there, at the top of the room.

CON: Be God, he's swaying to the music. He likes the music! *(To Mossie and Paddy)* I've been teaching him the tin whistle myself.

BRID: Let's go and ask if she'll let him play.

They move off, calling out 'Miss O'Leary'. The music grows louder as Con and Brid approach Miss O'Leary.

Scene 6

MISS O'LEARY: He's enjoying that.

POOR BRID: He is Miss O'Leary. It's lovely to see. He's been learning the tin whistle.

MISS O'LEARY: I have a spare whistle if he feels like playing?

CON: Will you give it a go Colm? *(Colm looks from one to the other and slowly accepts the whistle)* Take it, there's a good boy.

POOR BRID: He's taking the whistle, Con.

CON: He can play "The Dawning of the Day" Would you like to play that, son?

Colm shakes his head.

POOR BRID: Would you like that Colm?

He doesn't respond

MISS O'LEARY: Colm. Would you like to play 'The Dawning of the Day' with these children? *(No response, kindly)* I must be getting old. My hearing isn't as good as it used to be. You'll have to speak up.

TERESA: He can't speak. He's a mute.

POOR BRID: He's well able to speak.

TERESA: It is widely accepted that living in a workhouse slows down early childhood development.

POOR BRID: He's shy.

TERESA: And also living for so long without proper parents would not….

Brid is getting upset and through all this exchange, the joy leaves Colm. He begins to shake and puts his hands to his ears as if in pain. The others are oblivious.

POOR BRID: *(Voice rising)* Proper parents? What do you mean by that? We are his parents now, aren't we Con? We love him.

Colm's distress is growing slowly.

CON: It's alright Brid. Teresa -

TERESA: We all said it was a risk.

POOR BRID: Who is all? Are ye all talking about me? Is that it? For your information, he's always talking at home. We can't get a word in edgeways.

A scream form Colm. Mossie who has been observing Colm, jumps up and comes forward

MOSSIE: In the name of God, will the two of ye just stop it.

TERESA: Mossie, I am merely informing ….

MOSSIE: Ye ought to be ashamed of yourselves.

TERESA: I am merely informing …

MOSSIE: Will you just look at what you're doing to the young fella. Hands over his head, rocking like that. *(He bends down and puts his hand on Colm's arm)* You'll be alright son.

Colm stops shaking and looks at Mossie

POOR BRID: Leave my … my boy alone.

MOSSIE: It's not me should leave him alone…

POOR BRID: I'll decide what's best for him.

MOSSIE: Then bring him home, out of here. He's heard enough fighting in his life, he doesn't need any more.

POOR BRID: How would you know what he has or hasn't heard?

MOSSIE: He's workhouse, he'll have heard fighting. And seen things too. Bring him home.

CON: He's right, Brid, the boy needs to go home.

POOR BRID: Aye, come on, Colm love, we'll go. You stay on, Con, 'tis grand. Out of our way, Mr. Kinsella.

MOSSIE: With pleasure. *(With unexpected tenderness to Colm)* Take care now, Colm. Take care.

CON: Thanks again to Miss O'Leary and her class for the music. And now we have another treat for you all in the form of a puppet show.

His voice fades, music in background.

Scene 7

Anne Kilbride is sitting at a table. She is uncomfortable, glancing around to see if people are looking at her. There is an empty chair beside her. Mary approaches.

MARY: Are you alright there, Auntie Anne? You're hidden away in the snug.

ANNE: I have no need to display myself and be the subject of idle gossip. I'm entitled to be here as much as anyone else.

MARY: That's true. Can I get you anything?

ANNE: No thank you.

MARY: *(After a beat)* Did you hear Cissy had a baby girl?

ANNE: And why would I care about that?

MARY: Well, if it's Donnacha's baby and -

ANNE: Donnacha's baby! Donnacha is not that sort of a boy. He was going for the priesthood at one stage. Now if you'll excuse me, Mary, I want to be on my own.

MARY: *(Sliding into a seat)* Cissy is a good friend of mine. She doesn't tell lies and -

ANNE: Please don't sit beside me. Donnacha would never have dealings with a tramp like that. I know my son.

MARY: *(Hesitates)* You think you do. Mammy and Joseph don't know everything about me.

ANNE: Then they are not good parents, are they?

MARY: That's not what -

Footsteps as Brigid approaches.

ANNE: Has your mother put you up to this? Joseph said they'd support whatever I wanted and – ah, Brigid, can you tell your daughter to mind her own business.

BRIGID: Mary! I thought we talked about -

MARY: Cissy had the baby and I think she should know and meet her.

BRIGID: Mary, I am warning you -

ANNE: I've had enough of this. I came here for the entertainment. I'll find more suitable company. *(She stands up, sees Cissy. Beat – shock)* What is she doing here?

MARY: I told her to come. I thought maybe… Cissy! Cissy!

Footsteps as she runs towards her.

ANNE: Oh my God. Oh my God.

BRIGID: I'll sort this. Stay here. Mary!

Scene 8

CON: Well, we've come to the end of our celebration and I'm sure you'll all agree -

CISSY: *(Interrupting him)* I'd like to sing. I'd like to sing a song.

CON: Oh, well, we've finished and -

MARY: My friend, Cissy, would like to sing a song. Is there a problem?

BRIGID: Mary!

CON: *(Unsure what to do)* We're just finishing up ... but ... I suppose if you have a song ....

CISSY: I'll need someone to hold my baby. *(Silence. Cissy walks towards Anne)* Mrs. Kilbride?

She approaches Anne and offers her the baby. Anne turns her back.

ANNE: Go back to where you came from.

Cissy stands, staring at Anne in silence for a while.

CISSY: Will you not even look at her?

No response from Anne. There is an embarrassed silence.

TERESA: I'll hold your baby.

CISSY: Thank you, Teresa. *(To Con)* Where do you want me, Mr. O'Sullivan?

Con has lost control of the situation

CON: Most did it from up here ... so here ... if you like ... or would you prefer to sit?

CISSY: I'll stand.

She takes her position and looks at the audience, almost daring them to say something. She settles herself and begins to sing while focussing on Anne.

CISSY: My young love said to me, "My mother won't mind
　　　　And my father won't slight you for your lack of kind."
　　　　then he stepped away from me and this he did say:
　　　　It will not be long, love, till our wedding day.

Anne is enraged. She stands up, interrupts the song.

ANNE: If ye want to listen to this hussy, then ye're welcome to her but I'll not stay in the same room as that brazen bitch.

Footsteps as she leaves. Door opens, slams. Cissy falters briefly but carries on

CISSY: He stepped away from me and he moved thru' the fair

And fondly I watched him move here and move there.

And he made his way homeward with one star awake

As swan in the evening moves over the lake.

Last night, he came to me, he came softly in

So softly he came that his feet made no din,

And he laid his hand on me and this he did say:

It will not be long, love, till our wedding day.

The song ends. Mary applauds but no one else does. Cissy steps down from the performance area to Teresa who hands back the baby.

TERESA: Your baby.

CISSY: Thank you.

MARY: Come upstairs Cissy, you must be tired.

CISSY: I am, Mary. I could do with a rest before I go back to Dublin.

Mary begins to lead her away.

BRIGID: That's not a good idea Mary. *(Mary looks at her confused)* Moll is sick. *(Mary still puzzled)* It wouldn't be safe to bring the baby up there in case it caught something.

MARY: *(Realising)* Don't force me to take sides Mammy.

(Pause)

JOSEPH: It would be better for Cissy to go somewhere else, Mary.

MARY: She only had the baby last week. She came all the way out here from that place in Dublin on her own.

CISSY: It's alright Mary, I'll get the early train.

MARY: You'll do nothing of the sort. *(Turning to Brigid)* Mammy?

JOSEPH: *(Embarrassed)* I'm sorry, Cissy, but Anne is family.

TERESA: She can stay in my house. With me and Bartholomew.

CISSY: I can?

TERESA: It makes sense. You're a new mother and are in a weakened state after childbirth. If the body is not allowed to heal, there is a high probability of developing a postpartum haemorrhage which if not treated properly can lead to serious illness and even death. Well?

CISSY: Oh…right.

TERESA: Your baby needs a healthy mother to thrive. There are enough children dying in this country, or living in workhouses, without adding an innocent baby to the list.

Silence in the pub. Everyone is uncomfortable and not sure what to do. The celebrations have soured.

CISSY: Thank you. Thank you very much, Teresa.

TERESA: Any food, you'll have to cook it yourself. Come on. *(She starts to lead them out)* I hope you like cats.

Footsteps as they leave in silence.

MARY: I hope you're all proud of yourselves. Cissy, Teresa, wait for me.

She leaves – door bangs after her.

END OF EPISODE

EPISODE 29 – RECRUITING TERESA, AUG. 1921

Scene 1 – Barry's pub

MOSSIE: A pint there, Joseph, if you would. And one for Padraig here, too.

Joseph pours the drinks.

JOSEPH: There you are now, gentlemen.

Places drinks on counter.

MOSSIE: I see you've the poster about the rates up behind the bar.

JOSEPH: That's Tomas' doing, not mine, but I agree with it.

MOSSIE: How can we pay rates when we don't know whether to pay it to the Irish or the British?

PADRAIG: Well said, Mossie. Load of nonsense.

MOSSIE: Aye, Come on Padraig, we'll drink in the snug. That poster will leave a bad taste in my mouth.

Padraig laughs.

VOICEOVER: Fractured – August 1921

Scene 2 - Barry's pub. An hour later

Door to pub crashes open. Moll is screaming. Brigid and Teresa enter. Tomas and Joseph are behind the bar. Joseph is about to go out.

BRIGID: How many times? How many times have I told you not to be playing down by the river?

TERESA: Ten times in my hearing.

MOLL: Everyone is playing there. It's the fun place.

BRIGID: A dirty river that stinks up the whole town is not a fun place. Do you want to be sick?

MOLL: Yes!

BRIGID: Don't be so cheeky. Get upstairs and wash your hands and face and take off those clothes.

MOLL: *(Appeals)* Daddy?

JOSEPH: Is that my Moll, I thought it was a great big pile of smelly rubbish walking into my pub.

MOLL: It's me.

JOSEPH: I might have thrown you out, so I would.

MOLL: I would have shouted out to stop you.

TERESA: She's well able to do that alright.

BRIGID: *(With an irritated look at Teresa)* Thank you, Teresa, Upstairs. Now, Moll.

Moll is about to protest.

TOMAS: I'll count and see how long it takes you, Milly Molly Mae. Go – *(She runs off. Loudly)* One! Two! Three! Four - that's too long now.

We hear Moll laughing. Footsteps fading.

BRIGID: She's getting cheekier by the day. Mary was never like that.

JOSEPH: A bit of spirit is no bad thing.

BRIGID: *(Referencing the bottle of whiskey under his arm)* I see you've a bit of spirit yourself hidden under your arm. Are you off somewhere?

JOSEPH: Just to see Paddy. He's been a bit under the weather recently.

BRIGID: Then he should call on a doctor and not a publican.

JOSEPH: I'll pass your good wishes onto him, so I will. Mind the fort there now, Tomas. Bye now, Teresa.

Footsteps as he leaves. Door opens, closes. Beat

BRIGID: If I was lying dead in the bed upstairs, he'd hardly notice, but Paddy is 'under the weather' and he goes running off to him.

TERESA: He'd notice when the decomposition starts.

BRIGID: What?

TERESA: Decomposition starts within a few hours of death. It's worse in warm weather. If you were dead in the bed -

BRIGID: What is it you wanted, Teresa?

TERESA: Bartholomew has run off again. I think there's a bit of jealously there with Cissy's baby. I've a notice here describing him with details on how he is to be returned should he be found. Can you hang it up for me?

BRIGID: Tomas, take care of that, will you?

TOMAS: Hand it over there, Teresa, and I'll put up, slap bang beside the rates poster.

Teresa hands over her poster. Banging as Tomas puts it up.

BRIGID: I don't know why we have that rates poster up at all. Load of nonsense. If you pay rates to the British the Irish come after you, if you pay the Irish, the British come after you.

TOMAS: *(With grit – he's heard this already)* You're supposed to pay the Irish, Mammy. There now, Teresa, is that alright for you?

BRIGID: And what are they doing with our rates? Not cleaning rivers, that's for sure.

TERESA: The poster is excellently positioned, Tomas. And Brigid, the rivers are to be cleaned. They discovered that it's all the shit coming out of the College that's causing the problem.

Tomas laughs.

BRIGID: God forgive you, Teresa for saying such a thing. And you, Tomas, for laughing. It's priests and holy people above in the college.

TERESA: 'Twas reported in the paper. Let me try remember now - it said - 'there is a large amount - that was the pollution - running from the College but so far the District Council have been afraid to approach St Patrick's College Maynooth. They have been asked to have a certain amount of work done but have never done it'.

BRIGID: I can't believe that. Priests and bishops polluting our river.

TERESA: They use the toilets same as anyone else.

TOMAS: *(Laughing)* I think we should be on our knees, giving thanks that Maynooth has a better class of pollution than the average town. Maybe Moll has the right idea playing down there.

BRIGID: May God forgive you. You're worse than your father. That's blasphemous talk. Moll, I'm coming up now, ready or not.

Footsteps as Brigid runs off. Moll squeals, distant

TERESA: What you said wasn't blasphemous. A better class of pollution is a compliment.

TOMAS: Aye. Teresa, I've been meaning -

TERESA: Though I would say it's an inaccurate statement. Excrement is excrement no matter what way you look at it.

TOMAS: *(Laughing)* Aye.

TERESA: I'll be on my way.

TOMAS: *(Desperate to prolong the conversation)* Aw, now, stay. Have a drink.

TERESA: I have a cat to look for.

TOMAS: A drink to fortify your search. And besides, I'd really like to get to know you, Teresa

TERESA: It's not convenient.

TOMAS: I hear your talk the other week on taking care of gunshot wounds was very informative.

TERESA: That was four months ago. I've given talks on bandaging severed limbs, recognising shell-shock and how to keep your cat happy since then. I've also changed a few nappies and been on stage.

TOMAS: And you were excellent. Teresa, I was -

TERESA: I was - except my talk on how to keep your cat happy seems not to have resonated with Bartholomew.

TOMAS: Maybe your cat just has places to be. Teresa, you seem like -

TERESA: What places? He has a cosy basket, good scraps from the table, a toy I made him. Where would he get better?

TOMAS: I'd move in with you myself.

TERESA: No thank you, I have enough. I'll be off.

Footsteps as she moves on.

TOMAS: *(Trying to get her to stay)* Don't go. I hardly ever get a chance to chat with you, Teresa.

TERESA: That's because we have nothing to chat about.

TOMAS: I'm sure we could find something. Mammy is always saying what great..fun..she has with you.

TERESA: She did say she enjoyed my talk on bullet wounds.

TOMAS: There you go.

TERESA: She gave me a round of applause at the end.

TOMAS: She loved that talk.

TERESA: It was educational, informative and entertaining, all necessary ingredients for a lecture. Did you know for instance, Tomas, that if a bullet enters the head and bounces around, the damage formed is so bad because there is no room for the brain to move and the shock waves - from the bullet bouncing about - can cause irreversible damage.

TOMAS: Eh...no.

TERESA: That's what the RIC lad back in February died from. A bullet to the head. I met him once.

TOMAS: Look, I -

TERESA: He refused to look for my cat.

TOMAS: Did he?

TERESA: If Bartholomew had gone in with a gun in his paw and robbed the station, he'd look for him quick enough, I remembered thinking that at the time.

TOMAS: *(Seizing his chance)* Do you not like the RIC, Teresa?

TERESA: I didn't think much of them that day.

TOMAS: And what about the Volunteers?

TERESA: They were worse. They laughed, said they had better things to be doing than to be looking for my cat.

TOMAS: But.. in general, forgetting about the cat, what do you think of the Volunteers?

TERESA: I can't forget about the cat.

TOMAS: Do you agree with what the Volunteers and IRA are doing otherwise?

TERESA: Blowing things up and shooting people in the head and destroying the roads?

TOMAS: They're doing it for Ireland, don't you think?

TERESA: I have no idea why they're doing it. I'll have a whiskey.

TOMAS: Sorry.

TERESA: With a drop of water. I might need a drink if I'm to keep talking to you.

He goes to get it. Clinking, pouring, laying it on the counter.

TOMAS: And a fine drink it is too.

TERESA: I first had it back in 1890, after all the sheep were sheered on me father's farm.

She knocks it back.

TOMAS: Very nice.

TERESA: I was eight, been drinking it ever since.

TOMAS: Eight?

TERESA: Very young to be holding down a sheep, I know. I got kicked in the head twenty-two times. Have you ever been kicked in the head?

TOMAS: No.

TERESA: It's not a pleasant experience. There's the initial shock, of course. One is stunned. And it depends where the kick has landed as to how stunned one is. And a kick from an animal is very different than a kick from a human.

TOMAS: I didn't know.

TERESA: Oh yes. Say for instance a sheep, it has a particular kind of hoof. If it kicks you with the edge of the hoof, that's very painful. That happened me sixteen times out of the twenty-two. The other six times, the animal kicked me with the whole hoof, which is not as painful. Now a kick from a man, would depend on the size of his foot and his strength. A weedy lad like yourself, I imagine wouldn't do too much damage but a fine lad like your brother Sean, now there's a kick in the head I wouldn't like to get.

TOMAS: I see. Teresa -

TERESA: It's quite an interesting subject.

TOMAS: Oh, it is. Listen -

TERESA: You can calculate, with mathematics, the force of any given kick, did you know that?

TOMAS: No. Can we go back to the -

TERESA: The amount of damage done is the amount of energy absorbed and dissipated by the receiving body. And whether it is localised or not. Take for instance that soldier who was shot in February -

TOMAS: Let's not take that.

TERESA: Alright - just say, you were to kick me in the head.

TOMAS: But I wouldn't -

TERESA: *(Firmly)* I know that. It's an example. So, I'm on the ground and you lift up your foot and you're quite angry and you smash your foot into my skull. Have you got that?

TOMAS: Can we talk about -

TERESA: The amount of damage you do is caused by the force of your foot. Can we agree on that?

TOMAS: Yes, but -

TERESA: The formula for the damage done - we'll call it force - is measured as the mass of your foot by the acceleration of your foot.

TOMAS: You're a font of knowledge, Teresa, no doubt about that. Now, I was wondering if -

TERESA: What else can I tell you so you can get to know me?

TOMAS: Maybe I could ask you questions?

TERESA: That would certainly speed things up. Maybe I ask you one and you ask me. That way we're equal.

TOMAS: Right.

TERESA: I'll go first as I told you about the sheep on the farm and about the whiskey and about calculating force. So *(She thinks)* Is it true what the whole town is saying, that you and Lizzie O'Neill are courting?

TOMAS: Jesus!

TERESA: True or not?

TOMAS: The whole town?

TERESA: Eight-one percent of it certainly. Well?

TOMAS: I wouldn't say courting...

TERESA: So, no.

TOMAS: Well...no...yes.

TERESA: Your turn.

TOMAS: *(Thinking carefully)* If I asked you to memorise a series of random letters, could you do it?

TERESA: That's a very peculiar question. But yes.

We hear Tomas scrabbling for a pen and paper.

TOMAS: All right, just a second...just one second...I just have to get...*(Sounds of things being moved)* Ah, yes, one pen. *(Sound of paper)* One page.

TERESA: Me now - What do you think of the colour red.

TOMAS: *(Distracted)* That it's bright and cheerful. *(The scrape of a pen across paper)* Me now - can you memorise this?

He hands her the paper. She skims it as she speaks.

TERESA: Technically red can be many shades. There is scarlet and crimson, cerise and magenta, maroon, carmine, claret and burgundy, as well as carnelian and cherry and cardinal. Not all bright. My next question was to be if you're a bit narrow thinking but sure I know the answer to that now. Here's your paper back. *(Paper being handed back)* 432 56wfghityvlp 346 23gh4t9gow867bgfre

TOMAS: That's amazing.

TERESA: That's only a handful. There's Imperial, Ruby, Spanish, Indian, Rust -

TOMAS: I mean about memorising the letters.

TERESA: Mm. My question - do you like cats?

TOMAS: Love them. My question, do you think you'd like to do some memorising for the IRA?

TERESA: No. My question. What particular cats do you like?

TOMAS: Ones like yours. Black and white. My question - why wouldn't you like to memorise for the IRA?

TERESA: Because neither they or the RIC would look for Bartholomew last year. I told you that. My question, is it fluffy black and white cats you like or smooth haired black and white cats?

TOMAS: Eh....the smooth ones? My question - would you do some memorising for me?

TERESA: Yes. My question -

TOMAS: Yes?

TERESA: I haven't asked it yet. I wouldn't go rushing saying yes until you've heard it. *(Beat)* Do you like any other animals besides cats?

TOMAS: No. Just cats. My question - if I came to you and asked you to memorise something and then go and pass it on, would you?

TERESA: That's very vague. My question -

TOMAS: If I gave you some numbers to memorise would you pass it on to a man in Dublin if I gave you the train fare up.

TERESA: No. My question - would you help someone in need?

TOMAS: Yes. My question, why wouldn't you go to Dublin?

TERESA: There was no mention of a return fare. My question - is there anyone you wouldn't help.

TOMAS: I'd help everyone. My question, if I gave you the train fare there and back, a map of where to meet a man and a detailed description, would you memorise numbers and deliver them?

TERESA: Yes. My question - will you look for Bartholomew with me if I asked?

TOMAS: I would. My question - will you help me get some numbers up to Dublin, Teresa.

TERESA: Yes. My question, will you help me look for Bartholomew now?

TOMAS: *(Realising he's been played too)* Eh….yes, but I can't just now. I have to mind the pub.

TERESA: Your mother is here. Call her. *(Sensing reluctance)* Go on.

TOMAS: *(Calling weakly)* Mammy! I don't -

TERESA: Louder.

TOMAS: MAMMY!

Hurrying footsteps.

BRIGID: What in the name of God? What's wrong?

TOMAS: Nothing. I eh…

TERESA: I'm going to memorise numbers for Tomas and in exchange he's helping me look for my cat because we know one another now. You can mind the pub, Brigid. Come on Tomas.

BRIGID: *(With suspicion)* Tomas?

TOMAS: It's nothing…I just…

TERESA: He's very kind.

BRIGID: Isn't he? You go on Teresa, I'll send Tomas out after you in a minute.

TERESA: Grand so.

Footsteps as she leaves. Door opens, street, door closes.

BRIGID: What was that about?

TOMAS: Nothing.

BRIGID: You expect me to believe it? Memorising numbers?

TOMAS: It's just -

BRIGID: It's just nothing, you little…Jesus…Teresa is not like you and me. She's not like anyone else in this town.

TOMAS: Can I go now?

BRIGID: I see the people you call friends and I don't like them.

TOMAS: I wouldn't be too mad on your friends either, Mammy.

BRIGID: Don't be so smart. You know what I'm saying. You've always been a decent lad, don't compromise.

TOMAS: It was just…. *(Realising she's right - long beat)* I'm only looking for a cat, Mammy.

BRIGID: If you say so.

TOMAS: I do. *(Beat.)* I promise.

BRIGID: Then go.

As he leaves, Mossie Kinsella and Padraig Doran shuffle out of a corner up to the bar.

BRIGID: Oh my God, will it ever… *(She eyes Mossie in horror wondering what he overheard)* Oh … Hello, Mossie, I didn't know you and this gentleman were down there. What would ye like?

MOSSIE: Two whiskeys. One for me and one for Padraig. D'you know Padraig, Mrs?

Brigid goes to get the whiskey.

BRIGID: Can't say I do. Hello, Padraig.

PADRAIG: Mrs.

MOSSIE: Padraig knows Sean, don't you, Padraig?

PADRAIG: I do, indeed.

MOSSIE: Sean threatened him once, down at the railway, didn't he Padraig?

PADRAIG: He did.

BRIGID: *(Laying drinks on the counter)* That'll be -

MOSSIE: Now, you'll hardly charge me for that, will you?

BRIGID: And why wouldn't I charge you?

MOSSIE: I think we all know why. Let's just say...you'll be hoping that Teresa's cat got my tongue.

Both men down their drink and leave. Brigid is horrified.

BRIGID: Oh dear God...

END OF EPISODE

EPISODE 30 – CONFESSION, SEP. 1921

Scene 1 - Curragh, night.

Laboured breathing, running footsteps. A shot rings out.

ALAN: Oh, Jesus. *(Heavy breathing)* full of grace, the Lord is with thee, blessed art thou among woman and – *(Sounds of pushing, shoving)* I'm out. I'm out. *(Emotional)* Oh yes. Thank you God. A-bloody-men.

Running footsteps, laboured breathing fade into distance.

VOICEOVER: Fractured – September 1921

Scene 2 - Church. Intercut between church and confessional

ANNE: Who on earth is inside the confessional with the Father?

TOMAS: I'm waiting going on for twenty minutes.

ANNE: It's probably Cissy Boland.

TOMAS: Aw now, Auntie Anne -

ANNE: Or that murderer, Michael Collins. I heard they can't move in Dublin for tripping over bodies.

TOMAS: There was a war on.

ANNE: Shooting people in their beds and from behind bushes, that's thuggery, not war.

TOMAS: Ah, now Auntie Anne -

ANNE: Take a good look at whoever comes out of that box and say to yourself, that there's a person not to be trusted.

TOMAS: But sure, if God forgives them that should be good enough for us.

ANNE: You're trying to invoke Cesusbella, Tomas, but I don't think so.

TOMAS: I'm just trying to invoke -

They are interrupted by Maggie

MAGGIE: Are you not gone in yet, Tomas? Sure you were here when I came by ten minutes ago.

TOMAS: No one has come out, Mrs. O'Donoghue.

MAGGIE: That's because no one has gone in, you eejit.

TOMAS: Are you sure? I wouldn't want -

MAGGIE: I'll check. *(Footsteps to confessional. A knock. She bellows)* Father! Father! There's two here for the confessional. And myself as well now I've finished changing the bedclothes. Are you free?

FATHER DEMPSEY: *(Muffled)* I am.

MAGGIE: I'll send Tomas Barry in so.

TOMAS: Jesus!

FATHER DEMPSEY: *(Muffled)* Mrs. O'Donoghue, I do not need to know who is coming in to receive the sacrament.

MAGGIE: But sure, you know all the voices anyway, I'm only saving you the bother of trying to place them. In you go, Tomas. *(Footsteps as Tomas reluctantly gets up and goes in)* Don't be too long now!

Tomas opens and closes the confessional door. Inside confession box.

FATHER DEMPSEY: I apologise, Tomas. If you'd rather come back at some other stage?

TOMAS: It's grand and sure, you probably do know all the voices, do you, Father?

FATHER DEMPSEY: No and I don't try to guess them whatever Mrs. O'Donoghue might say. In your own time, Tomas.

TOMAS: Forgive me father for I have sinned, it's been…well…a while since my last confession.

FATHER DEMPSEY: Why would that be?

TOMAS: I've been afraid to come, Father.

FATHER DEMPSEY: Why?

TOMAS: I've done a fair bit of sinning, Father. I've done the usual things, annoyed me mother and father, upset me sister, quite a lot. I've had bad thoughts about belting a few of the boys I know. I get angry at -

FATHER DEMPSEY: Why have you come today, Tomas?

TOMAS: *(With difficulty, in a rush)* I have two awful ones, Father. I'll start with the least awful one. I've been having….thoughts…father.

FATHER DEMPSEY: Thoughts?

TOMAS: About a girl I like. I can't seem to stop thinking of her.

FATHER DEMPSEY: That's a common enough one. Read the bible when these thoughts strike. And make sure the girl is a good girl and doesn't lead you to sin.

TOMAS: She is a good girl, Father. I'm the problem.

FATHER DEMPSEY: The book of Revelations, that's the fellow to cure you. Read it before you meet the girl and hold the words in your head.

TOMAS: I will. That's great advice.

FATHER DEMPSEY: And the next sin on your mind?

TOMAS: That's the terrible one

FATHER DEMPSEY: Are you truly sorry for this sin?

TOMAS: That's the thing, that's why I haven't come before now, I am but I'm not.

FATHER DEMPSEY: A dilemma.

TOMAS: Aye.

FATHER DEMPSEY: That time, in your house, when I helped Sean, d'you remember?

TOMAS: Aye. My mother was so grateful to you. She keeps saying she'll never repay you.

FATHER DEMPSEY: Afterwards, that was my dilemma. In that moment, I knew what he was, Tomas. I knew he was a Volunteer, I knew he'd done terrible acts, but I also saw a man fighting for a cause he believed in. I did what was right at the time, even though now, I wonder. A dilemma. Was what you did right for you at the time?

TOMAS: I think it was, Father.

FATHER DEMPSEY: I don't believe God would hold it against you for doing what feels right.

TOMAS: You saved a man, Father...I, I killed one. How can it ever be right to break the fifth commandment?

FATHER DEMPSEY: There is blood on the hands of every man and woman in this country, Tomas, whether they admit it or not. Everyone who picks up a gun, any woman who takes a side, every person who hides a fugitive, who looks for a target, they all know the risks. Whoever you killed Tomas, he made that pact with himself, just like you did.

TOMAS: I know but -

FATHER DEMPSEY: Was it a soldier you killed?

TOMAS: RIC.

FATHER DEMPSEY: Then he knew what might happen.

TOMAS: So, it's alright what I did?

FATHER DEMPSEY: Killing a man is not alright, you know that. But the fault lies in the world and not in the boy. I look to Bishop Mannix when I say, God will forgive you if you truly want it.

TOMAS: I do want it but I can't promise not to shoot someone else if the time comes. I don't want to but -

FATHER DEMPSEY: That is for your own conscience. I believe Tomas that you want to live a good life, am I right?

TOMAS: Aye.

FATHER DEMPSEY: Then go in peace. You've made a great confession. A decade of the sorrowful mysteries. Say the act of contrition, now.

As Tomas bends to say the prayer, Maggie and Anne talk.

TOMAS: O my God, I am heartily sorry for having offended Thee, and I detest all my sins because I dread the loss of Heaven and the pains of hell,

Fade to outside confessional.

MAGGIE: He's an awful man for talking to everyone. I tell him not everyone wants to chat in the confessional, most people just want to confess and away with themselves. Mrs. O'Sullivan was in with him for an hour and a half one first Friday. I don't know what he'd talk to her about.

ANNE: Probably advising her to get rid of her workhouse brat. That child will come to no good.

MAGGIE: He's a grand little tin whistle player all the same. I heard him there -

ANNE: Donnacha was playing the piano at that age. Nurturing, it can't be beaten.

MAGGIE: I'm not a great fan of the piano, a lot of auld banging, do you not think so? No, give me a tin whistle anytime and a – *(Confessional opens)* Did you get much penance, Tomas?

ANNE: Really, Mrs. O'Donoghue. Excuse me, my turn.

Footsteps, then she closes the confession behind her. Inside confessional.

ANNE: Forgive me Father, for I have sinned, it's been a week since my last confession.

FATHER DEMPSEY: I can't imagine you have too much to tell me.

ANNE: Wrath, Father.

FATHER DEMPSEY: Wrath?

ANNE: Every day I have to battle against it. Every day, I have to force myself to go out my door and hold my head up high and pretend I don't hear the malicious rumours being whispered against me and my family on the streets of this town. I have to hold myself in, restrain myself. I want to scream, Father. I want to scream the most obscene words at these people. I have a pain in my chest from not screaming. Every day, Father.

FATHER DEMPSEY: And what has brought this on?

ANNE: You know what's brought it on, Father.

FATHER DEMPSEY: Is this Anne Kilbride?

ANNE: You know it is, who else in this place uses words like 'malicious' and 'obscene' and who else is being talked about all over town?

FATHER DEMPSEY: Cissy Boland is being talked about.

ANNE: With all due respect, Father, do not mention that girl to me.

FATHER DEMPSEY: I assume she is the reason for your wrath, Mrs. Kilbride?

ANNE: You assume right. Telling everyone that that fatherless child is Donnacha's. My son would not know one end of a girl from the other, Father. And if he did, he'd choose more wisely.

FATHER DEMPSEY: Thou shalt not judge, Mrs. Kilbride.

ANNE: I beg your pardon?

FATHER DEMPSEY: There is no doubt that Cissy has ruined herself, but that fellow whoever he is has let her down and she will have to live the rest of her life, ruined, because of his cowardice.

ANNE: As she should.

FATHER DEMPSEY: As she will, Mrs. Kilbride. I understand your anger but the whispers against Donnacha will pass. He will move on from this and do his studies and God willing, live a successful life. For Cissy, that will never happen. Now, put away your wrath and count your blessings.

ANNE: It still doesn't excuse what she's saying.

FATHER DEMPSEY: Nor does it excuse what you have said against her.

ANNE: I beg your pardon?

FATHER DEMPSEY: Look into your heart, Mrs. Kilbride. Ask yourself why you are so filled with wrath. Really. Ask yourself.

ANNE: I just told you. The whispers…that girl…I told you. *(Beat. Silence. More to convince herself)* Donnacha would not lie to me.

FATHER DEMPSEY: Then count your blessings. Be kind to those who don't have them. That is your penance. Be kind.

ANNE: I am kind, Father.

FATHER DEMPSEY: Then try to be kinder.

ANNE: I will.

FATHER DEMPSEY: *(Joking)* And less wrathful.

ANNE: Yes. Will I say my act of contrition now?

FATHER DEMPSEY: Do.

ANNE: O my God, I am heartily sorry for having offended Thee, and I detest all my sins because I dread the loss of Heaven and the pains of hell,

Fade out and back to outside confessional.

MAGGIE: Bye now, Tomas. Was it a decade you got?

TOMAS: That's between me and the Father, Mrs. O'Donoghue.

MAGGIE: Of course it is and sure, look at the little face on you, sure you never did a wrong thing in your life. He gave Mossie Kinsella three decades once and I know that because Mossie said he wasn't going to waste his time saying three decades and he didn't. Up and out he went, trailing them sins behind him like a cart. *(Door opens on confessional)* Here's herself. *(Anne moves to leave)* Are you not going to say your penance, Mrs. Kilbride?

ANNE: I got no prayer to say, Mrs. O'Donoghue.

MAGGIE: Tomas got a decade.

TOMAS: I didn't confirm or deny that now.

MAGGIE: You must be a fierce good citizen not to get any penance at all. Or maybe the Father regrets what he gave Tomas and is making it up somehow or -

ANNE: It really is none of your business – *(Remembers she has to be kind)* I have an alternative type of penance to do, Mrs. O'Donoghue because none of us is perfect. Tomas, can you walk back with me?

TOMAS: I will, Auntie Anne.

They walk out together. Maggie prepares to go in. During her confession, a young man, Alan O'Brien, arrives into the church, wary and scared. He is well wrapped up with a scarf concealing most of his face. He looks familiar.

MAGGIE: I'm coming in now, Father and that'll be the last, unless you get a crowd from the pub. *(She opens the confessional. Closes it. Kneels)* Bless me Father for I have sinned. It's been a fortnight since my last confession.

FATHER DEMPSEY: Off you go, Mrs. O'Donoghue.

MAGGIE: Now, I don't have many sins to be telling you but there's no point in waiting for them to build up because you and I know that when housework builds up, it's no fun clearing it, isn't that right, Father.

FATHER DEMPSEY: That's right.

MAGGIE: Which leads me to my first sin. The state of your bed sheets.

FATHER DEMPSEY: Mrs. O'Donoghue, please.

MAGGIE: They were filthy. And that's not a sin, there's many a person with filthy bed sheets but it made me terrible annoyed so it did Father and I cursed you, and for that I am heartily sorry.

FATHER DEMPSEY: And I'm heartily sorry for making you sin.

MAGGIE: That's no bother, I forgive you. Maybe you should bang out an act of contrition to me, Father, ey?

FATHER DEMPSEY: Anything else, Mrs. O'Donoghue.

MAGGIE: Yes. I'm still harbouring them suspicious thoughts, Father. I can't help it.

FATHER DEMPSEY: The suspicious thoughts against Mossie Kinsella?

MAGGIE: My husband died falling off the roof of his barn. How do I know he wasn't pushed?

FATHER DEMPSEY: We were over this the last time you were in confession, Mrs. O'Donoghue. Your husband had drink taken, wasn't that found at the inquest? Now you must -

MAGGIE: Mossie Kinsella owed my husband money, it's a great handy way to get out of paying him all the same, isn't it, to kill him?

FATHER DEMPSEY: I would advise you, for your own good, not to go about the town saying such things, Mrs. O'Donoghue.

MAGGIE: As if I would, Father. The soul of discretion, that's me. I'm just telling you, letting off steam. What made me suspicious this time was that two weeks ago, you gave Mr. Kinsella three decades, what did you give it to him for, if you don't mind me asking?

FATHER DEMPSEY: I do mind. The confessional is sacrosanct, Mrs. O'Donoghue. You need to banish these suspicious thoughts. Your husband is gone over twenty years now, he'd want you to get on with your life.

MAGGIE: With all due respect now, Father, he wouldn't. He would hate me to be getting on with my life and him cold.

FATHER DEMPSEY: These suspicious thoughts will only hurt you in the end.

MAGGIE: I do have an idea how I could banish or confirm them, Father.

FATHER DEMPSEY: That's very good, Mrs. O'Donoghue. God loves a trier.

MAGGIE: Marvellous, because I was hoping you could ask Mossie the next time he comes in for confession, that's if he hasn't confessed it already?

FATHER DEMPSEY: Even if he confessed I can't tell you, Mrs. O'Donoghue.

MAGGIE: A nod or a wink or something?

FATHER DEMPSEY: I'm sorry, no. Now, let me remind you that there is no foundation for your suspicious. Have you anything else to confess?

MAGGIE: Just that I am disappointed in you, Father. *(After a moment)* I shouldn't have said, that, I'm sorry, Father. But I am disappointed…in the whole confessional rules, but you have to follow them, I understand that.

FATHER DEMPSEY: Make me some stew this evening and we'll forget all about it. Now for your act of contrition.

MAGGIE: *(Laughing)* Isn't that taking advantage of your position? I'll try to ignore the thoughts, I will. Now, O my God! I am heartily sorry for having offended Thee; and I detest my sins above every other evil, because they displease Thee, my God, Who for Thine infinite goodness art so deserving of all my love; and I firmly resolve, by Thy holy grace, never more to offend Thee, and to amend my life. Amen

FATHER: Your sins are forgiven.

MAGGIE: Thank you, Father. I'll go now. Get the stew – *(Door opens, Maggie yelps!)* Bless us and save us!

ALAN: Sorry, Mrs. I didn't mean to frighten you.

MAGGIE: Well you did. I hope you weren't listening in. That's a sin. There's another one after coming in, Father. Young chap. I don't know him.

FATHER DEMPSEY: Thank you Mrs. O'Donoghue.

We hear Maggie leave and Alan take her place inside confessional.

FATHER DEMPSEY: Go ahead, my son.

ALAN: Father Dempsey, is it?

FATHER DEMPSEY: It is.

ALAN: I haven't come for the confession. I need your help. Can you help me, Father?

FATHER DEMPSEY: That depends on the help you need.

ALAN: I'm after escaping the Curragh Camp Father. Last night. There was about sixty or so of us got out. I've been there since last year Father and I won't lie, I held up the RIC station down the road with Sean Barry and maybe I deserved a bit of jail time but I did it for Ireland and 'tis a terrible place down there, Father and I can't go back. And if they catch me and -

FATHER DEMPSEY: What makes you think I can help you?

ALAN: I got your name off Sean Barry when I was in Ballykinlar before I was transferred.

FATHER DEMPSEY: What's your name?

ALAN: Alan O'Toole, Father, from out the Kilcock road. My parents will want to know I'm alive and that. Can you get word to them for me?

FATHER DEMPSEY: One thing at a time. You wait there, don't so much as poke your head out until I come back. Alright?

ALAN: You won't go turning me in, will you, Father?

FATHER DEMPSEY: No, I won't do that. Wait there. *(He leaves the confessional, crosses the church and kneels)* Forgive me Father for the things I do. Forgive me.

END OF EPISODE

EPISODE 31 – ALAN'S ESCAPE, SEP. 1921

Scene 1 - Parochial House.

ALAN: Father, she asked me when I was going to say mass. She'll remember me from the confessional, I know she will.

FATHER DEMPSEY: It's all right, Alan, put on the cassock and remember the three rules -

ALAN: Don't speak unless spoken to, keep my answers brief and my eyes off the ladies.

FATHER DEMPSEY: Good man. Come on. *(He opens a door. Street sounds)* We're off to a friend.

VOICEOVER: Fractured – September 1921

Scene 2 - Room off Barry's pub.

The sound of delph, clinking etc as Brigid organises tea for her visitors.

BRIGID: Make yourselves comfortable there, Fathers. This is a lovely surprise.

FATHER DEMPSEY: Thank you, Brigid. It's a delicate matter, I was wondering if Tomas was about?

BRIGID: What has that boy done?

FATHER DEMPSEY: It's more -

BRIGID: I knew it was too good to be true when he was carting the Holy Book everywhere. What has he done, Father?

FATHER DEMPSEY: Nothing, I was -

BRIGID: He must have done something. It's bad enough one priest looking for him, but two. I'll skin him, so I will.

FATHER DEMPSEY: There will be no need. I -

BRIGID: Is it that Lizzie girl he's stepping out with? Her brothers are wild and I'd say she's no better but there's no getting through to Tomas when he has his mind made up. He will -

FATHER DEMPSEY: He has done nothing, Mrs. Barry. Really. I am, well, I'm in a pickle.

ALAN: It's my fault.

BRIGID: And you a priest. I don't think so. Tomas is not the boy he was and -

FATHER DEMPSEY: Really, Mrs. Barry. It's not Tomas.

BRIGID: Then what's wrong, Father?

FATHER DEMPSEY: Can I ask for your total discretion in the matter, Mrs. Barry?

BRIGID: Always, Father. Is Tomas alright?

FATHER DEMPSEY: He's fine but...Father O'Leary...Alan here, well, he is no more a priest than Lloyd George.

BRIGID: I'm not following.

FATHER DEMPSEY: He's...well, on the run, is the term they use, I believe.

BRIGID: Jesus, Mary and Joseph. Why are you bringing him here, Father?

FATHER DEMPSEY: He came to me for help, I couldn't turn him away.

BRIGID: But bringing him here?

ALAN: I escaped the Curragh, Mrs. Barry. I can't go back. It's a terrible place, not as bad as Ballykinlar but -

BRIGID: You were in Ballykinlar?

ALAN: For a few months in the beginning. I'd be scared to -

BRIGID: Did you meet Sean Barry, my son?

ALAN: That's why I came to the Father. Sean told us about him, how he helps people.

BRIGID: How is Sean? He says the food is terrible and that he can't get the parcels we send.

ALAN: The food is terrible, Mrs. Barry but Sean is holding out. When I left, he was tight with Pat Colgan. He was in good spirits and him and Pat were reorganising the camp and drilling the men in secret and -

BRIGID: Drilling the men in secret! Has he learned nothing?

ALAN: Ah, now, it's nearly all over, once Dev and Lloyd George come to agreement about the talks, they'll be out and no need for drilling.

BRIGID: And when will that be? One looking for a republic and the other refusing it? Two children fighting over a toy.

FATHER DEMPSEY: They both have to make it work, Mrs. Barry. Dev has to save face and Lloyd George has to convince the world he cares.

BRIGID: Only he doesn't and sure they invented the language and they can twist it up down and sideways to make fools of us. I hold out no hope for this peace, Father.

FATHER DEMPSEY: I hope you're wrong. Neither country can continue like this.

BRIGID: They say the bishops are going to issue a statement, is that true?

FATHER DEMPSEY: I believe so. They're asking for the release of the prisoners. There'll be a novena in October sometime.

ALAN: Everyone is tired of the fighting, Mrs. Barry. The boys in the camps just want to go home.

BRIGID: I just want to see my son again. Do you still have parents, Alan?

ALAN: I do, Mrs. Barry. They live out towards Kilcock, on a farm there. I'm the youngest of five.

BRIGID: And have you seen your mother since you were imprisoned?

ALAN: No.

BRIGID: Take it from me, she just wants to put her arms around you now and never let you go.

ALAN: The Father got a letter to her to tell her I was safe. I just need to wait it out until we're all free.

BRIGID: And you think Tomas can help?

FATHER DEMPSEY: I'm hoping, Mrs. Barry, that Tomas might be able to arrange a safe passage for Alan. I was going to keep him with me as a visiting priest but Mrs. O'Donoghue is asking too many questions.

ALAN: The Tans wouldn't ask me as much as that woman. I'm afraid I'll slip up.

FATHER DEMPSEY: She wants him to say mass on Sunday and sure, that can't happen.

BRIGID: God forbid, wouldn't that be a sin! Still, I'm sorry to disappoint you, Father, I'm really not sure Tomas can help, he's not as involved with the Volunteers as Sean. And I'm not comfortable -

FATHER DEMPSEY: I just need to get Alan up to Dublin. He knows where to go after that.

BRIGID: Have you tried UaBuachalla?

FATHER DEMPSEY: He's away for the next few days.

BRIGID: I don't want Tomas getting in any trouble. *(Beat)* But sure, he'll make his own mind up when he comes. None of them listen to me anymore. Tea, Fathers?

FATHER DEMPSEY: That's be lovely, Mrs. Barry, thank you.

ALAN: Thanks very much, Mrs. Barry.

BRIGID: What did you do that you landed in Ballykinlar, Alan?

ALAN: Nothing too terrible. Not murder or anything. I held up an RIC station with Sean, Mrs. Barry.

BRIGID: My Sean?

ALAN: Aye. Did you not know?

BRIGID: I did not. Sure that's an awful thing to do. Is that the time Teresa was in it?

ALAN: I don't know a Teresa. And we were doing it for Ireland.

BRIGID: Ireland is worse than the devil. He at least just wants your soul. Were you on the run like Sean, that time? The milk is there Father.

FATHER DEMPSEY: Thank you, Mrs. Barry.

ALAN: I was picked up early on.

BRIGID: Was it you who gave Sean away?

ALAN: I did not! I'm not a rat, Mrs. Barry. They beat me and everything. But they knew. They have informers and spies everywhere.

BRIGID: I wasn't meaning to accuse - it's just my heart is broke and -

FATHER DEMPSEY: It's not easy times, Mrs. Barry.

ALAN: I just want it to end.

BRIGID: We all do. *(Footsteps outside)* That's probably Tomas now.

ANNE: *(From off)* You hoo! It's me. I've got some fantastic news and *(Door opens)* Oh hello, Fathers.

FATHER DEMPSEY: Hello, Mrs. Kilbride...eh, can I introduce you to a visiting priest, Father O'Leary.

ANNE: Father O'Leary, it's lovely to meet you. Where are you visiting from?

ALAN: The country.

ANNE: The country? That's a broad answer. Any particular part?

ALAN: All over.

ANNE: I see. *(A bit put out)* And you both came to call on Brigid? Isn't that nice for you, Brigid?

BRIGID: It's great, alright.

ANNE: You must both come to me in a day or two. I'll do a nice roast in honour of your visit, Father O'Leary. How long will you be here for?

ALAN: Not long.

ANNE: I hear the country is lawless, were you in Galway and Mayo and sure Cork is supposed to be a terrible place altogether.

FATHER DEMPSEY: *(Deftly stepping in)* It's more peaceful now since the truce. Father O'Leary is a man of few words, Mrs. Kilbride. He's just finished a vow of silence so he's not used to talking.

ANNE: My.

FATHER DEMPSEY: He's a great man for the praying, though.

ALAN: *(Nodding)* I am, God is good and thanks to his holy saints.

ANNE: Amen. Praying is important. Your mother must be so proud to have a priest in the family.

ALAN: Yes.

ANNE: Donnacha, that's my son, he was going for the priesthood at one stage, wasn't he, Brigid?

BRIGID: Was he? *(Laying sandwiches on table)* Some sandwiches, Fathers.

ANNE: Listen to her, was he! It was all the child could talk about from when he was two. He was an early talker. 'Mama, I want to be a priest,' he used to say.

BRIGID: Tea, Anne?

ANNE: Yes, not too strong. *(Tea pouring)* He used to bless the bread when I'd buy it from the shops and everything. And he knew his Latin like he knew his mathematics.

BRIGID: Milk?

ANNE: A smidgeon. *(More pouring)* Enough! Fathers, I was so disappointed when he said he wanted to study law in UCD, but what could I do. Children must follow their own path.

FATHER DEMPSEY: Indeed they must. That's lovely looking bread there, Mrs. Barry.

ANNE: When did you get the call, Father O'Leary?

ALAN: What call?

ANNE: From Our Lord?

ALAN: Right....eh..when I was two as well.

ANNE: That's remarkable. God calls early on the special ones. Did any of yours ever have a vocation, Brigid?

BRIGID: A vocation to driving me mad, maybe. Eat up there now, Fathers. What was it you wanted to tell me, Anne?

ANNE: I think our visitor should say Grace?

FATHER DEMPSEY: Of course. Blessed oh Lord -

ANNE: Father O'Leary, I meant.

ALAN: Of course. (*He is a bit panicky*)   Blessed oh Lord and these thy gifts which of thy mountain we are bound to receive. Amen.

ANNE: Mountain? I always thought it was bounty.

FATHER DEMPSEY: God's holy mountain, isn't that right, Father O'Leary.

ALAN: Indeed. His holiest of holy mountains.

ANNE: And what mountain would that be?

FATHER DEMPSEY: Mount Everest.

ANNE: Mount Everest is a holy mountain?

ALAN: Indeed.

FATHER DEMPSEY: A very important mountain. A symbol of all the vastness of the world.

ANNE: Of course. It must be my age than made me forget or that fact that I have so much on my mind, Donnacha and -

BRIGID: Is the tea alright for you, Fathers?

FATHER DEMPSEY: It is indeed.

BRIGID: What was it you wanted, Anne? You said you'd fantastic news when you came in? I'm sure we don't want to keep you.

ANNE: You're not keeping me at all, I'm enjoying myself. I tried to tell Joseph the news downstairs but Inspector Dwyer is there and - *(Alan yelps, his cup clatters)* What's the matter with you? Is it the tea? I think myself it's a bit off.

BRIGID: There's nothing wrong with the tea.

ANNE: The poor Father jumped. Nearly upended his tea.

ALAN: I'm grand.

BRIGID: What is Dwyer doing downstairs? He needn't think everything is rosy again because of the truce.

ANNE: He wasn't looking to be served, he's on duty. Are you sure you're alright, Father?.

ALAN: Yes.

ANNE: You don't look too good.

ALAN: I'm fine.

ANNE: If you say so.

BRIGID: What's this news, Anne?

ANNE: I have arranged a surprise for you and Joseph.

BRIGID: I'm not following.

ANNE: Listen to her, Father. You'd swear she never got a surprise in her life.

BRIGID: Not from you, I haven't. Are you sick or something?

ANNE: How funny you are! Mr. Kilbride has hired out a Landaulette from Dawsons for tomorrow. He's some business in Dublin and he was to take his secretary, but, I said, John, she has two legs, she can go up in the train. Denis, I said, wouldn't it be nice for Brigid and Joseph, who work so hard to come with us. I'm packing for a picnic in the Phoenix Park.

BRIGID: You want me and Joseph to go out with you and Denis?

ANNE: Yes. A treat.

BRIGID: Are you sure you're not sick?

ANNE: *(Laughing uneasily)* I'm as well as can be. Will you come?

BRIGID: It all sounds…unusual and -

ANNE: It's a trip in a car, how unusual is that? I really thought you'd be excited. Father?

FATHER DEMPSEY: It sounds lovely, Mrs. Kilbride. A very kind gesture.

ANNE: Yes, kind, exactly. What is the point, I thought, of being one of the richest women in town, with a very successful son and husband if you can't make others happy too.

FATHER DEMPSEY: Very noble.

BRIGID: Alright then, I'd be delighted. I'll tell Joseph to organise Tomas to mind the pub. Or Mary if she's not at the college.

ANNE: That's settled then. The car seats four so we might as well all use it. It's the biggest they had. I'll have another cup of tea, Brigid.

Pouring. More footsteps outside. Door opens.

TOMAS: Dwyer's up the wall asking questions down there, Mammy and – *(He sees Anne and the priests)* Fathers. Auntie Anne.

BRIGID: You were supposed to be back five minutes ago.

TOMAS: I'm early as it happens, Mammy. Miss O'Neill needed a hand with some clearing out and I was -

BRIGID: Helping Lizzie O'Neill clear out, aren't you the great fellow? You can do that for me later.

TOMAS: *(Ignoring her)* I'll just take a slice of bread and I'll get down to Daddy. Dwyer is asking everyone in the pub if they saw any of those Curragh escapees and everyone is sending him off on wild goose chases.

BRIGID: The Father was wanting to ask you something, Tomas.

TOMAS: Father?

BRIGID: Anne and I will get out of your way. Come on Anne.

ANNE: But I'm still drinking my tea. And I am not going down to that bar. Mossie Kinsella was there on the way in and … *(A look to Father Dempsey)* And even though he's a fine fellow, I'd rather not listen to him cast slurs on Mr. Kilbride.

BRIGID: The Fathers can hardly go down to the pub. We'll go to the kitchen, Anne.

FATHER DEMPSEY: It's a small matter but I'd say Tomas would rather we discuss it privately, Mrs. Kilbride.

ANNE: Of course. Indeed. *(She stands)* Excuse me.

BRIGID: We'll leave you to it, Fathers.

Footsteps, door opens closes. Beat.

TOMAS: Father? I've done nothing, Father.

FATHER DEMPSEY: But I have, Tomas. I need your help. Father O'Leary here is a Curragh escapee. Alan O'Brien.

TOMAS: You were the fellow squealed on Sean.

ALAN: I did not. Amn't I in prison the same as him. And wasn't it Sean told me about the Father. Would he have done that if I squealed on him? Tomas, you have to help me.

TOMAS: I'll help Father Dempsey. What do you need, Father?

Footsteps outside.

FATHER DEMPSEY: He needs a place to stay and transport to Dublin,

Door opens.

ANNE: Fathers, I'm sorry…I left my bag. I overheard the last piece. I'm sorry. I wasn't listening. But really …Tomas could hardly transport a Father to Dublin. Father O'Leary, you're welcome to come with me and my husband tomorrow in the Landaulette. We can drop you anywhere you want to go.

FATHER DEMPSEY: That's very kind Mrs. Kilbride, but -

ANNE: You should have just asked me, Father. What is the point of being the richest person in the town, with the biggest house, if the clergy can't come to me for help? Myself and John will be delighted to have a real Father come to Dublin with us.

FATHER DEMPSEY: But you said the car only holds four and you've got Joseph and -

ANNE: Joseph and Brigid won't mind giving up their day out for the clergy. *(Calling back)* Isn't that right Brigid?

More footsteps, Brigid enters. Breathless

BRIGID: I said I'd get your bag when the Fathers were finished with Tomas and – I'm sorry Fathers.

ANNE: Father O'Leary needs a lift to Dublin. I was just saying that you and Joseph will be glad to give up your seat in the Landaulette to help the clergy.

BRIGID: I might not be glad.

ANNE: May God forgive you. She's only joking, Fathers. Now, I won't hear another word about it. Tomorrow at twelve. You can come yourself Father Dempsey if you'd like now we've a spare seat.

FATHER DEMPSEY: I think I'd better.

ANNE: That's settled then. Thanks for the tea, Brigid.

Footsteps, door opens, closes as she leaves. Footsteps fade.

BRIGID: That's a great mess, now.

TOMAS: No one will suspect Auntie Anne, it'll be fine.

BRIGID: Is every member of this family to be dragged into this war?

FATHER DEMPSEY: I'm sorry Mrs. Barry -

BRIGID: You should be, Father.

TOMAS: You weren't saying that when he did it for Sean, Mammy.

BRIGID: I know. I know. Go downstairs you, your father will be bellowing up for you in a minute.

TOMAS: *(To O'Leary)* Don't you go doing anything to put my Auntie Anne in danger.

ALAN: I wouldn't.

Footsteps as Tomas leaves. Silence.

BRIGID: You and I are even now, Father. Do not ever come back here looking for one of my sons to do any more. I swear, I'll lock that eejit of a boy up in this house before I'll let him be killed. I'll turn you all in before I let one hair of his head be harmed. And you *(To Alan)* you stay away from all this now. Don't destroy your mother. Go on. The pair of ye.

They leave. Brigid begins tidying up the delph. After a moment, she lets them drop with a crash and buries her head in her hands.

END OF EPISODE

EPISODE 32 – MOSSIE GETS FOLLOWED, OCT. 1921

Scene 1 - Street in Maynooth

PEADAR: That's him. See? Matches the photograph. He's just walked into Barry's pub.

PETER: From all accounts, he'll be there awhile. We'll leave it about half an hour, Peadar, then go in and see how the land lies.

PEADAR: It won't be lying too well for him, that's for sure, Peter.

Laugh

VOICEOVER: Fractured – October 1921.

Scene 2 - Barry's pub

In the pub. Tomas is behind the bar. Mossie is seated at the bar.

MOSSIE: 'Mossie Kinsella wouldn't be seen dead on a stage' says I. 'The stage is only for fools and fairies', says I.

TOMAS: Is that right?

MOSSIE: That's right, Tomas. 'Fools and fairies', says I. 'And I don't know which one of them you are, Paddy Dooley – but that's your own business!' *(He laughs uproariously)* Paddy Dooley didn't know what hit him, so he didn't – arrogant gobshite that he is.

TOMAS: Ah now Mossie..

MOSSIE: Ah now Mossie me arse! Bringing his neighbour to court. Sending the Volunteers after me. Say what ye like about Mossie Kinsella – I pay what's due. Honest as the day is long, so I am.

TOMAS: The clocks are going back next week Mossie. The days are getting fierce short now.

MOSSIE: Ah would ye shut up with yer smart comments.

TOMAS: And here's me having to listen to yours all evening.

MOSSIE: I've a mouth on me alright, but I know when to keep it shut. *(Pause. An undertone of warning)* That's a lesson Paddy Dooley might choose to learn.

TOMAS: What's that supposed to mean?

MOSSIE: I'm saying nothing. I don't spend all me time talking ye know – I spend a fair amount of it watching, and listening too. Oh, the things Mossie Kinsella could tell ye...

Door opens. Poor Brid rushes in, all in a dither. Colm is with her, carrying a home-made wooden sword that is broken.

POOR BRID: Colm we're going to be late! Come on love, we have to hurry. Hello Tomas! Mr. Kinsella.

TOMAS: Mrs. O'Sullivan. Mammy's housecoat gang are meeting upstairs.

POOR BRID: The housecoat gang! Would you go on with yourself ye cheeky little pup. We're the Women's Group, don't ye know. Doing very important work.

TOMAS: Ah that's right. I believe Mick Collins himself is arriving today for consultations on the Treaty. Wait until he hears about your cake sale!

POOR BRID: Wait until he hears about your black eye!

MOSSIE: She got you there Tomas! She got you there.

POOR BRID: Come on Colm. *(Colm is sulky. He holds up his sword)* There's no use holding up that sword, Colm. It's broken. There's nothing I can do about it. Upstairs, I said. *(impatient)* Now!

TOMAS: What's wrong with you, Colm?

POOR BRID: He's in a mood because his sword is broken. Daddy will fix it when he gets home. Come on, Colm. We have to go to that meeting now. Maybe Moll with be there. You can play with her.

MOSSIE: Ah – is that his little girlfriend?

Colm stops immediately.

POOR BRID: Mr. Kinsella! That's not helpful. *(Mossie chuckles)* Colm please.

TOMAS: Sure leave him here if you want Mrs. O'Sullivan. I'll keep an eye on him.

POOR BRID: Are you sure? I don't want him to be any trouble.

TOMAS: Ah it's no trouble. It's not like there's a rush on.

BRID: Thanks Tomas. You're very good. *(To Colm)* You can stay here love. I'll be back soon. Behave yourself now. *(She gives him a loud kiss and footsteps as she leaves, which fade)* I'm here, ladies

COLM: Ugh!

Colm promptly wipes the kiss away. Mossie gives a huge laugh.

MOSSIE: Look at him, wiping off that kiss. God man. Set your standard a bit higher. Come over here now and I'll see what I can do about that sword. *(A hesitant footstep)* Come on, I won't bite. *(More footsteps)* Good lad. You're dead right to be suspicious. People are far too trusting these days. Makes for nothing but pain, believe you me son. Let's see your sword. *(Sound of sword being passed over)* Broken is it? What were you doing with it at all? Catching rats in the shed? No. Fighting the fairies?

(Colm looks disgusted) That's annoyed you, huh. Ah no I can see now. This is a very strong sword. It was probably broken in a fierce battle. *(Colm nods)* By a very brave fighter. *(Colm smiles)* I'm right, amn't I. Was it your Daddy who made it? *(grunt)* It was, ey? He's alright your daddy. Not like some of the arseholes around here. Bit soft though. Watch out or he'll have you prancing around on the stage with Paddy Dooley before ye know it. Hang on, now until I get my magic hands on this sword.

We hear him taping up the sword. He starts to whistle. Colm copies him.

MOSSIE: Whistling is it? Begod, we could make a man out of ye yet. Here, hold this end of the sword. That's the boy. There you are now, all fixed.

Colm is delighted. He waves it around and pretends to kill Mossie.

COLM: Ya! Ya! Ya!

MOSSIE: Ye bastard! Ye've killed me. A dumb fucking mute has killed Mossie Kinsella. Did we ever think we'd see the day!

Colm laughs. The door opens. Squeaky pram. Cissy enters, pushing a huge pram. She has difficulty with the door.

CISSY: Jesus Mr. Kinsella, would ye not think of giving me a hand in the door.

Tomas goes to her aid.

TOMAS: Sorry Cissy. Let me help you there.

CISSY: Thanks Tomas. At least there's one gentleman around here.

MOSSIE: I didn't know it was in search of a gentleman you were Cissy. I'd have warned you to avoid Donnacha Kilbride if that was the case.

TOMAS: Mossie…

CISSY: It's alright Tomas. I've heard worse. Is Teresa upstairs? She's gone off without leaving me a key. I can't get in and the baby needs to be fed.

TOMAS: I'll run up and ask her.

CISSY: Thanks Tomas – you're a pet. *(Tomas goes)* I'll just use the toilet while I'm waiting. I'm bursting!

She runs off to the toilet. Mossie shakes his head.

MOSSIE: Women these days Colm – not the quality they used to be at all. *(Colm shakes his head)* That's right, shake yer head, yer not stupid, are you? Sit up here beside me now young man and let Mossie Kinsella instruct you on the ways of the world. *(Colm climbs on stool)* Good man. Now, there's two types of people in this world young Colm – the gombeens and the gobshites. If you're anyway clever at all you'll make sure to be a gobshite. Gobshites…

Door opens, street, closes. Anne walks in.

MOSSIE: Well, good afternoon Granny Kilbride! Or is it Grandmama these days? I forget sometimes. *(In the pram the baby stirs)* Aren't you going to say 'hello' to your grandchild over there in the pram?

ANNE: That's, that's not – *(The baby cries louder)* Where's her mother? *(Crying gets worse)* Oh, for goodness sake. Hush there now. *(Rocking the pram)* Hush. *(More tenderly)* Hush. That's it. Hush now. *(The baby settles.)* There now, all better. All better.

MOSSIE: You've the touch there now, Granny Kilbride.

ANNE: Mrs. Kilbride to you Mr. Kinsella

MOSSIE: Wasn't always that way. *(Under his breath)* Annie.

Anne starts. She is caught off guard. For a long moment they stare at each other. She finally breaks contact and goes upstairs.

ANNE: *(Composing herself)* It's Anne. Good day, Mr. Kinsella.

Footsteps moving off, fading.

MOSSIE: Like I said Colm. They don't make women like they used to.

Cissy exits toilet as Tomas footsteps on stairs.

TOMAS: I'll tell her Teresa, don't worry!

CISSY: Oh God. How many rules do I have to obey to get into the house? *(Bending over baby)* Hello, baby. Go on, Tomas, tell me.

TOMAS: Just one. Don't let the cat out on your way in.

CISSY: I'll do my best.

TOMAS: How are you getting on?

CISSY: Ah ok. Teresa's very good to have me. I just…I don't know if she likes me very much.

TOMAS: That's just Teresa. She wouldn't have you if she didn't want to. You know that.

CISSY: I suppose. Can you open the door to let me out? It's a bit of a squash. *(Footsteps as they move to the door, the struggle to get out)* Thanks Tomas. Tell Mary to come and visit me will you?

TOMAS: I will. Bye Cissy.

Footsteps as Peter and Peadar enter. Tomas is shocked to see them.

TOMAS: *(Undertone)* Peter. Peadar. What are you two -

MOSSIE: *(Calling over)* There's two men over here in need of a pint Tomas!

TOMAS: What?

MOSSIE: Meself and young Colm here. Pints on the double! *(Laughs)*

TOMAS: In a minute, Mossie. Boys?

PETER: Tonight.

PEADAR: That's our orders.

TOMAS: Are they sure?

PETER: Must be.

TOMAS: They did all the checks?

PETER: I don't know. We just do what we're told.

TOMAS: Yeah but…

PEADAR: The way I heard it, it was you made the report.

TOMAS: Well, my mother said…yes, I made a report. I didn't expect..

PEADAR: What?

TOMAS: Nothing.

PEADAR: We'll just sit over here, keep an eye.

Footsteps as they move off. Seats being pulled back.

TOMAS: Jesus. *(Sounding a little shell shocked)* Pints coming up, Mossie. *(Pouring)* Here you go Mossie. On the house.

MOSSIE: Save your charity for someone who needs it Tomas Barry. Never let it be said that Mossie Kinsella couldn't pay his own way. Some people Colm would be in the habit of telling lies about a man – spreading stories if ye like. Never let that happen to you, do ye hear me? *(Shouts)* Mossie Kinsella pays his bills! *(Confidentially)* A man's good name is all he has, ye see. Take that away and there's nothing left. Isn't that right Tomas?

TOMAS: That's right Mossie.

MOSSIE: Hold on to your good name Colm. Talk as much shite as ye like - when you get around to talking - but let it be harmless shite. Isn't that right Tomas?

TOMAS: That's right Mossie.

MOSSIE: Hold yer secrets inside, where they belong. *(He puts his fist to his chest. Colm copies him)* Never let it be said that Mossie Kinsella betrayed a secret. *(He drinks)* Ahhhhhhh...

He pats Colm on the back, picks up his cap and makes to leave.

COLM: Ahhhhhhh.

MOSSIE: *(Laughs)* Well, do ye know what, but you're great company, young Colm. Maybe we might meet up for another pint some evening?

COLM: Uh-huh

MOSSIE: You're buying the next time though. Never trust a man who doesn't get a round in. I'll be off.

TOMAS: One for the road Mossie?

MOSSIE: Christ almighty, are you Barrys ever finished trying to squeeze the last few shillings out of me? Don't think I haven't noticed that your bread is tuppence dearer than it was two weeks ago. I've a mind to do all my shopping in Kilcock from now on. Money grabbing bastards the lot of ye!

Footsteps. He opens the door and exits.

PEADAR: *(Getting up)* That's us. Be seeing you Tomas.

TOMAS: Boys, please...

PETER: We have our orders. *(Door opens)*

TOMAS: I know, but... *(Door closes)* Oh Christ. Oh, Christ. I have to find O'Reilly.

Tomas goes to door and exits. Colm is alone. Beat

COLM: M-m-mossie? *(Climbing down from stool. Footsteps to door)* 'amos? Mossie? *(he exits)*

BRIGID: *(Distant but growing closer)* Thanks ladies. It should be a great fundraiser. We'll be baking for the next week!

Footsteps as they enter bar.

POOR BRID: I'm always baking anyway. Con loves my fruitcake.

ANNE: I really don't have time for baking. I think I'm better suited to a marketing role.

BRIGID: Whatever you can do, that would be great. There's so many families out there who need our help.

TERESA: Baking is a simple matter of chemistry. Follow the instructions and achieve a result. I'll get Cissy to help. She's really quite a good companion.

ANNE: Huh! If you like that kind of thing.

TERESA: I do. And the baby is very well behaved. It made a two-syllable gurgle yesterday– which is quite advanced. She shouldn't be doing that sort of thing until at least six months old.

POOR BRID: What's the baby's name, Teresa?

TERESA: Mary Anne. Mary for Cissy's mother, who wants nothing to do with the child, unfortunately. And Anne for her other grandmother who feels exactly the same.

Anne is stunned. There is an awkward silence.

ANNE: Time I was getting on.

BRIGID: Yes. Cakes won't bake themselves.

POOR BRID: I'll just get Colm and we'll be off.

TERESA: I'll be in for some of the ingredients tomorrow Brigid. Will there be a discount?

BRIGID: I'll give them to you for cost.

ANNE: I'll be going.

She exits

POOR BRID: *(Calling)* Colm! Where's Colm? *(Door opens as Tomas enters)* Tomas, is Colm with you?

TOMAS: *(Jumpy)* Colm? I..eh...

POOR BRID: Did he go in the kitchen? He's always after your sponge cakes Brigid.

TOMAS: He must have. I'll go get him.

POOR BRID: The divil.

Footsteps as Tomas moves off.

BRIGID: Ah, he's welcome to it. I'll remember to put a few sponges on my list. You can buy them all!

POOR BRID: If Colm doesn't eat them first.

TERESA: You know it's really not healthy to have an excess of sugar in one's diet. It can lead to childhood weight problems, diabetes and heart problems in later life.

BRIGID: Oh for goodness sake Teresa. A bit of sponge cake never did anyone any harm.

TOMAS: *(Footsteps as he emerges)* He's not in there. Did he go into the toilet do ye think?

POOR BRID: I'll check *(She goes, distant)* Colm! Colm! *(From the toilet. Distant)* He's not here!

BRIGID: I thought you were watching him, Tomas.

TOMAS: I was, I – I just slipped out for a moment, couldn't find who I wanted and came back. I was only a minute.

BRIGID: Are you some class of an eejit?

BRID: *(Returning)* He's not in there with you? Is he hiding behind the bar?

TOMS: No.

POOR BRID: Did he go out the door Tomas? He'd never do that, would he?

TERESA: If he did, his poor communication skills really wouldn't aid his return.

TOMAS: He was here Brid. He was here all the time. Up at the bar, with Mossie. They were laughing away together, having a great time. He…. *(He realises what has happened)* Oh Christ.

POOR BRID: What? What's wrong? What did Mossie do?

TOMAS: Nothing. Colm liked Mossie. He just…may have followed him home.

POOR BRID: What?

TOMAS: I don't know. I didn't see. I was only out for a second. I got distracted.

BRIGID: Tomas!

POOR BRID: Colm!

TOMAS: I'll go get him back. I'll find him. He's not gone long. I swear Brid. I'll have him back.

He runs out.

BRIGID: Tomas! *(Goes to door)* What way are you going? Mossie doesn't live down that way at all.

POOR BRID: I can't wait around while Colm is out there on his own.

BRIGID: I'll come with you. Let me just grab my coat.

TERESA: It's possibly a waste of resources for everyone to go off in different directions, with no form of communication between the various parties.

POOR BRID: *(Screams)* I don't care about resources! I'm going to find my son. Colm! Colm!

Door opens, closes as she runs out.

TERESA: I was only going to suggest that someone should remain here in case he should chance to return on his own.

BRIGID: Good idea. You stay. I'll go with Brid. *(As she exits)* Brid! Brid!

END OF EPISODE

EPISODE 33 – MOSSIE'S DEMISE, OCT. 1921

Scene 1 - Outside Mossie's house

Hammering on door.

POOR BRID: Mossie, Mossie, if you're in there. Have you got Colm? *(More hammering)* Mossie!

BRIGID: Mossie's not there, Brid. Let's go. Come on.

POOR BRID: Colm can't have gone, Brigid, he can't be gone. We've waited so long and -

BRIGID: We will find him and look, if he's with Mossie, he'll come to no harm. Come on.

Brid sobbing. Footsteps

Scene 2 - Exterior, Maynooth, off Main St

Footsteps. Mossie is whistling a tune. He is joined by two other sets of footsteps. Whistling fades.

MOSSIE: Yer walking very close, boys there, if you don't mind me saying.

PETER: A word if you please, Mr. Kinsella.

Footsteps stop.

MOSSIE: Mossie Kinsella is always ready to talk to anyone if they're buying him a pint.

PETER: That's what we heard alright.

PEADAR: Talking to a lot of people aren't you, Mossie?

MOSSIE: Who are you?

PETER: Come with us.

MOSSIE: I'll go with no one if I don't know their name.

PETER: I said come with us.

MOSSIE: What do ye want?

PEADAR: Just do as we say.

MOSSIE: Did Paddy Dooley send ye? *(No answer)* How many times must I tell ye lads, I will pay Dooley when I have the money.

PEADAR: Move.

MOSSIE: How can I pay him if I don't have it? You can't get blood out of a stone, can ye?

PETER: Come on.

MOSSIE: Will ye go away and stop wasting my time.

PEADAR: We're not asking you.

They catch hold of him. Sounds of struggle.

MOSSIE: Hey, go easy. What are ye doing?

PETER: We have business with you.

MOSSIE: Well, I have no business with you.

PEADAR: Don't make this any harder than it needs to be.

MOSSIE: Go back to your Mammies. Look at the two of ye, playing soldiers. Let me go.

Sound of a gun being clicked.

PETER: Playing are we?

MOSSIE: Threatening a man with a gun in his own town. Paddy Dooley has stooped low now. I told you, he'll get his money.

PEADAR: We know nothing about any money.

MOSSIE: *(With real fear)* What is it then? I'm just an ordinary decent man trying to earn a living in these hard times and -

PETER: The word is you've been doing a lot of talking Kinsella.

Sound of a stumble.

MOSSIE: Talking? What are you on about? Where are you bringing me? What I have done?

Sound of footsteps on grass, then into forest.

MOSSIE: What have I done, I'm asking ye?

PETER: You've talked to the wrong people. Stand there. *(Footsteps stop)* Doing a bit of informing, were you?

MOSSIE: *(Laughs)* Me, an informer. To who? The British?

PETER: To anyone who'll listen.

MOSSIE: Who said that?

PEADAR: We have good information.

MOSSIE: If you lads knew me, you'd know that there's no love lost between Mossie Kinsella and the Volunteers but I like the British even less.

PETER: We wouldn't expect you to say anything different.

MOSSIE: Who accused me? A man has a right to know who his accusers are. Was it that eejit Paddy Dooley?

PETER: You've been too clever by far, Kinsella. You should have kept yourself to yourself. You picked on the wrong people this time.

MOSSIE: *(It dawns on him)* Wait a minute. You don't mean it came from the Barrys? *(No answer)* Jesus Christ, that fella is even younger than ye lads. It's all lies …. Bring him down here. Let him say it to my face. I don't believe this. I was just havin a bit of … all I got was a few free drinks from his stone faced bitch of a mother. I didn't mean anything by it.

PEADAR: Ah, you got your memory back.

MOSSIE: It was nothing. Go on up there and ask him. I never said anything to anyone.

PETER: It's not just that. There's been an informer in this town for a long while now.

MOSSIE: It's not Mossie Kinsella.

PETER: That's not for us to decide.

MOSSIE: What are ye going to do?

PEADAR: *(Nervously)* You know how we deal with informers.

MOSSIE: No, no. This is all wrong. I haven't done anything.

PEADAR: We've a job to do.

MOSSIE: So I'm to be executed without a fair trial?

PETER: We're just doing ….

MOSSIE: For fucks sake, don't give me that whole duty line. You can't hide behind that. Do you not care that I'm an innocent man?

PEADAR: Don't make this …

MOSSIE: You're no better than the British. At least they'd give me a trial and a chance to defend myself.

PEADAR: We have our orders.

MOSSIE: I swear to you. I've done nothing. Give me a chance to prove it. You can do what you like with me then.

Peadar is having doubts and turns to Peter.

PEADAR: *(To Peter)* Maybe Peter, we should …

PETER: *(Interrupting)* No names!

PEADAR: Maybe he is telling the truth.

PETER: How many of them ever admit it?

MOSSIE: At least listen to him Peter.

PETER: Don't you use my name. *(A sound. It's Colm)* What was that? *(Shouting)* Anyone there? *(To Peadar)* Go see if there's anyone there.

PEADAR: Right. *(Footsteps as Peadar moves away)*

MOSSIE: All I'm asking is for a chance to defend myself. *(No response)* Lock me up wherever you like. Put me before any court. Just don't do anything now that you'll regret for the rest of your lives.

PETER: Shut up, old man. *(Footsteps as Peadar returns)* Anything?

PEADAR: Not that I could see but there's trees everywhere.

PETER: Probably just an animal. Put -

MOSSIE: You know this isn't right. I can see it in your faces. *(No response)* What's your name, son?

PETER: Shut up, old man, I said.

PEADAR: I think...maybe we should...what's the harm in waiting?

PETER: He knows us now. He'd have the RIC down on us before we'd get to the end of the street.

MOSSIE: I'm not asking you to let me go. Just give me more time. A chance to ...

PETER: That's enough. *(To Peadar)* We have our orders. We can't go back without carrying them out.

MOSSIE: There you go again, orders and duty! Where does common sense come into it? Why can't you make up your own mind? I've never let anyone tell me what to do.

PETER: And I'll certainly not let you tell me what to do. There's been enough talk.

Takes a black hood out of his pocket and throws it to Mossie.

PETER: Put that hood on.

MOSSIE: You're really going to do this? *(No reply)* Why should I put it on?

PETER: For Christs sake. Just do it!

MOSSIE: Or what? *(Pause)* I told you, nobody tells me what to do. *(He looks at Peadar)* If you're planning to pull that trigger son, you'll have to look me in the eyes while you're doing it.

PEADAR: *(To Peter)* I can't watch this.

PETER: For fucks sake!

PEADAR: It's not too late. We don't have to.

PETER: If you want to go, then go but you know what will happen if you do.

PEADAR: Then you'll have to shoot him, I can't.

PETER: I'll have to report this.

MOSSIE: *(Sarcastically to Peter)* A report? You'll be a big hero.

PETER: *(Pointing the gun at Mossie)* I've heard enough out of you. If you have any prayers, you'd better say them now.

MOSSIE: *(He laughs)* I never had much time for prayers. If there is a God, he was never a friend to me. Do ye lads believe in God? *(No response)* Ye look like ye do. God and country, they go together, don't they? Well, I hope when ye get in front of whatever God ye believe in, ye'll be able to justify what ye're planning on doing today. Although, I don't think any God would forgive the murder of an innocent man.

PETER: Get yourself ready.

MOSSIE: I haven't finished talking yet. You can't deny a man his last words.

PETER: You have too many words, Kinsella.

PEADAR: *(Hoping to delay the inevitable)* Leave him have his say.

Unseen by the three men, Colm will appear and observe from a distance.

MOSSIE: You can tell the good people in this kip of a town that I curse them all. I curse the woman who brought me into this world and the man who helped her. I never even knew their names. I curse everyone who looked down their noses at me as if it was my fault I was born in a workhouse. *(Pause)* I might have died there if it wasn't for John and Mary Kinsella, the only people who ever showed any kindness to me. The one regret I have is that I wasn't as good to them as I should have been. They gave me everything I have.

Pause as he thinks.

PETER: Are you finished?

MOSSIE: You're in a fierce hurry to put a bullet in me. Am I keeping you from your dinner? *(Pause)* Will I be your first? *(No response)* What's it like to kill a man? *(No response)* They all thought that I killed a man once. There was no proof and I never denied it. I enjoyed seeing the look on their faces, wondering "did he or didn't he". Well you can tell them that Mossie Kinsella never harmed anyone in his life.

PETER: That's not what we heard.

MOSSIE: There's not many who'd have a good word to say about me. I had no need of friends, they only ever let me down. There was one time…but…I think she thought that I wasn't good enough. Maybe I should have fought for her. Maybe I let her down too. The thing is boys, if you spend your life thinking you're not good enough, you never will be.

Silence. The two men are not sure how to proceed.

MOSSIE: *(With dawning realisation)* I never wrote a will. Didn't see any reason to. There's no family about. *(He looks at Peter)* You are going to do this?

PETER: I am.

MOSSIE: I want my final wishes recorded. Have ye got something to write with?

PETER: Oh, for the love of God!

MOSSIE: I've been in court many times in my life and I know that if it's not written down, it means nothing.

PETER: We don't have time for this.

PEADAR: We can use the photograph I have of him and I have a pencil. *(Rummages in his bag)* There we go.

PETER: *(Exasperated)* Jesus! Be quick about it.

MOSSIE: Ye lads better swear that this will be passed on.

PEADAR: I swear

MOSSIE: Are you ready? *(Slowly)* I want the house and land to go to …. Anne Kilbride … she'll understand. The cattle are to be sold and Paddy Dooley is to be paid the £100 I owe him plus £10. I swear to God that fella would follow me to hell for the money *(Laughs)*He wasn't the worst and I always enjoyed getting a rise out of him. Any money left over will go to Con O'Sullivan for the young lad Colm. He's to have a good education so he can escape from this Godforsaken place. Let me sign it.

Peadar hands Mossie the paper and pencil. He signs and hands it back. Suddenly, a noise. Colm has moved into view and Peadar spots him

PETER: Jesus Christ, how long has that child been there?

PETER: *(Cocking gun)* You said there was no one there.

PEADAR: Go easy. He's only a child.

PETER: He's seen us.

MOSSIE: Colm?

PEADAR: Is that …

MOSSIE: Don't point that thing at him. Let him go. He's a simple young lad. He can't even speak. He's a mute.

PEADAR: *(Panicking)* Come on. We'd better go. Do what you have to do.

PETER: But the child...

PEADAR: You can't!

PETER: He's seen us. *(Cajoles)* Come here Colm. Come on, I've got sweets. *(Light hesitant footsteps)* That's it, that's the lad. Come here.

MOSSIE: No. Run Colm. Run and get help. RUN!

Colm runs

PETER: You bastard! *(Gunshot. Sound of body falling)* Done. Now for the child.

Starts running after him. In the distance, we hear Brigid / Brid calling Colm's name

POOR BRID: *(Distant)* Colm! Colm!

PEADAR: We don't have time. Come on. Peter. He's a mute, you saw yourself earlier. Come on

BRIGID: *(Getting nearer)* Colm! Colm!

PEADAR: Come on, leave it. There's people coming. Come on.

They run off. Footsteps fade.

Scene 3 - Other part of wood

Sound of stumblin footsteps, panicked breathing.

BRIGID: Oh God almighty, Brid, it's Colm. Colm, pet. Colm. What's happened? Are you alright Colm? Was that a gunshot we heard?

POOR BRID: We were so worried. Why did you go off like that? What are you doing up here?

COLM: *(Quietly)* Mammy.

The women are stunned.

POOR BRID: Did he just ….

BRIGID: Yes.

COLM: *(Beginning to weep gently)* Mammy!

POOR BRID: I knew it. Didn't I tell you?

COLM: Man. The man.

POOR BRID: What man. What is it son? *(They now look in the direction Colm is pointing)* He wants us to follow him.

Footsteps as Colm leads them a few feet.

BRIGID: Jesus, Mary and Joseph! Brid, take Colm away from here and get help. Go now, Brid. NOW!

Brid runs off.

BRIGID: Oh, Mr. Kinsella. *(Sound of kneeling)* "Through this holy anointing may the Lord in his love and mercy help you with the grace of the Holy Spirit. May the Lord –

Fades out.

END OF EPISODE

EPISODE 34 – CISSY AND MARY, NOV. 1921

Scene 1 - Outside Teresa's house.

Door opens.

CISSY: *(Calling)* I'm just leaving the baby in the garden, Teresa, it's a nice sunny day. *(Pram being wheeled into position)* There now, Mary Anne. There now.

Baby coos. Sound of Cissy walking off. Door closes. Beat. Hesitant, furtive footsteps. Anne enters.

ANNE: Hello, Mary Anne. I'm Anne. I'm your grandmother. Not Teresa. *(The crinkle of paper)* That's for you. *(Beat)* Goodbye for now.

Footsteps walking quickly away.

VOICEOVER: Fractured – November 2021

Scene 2 - Teresa's house. A day later

Mary and Cissy are sitting at the kitchen table, having a cup of tea. Woodworking sounds come from another room.

CISSY: *(Reading from a newspaper)* Oh look. 'The bride wore a graceful gown of ivory satin beaute, draped in front, and falling in the new loose pouch at back, with long pointed train, a knot of orange blosson at waist, and a horseshoe of orange blossom at end of train completed the toilette.'

MARY: A horseshoe of orange blossom at the end of the train? I can't imagine that.

CISSY: 'The veil was of white tulle, with wreath of orange blossom.'

MARY: She likes orange, doesn't she?

CISSY: It's called co-ordination Mary. A commoner like you wouldn't know anything about that.

MARY: Commoner is it? And I suppose you're Maynnoth's answer to Countess Markievicz!

CISSY: No, but I think Eileen Brady must be. Listen to this – 'The bridesmaid wore a charming frock of mauve georgette, made in a design of floating petals, with velvet flowers around waist. Her hat was of black velvet with ostrich plume'.

MARY: Who paid for all this?

CISSY: It says here that the reception was held at the Hibernian Hotel by her mother Mrs. Brady of Greenfield, Maynooth.

MARY: She must have been left a fair amount of money when her husband died.

CISSY: The merry widow! I'd be fairly merry if that happened to me!

MARY: Don't say things like that.

CISSY: If Donnacha went and died and left me a load of money I'd be delighted. Jesus, if he just went and died I'd be delighted.

MARY: *(Getting upset)* You don't mean that.

CISSY: I do so. And I hope it's painful.

MARY: No.

CISSY: I have these daydreams where he goes off with some woman and she happens to be the girlfriend of a volunteer or something, so he gets shot through the head.

MARY: Will ye stop!

CISSY: And the blood is pouring out of him and he's roaring in pain.

MARY: For God's sake Cissy..

CISSY: And he's sorry then. Sorry for hiding our relationship, pretending I didn't exist.

MARY: Shut up!

CISSY: But it's too bloody late. And he bleeds to death in the street. No precious mammy to…

MARY: *(Screaming, in tears)* Shup up! Shut up! Shut up!

CISSY: *(Shocked).* What? Mary…oh I'm so sorry. I forgot he's your cousin, isn't he?

MARY: No, it's…

CISSY: I know he's not your real cousin, but still. That was really mean of me.

MARY: I'm not talking about…

COSSY: Don't pay any heed to me. I'm just bitter. I'm never going to be completing my toilette with a horseshoe of orange blossom. *(She laughs)* A horseshoe of baby shit maybe…

MARY: Neither will I…

CISSY: Of course you will. You and your secret boyfriend. 'A stor mo chroi'!

MARY: Stop!

She dissolves into tears again.

CISSY: Mary! What's the matter?

MARY: He's gone.

CISSY: The bastard. You're better off without him, you know that.

MARY: He's not a…

CISSY: Did he go off with someone else? Honestly, they're all the same.

MARY: He didn't go off with anyone else.

CISSY: Yeah – that's what he told you. Donnacha did that too. He…

MARY: He's dead.

CISSY: Dead?

MARY: Shot in the head. Bled to death in the street.

CISSY: Oh Jesus. *(Pause)* Me and my…I'm so sorry. How? When?

MARY: February. Remember that Volunteer ambush?

CISSY: Was that the one where the RIC man was killed? *(Mary nods)* I don't remember anyone else getting killed though.

MARY: No.

CISSY: RIC?

MARY: You're shocked.

CISSY: I'm hardly one to pass judgement. It's just…

MARY: I loved him. He loved me.

CISSY: I can see why you kept it a secret.

MARY: We were going to get married.

CISSY: You were taking your life into your hands.

MARY: Oh but Cissy, he was so kind, and so sweet. He just wanted to help people. If you only knew him. He was brave, and strong, and funny, and handsome. It's so unfair.

CISSY: You've been going through this all alone?

MARY: Tomas knows.

CISSY: Tomas knew about it?

MARY: You know Tomas. He picks up on these things. For a while there I was so mad I thought he was the one pulled the trigger.

CISSY: Mary!

MARY: I know.

CISSY: Tomas would never do anything like that. He's so kind.

MARY: I needed someone to blame.

CISSY: Poor Tomas.

MARY: It wasn't fair. Tomas would never do anything like that. He reminds me of my Joseph actually.

CISSY: That was his name?

MARY: Joseph. Joseph Hughes.

CISSY: Mary Hughes. *(She takes her hand)* It suits you.

MARY: I have daydreams too you know. Whatever bastard it was that killed my Joseph gets shot himself.

CISSY: If I'd known..

MARY: You didn't.

CISSY: I wouldn't have burdened you so much with my own problems.

MARY: It's okay.

CISSY: You've been so good to me Mary. I don't know what I would have done without you these past months. Standing up for me in the pub that day and -

MARY: You're my friend.

CISSY: I would have listened, that's all I'm saying. I would have tried to help you. *(Mary breaks down again)* Come here! *(She hugs her)* You poor thing.

The sound of sawing stops for a moment.

TERESA: *(From outside, muted)* Fuck and shit. *(Teresa enters the kitchen, blood coming from her finger)* I've cut my finger. A recent study says that swear words are supposed to lessen the pain of an injury. It does not seem to have worked.

CISSY: *(Jumping up)* Teresa, what happened?

TERESA: The saw slipped. Foolish of me.

CISSY: Here, let me wash that out. Come over to the sink and I'll pour water on it.

Teresa and Cissy move to sink. Sound of water.

CISSY: It doesn't look too bad. I wouldn't say it's very deep.

TERESA: A superficial wound only. However, it's important to keep it clean lest any infection be allowed to fester.

Cissy starts to clean and bandage the wound.

CISSY: I don't want you to injure yourself on my account Teresa. You're working too hard.

MARY: What are you working on?

CISSY: She's building a crib for Mary Anne.

MARY: A crib? Do you know how to build a crib Teresa?

TERESA: Of course not. Nobody knows how to do anything until they've attempted it for the first time.

MARY: Oh right.

TERESA: It's going quite well. The dados have all been cut at this point, but I've never worked on a blind dovetail joint before, and it's proving problematic.

CISSY: If anyone can do it you can Teresa. Mary Anne is a very lucky little girl.

TERESA: Well she can hardly sleep in her pram for the rest of her life, can she? Aside from anything else, it can increase the incidence of accidental smothering.

MARY: She's a little dote.

CISSY: She is, isn't she. You should see her when she smiles – her whole face lights up.

MARY: Your face lights up just talking about her.

CISSY: She reserves her best smiles for Teresa though. Just hold steady there, Teresa.

Sound of bandaging.

TERESA: An instinctive reaction, brought about by an innate desire by the vulnerable to be accepted into the tribe.

CISSY: There you go – all sorted. Will I make you a cup of tea for the shock?

TERESA: You can heat the water. Call me when it's boiled. I'll make another attempt on the blind dovetail joint.

CISSY: Ok. Be careful.

Footsteps. Teresa exits. Door closes.

MARY: She's building you a crib.

CISSY: She's amazing.

MARY: You've fallen on your feet.

The sound of sawing recommences, with hammering.

CISSY: I'll have to move on eventually though. I can't expect her to put us up forever.

MARY: Your aunt in Dublin?

CISSY: She never wanted me.

MARY: She took you in.

CISSY: Didn't have much choice, when I turned up on her doorstep in labour.

MARY: Was it awful?

CISSY: Horrible. And she and my uncle wanted to take her off me. Said it was better for the baby, that it was selfish of me to deprive her of a proper family.

MARY: You are her family.

CISSY: I am. When I arrived in your place that night – the night of the Truce party – I didn't have anywhere to go. Mammy and Daddy wouldn't answer the door to me.

MARY: My mammy wasn't much better. I was really cross with her for not letting you in.

CISSY: She has your Auntie Anne to think about.

MARY: Auntie Anne can mind herself.

CISSY: You were so brave to stand up to them, Mary. I'm so glad you're still talking to me.

MARY: For goodness sake. Why wouldn't I be talking to you?

CISSY: No one else is. It's like I've got TB or something. People cross the road to avoid me. A young lad spat at me yesterday.

MARY: The brat.

CISSY: Lily from work ignored me in the post office last week.

MARY: Lily?

CISSY: She was standing in the queue behind me. Couldn't miss me. I said hello and she just turned her back.

MARY: I can't believe that.

CISSY: Just as well I got the sack I suppose.

MARY: Oh Cissy. How are you managing for money?

CISSY: It's really strange actually. I keep finding money in odd places.

MARY: What?

CISSY: There was a five pound note in Mary Anne's pram the other day. I'd never even seen one in my life before. Five pounds!

MARY: That's more than two months wages.

CISSY: I couldn't believe it.

MARY: Somebody must have lost it.

CISSY: And last Friday I went out to take in the clothes and there was two pounds stuffed into my blouse pocket.

MARY: How would that happen?

CISSY: I think someone is giving it to me.

MARY: Who though?

CISSY: My mammy? I keep thinking that maybe she wants to help me but my daddy won't let her.

MARY: Would she have five pounds?

CISSY: I wouldn't have thought so but maybe she saved it. And I did try to thank her yesterday and she said she didn't know what I was talking about and to leave her alone.

Pause. Cissy is emotional.

MARY: Could it be Teresa, do you think?

CISSY: I don't think so. If Teresa wanted to give me money she'd just give it to me.

MARY: Auntie Anne?

There is a pause. Cissy looks at Mary, incredulously. She begins to laugh. Mary joins in, despite herself.

CISSY: You say the funniest things, Mary!

They laugh again. A smash. Hammering stops.

TERESA: *(From outside)* Fuck and shit and bastard. *(Teresa enters, holding her left hand)* I've hurt my other hand, now.

CISSY: Teresa!

TERESA: My grip on the hammer must have been faulty. It slipped from my grasp and landed on my wrist.

CISSY: Sit down there now and I'll have a look at it. Mary will you make the tea? Plenty of sugar for Teresa.

MARY: Will do. *(Sound of tea making)* Where is the sugar?

TERESA: In the press under the sink, behind the strawberry jam. An excess of sugar has been proven to have negative effects on the digestive and olfactory systems, you know.

CISSY: Taking a hammer to your hand isn't too good for them either.

Teresa laughs. It is very unexpected and the girls have never witnessed it before.

TERESA: What?

MARY: You laughed.

CISSY: I've never seen you laugh before Teresa.

TERESA: Haven't you? Perhaps you've never been funny enough.

CISSY: I'll have to try harder so.

Mary hands Teresa tea.

MARY: Here's your tea. Take a good sip for the shock. How's that hand looking Cissy?

CISSY: I think it's ok – just bruised. We might need a painkiller.

MARY: I'll get some from the pub. Mammy has loads for when Moll gets her headaches.

CISSY: Are you sure? Will I go with you?

MARY: Not at all. I'll be back in a jiffy.

CISSY: Just be careful. Don't go through the wood. After what happened to Mossie Kinsella I'd be nervous for you.

MARY: Yeah. Grouch and all as he was, I do miss him from the pub a little bit. Poor Mossie.

TERESA: I liked Mossie. He said what he thought.

MARY: That he did. I'll be back in ten minutes.

Footsteps, door opens, closes.

TERESA: Mary Anne is due a feed in 13 minutes.

CISSY: I hope you're not going to be too badly bruised.

TERESA: As long as it doesn't affect my mobility. I would like to have the crib ready by tomorrow evening.

CISSY: *(Pause)* I don't know what I would have done without you Teresa.

TERESA: You would probably have had to give up Mary Anne for adoption.

CISSY: Eh…yes.

TERESA: And you might have had nowhere to live.

CISSY: Yes.

TERESA: So you would have gone into one of those mother and baby homes.

CISSY: Right.

TERESA: That probably wouldn't have been very pleasant for you. You would have had to…

CISSY: Thank you Teresa.

TERESA: Pardon?

CISSY: Thank you. What I meant to say was thank you. You have been so kind to me and Mary Anne. I can never repay your goodness, but I will always be grateful.

TERESA: *(Teresa is caught off-guard by this effusiveness)* You're welcome.

CISSY: I was talking to Father Dempsey the other day.

TERESA: Yes?

CISSY: I wanted to have Mary Anne baptised. I didn't know if he could do it or not, what with her being…well. He said he'd do it privately.

TERESA: Excellent idea.

CISSY: Just me and the godparents.

TERESA: Yes.

CISSY: I was wondering….do you think you might be able to come along?

TERESA: I don't think so.

CISSY: *(Disappointed)* Oh.

TERESA: Father Dempsey said it should just be you and the godparents. You should do as he says.

CISSY: But..Teresa, that's what I meant. I was hoping you would be her godmother.

TERESA: Me?

CISSY: I can't think of anybody better than you. You're so strong and capable. You're kind. You're generous. You can teach her so much.

TERESA: A godmother?

CISSY: She has a hard road ahead. And that's my fault. But with someone like you in her life, it'll be that much easier. Please?

TERESA: I've never been a godmother before. I don't know what to do.

CISSY: Nobody knows how to do anything until they've attempted it for the first time. Isn't that right?

TERESA: Perhaps Father Dempsey has a book on the subject.

CISSY: Is that a yes?

TERESA: *(Thinks for a moment. Her voice is a bit shaky)* Yes. Thank you Cissy.

CISSY: *(With feeling)* Thank you, Teresa.

END OF EPISODE

EPISODE 35 – MOSSIE'S LAST WISHES, NOV. 1921

Scene 1 - Brid's house.

Scream. Crying Hurried footsteps. Door flung open. Footsteps across room.

BRID: Colm! Colm! It's all right, Colm! It's just a nightmare. *(Colm sobs)* It's just a nightmare.

COLM: The m-m-man. The man.

BRID: It's just a nightmare.

Sobbing fades.

VOICEOVER: Fractured – November 1921

Scene 2 - Barry's pub

BRIGID: Mind him well now, Tomas. Brid is very good trusting you with him again.

TOMAS: I won't let him out of my sight, I promise. How's he doing anyway, Brid?

POOR BRID: He's talking but he's fixated...he saw something no child should have to see. This country...

BRIGID: Don't upset yourself, Brid or you'll only upset him. Anne is upstairs. Come on.

Footsteps as she starts to lead her away.

POOR BRID: *(Her voice fades so end of sentence is indistinguishable)* I blame Paddy Dooley, if he hadn't wanted his money so badly none of this would have happened.

TOMAS: Well, young man, what would you like to do? *(Colm says nothing)* Would you like to draw? Is that a nod? Can you say 'yes?' Someone told me that you found your voice but I think they were telling lies. Were they? *(Colm shrugs)* I didn't hear that. I'll tell you what. This time I'll close my eyes really tight and listen very carefully. *(Tomas turns. Colm giggles)* I thought I heard a noise there but it could be anything. Did you laugh, Colm?

COLM: *(Quietly)* Yes

TOMAS: *(Eyes still closed)* That's better. Try it a bit louder.

COLM: *(Still low)* Yes.

TOMAS: Naw, I can't hear that.

COLM: *(Louder)* Yes.

TOMAS: Didn't get that, sorry.

COLM: *(Laughing) YES! YES! YES! (Door opens, street, door closes. Peter enters)* YES! YE -

Colm's laughing stops suddenly.

TOMAS: Not loud enough. Am I deaf? Colm? Colm? *(Tomas turns around)* Colm?

COLM: *(Whisper)* The Man. Man.

PETER: *(Indicating Colm)* Is that …

TOMAS: *(Interrupting him)* Peter! You shouldn't be in the town.

PETER: I didn't expect to see -

Tomas interrupts him again and tries to make light of the situation in front of Colm.

TOMAS: This is Colm. His mother is upstairs.

PETER: *(Looking around)* Anyone else here?

TOMAS: They're all upstairs. It's not a good idea for you to be here. *(Colm is frightened and hiding behind Tomas)* It's all right, Colm.

PETER: I thought he was mute.

TOMAS: He may as well be. He hardly says anything.

PETER: He was talking grand when I came in.

TOMAS: He was saying one word. He's a bit simple, so he is. *(Muted to Peter)* You need to go before anyone …

PETER: He better not have too many other words, d'you hear me?

TOMAS: What is it you want?

PETER: I have a message for you. I certainly didn't expect the young lad to be here.

TOMAS: I'm only looking after him while his mother … his foster mother is upstairs.

PETER: Is he mute at home, do you think?

TOMAS: He hadn't spoken at all since they took him out of the workhouse. *(Peter moves toward Colm)* Stay back, Peter. You're scaring him.

PETER: What's that you're doing there Colm?

No response.

TOMAS: Just leave him be. You don't have to worry.

PETER: I think I've seen you somewhere before Colm.

TOMAS: That's enough! I'm handling this. Just give me the message and go.

PETER: What's the hurry? I'm having a chat here with Colm. *(To Colm)* Have you seen me before, Colm?

Colm is frozen.

TOMAS: For Christ's sake. *(To Colm)* It's OK Colm, he's only joking with you.

PETER: *(Pointedly)* I just want to know if the lad has seen me before. I'm told I have a common face. People are always mistaking me for someone else. That could lead to all sorts of trouble.

TOMAS: There'll be trouble here if you don't go.

PETER: You're quite the big man, now, Tomas, ey?

TOMAS: What is the message?

PETER: Now that I look closely at you Colm, I don't think I have seen you before. It's very easy to make a mistake though, isn't it, Tomas?

TOMAS: It is.

Poor Brid's voice is heard off.

POOR BRID: *(Off)* Thanks Brigid. I'll see myself out.

Footsteps as she nears.

TOMAS: For God's sake, Peter. Give me the message and go.

BRID: *(Entering bar)* How did he get on, Tomas? *(Colm races to her)* Oh Colm, a big hug for my legs. That's a lovely greeting to get. *(To Colm)* Moll was asking for you. You might be able to see her soon when she's feeling better. Thanks for minding him, Tomas.

TOMAS: He was no trouble Brid.

PETER: You're Colm's mother?

Brid looks at him suspiciously.

TOMAS: This is a friend of mine, Brid.

Pause.

PETER: Patrick … Feeney …… from Carlow.

POOR BRID: Pleased to meet you. I'm actually Colm's foster mother.

PETER: Aye. Tomas told me that. He's a great lad, a credit to you.

POOR BRID: We do our best.

PETER: Tomas was telling me that he had a terrible experience a few weeks back?

POOR BRID: I'm not the better of it myself. I was one of the first to find the body, you know.

PETER: Did you see anything?

TOMAS: She didn't.

POOR BRID: I wouldn't say that now, Tomas. I saw a leg. Purple with the beating they gave him. Tortured, they're saying. The poor man must have been in fierce pain with what was done to him.

Peter shoots a glance at Tomas.

PETER: Really?

POOR BRID: They say that both his legs were broken and all his toes bar the big one on his left foot. That one though, was half sawed off.

PETER: Aw now -

POOR BRID: And that wasn't the worst of it.

TOMAS: Brid hears lots of things from a lot of unreliable sources, don't you, Brid?

POOR BRID: I resent that. I wouldn't say it if it wasn't true. Paddy Dooley has a lot to answer for.

PETER: Paddy Dooley?

POOR BRID: He might not have pulled the trigger but he knows them that did.

TOMAS: Brid, you can't go around accusing people.

POOR BRID: I'm only repeating what the whole town knows. Didn't Mossie owe Paddy a lot of money and weren't they always fighting over it?

TOMAS: That proves nothing, so it doesn't.

POOR BRID: He didn't even go to Mossie's funeral. The sure sign of a guilty conscience.

PETER: Has Colm said anything to you about what happened?

POOR BRID: Not yet, but if he knows anything, I'll get it out of him.

Another look between the two men.

TOMAS: I wouldn't go trying, Brid. You might upset him. Sure, he's mute anyway.

BRID: Amn't I after telling you, he's not as mute as he was. If Colm has anything to say, he'll tell me, won't you pet?

PETER: You'd want to be careful there missus.

POOR BRID: It's them that did it need to be careful. Torturing a lovely man like Mossie.

PETER: I have a cousin down in Carlow. Same as yourself, took a child out of the workhouse. The young one started telling stories about the neighbours, maybe she made them up or maybe she overheard the parents talking, I don't know. The next thing, didn't they come and take the child back off her. Workhouse children can be terrible liars and liars cost lives in these times.

POOR BRID: They took the child?

PETER: Sure as I'm standing here. She never saw the child again. They think she might have been taken to Cork. *(Brid, lost for words looks at Colm who is still clinging nervously to her)* It happens more often than you think. Have you ever heard of anything like that Tomas?

Tomas glares at him.

TOMAS: *(Feeling terrible)* Maybe.

PETER: The best advice I can give you is to leave matters as they are. Let him forget about the whole thing.

POOR BRID: Hmmm. I think I'll be going. Come on, Colm. *(Colm is reluctant)* Come on.

COLM: The man.

BRID: Don't be silly, come on now. Good boy. Oh, you're shaking.

Beat

COLM: The man. The man.

BRID: The man?

COLM: Yes.

PETER: I hope I didn't frighten you or him missus?

POOR BRID: *(Distracted, realising)* Well … no … no … its grand. Nice to meet you Mr. Feeney. I have to be going. *(Beat)* I'll not be asking my son anymore questions. Come on, Colm.

She exits.

PETER: Goodbye now.

Door closes.

TOMAS: You're a bastard.

PETER: Which is worse, an upset mother or a dead child? *(Tomas is shocked)* Don't look so shocked. What would you expect us to do? Now, here's the message. Take a good hard look at it. *(Paper sounds. Passes it to Tomas)* Last will and testament of one Mossie Kinsella. Notice anything?

TOMAS: He left his farm to my Auntie Anne? Jesus.

PETER: Not that. Further down. Why would he leave anything to that young lad?

TOMAS: Money for his education. Fair play to him. I know he took a shine to Colm.

PETER: If his wishes are carried out, the prospect of money might help to loosen the young lad's tongue.

TOMAS: You heard Mrs. O'Sullivan, that won't happen. Is this legal?

PETER: They were his wishes. I'd not deny that to a condemned man. *(Pause as Tomas re-reads)* You are sure that he was the informer?

TOMAS: There was information that he was… saying things…threatening things…

PETER: He struck me a too much of a loudmouth for an informer.

TOMAS: Our source was reliable. *(Door opens, Paddy enters)* Howya Paddy? *(Beat)* Are you all right?

PETER: I'll be off Tomas.

TOMAS: Right. Bye now. *(Peter leaves)* What is it, Paddy?

PADDY: You tell me. I bumped into Mrs. O'Sullivan outside and she nearly took the head off me. When I tried to reason with her, she started crying and said I should ask you. What's she on about?

TOMAS: No one believes it.

PADDY: No one believes what?

Pause.

TOMAS: She has some notion that you were behind Mossie getting killed. And Colm saw it so -

PADDY: Jesus Christ. Is she serious?

TOMAS: She probably heard some of the women talking and picked it up wrong

PADDY: There's others talking?

TOMAS: I..eh...think so.

PADDY: I had nothing to do with it.

TOMAS: I know that.

PADDY: Is your mother upstairs? I want to hear what she has to say.

TOMAS: That mightn't be a good idea … you know my mother.

PADDY: I'm not having people accusing me behind my back.

TOMAS: Leave it for a while Paddy. My aunt Anne is up there with her.

PADDY: Was the whole bloody women's group talking about me?

TOMAS: No. It'll blow over. *(Paddy crosses bar)* Paddy, I wouldn't.

PADDY: *(Opening door, Shouting upstairs)* Mrs. Barry. Can you come down! Come down now, Mrs. Barry! *(realising it's Brigid he's talking to)* Please?

TOMAS: Paddy!

Footsteps as Brigid comes down.

BRIGID: *(Distant, growing closer)* What in the name of God is all the shouting about? *(Entering)* Oh, it's you, Paddy.

PADDY: I want to know what's being said about me.

BRIGID: And you can't just ask like a sane person? In here shouting and roaring like a madman.

PADDY: I heard that there's rumours circulating saying I'm responsible for Mossie's shooting.

ANNE: The evidence is circumstantial but you had motive and probable cause which would stand up against any inquisitorial procedure.

PADDY: Will you stop it with your fancy talk! I did nothing.

BRIGID: We've all heard you and Mossie fighting over that money.

PADDY: He owed me.

ANNE: Motive.

PADDY: What?

ANNE: You didn't even go to his funeral.

Footsteps distant but getting closer.

PADDY: I am not a hypocrite. I didn't like the man and I certainly didn't mourn him when he died but I had nothing to do with his killing.

Door opens. Joseph enters.

JOSEPH: What's going on?

PADDY: Joseph, tell them I had nothing to do with Mossie's killing.

JOSEPH: No one believes that Paddy.

PADDY: Your wife does. Your sister does.

ANNE: I don't want to believe it. I'm trying to see the best in people but

BRIGID: As a matter of fact, I have spent the past half hour defending you, Mr. Dooley. But with your carry on now, shouting and roaring, well, I have to wonder.

PADDY: Wonder no more. I did nothing. And if anyone says otherwise, I'll have them up on slander charges. Maybe you know what that is, Mrs. Kilbride?

JOSEPH: No one will say anything, Paddy. You've been a good friend to us for many years.

BRIGID: A good friend to you, you mean!

JOSEPH: To our family

BRIGID: To you! Maybe you should have married him.

JOSEPH: Brigid, please -

BRIGID: Don't 'Brigid please' me. He's after coming here shouting and roaring at your wife and what do you do – stand up for him as usual.

JOSEPH: He doesn't want the whole town telling lies about him.

BRIGID: And I don't want the whole town saying my husband thinks more of his friend than he does of his wife.

JOSEPH: For God's sake, Brigid, that's -

PADDY: It's alright Joseph. I'll not come between a man and his wife. I'll not set foot here again.

JOSEPH: Ah Paddy!

PADDY: I know where I'm not welcome.

He starts for the door.

JOSEPH: Brigid? *(No response. Door opens)* Brigid! *(Door closes)* You've gone too far this time.

BRIGID: He barred himself. Why don't you run on after him if you're so worried.

JOSEPH: What has he ever done to deserve your abuse? Is it jealous, you are? Jealous of our friendship?

BRIGID: I don't have to listen to this.

TOMAS: *(Exploding)* For God's sake, will you both stop it! Can ye hear yourselves.

BRIGID: Tomas!

TOMAS: I can tell you now Mammy and Auntie Anne that Paddy had nothing to do with Mossie's killing.

ANNE: How would you know?

TOMAS: Because the volunteers were operating on other information. From someone else.

BRIGID: *(Slightly wary)* What information?

Tomas hesitates, unsure of how to proceed.

TOMAS: *(Pointedly)* It seems someone saw Mossie acting suspiciously and reported him as an informer. They were concerned for a family member.

BRIGID: *(Realising it was her)* You're making that up.

TOMAS: No.

BRIGID: *(Panicking)* Trying to defend Paddy like all the men in this house!

TOMAS: If Paddy was behind it all, why would Mossie ask for his debt to be paid in full?

BRIGID: Mossie never asked for that. He never, sure we all know he never paid and …

TOMAS: I have Mossie's last wishes. *(Holds up photograph)* He wanted Paddy paid the money he was owed.

JOSEPH: How did you get that?

TOMAS: It was passed on to me.

ANNE: It doesn't look very legal.

Tomas hesitates but this is his opportunity to show Anne

TOMAS: You're the family expert in legal matters, Auntie Anne. Maybe you should check it.

He holds it out to her. She's not sure but is chuffed to be asked. She takes the paper.

ANNE: *(Initial examination)* It's only a piece of scrap paper. A photograph of Mossie. 'I Mossie Kinsella being of sound mind and body do bequesth my farm and house to …oh my God. Oh my God.

(Beat) Tomas?

TOMAS: That's what he wanted.

JOSEPH: Annie? Are you ok?

ANNE: *(Visibly upset)* Don't call me, Annie. I have to go, now. Here, here, Tomas, take it back.

She slams the paper on the counter and goes to leave.

JOSEPH: Anne! Anne!

Door opens, street, closes.

TOMAS: Go after her Daddy.

JOSEPH: But sure, I don't know what's going …

TOMAS: Just go.

JOSEPH: Right so.

He follows Anne. Beat

BRIGID: What you said earlier about...well, is it my fault?

TOMAS: You've told us often enough Mammy. All actions have consequences.

BRIGID: *(Horrified)* Oh, dear God...

END OF EPISODE

EPISODE 36 – SEAN'S RETURN, DEC. 1921

Scene 1 - Radio

REPORTER: "This is the happiest day of my life. An age old problem solved,". Such are said to have been the first words of the Prime Minister when the agreement which he and the Government have reached with Sinn Fein was signed in the early hours of yesterday morning in the cabinet room at number 10 Downing Street.

VOICEOVER: Fractured – December 1921- under the terms of the treaty, all the prisoners held in internment camps were released.

Scene 2 - Train station.

Big celebratory crowd. Music. Flows through outside scenes.

MARY: Are you sure it's this train he's on?

TOMAS: Will you stop asking me that.

MARY: This is the third time we've been down and no sign. Mammy's going mad.

TOMAS: I know well she is. Isn't she always mad about something?

MARY: What happened between you and her?

TOMAS: Nothing.

MARY: Fine. Keep your secrets. *(Beat. Tomas shrugs)* I wonder if Sean has changed.

TOMAS: Sean will never change.

MARY: We've changed. You've changed.

The faint sound of a train in the distance. Poor Brid runs on.

POOR BRID: Tomas, Mary. I haven't missed it, have I?

TOMAS: No, Brid, you haven't.

POOR BRID: I hope you have it right this time, Tomas.

MARY: He says he's still not sure.

POOR BRID: Tomas Barry, you'll kill me so you will.

TOMAS: Hard to kill a bad thing like yourself.

POOR BRID: Go away with you now.

TOMAS: Don't you know I'm only joking with you.

POOR BRID: I do. Isn't this a grand crowd here all the same? Aren't we lucky to be alive to see this day.

MARY: *(With upset)* Aye.

POOR BRID: When you think of poor Mossie, shot through the head. I heard his left ear was ripped right off and they found it down by the river -

MARY: Aw now, I doubt -

POOR BRID: It's true. And then when you think of my Colm seeing things he shouldn't see -

TOMAS: I know.

POOR BRID: - you have to be glad there's an end to it.

MARY: Aye.

TOMAS: How is the little fellow?

POOR BRID: He's like a shadow to me.

MARY: Poor Colm.

BRID: And the screams out of him at night. I think it's worse he's after getting.

TOMAS: He'll forget it, in time.

POOR BRID: You don't always forget. I was born sideways, they say. I have an aversion to turning sideways now.

TOMAS: *(Trying not to laugh)* Brid, don't -

POOR BRID: What?

TOMAS: Just…don't.

POOR BRID: Are you laughing, Tomas Barry?

TOMAS: No.

POOR BRID: Because that's the God's honest truth. You try living your life not being able to turn sideways.

MARY: *(Giggling)* I'm sure it's terrible hard.

POOR BRID: Now you're at it. You're worse than Mr. O'Sullivan.

TOMAS: I've seen you turn sideways, Brid.

POOR BRID: You have not, not properly. Oh, laugh away. It's an affliction.

MARY: We're sorry, aren't we, Tomas?

TOMAS: You know we love you.

POOR BRID: I do and sure aren't the Barry's my own blood in everything but…..blood.

TOMAS: Aye.

POOR BRID: But by God, you're trying to kill me with all this waiting.

Unmistakable sound of a train now.

TOMAS: This is it! Here they are!

People cheering.

MARY: You said that the last two times.

TOMAS: There's fellas poking their heads out the window! *(Band strikes up)* This is it!

MARY: Is one of the fellows Sean? Can you see?

TOMAS: I don't know. I don't -

MARY: Oh Tomas! *(She hugs Tomas)* Oh, Tomas.

TOMAS: *(Pulling away)* Stop hugging me there now. Sean won't want any tears. This is a great day, Mary.

MARY: It is. The boys all coming home.

TOMAS: In time for Christmas. A real Christmas, not like last year when he was in and out, d'you remember.

MARY: Aye. I remember.

A moment of awkwardness.

TOMAS: Then remember that this will be a great Christmas. You, me, me father, Mammy and Moll all together.

MARY: Like before all the trouble.

TOMAS: Yes.

Cheers grow louder.

POOR BRID: I think they're getting off now. Is that Patrick Colgan, oh, his mother and his clatter of brothers will be only delighted!

TOMAS: He's gone fierce thin.

A huge cheer.

MARY: He was never a big fellow.

TOMAS: That's true. He's coming over. *(Calling)* Hello, Sir.

COLGAN: *(Shouting over crowd)* It's Pat today, Tomas Barry. How are you! And Mary! Sean is here somewhere. Mrs. O'Sullivan, would you look at yourself, how's that little boy?

POOR BRID: Grand. Grand.

TOMAS: Will you be joining us for a drink later in the pub, Si – eh Pat.

COLGAN: If I can get away, me Mother is determined to lock me up now.

TOMAS: You're going from being locked up in Ballykinlar to being locked up in your mother's front room!

COLGAN: I'd take Ballykinlar any day.

Laughter.

MARY: There's Sean. Sean! Sean! Over here!

COLGAN: I'll leave ye to it. I'll catch up with ye in a day or so.

He leaves as Sean pushes his way through the crowd.

MARY: Come on, Tomas. *(Mary runs. Footsteps)* Sean!

Sean embraces Mary in a huge hug, swinging her around.

SEAN: Mary, I never thought I'd miss you, but I did.

MARY: *(Thumping him, laughing)* Put me down, you brat! I didn't miss you one bit!

SEAN: I missed your moaning and sniping and whinging.

MARY: I didn't miss the way you bossed us all about.

SEAN: Someone had to. *(Beat)* And how's my little brother?

TOMAS: Sure, I'm grand.

SEAN: Sure I'm grand. Come here. *(They embrace. Thump on back)* I'm proud of you. So bloody proud.

TOMAS: And I'm proud of you, can't have been easy in that place.

SEAN: It wasn't but sure we kept up the drilling and men's fitness, so at least we still have an army.

POOR BRID: How's my baby boy?

SEAN: Aw, Brid, gimmie a hug. You're getting better looking by the month, d'you know that?

POOR BRID: I do. Mr. O'Sullivan tells me that every morning.

SEAN: Is that before or after you make him breakfast?

POOR BRID: G'way outa that. You'd want to make tracks back to the pub, Brigid and Joseph will be dying to see you.

SEAN: They didn't come down?

POOR BRID: Moll isn't well and your mother was afraid to leave her. Joseph is minding the pub. Come on.

Footsteps as they begin walking. The big crowd sounds fade slightly.

SEAN: Is Moll alright?

POOR BRID: She's got a bit of an upset stomach.

TOMAS: She'll be grand in a few days.

POOR BRID: Your mother was relaxed about it until Teresa arrived and you know what she's like.

TOMAS: The grim reaper.

MARY: Told Mammy that Moll had one foot in this world and one foot in the next.

TOMAS: So Mammy told her to have her two feet outside the door and onto the street or she'd wallop her.

SEAN: *(Laughing)* She did not.

POOR BRID: She did so! But it spooked your mother.

TOMAS: Didn't knock a bother off Teresa, she just wondered why Mammy would want to do that when all she was doing was giving her expert opinion.

MARY: To which Mammy said 'But you're not an expert!'

TOMAS: And that's when Teresa took offense.

They all laugh.

SEAN: But Moll, she is alright?

POOR BRID: Won't you see for yourself in a minute. Come on, your mother told me to get you back as quick as I could.

SEAN: It's great to be home, stinking river and all.

As they make their way from the station, Sean calls out greetings.

SEAN: There's Mrs. Kenny? How's the boys? And Ellen? I hear she's doing great work for the cause. *(Looking around)* Nothing's changed..

TOMAS: Is that a good thing or a bad thing?

SEAN: Good. Definitely good.

POOR BRID: Will you come on and stop looking about!

Footsteps behind them. UaBuachalla hurrying towards them.

UABUACHALLA: Sean Barry, conas ata tu?

SEAN: Ah Domhnall. Ta me go maith, go maith. Tu fein?

UABUACHALLA: Go maith freisin. I got held up in the shop, I meant to be down for the train. Great to see all our boys out.

SEAN: The army back on the streets again!

UABUACHALLA: Where we need them.

SEAN: I saw the paper on the train.

UABUACHALLA: Clever of Dev, ey? Get the boys released, then publish that letter.

TOMAS: What letter?

UABUACHALL/SEAN: Dev's letter.

UABUACHALLA: In the paper today. You should read it.

TOMAS: Is it a rant against the Treaty?

UABUACHALLA: I'd hardly call it a rant.

SEAN: Dev doesn't rant.

MARY: Mammy does though, come on.

TOMAS: What did he say?

UABUACHALLA: That the great test has come, Tomas.

TOMAS: That's true enough.

UABUACHALLA: That he can't recommend the Treaty -

TOMAS: That's bollix

MARY: Tomas!

SEAN: My little brother all grown up.

TOMAS: Of course, he can recommend it. He just can't move his ego out of the way.

UABUACHALLA: How could he recommend an oath of allegiance to the King? How can he -

MARY: *(Knowing a row is coming)* Mammy is expecting you home, Sean. Let's leave the politics alone for now.

UABAUCHALLA: Gabh mo leithsceal. Ta failte romhat arais, Sean. I'll see you across the week for more debate, ey?

SEAN: I'll look forward to it.

UABUACHALLA: Did Pat Colgan come back with you at all?

SEAN: He did. He said he was going to his mother.

UABUACHALLA: I'll call in there so. Welcome back again. *(Footsteps as he moves off)* Hello, Paddy

PADDY: *(Distant)* Domhnall. *(Footsteps crossing to Sean)* The wanderer returns! How are you, Sean?

SEAN: Hardly a wanderer, Paddy, unless you're counting walks around and around a yard.

PADDY: I am! *(Laughter)* Let me see you. Boy, but you're looking fierce thin. You'll have to get a bit of meat put on them bones.

POOR BRID: Brigid will do that if we can ever get him back to her.

SEAN: Brid, don't be looking all cross with me now, it spoils your lovely face.

POOR BRID: I'll spoil your lovely face if you don't hurry up. Your mother will think that's another train you haven't arrived on.

SEAN: Another train?

POOR BRID: Tomas had us out three times so far. Your poor mother's nerves are in tatters.

SEAN: Join us, Paddy.

PADDY: Oh now, I'm not exactly welcome in the pub these days. Your mother -

POOR BRID: Paddy's working.

PADDY: I am not, it's just your mother, Sean -

SEAN: Forget about me mother, will you? She'll hardly refuse me anything today.

MARY: You'll have one drink at least.

PADDY: Oh, at least!

Laughing.

POOR BRID: *(Pointed)* Did you hear about Mossie Kinsella, Sean? Shot like a dog in the street a month back.

PADDY: *(Pointed back)* And did you also hear that it had nothing to do with me!

MARY: We all know it had nothing to do with you, Paddy, don't we, Brid?

POOR BRID: Well...yes, But you could hardly be blamed for thinking -

SEAN: This man is a hero. Doesn't Tomas owe him his life since Bloody Sunday. Mammy said she was indebted to him.

PADDY: Your mother said that?

SEAN: Yes, in one of her letters. Indebted, she said.

PADDY: No offense to your mother Sean, but she certainly hasn't acted indebted.

MARY: You know Mammy, she shouts her mouth off. Come on, Paddy.

PADDY: I haven't set foot inside that pub since I got accused of murder.

They look at Brid.

POOR BRID: I'm sorry about that.

PADDY: You should be. Only for that will showing up, people would still be believing it.

SEAN: What's this about a will?

PADDY: You've a fair bit of catching up to do, Sean Barry.

SEAN: And you're the man to do it, come on, my mother won't say a word if you're with me.

PADDY: For you, Sean. For you.

Scene 3 - Moll's room in Barry's

Brigid is with a sick Moll. Sound of laboured breathing.

JOSEPH: *(From bar, distant)* I think the train is in Brigid. I'll give you a shout when he arrives.

BRIGID: Grand Joseph. Did you hear, Moll? Sean is home! What do you think of that now?

MOLL: *(With difficulty)* Good. Sean is funny.

BRIGID: He is and he'll have a lot of stories and jokes for you. *(Beat)* And when you get better, he'll take you maybe on the train somewhere. Or get conkers for you in the College.

MOLL: Or a picnic, maybe?

BRIGID: Or a picnic.

MOLL: I'd like that.

BRIGID: I know you will, pet. I know you will.

JOSEPH: *(Calling)* I caught sight of Tomas coming up the street, Brigid. They'll be here in a minute.

BRIGID: I'll be down now. *(Kisses Moll)* You get some sleep and I'll send Sean up to you in a bit.

Footsteps as she crosses floor. Opens door softly, closes it softly.

Scene 4 - Barry's pub

Brigid enters

BRIGID: Where is he? Is he not back? I thought you said –

JOSEPH: He's gone off with JJ Fitzgerald drinking in Dublin.

BRIGID: Drinking in Dublin! I'll drink him in Dublin! Get me my coat. *(To Paddy)* And what are you doing here, Paddy Dooley?

JOSEPH: Brigid!

BRIGID: He said he wouldn't set foot in the place, yet here he is. Get me my coat.

PADDY: It's a special day. I thought I'd celebrate Sean's homecoming.

BRIGID: Then wait until he comes home at least. It's not funny, Mary, I can see you laughing behind that scarf. That boy hasn't seen his family in months and he takes off drinking in Dublin. I'll bring him back. Go up to Moll, Mary.

Soft footsteps that she doesn't notice as Sean walks up behind her. He motions for the others to be quiet.

BRIGID: *(To Tomas)* And you, Tomas you useless eejit, go and get the bar and make sure everyone pays for their pints. Yes, I'm looking at you, Mr. Dooley. Joseph, get the cart around the front. If I have to drag that boy back by the hair on his head, I will. A good kick up the -

SEAN: I think I'm too old for a kick up the arse now, Mammy.

Brigid stops and turns

BRIGID: Jesus Christ. Oh, Jesus Christ.

SEAN: Sorry to disappoint you, it's just me.

BRIGID: Come here, you eejit. That was a terrible trick to play on us. Joseph, look. *(She hugs him hard. Touches his face)* You're all thin and pale. Your lovely face is all sunken. I'll soon have you back to the man you were. Joseph, he's back. He's back. Look at him.

JOSEPH: Good to have you home son.

PADDY: It deserves a pint.

BRIGID: Will you serve that fellow a pint, Joseph before he dies of the thirst? *(A smile for Paddy. She pulls out a seat)* Sit down there, Sean. Mary, will you go up to Moll, let me have a moment with my son.

MARY: I will.

Footsteps as Mary leaves. Joseph serves Paddy a pint. Paddy stays at the bar.

POOR BRID: I'll be getting back now. It's grand to see you again Sean. I'm happy for you Brigid.

She goes

BRIGID: Sit in here. *(Chairs being moved)* Tomas, you sit there. *(Calling)* Joseph, have you got those sandwiches Mary ran up this morning. Your favourite, son, ham and egg.

SEAN: *(A little emotional now)* Thanks, Mammy. It's a good while since I had anything decent to eat. The food was shocking.

BRIGID: You're home now, that's what matters. I can't believe you're here. My boy.

Footsteps as Joseph crosses. He deposits sandwiches on the table.

JOSEPH: There you are son, eat up.

BRIGID: Yes, eat up Sean and promise me, no more robbing RIC stations.

SEAN: *(Beat)* Who told you that now?

BRIGID: That lad you did it with. Alan from out Kilcock way.

SEAN: *(Shock)* What were you doing talking with him?

BRIGID: He escaped from the Curragh last month. Came to Father Dempsey for help and that stupid eejit brought him here.

JOSEPH: Don't be calling the priest that now.

BRIGID: Joseph, go back up to the bar before your friend has it drunk dry. And I'll call the priest that if I want.

SEAN: You helped that little rat?

JOSEPH: Don't be calling the priest that, Sean. He saved your skin.

SEAN: I'm indebted to the Father. It's Alan I'm talking about. That's not a fellow to be trusted, Mammy.

TOMAS: He swore he never told on you, Sean. Said he was beaten up by the Tans and everything.

SEAN: Someone told. *(There is an uncomfortable silence)* How did you get him out of here anyway?

TOMAS: That was the funny part. We didn't. Auntie Anne offered him a lift to Dublin.

SEAN: Why would she do that?

TOMAS: She thought he was a priest needing a lift and sure, we couldn't tell her the truth.

SEAN: *(Laughing)* Auntie Anne doing her bit for the cause. How's the bold Donnacha?

TOMAS: If the rumours are to be believed, very bold.

BRIGID: *(Snapping)* Don't be joking about your cousin like that. *(Beat)* Cissy says he fathered her child.

SEAN: Aw Jesus, I've missed this place.

TOMAS: And Cissy had the baby and is now living with Teresa.

SEAN: And her cat?

TOMAS: And her cat.

They laugh.

PADDY: *(Calling over)* And Tomas finally plucked up the courage to go stepping out with Lizzie O'Neill much to the relief of the whole town.

TOMAS: Feck off, Paddy.

As Sean laughs and Tomas glowers, Paddy stands up to leave.

PADDY: *(Calling from bar)* That I will, Tomas. Slainte Sean and I'll see ye over the Christmas.

Footsteps as Paddy and Joseph move to door.

JOSEPH: Good day, Paddy. *(He locks the door)* There'll be no more work today. If a man can't take a day off to celebrate his son coming home, then things are in a bad way. *(Becoming a bit emotional)* We're delighted to have you back, so we are. I heard it was terrible up there.

SEAN: Only for the bravery of the men, it would have been. Ye heard about poor Tadhg Barry.

TOMAS: The whole country heard.

SEAN: I was there. Seen the whole thing, so I did.

TOMAS: What happened? Some boys were being released, we heard?

SEAN: That's right and Tadhg and a few of the others were just standing by the fence looking out and then the next thing, the bastard - sorry Mammy - on sentry duty, shot Tadhg right through the heart. One of men dragged him back but sure it was too late.

JOSEPH: The reports in the newspaper said he disobeyed an order to move away from the fence.

SEAN: That's true but to kill a man over it?

TOMAS: He got a good send off anyway.

SEAN: He did, there were a few British were sorry it happened so they let the tri-colour go on the coffin. But we were all worried after.

TOMAS: There's to be an inquest. He'll get justice there.

SEAN: I wouldn't trust anyone but our own to get justice for one of our own. *(Getting riled up)* There was no justice when they shot Tormey and Sloane, was there?

BRIGID: *(Diffusing)* You're home now anyway.

JOSEPH: And sure peace is on the horizon.

SEAN: If you'd seen what I seen today, you wouldn't say that.

BRIGID: What did you see?

SEAN: Stones and missiles fired at the train in Portadown and in Banbridge, some Unionists climbed aboard and started fighting. We got the better of them but they'd rather die than come in with the south. And there's many fellows would rather die than swear allegiance to a British King.

BRIGID: The cheek of them Unionists.

SEAN: They hate us, Mammy as much as we hate them.

BRIGID: I don't hate anyone. Your father was a proud soldier.

SEAN: Peace will be a long time coming so don't hold your breath.

BRIGID: I won't listen to this today. Come on up and say hello to Moll. She might be awake now.

Footsteps as Sean leaves with Brigid.

JOSEPH: He's not to be talking like that in front of your mother.

TOMAS: I can't stop him.

JOSEPH: He'll be back out with a gun in his hand again, if we're not careful.

TOMAS: It might not come to that.

JOSEPH: What's your thoughts on all this?

TOMAS: This Treaty is better than anything we ever had before. Better than Home Rule. We need to at least give it a chance.

JOSEPH: Dev doesn't think so.

Footsteps as Sean comes back.

TOMAS: Mick Collins ran the war, he knows how far we can push it, he wouldn't have signed unless it was the best he could get.

JOSEPH: That's true.

TOMAS: Dev's just a blow in with an ego problem.

SEAN: *(Footsteps crossing, sits down)* Dev is the man who raised the money for this war.

JOSEPH: I thought you were upstairs.

SEAN: Moll's still asleep. Is she all right? She looked very pale.

JOSEPH: She'll be grand. I'll go up, give your mother a break, if she'll trust me.

Footsteps as he leaves, fading.

SEAN: You're all for the Treaty, ey, Tomas?

TOMAS: Peace will come if we all work at it.

SEAN: You always loved your fairytales.

TOMAS: *(Beat)* You can't talk to me like that anymore.

Beat. In the brief silence, we hear footsteps. The boys don't.

SEAN: That's right, sure aren't you the great boy, got promoted and everything.

TOMAS: That's not what -

They eyeball each other. Their conversation continues over Mary's dialogue and footsteps.

MARY: *(Distant)* I'll go on down now, Mammy.

SEAN: Higher than me, now, ey?

TOMAS: Aye, I am.

Mary's footsteps coming closer.

SEAN: *(After a beat, grudgingly proud)* You did good, though. Shooting that RIC fella clean through the head.

TOMAS: *(Uneasy)* It was a lucky shot.

SEAN: Word was he went down like a sack of spuds.

TOMAS: I don't remember rightly.

SEAN: One less RIC man in Maynooth, we had celebrations in Ballykinlar that night.

MARY: What's that you're saying?

SEAN: That's not for repeating, Mary, there only a few knows it was Tomas.

MARY: Knows it was Tomas what?

Silence.

TOMAS: Nothing.

MARY: One less RIC man in Maynooth? Tomas?

TOMAS: He's talking rubbish.

SEAN: I am not. This fella here, Mary, he shot –

Mary's hysteria grows during this exchange

MARY: You?

SEAN: Yes, him. He's a –

It becomes a full-blown attack - tearing at him, pulling at him. He makes a half-hearted attempt to hold her off, but part of him feels he deserves it.

MARY: *(Light thump)* You!

SEAN: Jesus, Mary what -

MARY: *(Harder thump)* It was you! You bastard!

SEAN: What's got into you?

MARY: *(Wallop)* How could you?

TOMAS: Mary I – stop!

MARY: *(Shaking him)* How could you? He was a good man. A good man. I swear. I will kill you, report you. I will - kill you. I -

SEAN: *(Grabbing Mary. Holding her. She pants)* Stop it, would you, Mary? Tomas is a hero.

MARY: *(Pushing against him)* And you, celebrating? Celebrating. You make me sick.

SEAN: I'm only talking about the RIC man that Tomas shot.

MARY: Joseph Hughes was his name.

SEAN: What?

He releases her.

MARY: He was of Wolfhill and he came from a family of six. Two girls, four boys. His mother and two brothers, one of whom is a dumb mute lives on a farm and Joseph used to send her money.

SEAN: What are you on about?

MARY: I'm telling you his name. I'm telling him *(Referencing Tomas)* who he shot that night. His name was Joseph Hughes and when he died, his life, to the state was worth only five hundred pounds. It was worth so much more to me.

SEAN: You knew him?

MARY: We were engaged.

SEAN: *(Beat).* Jesus. *(To Tomas)* How could you let her do that?

MARY: Let me? Let me! I can do what I want.

SEAN: Stepping out with the enemy, you're a disgrace.

MARY: Our own father was a British soldier.

SEAN: And he was a disgrace too.

MARY: His job put food in your mouth, drink in your belly.

SEAN: I would rather have starved.

MARY: That's not what you were saying with all your moaning in Ballykinlar. Oh, the food is bad. Oh the food -

TOMAS: Can we just -

MARY: *(To Tomas)* All I did for you -

TOMAS: Mary, I didn't know, I -

SEAN: You did your duty, Tomas.

MARY: I'll tell you about duty. When Mammy got depressed after Joseph Junior died, I was the one looked after you, Tomas.

TOMAS: I know but it was dark that night and -

MARY: I fed you and played with you -

TOMAS: He was at the head and -

MARY: I gave up my time for you.

TOMAS: They told me to shoot.

MARY: You killed him.

TOMAS: Yes.

MARY: Murdered him.

TOMAS: Yes.

MARY: Shame on you.

SEAN: You're a fine girl to be talking about shame. By God, if I'd been here, I'd have put a stop to it.

MARY: You might have tried but I loved him. He loved me. And I'm proud to say it.

SEAN: You bitch.

He lunges at her.

TOMAS: Let her go!

SEAN: All the men that have died for the cause of freedom and you, you tramp, defending a lacky of the English.

MARY: He was no lacky. He was Irish. He was a better man than you.

SEAN: You say that again and I'll clatter you.

MARY: *(Taunting)* Aye, you will!

TOMAS: Let her go.

SEAN: *(He throws her from him, she staggers)* You should have put a stop to it.

MARY: Didn't he slaughter him.

TOMAS: I'm sorry, Mary.

SEAN: What are you sorry for? Jesus Christ. Have you all gone soft.

MARY: It's too late for sorry. I loved someone and you took him away. I won't ever forgive you, Tomas. *(To Sean)* And as for you, I hope Ireland is worth it.

Footsteps as she turns to leave.

TOMAS: I'm done with killing now, Mary. *(Mary keeps walking)* Mary!

SEAN: Leave her. She'll be alright.

TOMAS: How will she ever be alright again? I killed her sweetheart.

SEAN: And a good thing too.

TOMAS: *(Pushes chair away. Stands)* Have you no heart left?

SEAN: I saw fine men executed for no reason. I saw men ill and not tended to. Men starved. Men beaten. I saw grief when Barry was shot. I have no heart for those who serve or love those who serve the empire.

TOMAS: Would you listen to yourself. What about a heart for your own sister? Your own flesh and blood?

SEAN: Did you ask her where her heart was when she was chasing an Englishman?

TOMAS: She loved him Sean, same as I love Lizzie. But you wouldn't understand about that sort of love, would you? You're far too busy loving Ireland.

SEAN: Lizzie was with me before she ever was with you.

TOMAS: Liar.

SEAN: Prove it.

TOMAS: Get lost, Sean. *(Pushes him)* Just get lost!

A keening noise is heard, loud but distant. The boys stop.

TOMAS: What's that? *(The sound again. Running across floor)* Mammy? Mammy!

Urgent footsteps getting closer. Joseph runs in carrying Moll.

JOSEPH: Tomas, open the door there, good boy, I'm taking Moll up the road to the doctor. She's after taking a turn.

BRIGID: Hurry, hurry, oh my God. You'll be alright Moll, you'll be alright. You will. You will. Mammy promises. Hurry up with that door.

Tomas struggles as he unlocks the door amid Brigid's keening.

SEAN: Here. Put my jacket over her. *(He does so)* Aw Jesus, little Molly Mae, aw Jesus.

TOMAS: I'll lock up here. We'll all go.

Footsteps. The door of the pub crashes closed.

END OF EPISODE

EPISODE 37 – JOSEPH AND PADDY, JAN. 1922

Scene 1 - Paddy's farm, Maynooth

Farm sounds, Footsteps. Knocking on door. Door opens

PADDY: I wasn't expecting you tonight, Joseph. Come on in.

JOSEPH: I can't, Paddy. Not tonight. Not ever again.

PADDY: Oh, aye?

JOSEPH: I'm to be married. To that girl I was telling you about. Father Dempsey has it all arranged.

PADDY: I see.

JOSEPH: I'm sorry, Paddy.

Footsteps as Joseph walks away.

PADDY: *(To himself, bitter)* Of course you are, Joseph.

VOICEOVER: Fractured , Janurary 1922

Scene 2 - Barry's pub

BRIGID: Mary, what are you standing there for. I told you. Just do it! Take that box away out of my sight.

MARY: Mammy. Please. Leave it for a bit. See how you feel in a week or two.

BRIGID: A week or two is it? A week or two? I know exactly how I'll feel in a week or two.

MARY: I didn't mean…

BRIGID: You think it's all going to get better in a couple of weeks?

MARY: I never…

BRIGID: Come February we'll forget all about it?

MARY: No! Mammy… I just…

BRIGID: Nice knowing ye Moll. Close the door on your way out.

MARY: That's not what I meant.

BRIGID: I'll never forget. D'ye hear me Mary? Never! And all this stuff of hers is going to cause me nothing but heartache.

MARY: But Mammy, I…

BRIGID: *(Calls)* Tomas! *(Footsteps as Tomas climbs the stairs)* Tomas!

TOMAS: Yes Mammy.

BRIGID: I want you and Mary to take these boxes down to Father Dempsey. Tell him to donate it to whoever he sees fit.

TOMAS: Father Dempsey?

BRIGID: Now Tomas. Please. Go on.

TOMAS: Mammy are you sure?

BRIGID: Oh course, I'm sure. Here's a box for you. And you, Mary. Now go. *(Footsteps to door)* And come straight back when you're finished. I'll have more for ye.

The sound of things being pulled from drawers fading into footsteps as they descend stairs, cross into bar.

MARY: Daddy, she's throwing out all Moll's clothes! *(Joseph with a drink stares into the distance)* Joseph! Daddy! Will you put the bottle down and listen. She's throwing out Moll's clothes.

JOSEPH: They're no good to her now Mary.

MARY: But there'll be nothing of Moll left!

TOMAS: Mary, it's what Mammy wants. She told us to do this.

MARY: And you always follow orders, don't ye, Tomas Barry? Well, I'm not doing it.

She drops the box on the bar and marches off. There is a silence.

TOMAS: Can you put Mary's box on top of mine, Daddy and I'll get going.

Sound of boxes being manoeuvred.

JOSEPH: There you go. *(Knock on door)* We're closed.

PADDY: *(Distant)* It's me. *(Joseph opens door)* I thought I might give ye a hand with the stocktaking.

JOSEPH: Stocktaking?

TOMAS: Excuse me there, Daddy. Paddy

We hear him squeeze out the door.

JOSEPH: Moll's things. He's eh…taking them to Father Dempsey.

PADDY: Oh aye…

JOSEPH: Come in.

Footsteps. Door closes.

PADDY: How far have you got? With the stocktaking.

JOSEPH: *(Shaking a bottle of whiskey)* Half a bottle of whiskey far.

PADDY: Pour one for me and we'll get started so. *(As Joseph pours)* Do ye want to count or write?

JOSEPH: I've a pen and paper here, so I'll write. *(Picks up his drink)* Slainte.

PADDY: Slainte. *(Clink. Paddy drains his whiskey)* I'm ready to go. *(Claps hands together)* So…we have… large bottles of stout. Four, eight, twelve – two dozen. Small bottles of stout. Two, four. Four! Holy God. Was Con O'Sullivan on the rampage again? *(No reaction from Joseph)* That was a joke, Joseph. Was it Maggie O'Donoghue? Is she still buying them for Father Dempsey?

JOSEPH: Aye.

PADDY: The poor man. I wonder does she leave any for him at all. Anyway, small bottles of stout four, eight, twelve…twenty six. Bottles of ale – who drinks that poison – six, twelve, fifteen. Are ye writing this down?

JOSEPH: I am.

PADDY: *(Footsteps)* Cider. Not your most popular tipple. *(Sound of clinking bottles)* Sure there's dust all over them. Three dozen. Bottles of orange. Little Moll must have been at these. Only five. The divil. I always used to catch her… *(Long pause)* Sorry.

JOSEPH: She was a divil.

PADDY: Twist ye round her little finger so she would. 'Mr. Dooley', says she. 'you're here again. Do ye have no home to go to?'

JOSEPH: Took after her mother in that respect.

PADDY: Glad you said that and not me! *(Pause)* How is herself?

JOSEPH: Not great.

PADDY: Early days I suppose. *(He doesn't know what to say. Footsteps)* Powers, one, two, three, four, five bot.. We'll call it four. Jameson six bottles. You'd know Mossie Kinsella wasn't around. Miserable bastard, the Lord have mercy on him. I don't know if I'll ever get my money out of that will of his. They need two witnesses apparently. Did ye ever hear such a load of shite? I'm sure the boys who killed him will be only too delighted to sign their names to the document. *(Pause)* Sherry. Five bottles. Gin…you don't have any gin here. We'll check the cellar after.

JOSEPH: There should be gin, on the bottom shelf.

PADDY: Under the sink?

JOSEPH: No, the far end.

PADDY: *(Footsteps)* I can't see any.

JOSEPH: It's not that popular. In there, behind the red lemonade.

PADDY: Ah for fecks sake Joseph. You'd need to be a contortionist to get down there.

JOSEPH: I don't have any problems.

PADDY: You're not carrying as much muscle as me. You're gone soft so ye are, stuck behind this bar all day. Come out on the farm with me some time and ye won't last five minutes.

JOSEPH: I can bale hay as well as the next man.

PADDY: *(Showing off his biceps)* Look at my muscles here, sure! You won't get that definition pulling pints. I'd say I have the physique of a man twenty years younger.

JOSEPH: *(Smiling despite himself)* If Dan Donnelly was still around you could challenge him to a fight.

PADDY: Dan Donnelly up in the Curragh? He'd have nothing on me. Sure he was only a Jackeen – what do they know of real work. *(The light footstep of a boxer, throwing punches)* And Paddy Dooley moves in again, with a double jab and an incredible right hook to the head. What a man! And dodge, dodge. *(Light footsteps)* Dan Donnelly – world champion bare knuckle boxer is in trouble. The amazing Paddy Dooley takes him on again with a series of swift hard punches to the body – one, two, three, four, five punches, and then that devastating uppercut to the chin... he's down!!!!

Paddy turns to put his hands in the air, gets his legs twisted, crashes into a table and falls over in a heap.

JOSEPH: He's down alright. Ye fecking' eejit! *(Laughing)* I'd say Dan Donnelly is running for the hills!

PADDY: *(Dragging himself up)* Give me a hand up, would you?

JOSEPH: *(Dragging him up)* There. Sit down.

He pulls out a chair.

PADDY: Dan Donnelly didn't have great bloody tables getting in the way. Christ, me ribs! I think they're broken. *(Joseph continues to laugh)* Don't make me laugh. Oh Jesus, the pain! Shut up will ye.

Paddy starts to laugh too. The laughter gets louder and more hysterical. Footsteps growing closer. Enter Brigid, who can't believe the sight of Paddy on the floor and Joseph in stitches. The men are immediately silenced.

BRIGID: What's going on?

PADDY: *(Jumping up. In obvious pain)* Mrs. Barry. We were just…stocktaking. I eh…my leg and…

BRIGID: Stocktaking? *(Turning on Joseph)* You might try taking stock of your family sometime. You obviously haven't noticed. One of them is missing.

Footsteps as she leaves. Door closes. Joseph closes his eyes, and turns back to the bar. Paddy slowly rights the table and awkwardly stands behind Joseph, not knowing what to do. He makes to speak, then stops. He lifts his hand to put it on Joseph's shoulder, and then draws it back. He turns to leave, then thinks better of it. Finally, he walks to the bar, sits beside Joseph, downs the last of his whiskey and places his hand tentatively over Joseph's. All we can see is the two men from behind. Neither looks at the other. Joseph gradually starts to grip Paddy's hand, their fingers slowly entwining. It is clear this is more than a supportive gesture. Finally, Joseph turns to look at Paddy and the spell is broken. Paddy leaps up, and there is a tense moment.

PADDY: I righted the table there.

JOSEPH: Thanks.

PADDY: I'd better…

JOSEPH: *(Tearful)* Aye.

PADDY: I'm terrible sorry, Joseph.

JOSEPH: Aye. Aye. Go. Go now.

PADDY: Joseph…don't… *(Catching Joseph in an awkward embrace)* Come here. Come here.

Sound of him comforting Joseph

JOSEPH: Paddy, no. *(Pulling away)* We can't. It's wrong. Brigid….

PADDY: *(Beat)* Aye. I'll…go.

He moves to door. Door opens.

JOSEPH: Paddy – I *(Paddy stops)* I just want to say…I just…

Footsteps as Mary barges in.

MARY: This is Moll's stuff. Mammy has no right to throw it out. Are you going in or out Paddy?

PADDY: I'll be seeing ye.

Paddy exits. Door closes.

MARY: Will you talk to Mammy, Joseph, please. Daddy are you listening?

JOSEPH: Sorry… eh…Mary, yes, yes, I am listening. She did the same when Joseph Junior died, God rest him.

MARY: And you just let her?

JOSEPH: People have different ways of grieving Mary.

MARY: And what about how I want to grieve?

JOSEPH: Your mammy is having a very hard time of it.

MARY: We're all having a hard time! And do you know what? She's even throwing out the teddy I bought for Moll out of my first wage packet. I hid it but she'll find it. Moll really liked that teddy.

JOSEPH: It was her favourite.

MARY: I know.

JOSEPH: She took it everywhere with her.

MARY: She did. *(Beat)* I think she was starting to grow up a bit though. Bits of my make-up kept going missing.

JOSEPH: Sorry love. You know how I always like to look my best behind the bar!

MARY: Stop! I'm not going to feel better about this. It's just wrong. Mammy is wrong.

JOSEPH: Tell me where the teddy is hid love, I'll sort it. *(Mary looks at him, quizzically)* The cellar is a big, cold place, full of spiders. Your Mammy was never a fan of spiders.

MARY: Neither was Moll.

JOSEPH: I'll put the teddy down there and keep it safe. I promise. It'll be on the shelf beside Joseph Junior's blanket and his little woolly shoes.

His voice breaks a bit. Mary links his arm.

MARY: Aw, Joseph…

She catches hold of him.

JOSEPH: You're a good girl, Mary. *(They sit in silence)* One thing though. *(Pause)* Tomas?

MARY: Daddy, it's not your business.

JOSEPH: It's a terrible time Mary. We all need each other. And whatever's going on between you and your brother…

MARY: Ask him why don't you?

JOSEPH: It's not helping your mother to have ye all at each other's throats.

MARY: Why is it always all about Mammy? I have feelings too. Does nobody care about me?

JOSEPH: If ye could go some way towards making peace.

MARY: No!

JOSEPH: I can see he wants to.

MARY: Oh so it's all my fault, is it?

JOSEPH: I didn't say that.

MARY: You have no idea what he did!

JOSEPH: I could take a good guess. *(Mary looks at him, stunned)* You don't work all your life behind a bar without hearing a few things you're not supposed to.

MARY: You knew?

JOSEPH: Not until Tom Dwyer came barging in the night of the ambush. I saw your face. I saw Tomas'.

MARY: You said nothing.

JOSEPH: How could I? I thought if I leave it alone, it'll all settle. But that was foolish.

MARY: 'It wasn't me Mary, I swear'. Tomas is a liar. And a murderer. I hate him. I hate him so much.

JOSEPH: He's made mistakes.

MARY: A mistake?

JOSEPH: But I get the feeling he's learned from them.

MARY: Oh well that's alright then. If Tomas has learned something. Jesus!

JOSEPH: I didn't really know your … young man.

MARY: Fiance.

JOSEPH: Fiance? *(A bit taken aback)* I didn't know him.

MARY: How would you, when he wasn't even allowed in the door.

JOSEPH: Tom Dwyer seems to have thought very highly of him.

MARY: He was RIC Joseph – just like Mr. Dwyer. You would have hated him.

JOSEPH: I don't … He was fighting for the British, Mary.

MARY: He wasn't fighting for anybody. He was trying to keep the peace.

JOSEPH: We were on different sides. Tomas and himself were on different sides.

MARY: He'd never have shot Tomas.

JOSEPH: *(Gently)* Was it him came here with Tom Dwyer to arrest Sean that time?

MARY: That's different! He didn't know Sean was my brother.

JOSEPH: And Tomas didn't know who he was shooting at that night either.

MARY: It doesn't make it right.

JOSEPH: It's a war Mary. Your own Daddy got killed the same way.

MARY: I just can't forget about it.

JOSEPH: Blame the war. Not the man that shot him.

Tomas enters.

BRIGID: *(From within)* Is that Tomas back?

TOMAS: Yes Mammy.

BRIGID: Come here, I've another box for you.

TOMAS: *(Sigh)* All right, mammy.

Footsteps as he moves off. We hear the sound of Brigid starting to cry.

JOSEPH: Ye were to be married?

MARY: We were.

JOSEPH: I'm sorry.

MARY: No you're not. The trouble it would have caused.

JOSEPH: It would have been a hard road for ye.

MARY: Anything's better than this one.

JOSEPH: Ah Mary…

MARY: What kind of a world is it that stops you from being with the person you love?

JOSEPH: There's nothing we can do about it. It's just the way it is.

Brigid's keening rises to a roar.

END OF EPISODE

EPISODE 38 – UABUACHALLA'S SPEECH, JAN. 1922

Scene 1 - Radio

REPORTER: *(English)* This historic building, which for seven centuries has been a symbol of British power in Ireland, has today, 16th January, been handed over to the Government of Southern Ireland. At five minutes after the appointed hour, Mr. Collins arrived to, as he said, 'take over'. Lord FitzAlan, the Viceroy and the Black and Tans made a swift exit afterwards through cheering crowds and the last guard at the castle was dismissed. Ireland is now at peace.

VOICEOVER: Fractured - Janurary 1922

Scene 2 - Domhnall UaBuachalla's house

Mullaney and O'Reilly are waiting.

MULLANEY: What do suppose UaBuachalla wants?

O'REILLY: No idea, Mullaney. He said he'll come into us once he finishes in the shop.

MULLANEY: Maybe he wants to talk about what happens next.

O'REILLY: Maybe.

MULLANEY: He can't be too happy about it all.

O'REILLY: He can't.

MULLANEY: I'm not happy about it.

O'REILLY: They say there was a fair crowd in Dublin today all the same.

MULLANEY: A fair crowd of eejits. Turkeys voting for Christmas.

From the shop, UaBuachalla's voice..

UABUACHALLA: *(Distant, underneath following conversation)* I'm going to have to stop you there, a chairde - I'll read it and get back to you. Bye now. Bye.

O'REILLY: I always had Collins down for a sensible man. He won't blink, I thought. He won't blink. I could have done better by the Brits myself.

MULLANEY: There was five of them in it. What were they thinking?

O'REILLY: Signing their names to that piece of…shite.

MULLANEY: UaBuachalla won't be happy at all.

Footsteps from outside, growing closer.

O'REILLY: Can you imagine it, him swearing an oath of allegiant to the Crown.

They allow themselves a laugh

MULLANEY: But it's not funny all the same.

O'REILLY: It's tragic is what it is.

Door opens. Footsteps

UABUACHALLA: Boys! Conas ata sibh?

Door closes. They mumble their 'go maith, go raibh maith agat'

UABUACHALLA: Sorry for holding ye up. I had Teresa in the shop down there -

MULLANEY: The one with the cat?

UABUACHALLA: The very one. She had me quizzed up down and sideways about the Pope dying and what did I think of his views and I had to admit that I didn't tend to think on his views at all.

O'REILLY: That went down well, I'd say.

UABUACHALLA: She didn't bat an eyelid, just quoted, verbatim, his last letter to Cardinal Logue and then asked what I thought of it.

O'REILLY: The world needs Teresa like it needs an Irish Treaty.

UABUACHALLA: She's not the worst, you know where you stand with her at least.

O'REILLY: Which is more than can be said for the Treaty. Is that why we're here, Domhnall?

UABUACHALLA: Yes. I'm waiting on a couple more. I've a proposal for ye and a speech to – *(A knock on the door)* Who is it?

SEAN: Sean and Tomas Barry.

UABUACHALLA: Come in, boys. Come in.

Enter Sean and Tomas. They are not really on speaking terms.

SEAN: How are ye all?

Beat.

O'REILLY: Fierce sorry for your loss, boys.

MULLANEY: It was a hard blow, how are your parents?

SEAN: Not good, sure, she was the light of the house.

UABUACHALLA: Cailin alainn. A smile always on her face. It was a grand funeral.

Beat

SEAN: How have things been here then?

O'REILLY: Doing our bit for the cause, you know yourself.

MULLANEY: Your brother helped. He was a credit to you.

TOMAS: *(Abrupt)* What are we here for? Can someone tell me?

UABUACHALLA: I like a man that gets straight to the point. Sit down everyone. Colgan said he'd be here too, but I don't want to keep ye so -

SEAN: I saw Colgan down at the station this morning.

Uneasy beat.

O'REILLY: Heading to Dublin, was he?

SEAN: I think so.

UABUACHALLA: It's a big day, I suppose.

TOMAS: Historic, I'd say.

UABUACHALLA: I asked ye here, and you too Tomas, though I know we don't see eye to eye on this Treaty business -

TOMAS: Treaty business? Is that what you're calling it? Today the British handed over Dublin Castle. That's a fair business I'd say.

Tomas and Sean will snipe at each other but their sniping goes deeper than just the Treaty.

SEAN: Domhnall was speaking.

UABUACHALLA: Let the boy have his say. I'm not for falling out with anyone over this, I want that clear. We've been on the same side this long time.

TOMAS: Aye.

UABUACHALLA: And we're all entitled to our opinions. Having said that, I should warn you, Tomas that I'm making a speech against the Treaty at the Sinn Fein conference in a couple of weeks. I thought I might run it by you boys.

ALL BAR TOMAS: Fire away/great / I'm listening.

TOMAS: Are you trying to convert me?

UABUACHALLA: *(With affection)* Maybe.

TOMAS: *(Affection back)* It better be some speech so.

UABUACHALLA: An open mind, an open heart. *(Paper rustling)* Here we go. Now I start off with a cupla focail on the delegates leaving for England with the instructions that they were to report back to the Cabinet in Dublin for approval. Have ye got me? Then I go on to say that Lloyd George's threat of an 'immediate and horrible war' was just bluff -

TOMAS: You know that for a fact?

UABUACHALLA: No nation calling itself civilised threatens war on delegates who won't sign a Treaty. Pure bluff.

TOMAS: If England is so civilised then why have we been fighting them all these years?

SEAN: Will you shut up and listen!

TOMAS: Don't talk to me like that. You were saying, Domhnall?

O'REILLY: *(Teasing)* Isn't Tomas in fierce bad form. Is Lizzie O'Neill not letting you court her now or something?

Sean flinches. Mulanney sniggers.

TOMAS: Shut your mouth about Lizzie.

O'REILLY: You'd want to rein your brother in there, Sean.

TOMAS: You'd want to rein your mouth in.

UABUACHALLA: Boys. What's going on at all?

SEAN: Apologies, Domhnall. What with Moll and -

TOMAS: Don't use Moll in this. Don't you dare. *(Beat)* We have a Treaty. It brings peace and I for one, can't understand why we can't work with it.

UABUACHALLA: Then listen to what I have to say, hear me out. Will you do that for me, Tomas?

TOMAS: Aye.

UABUACHALLA: Maith an buachaill. Right …. I've a piece here on the articles of agreement and you're right, Tomas, the British handed over Dublin Castle today and they will withdraw but they're keeping some of our ports for their own security, the King will be our head of state, he'll be represented in Ireland by a Governor General - an Irishman who will perform his duties for him.

MULLANEY: There's a man looking to be assassinated.

UABUACHALLA: Only a fool would take it on. There's more, the Dail will have to swear an oath of allegiance to the King, who will be head of the state -

TOMAS: We know all this. It's a stepping stone.

UABUACHALLA: To what? What it will mean, and I have it here in my speech is that, 'for the first time in history, Ireland will, of its own free will walk into the British Empire with their heads held high and become British Citizens.' Now think on, boys, what will your children make of that? Or your children's children?

SEAN: That's the point, isn't it? It's the future generations we need to be thinking about.

MULLANEY: I'm not going to have my grandchildren asking where was I when they were sold out.

UABUACHALLA: That's what I was saying to Joe last night. Think on. Why have people embraced this Treaty?

SEAN: Because they're afraid of war.

UABUACHALLA: Exactly. The papers have sold it to them like that. If there's no Treaty, there will be war. England controls most of the press and that's the message they're selling.

TOMAS: If there's no Treaty, then what will there be?

UABUACHALLA: For the last four years, we have made a great, stand-up fight against the British Empire and we took our place among the countries of the world and I think you'll agree, Tomas, it was a proud place and other countries looked to us and our example - especially countries trying to get out of the clutches of England.

MULLANEY: And we've let them down.

O'REILLY: We have.

SEAN: What was the fight for? To become British? Were Pearse and Kevin Barry led to their deaths for this?

UABUACHALLA: That's a great bit of rhetoric, Sean. I'll put that into the speech.

TOMAS: Can you put in your speech that I went out and killed a man.

O'REILLY: We all went out and killed, Tomas.

TOMAS: Don't you want your killing to count for something? Yes, they were RIC or Tans. Yes, they were the enemy, but they were still men who had lives. And families. I killed an RIC man to get the British out, to get the British to take notice. Well, they have and now we can move on.

O'REILLY: There was plenty of Irish shot by the British who had a family and life too. You're gone soft.

TOMAS: I've never been soft. I'm a realist. Let those Irish lives count for something as well.

UABUACHALLA: They will always count.

TOMAS: How will they count if we get to blowing each other up instead of the English?

O'REILLY: That won't happen.

TOMAS: Oh, but it will. Even the politicians are tearing each other apart.

UABUACHALLA: That's not true. That's the press again. You read that in the papers, didn't you?

TOMAS: You're saying they're all getting on grand and having cake and tea, is that it?

UABUACHALLA: *(Trying to diffuse)* Maybe not cake.

TOMAS: I'm sorry for my tone, Domhnall. You're a Dev man, and I was too. But I firmly believe that the boys got the best they could out of England and that sacrificing anymore lives is useless, which is what you're asking.

UABUACHALLA: I was never a man of violence, Tomas. I fell out with Colgan over the lockout way back in 1913.

TOMAS: I know you did but -

UABUACHALLA: I used to think Pearse was a madman. But in time, I learned that the British and their business here only listen to one thing. And that's the sound of a gun.

TOMAS: But what Dev is asking -

UABUACHALLA: Dev has been right twice before, Tomas. Once, with a minority in 1914 and again with a minority in 1916.

SEAN: And now, for the third time, he's in the minority but he will be proved right.

TOMAS: At what cost? More lives?

SEAN: Get over it, Tomas.

TOMAS: Get over what?

SEAN: You know.

TOMAS: I don't. Maybe you'll enlighten me.

Long beat.

SEAN: Tomas is for the Treaty because he doesn't like killing British men.

TOMAS: Bastard. Take that back.

SEAN: It's true isn't it?

UABUACHALLA: No one likes killing, but it's necessary at times. What I'm saying is, there will be no war if we all stick together.

TOMAS: If we all go for the Treaty there will be no war.

O'REILLY: I've had enough of this. You're wasting your time, Domhnall.

TOMAS: Sorry, Domhnall, but you are. I'll see myself out.

He stands up. Knock.

UABUACHALLA: That'll be Colgan now. *(Door opens)* Come in, you're welcome.

COLGAN: How is everyone? Sorry I'm late Domhnall, I was up in Dublin, having a look at things for myself. God, it's cold out there.

TOMAS: How was it?

COLGAN: I wasn't full sure it would happen.

TOMAS: And it did?

COLGAN: It certainly did. Boys, this is a great day. Dublin Castle, the seat of British power, is now ours.

UABUACHALLA: But the country isn't, Pat. I've a speech -

As himself and Tomas talk, the others remain silent.

COLGAN: There must have been about a thousand people along Dame Street, Domhnall, just waiting to see what would happen - men like yourself who don't believe in the Treaty. First off, there were parades and that in the Castle yard and everybody waiting for our boys to show and the excitement is mounting and then…about half-one, up sweeps three cars. The first is Mick Collins and he gets out and he waves and the cheering…well, you never heard anything like it.

TOMAS: I'd love to have witnessed that.

COLGAN: It was marvellous altogether. And when the rest of the boys got out and waved at the crowd, the cheering was so loud, I thought I was going to be deafened. Then into the Castle with the boys - men who were on wanted lists not six months ago. Mick Collins as leader of the state. A great day.

TOMAS: And is the Union Jack gone?

COLGAN: Aye and a tri-colour up in its place. All these years chasing that dream. And here it is.

TOMAS: I'll take a trip into Dublin and see that for myself.

COLGAN: They're leaving Beggar's Bush in the next week or two, they'll be moving out thousands of men every day until they're all gone. The booing when the British left the Castle, 'twas great and they not able to do a thing about it.

TOMAS: *(To the others)* D'you see? This is what we've achieved.

COLGAN: Our own army and all. They'll be advertising for that soon. Ye should join boys.

MULLANEY: And defend the British ports that are left here?

COLGAN: Are you still at that? Can't you see -

UABUACHALLA: I was in the middle of reading my anti-Treaty speech, Pat. Would you like to hear my side?

COLGAN: Indeed, I would not because that way lies ruin. And war and -

TOMAS: I agree.

COLGAN: If any of ye had bothered to come today, and I did ask you Sean, you would have changed your minds about this.

UABUACHALLA: It takes more than one gesture to change seven hundred years of barbarity.

TOMAS: It's not a gesture, it's real.

COLGAN: The people of Kildare want the Treaty.

UABUACHALLA: The people don't understand the articles of agreement and if they go wrong there is no reason why I should.

COLGAN: You were elected, Domhnall, to represent the people.

UABUACHALLA: The people are making a mistake, walking blind into a mangle.

COLGAN: I'm not stupid or blind. I canvassed for you, along with Paddy Dooley and JJ Fitzgerald and you said, and I'm quoting here, that your mandate was to try to 'win the freedom of Ireland as best you could.' There was no mandate for a Republic.

UABUACHALLA: A Republic was always the mandate.

COLGAN: Then how come no one told me?

SEAN: Maybe you weren't listening?

COLGAN: *(Pointing)* Out there, beyond that window, is a new country forming. Put away your ego boys.

O'REILLY: It's a sad day when the desire for freedom is called ego.

COLGAN: It's not the desire for freedom you have, O'Reilly, it's the desire to see an empire humiliated.

SEAN: They humiliated us for long enough.

COLGAN: No one is denying that. But they have given way now, we just need to keep pushing harder at the door.

MULLANEY: Aye, by resuming the fight.

COLGAN: For a school teacher, you're a fool.

MULLANEY: You'll take that back.

COLGAN: I will not.

Footsteps, pushing. Colgan is banged against a wall.

MULLANEY: I'll not be called a fool by a coward.

Footsteps as Tomas rushes at him

TOMAS: Get off him, Mullaney.

He joins in. Mullaney staggers.

SEAN: You get off, Mullaney, Tomas.

He pulls Tomas off.

TOMAS: And you get off me, Sean.

SEAN: Aw, my little brother raising his fist to me. Go on, you know you want to.

UABUACHALLA: Boys, let's not fall out over this.

TOMAS: Too late for that Domhnall. I'll be going.

COLGAN: I'll be off too. Think on what I've said, ey? Come on, Tomas.

They leave.

UABUACHALLA: This is a terrible state of affairs. Sean, you should go after your brother.

SEAN: He's not himself…there's a lot happening.

MULLANEY: He was close to the little one, wasn't he?

SEAN: He was.

Beat

UABUACHALLA: Are we wrong, boys?

ALL: No / Never / Not at all…

UABUACHALLA: Because if I'm blinded by ego, I'd like to know.

O'REILLY: You are as straight as an arrow. You see things clear. We need that.

MULLANEY: We'll also need money and arms and - *(They look at him)* We need them whether we end up fighting the English or each other.

SEAN: It won't come to that.

MULLANEY: Would you look at what just happened, would you? Tomas was ready to belt you. I went for Colgan.

SEAN: Still and all…

MULLANEY: Still and all, we need to be ready, just in case. There's a mail train coming through next month, could you arrange to be on shift Sean.

SEAN: I could. Will I say it to Tomas and Colgan?

O'REILLY: No.

UABUACHALLA: They've been good boys.

O'REILLY: They've taken their sides.

UABUACHALLA: Colgan is full of the flag being taken down, the shine will go off in a couple of days when he realises that for all that, we're still British subjects. And Tomas will lose the love for the Treaty for the same reason. They've always been good Irishmen. Have a word Sean.

SEAN: I will.

UABUACHALLA: Good boy. Here's the tail end of the speech, it'll rouse them, I think. 'Expediency or compromise never led a people to the goal of freedom. The straight path will lead us there. The fight will have to be continued. This Treaty, if put into force, will give us some good things -

MULLANNEY: Pre-empt the arguments, good man.

UABUACHALLA: Control of education and finance and a little army of our own, but our country will be dishonoured and I put honour above anything else, especially the honour of my country.

The men clap, Domhnall bows.

MULLANEY: Let the fight continue.

They agree, rousing.

END OF EPISODE

EPISODE 39 – THE PROPOSAL, FEB. 1922

Scene 1 - Maynooth Street

COLGAN: Think about it, Tomas. You'll get three and six a day plus maintenance. If you get married, your allowance increases.

TOMAS: But what chance would I have of getting in?

COLGAN: Every chance. You're the kind of man we need in this new country.

TOMAS: I've the pub and that but...I'm definitely interested. I'll talk to Daddy.

COLGAN: Just let me know and I'll put a word in with Mick Collins.

Footsteps as he walks away.

TOMAS: Thanks! Thanks! Fantastic.

VOICEOVER: Fractured Feb 1922

Scene 2 - Barry's kitchen

Tomas is sitting at the table. Reading the National Army Circular

TOMAS: Dependents pay four shillings a -

Sean enters

SEAN: What's that you're reading?

Paper folding.

TOMAS: Don't sneak up on me like that. *(Pushes paper into pocket)* It's nothing.

SEAN: Stuffing it away in your pocket, it can't be nothing. Is it top secret stuff meant for the higher ups? *(Tomas doesn't respond)* Is that tea fresh?

TOMAS: Just made a few minutes.

Footsteps. Sean gets a cup. Footsteps. Sits down.

SEAN: Want a hot sup?

TOMAS: I'm grand.

Sean pours.

SEAN: You're not working this morning?

TOMAS: Doesn't look like it, does it? *(With bad grace)* Daddy's behind the bar at the minute.

SEAN: We better check all the whiskey bottles so. *(He laughs as Tomas glares at him)* I'm only jokin. *(Pause)* How long will you keep this up?

TOMAS: What?

SEAN: This silent treatment.

TOMAS: Maybe when you open your eyes and see some sense.

SEAN: Is that my little brother talking?

TOMAS: (*Irritated*) What is it you want Sean?

SEAN: Nothing.

TOMAS: We've been avoiding each other for days, now you're sitting in beside me having tea. You want something.

(*Pause*)

SEAN: All right, I had a few drinks with Mullaney and the lads last night.

TOMAS: I saw ye. Ye were fierce loud altogether.

SEAN: He's some man to tell a story. Says one time his school got raided and he had to hide in a cupboard and the poor principal was so nervous he pissed himself.

TOMAS: A good man for the stories alright … if you can believe them.

(*Pause*)

SEAN: He's called a meeting for tonight. He asked me to tell you about it.

TOMAS: I'm not interested.

SEAN: Come on, Tomas. He thinks highly of you. He'd like to have you involved.

TOMAS: What's his big idea this time?

SEAN: A mail raid next month.

TOMAS: Is that the best he can come up with?

SEAN: Why don't you come along? If you have other ideas, the lads would be keen to hear them.

TOMAS: No.

SEAN: We have to get things moving again.

TOMAS: For what? So we can kill more people? We have a solution. Why can't we try and make that work?

SEAN: The Treaty is no solution.

TOMAS: I'm not fighting over this again. We're going around and around in circles. (*He stands*) I've to meet Lizzie off her train..

SEAN: You're not thinking straight.

TOMAS: You're not thinking at all. What about Mammy? It'll break her heart if she hears you're going to carry on fighting. You don't know what she's been like this past year when you were locked up. She hasn't been herself … and now after Moll, she can't take much more.

SEAN: Mammy will never know.

TOMAS: I'm sick of it all. I've lost Mary. She'll never speak to me again … and poor little Moll. I don't want to lose you Sean.

SEAN: Don't talk stupid.

TOMAS: I'm serious. What do you think is going to happen? Instead of fighting the English, we'll be fighting each other.

SEAN: That's rubbish.

TOMAS: I'm not changing my mind but I pray to God that you and Mullaney and the others see sense and change yours. *(Silence between the men)* Now, I have to go meet Lizzie from the station.

Footsteps as he moves away.

SEAN: *(Laughing)* The big romance! *(Tomas ignores him)* Where was she anyway?

TOMAS: Down in Sligo minding her aunt.

SEAN: Ooooh, will she be wearing a nurses uniform when she meets you? That'd be nice, ey?

TOMAS: Shut up, Sean.

SEAN: What special operations will she have in mind for you tonight?

He chuckles at his joke

TOMAS: We're not all like you.

SEAN: Can I give you some advice?

TOMAS: No.

He opens the door.

SEAN: Eat your greens because she can wear a man down.

TOMAS: Don't you talk about her like that

SEAN: Like what? Like she's a Cissy Boland?

TOMAS: Jesus! *(Tomas crosses back towards Sean)* Shut up!

SEAN: Are you going to actually hit me this time, Tomas. Are you going to man up?

TOMAS: You're jealous. You're just jealous. That's what's wrong with you.

SEAN: Jealous of what? What have you got that I'm so jealous about?

TOMAS: I'm higher rank than you in the IRA. Your bosses beg me for ideas. I'm cleverer than you. I've got a girl who likes me.

SEAN: Let me tell you something. Lizzie O'Neill is a stray dog. She'd like anyone who pats her head and tickles her belly.

TOMAS: You bastard!

He lunges at Sean.

SEAN: Get off me. Get off me.

Footsteps approaching.

TOMAS: You bastard!

SEAN: I wasn't the first and you won't be the last.

TOMAS: Take that back! You hear me, take it back!

LIZZIE: *(From outside door)* Tomas!

The men stop fighting.

TOMAS: *(Forced brightness)* In here, Lizzie. *(To Sean)* You say one word to her and I swear I –

Door opens.

SEAN: Lizzie. We were just talking about you.

LIZZIE: All good I hope. The train got in early and - *(Beat)* Are you okay Tomas?

SEAN: He's grand. We just had a difference of opinion. I'm sure you see it with your own brothers all the time. *(Lizzie is looking at Tomas)* I'll leave the two of ye. I'm sure ye have lots to talk about. Oh, and if you've nothing better to do tonight Lizzie, Mullaney is having a meeting. Tomas can tell you all about it.

(Tomas snaps)

TOMAS: Will you just go.

LIZZIE: Tomas!

SEAN: He's just dying to be alone with you, Lizzie. Goodbye now.

Footsteps.

LIZZIE: Goodbye, Sean. *(Sean exits. Tomas is still quiet)* Thank God, I'm back. That woman had me worn out and - *(No response from Tomas)* What's wrong Tomas?

TOMAS: Nothing.

LIZZIE: Are you not glad to see me?

TOMAS: I am. I'm delighted to see you. It's just … Sean. Since he came back, he's been … *(Tomas is lost for words)*

LIZZIE: What did he do?

TOMAS: *(Hesitates)* This and that. He was on at me to go to Mullaney's meeting tonight.

LIZZIE: Are they planning something?

TOMAS: A mail raid. I think.

LIZZIE: Another one! For when?

TOMAS: I don't know.

LIZZIE: It's probably next month.

TOMAS: *(Sharply)* If you want to know so badly, why don't you go along to the meeting yourself.

LIZZIE: *(Annoyed)* That's lovely.

TOMAS: I'm sorry Lizzie. I didn't mean it. It's bloody Sean, he -

LIZZIE: Just ignore him.

TOMAS: *(Again hesitating)* It's not just that. He was saying things about you too. I can't ignore that.

LIZZIE: What?

TOMAS: Just about … you and him …

LIZZIE: There was no me and him. I told you this.

TOMAS: I know … sorry…

LIZZIE: Look, he did chase me for a couple of weeks. He thought that he could click his fingers and I'd fall at his feet.

TOMAS: And you never … ?

LIZZIE: One night .. *(Hesitates)* we had a kiss. One kiss, that's all. He said he'd stop chasing me if I gave him a kiss.

TOMAS: *(A little devastated)* You kissed him.

LIZZIE: It meant nothing. I'm only interested in one of the Barry brothers.

TOMAS: Really?

LIZZIE: Cross my heart and hope to die. Come here,

They kiss

TOMAS: *(Awkwardly)* I'm very fond of you, Lizzie.

LIZZIE: Fond? Like you're fond of walking in the College?

TOMAS: *(Struggling)* I'm not really … I mean … I love you Lizzie

LIZZIE: You're a big eejit Tomas Barry. I've known that for ages. I love you too.

They kiss

TOMAS: *(Blurts out)* Will you marry me?

LIZZIE: What? Bless us and save us, that's a bit...sudden.

TOMAS: I know, but what's stopping us?

LIZZIE: My brothers?

TOMAS: They're big enough to look after themselves.

LIZZIE: They're big enough to be annoyed about it.

TOMAS: Tell them to come to me. You deserve more than being their housekeeper.

LIZZIE: What's brought this on?

TOMAS: Do you remember the time you asked me if I ever wanted to escape and just start again?

LIZZIE: I remember. You were a shy boy then.

TOMAS: At that time, I couldn't understand why anyone would do that but after all that's happened in the last year, I just want to get away from all this. Be with someone who makes me happy.

LIZZIE: That is just the nicest thing anyone has ever said to me.

TOMAS: Then what are we waiting for?

LIZZIE: Where would we go? What would we do?

TOMAS: Look at this. *(Unfolding of paper)* Have a look.

He hands it to her.

LIZZIE: The National Army?

TOMAS: Yes, the ad has been in all the papers. Colgan thinks I should go for it. He said he'd put in a good word for me. They need one thousand men.

LIZZIE: I thought you wanted to leave all that army stuff behind you?

TOMAS: This is an army for peace not war. Look at the pay, three and sixpence a day and if I was married, I'd get four shillings. I'd never see money like that in the pub and there's extra for maintenance. We'd be able to rent a nice house somewhere.

LIZZIE: That sounds lovely. I never dreamed...that sounds...wonderful Tomas. We could go to Sligo, be near my aunt.

TOMAS: *(Laughing)* The one you came here giving out about?

LIZZIE: I'm the only family she has.

TOMAS: There are postings all over the country. I could look to be stationed in Sligo so you'd be near her.

LIZZIE: It sounds... too easy. Can this really happen?

TOMAS: Yes. I mean, I have to get the job first but with Colgan behind me, I have a great chance.

LIZZIE: What about your mother and father? Will they mind you leaving?

TOMAS: Sean's always been Mammy's favourite so if she has him, she'll be grand.

LIZZIE: Your mother loves you too.

TOMAS: Yeah, just not as much. Are you going to come with me?

LIZZIE: I'd...I'd love to, Tomas

They laugh together

TOMAS: Brilliant. I'll talk to Colgan straight away and get things moving and then we'll go to Fr. Dempsey to see what we need to do about getting married.

LIZZIE: Now?

TOMAS: Yes. Now!

LIZZIE: Lizzie Barry. I like the sound of that.

TOMAS: I love the sound of that. Oh, Lizzie, we'll be so happy together.

LIZZIE: We will Mr. Barry. We will.

END OF EPISODE

EPISODE 40 – LAST WOMENS MEETING, MAR. 1922

Scene 1 - Priests House

FATHER DEMPSEY: That's incredibly generous, Mrs. Kilbride. Very kind.

ANNE: I'm doing it anonymously, Father. All bona fida. And...fiat. That means 'let it be done, father.

FATHER DEMPSEY: Well fiat it shall be, Mrs. Kilbride.

ANNE: And not a word.

FATHER DEMPSEY: I will abide by vinculum iurtis.

ANNE: What?

FATHER DEMPSEY: The chain of the law, Mrs. Kilbride.

ANNE: Yes! Yes of course. *(Beat)* I knew that.

She walks away. Father Dempsey chuckles.

VOICEOVER: Fractured – Mar 1922

Scene 2 – Barry's parlour

POOR BRID: Who's for tea?

MAGGIE: I'll have a little drop Mrs. O'Sullivan. I'm gasping, so I am. The Father has me run ragged this past week.

POOR BRID: Has he now Mrs. O'Donoghue? Sugar?

MAGGIE: I'm sweet enough, as the Father says himself. A terrible chest he has on him.

ANNE: I saw him yesterday. He seemed fine to me. No milk thank you Mrs. O'Sullivan.

MAGGIE: *(A bit put out)* You saw the Father yesterday?

ANNE: We had a meeting in the parochial house. He didn't appear to be...

POOR BRID: Tea, Mrs. Barry?

MAGGIE: What kind of a meeting? He never mentioned any meeting.

POOR BRID: Brigid?

BRIGID: Sorry. Yes please.

ANNE: It was a private meeting Mrs. O'Donoghue. Why would he?

MAGGIE: Well I...if you'd asked me first I could have made an appointment for you, that's all.

ANNE: No need.

MAGGIE: He likes me to keep a track of these things. He can be very forgetful, so he can. Head like a sieve! *(Pause)* That's why it's always good to keep me informed. In confidence of course. Private meeting?

ANNE: *(Smiling)* Yes. My lips are sealed.

MAGGIE: I'm sure he'll fill me in. I've been very busy, organising his diary and –

A knock, followed by the door opening. Betty Dwyer enters.

BETTY: Hello? Eh...sorry. Excuse me.

BRIGID: Come in Betty. You're welcome. I've asked Mrs. Dwyer to join us.

There's an awkward silence. Door closes, footsteps across room.

BRIGID: There's a seat there for you, Betty.

BETTY: Thank you.

POOR BRID: *(Trying to restore atmosphere)* The more the merrier, isn't that right Mrs. Kilbride, Mrs. O'Donoghue?

ANNE: Well I..

POOR BRID: Would you like tea Mrs. Dwyer? I'd say there's a cup left in the pot.

BETTY: Thank you Mrs. O'Sullivan. That would be lovely.

POOR BRID: We're just waiting on Teresa now. She's never usually late. *(Pause)* I'd say Mr. Dwyer is delighted to have you home, Mrs. Dwyer.

All look at Poor Brid in shock.

ANNE: Mrs. O'Sullivan!

POOR BRID: Sorry, I didn't mean...

BETTY: It's fine. He is. I just...had to visit my mother for a while, is all.

POOR BRID: Sure everybody needs a break now and them, don't they? A little holiday? Did you have a nice time?

BETTY: Well...

Door slams open as Teresa rushes in.

TERESA: Apologies everyone. I was delayed due to.. *(She sees Betty)* You're back, Mrs. Dwyer. I was under the impression you had separated from your husband.

BETTY: No..

TERESA: Because of his position in the RIC.

MAGGIE: Traitors to the cause

TERESA: That's a matter of perspective. What is the cause and -

POOR BRID: The RIC is being disbanded, Mrs. O'Donoghue. So Mr. Dwyer isn't going to be a traitor any more. Isn't that right, Mrs. Dwyer?

BETTY: Well .. I don't believe he ever..

POOR BRID: So we can all be friends again. Isn't that fantastic.

BETTY: Em...yes.

MAGGIE: Friends might be -

TERESA: I don't have any friends. *(She sits)* Can we get on with the meeting? Mary Anne is sick and I've left Cissy on her own in the shop.

ALL: Sick? / Oh dear me is she alright? / Poor thing / Is she very bad? / Have you seen the doctor?

TERESA: She's fine. Upset tummy. It'll clear up in a few days.

BRIGID: Are you sure Teresa? Is that what the doctor says?

TERESA: Oh we didn't bother with the doctor. I know the procedure.

ANNE: Does she have a temperature?

TERESA: Slightly elevated. Nothing to be concerned about.

ANNE: Is she off her food?

TERESA: Well of course she's off her food. She's sick.

ANNE: Babies can become dehydrated very quickly. I really think...

TERESA: She's getting plenty of fluids.

ANNE: Dr. Grogan is a good friend of mine. I'll ask him to visit.

TERESA: Cissy is an excellent mother. If she wants the doctor to visit she can ask him herself.

POOR BRID: We're just concerned Teresa, that's all. After..

She stops just before she says 'Moll' There's a pause.

BRIGID: You can say it. Moll. Promise me, Teresa, you'll call the doctor if Mary Anne gets any worse.

TERESA: Of course. *(She takes some papers from her bag)* We have three items on our agenda for this meeting..

POOR BRID: Have you seen her Betty? Cissy's baby. She really is the sweetest little thing.

ANNE: Do you think so?

BETTY: Those little curls!

POOR BRID: And the big brown eyes.

MAGGIE: I'm sure she's as pretty as they come, but at the end of the day...

ANNE: *(Icily)* At the end of the day?

MAGGIE: Well…we all know…

ANNE: What do we all know Mrs. O'Donoghue? Enlighten us please.

POOR BRID: Very bright little baby. Sleeps right through the night.

MAGGIE: It's only what everyone's saying.

POOR BRID: Tall for her age too.

MAGGIE: I wouldn't be one to talk badly of anyone now, but..

ANNE: But?

BETTY: She has some words too, I believe.

MAGGIE: Ah come on now Mrs. Kilbride. You know full well what I'm talking about.

TERESA: The child is illegitimate. Cissy is an unmarried mother, the stigma of which will undoubtedly harm her own prospects and those of the child. Was that what you meant to say Mrs. O'Donoghue?

MAGGIE: Well..

TERESA: Good. Now we all understand that we can move on. First item on the agenda – our cake sale.

ANNE: No reason why the child should suffer.

MAGGIE: She was conceived in sin.

ANNE: That's not her fault.

POOR BRID: Always smiling, God bless her.

MAGGIE: She doesn't stand a chance, that's all I'm saying.

ANNE: If everyone were kinder, she would have as much chance as..

MAGGIE: She hasn't even been baptised.

TERESA: Father Dempsey baptised Mary Anne six weeks ago. I am her Godmother.

ANNE: There!

MAGGIE: Six weeks ago?

POOR BRID: How lovely for you Teresa.

MAGGIE: I would have known about it.

ANNE: Well clearly you didn't.

MAGGIE: Father Dempsey tells me everything.

POOR BRID: Perhaps he just forgot this time.

TERESA: He probably just didn't want you to know. Now, the cake sale. We had to postpone..

BRIGID: Cissy made a very good choice for godmother.

POOR BRID: An excellent choice.

BRIGID: You put me to shame Teresa. There I was, thinking I was great setting up a 'women helping women' group and I didn't lift a finger to help Cissy, and she in a desperate situation.

POOR BRID: I feel ashamed myself Mrs. Barry, when you put it like that.

BRIGID: Mary asked me to take Cissy in. I should have. Maybe the house wouldn't be so empty now. *(Her voice breaks)* I don't know why I didn't.

ANNE: We all know why you didn't Brigid. I didn't want you to. *(She takes a breath. This is difficult)* Thank you Teresa.

TERESA: You're welcome. Our cake sale had to be postponed because of Mossie Kinsella's funeral.

POOR BRID: Well it didn't seem right to be selling sponge cakes the morning after the poor man was murdered.

MAGGIE: Good enough for him. Give him a taste of his own medicine. My poor Jack..

ANNE: Your poor Jack drank too much whiskey and fell off that barn roof. Mr. Kinsella was an honourable man.

MAGGIE: You would say that and you after inheriting a fine house and 20 acres of farmland from him.

ANNE: I would not..

POOR BRID: Ah now Mrs. O'Donoghue. Mr. Kinsella was very kind in his last moments to think of my poor Colm. Leaving him money for his education. That was a very noble thing to do.

MAGGIE: Sure what good is that, when it's not worth the paper it's written on? He won't get a farthing.

POOR BRID: Oh but he will! I haven't mentioned this to anyone except Father Dempsey, but Con and I got a letter from the executioners yesterday, and they said they were going to honour Mr. Kinsella's final wishes.

BETTY: The executioners?

MAGGIE: Father Dempsey?

POOR BRID: Yes. And they're going to pay for the very best education.

BETTY: Good God. The executioners are going to pay for Colm's education?

POOR BRID: Yes! Get him help with his speech and everything.

BETTY: So you know who these people are?

POOR BRID: Yes of course. They signed the letter. We have to meet with them next week.

BETTY: You can't meet them! These are very dangerous people.

POOR BRID: They were very polite in the letter.

MAGGIE: Father Dempsey never said.

BETTY: They killed Mossie Kinsella!

MAGGIE: Why didn't he just tell me?

POOR BRID: Did they? Oh my God. How do you know?

BETTY: They're the executioners! That's what executioners do!

POOR BRID: Don't go telling your husband, then, I mean, Father Dempsey seems to think it's okay. He said he'd come to the meeting with us.

MAGGIE: Jesus Christ! Father Dempsey said he would go to a meeting with Mossie Kinsella's executioners and never said a bloody word to me!

ANNE: Oh for goodness sake! They're not executioners, they're EXECUTORS. It's a firm of solicitors, and they're responsible for implementing Mr. Kinsella's will.

MAGGIE: How do you know that? I suppose Father Dempsey told you.

ANNE: No of course Father Dempsey didn't tell me. I know because I'm dealing with them myself. I also have considerable legal knowledge.

MAGGIE: I've legal knowledge enough meself to know that Mossie Kinsella's final wishes don't matter a damn.

POOR BRID: But my letter says…

MAGGIE: There weren't any witnesses.

POOR BRID: We've told Colm all about it.

MAGGIE: So it doesn't matter what any executor says.

POOR BRID: *(Really upset)* He's really excited.

MAGGIE: Colm gets nothing.

Poor Brid starts to cry. Betty tries to console her.

POOR BRID: This was his one big chance in life. What are we going to do now?

BETTY: Maybe there's been a mistake.

ANNE: Colm will get his money.

MAGGIE: No he won't.

ANNE: Colm will get his money because I have informed the executors that this is what I wish to happen. *(Annoyed. Directed at Maggie)* I had hoped to do it confidentially, Mrs. O'Donoghue.

POOR BRID: Really?

ANNE: Mr. Kinsella's final wishes are very clear. I intend to carry them out, irrespective of their legality.

POOR BRID: Oh Mrs. Kilbride! How can I ever..

ANNE: Mr. Kinsella's wishes, not mine. You were saying about the cake sale, Teresa?

TERESA: We intend to hold the cake sale two weeks from Sunday, after 11 and 12 Mass. Is that ok with everybody? Good. Item two on the agenda. Tell…

BRIGID: Do you think is there any point?

TERESA: Any point?

BRIGID: In having the cake sale. What'll we raise? Ten shillings if we're lucky. What are we going to do with ten shillings? I just don't see…

POOR BRID: We could add it to the twelve shillings I got in a door-to-door collection last month.

TERESA: *(Frustrated)* Fundraising. That's item three on the agenda!

MAGGIE: Yes. And then we can add on the twenty shillings or so we hope to get from next weeks's church gate collection.

BRIGID: When did -

TERESA: We haven't dealt with item two yet!

POOR BRID: Tell her about the shop Teresa. Go on!

MAGGIE: Wait till you hear this!

TERESA: I really feel..

POOR BRID: It was Cissy's idea. Teresa made such a lovely crib for Mary Anne and so -

TERESA: The child needed a crib. I don't know what all the fuss is about.

POOR BRID: So now she's made another one and it's being raffled in the shop.

TERESA: We ran out of tickets yesterday. The plan is to hold a similar raffle each month. Different prizes of course. I'll have to expand my repertoire.

POOR BRID: I hope you don't mind Mrs. Barry. You weren't able to come to our last two meetings – we just…

MAGGIE: Wanted to do something.

BRIGID: I can't bel…You collected twelve shillings in a door-to-door collection for our women's group?

TERESA: Item two on the agenda.

MAGGIE: We had a little chat about that ye see.

POOR BRID: Thought about what's really important to us.

TERESA: 'Inform Brigid of our Change of Name.' Item four.

BRIGID: Change of name?

All look nervously at each other. No one wants to speak.

POOR BRID: The Moll Barry Remembrance Fund.

Silence. Brigid is unable to speak.

MAGGIE: What do you think Brigid? We can change it back if you want.

TERESA: Too soon. It was a bad idea.

POOR BRID: Brigid?

BRIGID: I am...well – *(Knocking on door)* Come in. Please.

Door opens. Father Dempsey enters.

FATHER DEMPSEY: God Bless all here! *(There is a chorus of greetings. Maggie is visibly cold towards him)* I hope I'm not disturbing important business! A little bird told me you were all meeting here today.

MAGGIE: Your little bird is obviously much better informed that mine!

BRIGID: Sir down, Father. Will you have a cup of tea?

FATHER DEMPSEY: No thank you. I'm on a flying visit. And I'm still recovering from the delicious feast served up to me by Mrs. Dwyer yesterday evening.

BETTY: Ah it was nothing Father. We were delighted to have you.

MAGGIE: Anything else you'd like to share with us Father?

FATHER DEMPSEY: I do have a little bit of news for you as it happens.

MAGGIE: Oh! *(She is mollified. Glances around triumphant)* If you'll excuse me and the Father, ladies, please. Duty calls!

FATHER DEMPSEY: Do you not want to hear the news, Mrs. O'Donoghue?

MAGGIE: Oh, I … *(She turns. Realises her mistake)* No Father. Haven't I a private meeting of my own to attend.

She leaves.

FATHER DEMPSEY: Have I done something wrong?

BRIGID: She didn't mention anything about a private meeting earlier.

FATHER DEMPSEY: Strange. Anyway, ladies, my news! It's about the Moll Barry Remembrance Fund. *(There's an awkward pause)* I hope I haven't spoken out of turn?

BETTY: It's just..

BRIGID: You haven't Father. It's a lovely tribute. Thank you.

FATHER DEMPSEY: A very generous parishioner has – anonymously – contributed the sum of thirty pounds to the Fund.

All gasp in astonishment. Anne's is a little too dramatic.

BETTY: How wonderful!

ANNE: I can't believe it!

FATHER DEMPSEY: Indeed. You'll be able to do great work with all that money. The Lord always provides!

BRIGID: Thank you Father. I'm a bit overwhelmed.

FATHER DEMPSEY: Nothing to do with me Mrs. Barry. I'm just the messenger. Now I'd better go after Mrs. O'Donoghue. I seem to have offended her. I'll see you all on Sunday for the church gate collection!

He exits

TERESA: I must go too. That took longer than expected. We'll meet at 10.45 on Sunday. Will you be joining us Mrs. Dwyer?

BETTY: I'd be delighted – if ye'll have me.

TERESA: I'll make another collection box.

POOR BRID: You can help with the cake sale too Mrs. Dwyer if ye like. You make a lovely brack so ye do.

BETTY: I made a couple this morning. Would ye…have ye time to…come over for a little slice?

POOR BRID: I .. I will so. That would be very nice so it would.

BETTY: I'll give you one to take home. Colm might like a bit. *(Door opens)* Goodbye Mrs. Barry.

BRIGID: Goodbye, God bless.

POOR BRID: I'd say Colm would love a bit of cake. Goodbye, Brigid, Mrs. Kilbride. *(As she is leaving)* Can ye believe it? Thirty pounds!

Door closes. There is a silence as Anne prepares to leave.

ANNE: I'll be off too, Brigid.

BRIGID: I'd say poor auld Mossie Kinsella is turning in his grave.

ANNE: He wanted to give Colm that money.

BRIGID: Not too sure our women's group was top of his priorities though.

ANNE: *(Lying badly)* Nothing to do with me.

BRIGID: We'll be able to help the next Cissy.

ANNE: And the next Mary Anne.

Pause. She goes to the door.

BRIGID: It's not too late you know.

ANNE: She has Teresa.

BRIGID: Teresa's not her grandmother.

ANNE: What kind of a grandmother would I be?

BRIGID: That's up to you.

ANNE: I'm not very good at apologies.

BRIGID: Really?

ANNE: Believe it or not. *(They laugh. Anne thinks about it. Comes to a decision)* Thank you Brigid.

BRIGID: Thank you Anne.

END OF EPISODE

EPISODE 41 – INFORMER PLAN, MAR. 1922

Scene 1 - Field, countryside, night.

Police activity. Shouting, dogs. Footsteps creeping through undergrowth.

MULLANEY: What the -

CIVIL GUARD: *(Shouting)* Over here, Sir. Over here. I've got something. Guns, sir. I've got guns.

MULLANEY: Bollix.

Footsteps retreating.

VOICEOVER: Fractured – March – 1922

Scene 2 – Small room in safe house

Sean, O' Reilly and Farrell are waiting for Mullaney as they plan to raid a mail train that evening. They are playing cards. The sound of card playing. Cards being laid down.

SEAN: Now you have to take up six cards, O'Reilly.

O'REILLY: You're making that up, I just put down a two on top of yours.

SEAN: And I put another two down. That's the way it works.

O'REILLY: That's bollox. *(He picks up the card)* Your turn Farrell.

FARRELL: *(Lays down a card)* There. What's keeping Mullaney? He should have been here ages ago.

O'REILLY: He'll be here. *(Laying a card down)* Do I get anything for a Jack?

SEAN: No.

FARRELL: He's cutting it fine so he is.

SEAN: Are you playing or not, Farrell?

FARRELL: *(Playing second last card)* Am I supposed to say "last card"?

SEAN: *(Nods)* Now, yez are getting it. *(He plays a card)*

FARRELL: *(Playing his last card)* I win!

SEAN: That's an ace. I told you that you can't finish on a trick card. You have to take another card from the deck.

FARRELL: For fucks sake. Another rule. I think you're making it up as you go along.

SEAN: *(To Farrell)* Are you going to finish the game?

FARRELL: I'm tired of it. *(Throws down cards. There is the sound of a coded knock)* Here's Mulanney now.

Footsteps as he goes to answer door. Door opens.

O'REILLY: You took your time.

Door closes.

MULLANEY: Fuck it.

Footsteps

FARRELL: What's wrong, Paddy?

MULLANEY: The raid is off boys.

Sound of chair being pulled up.

SEAN: What?

MULLANEY: They're up there waiting for us.

SEAN: How do you know?

MULLANEY: I saw them so I did. I went up there last night to hide a few rifles in the ditch.

SEAN: You were supposed to bring them here.

MULLANEY: It was safer to leave them up in the dark. Just as well I did. On the way here this evening, I went by to have a look and the place was swarming with the new Civic Guards.

FARRELL: Did they see you?

MULLANEY: *(Sharply)* Do you think I'd be here if they did? They found the guns.

O'REILLY: Shite! You shouldn't have left them there.

MULLANEY: How was I to know? They must have got a tip off. I can't believe this has happened again.

FARRELL: Maybe they were just out on a routine patrol and came across the guns.

MULLANEY: There was too many of them. They knew.

FARRELL: They must have followed you last night.

MULLANEY: I wasn't followed.

FARRELL: I swear I was followed home meself two nights back.

MULLANEY: I'm telling you I wasn't followed.

FARRELL: I'm just saying …

MULLANEY: What are you just saying?

Farrell doesn't respond. There is tension in the room

SEAN: Boys, we'll get nowhere fighting among ourselves.

MULLANEY: *(To Farrell)* Just remember, Farrell, I'm the officer in charge here.

FARRELL: Sorry.

SEAN: What do we do now?

MULLANEY: Someone is passing on information to the other side.

O'REILLY: I don't think it's Mossie Kinsella unless he's communicating from the grave.

MULLANEY: We can't carry on operations until we take care of it.

O'REILLY: Who can it be? There's not that many of us.

FARRELL: It could be anyone. It's hard now to tell what side people are on.

MULLANEY: Apart from us here, who else knew about the raid?

O'REILLY: There was a fair crowd at your meeting a few weeks back.

MULLANEY: We didn't go into details.

FARRELL: It was known that we were planning to raid a mail train and there's not many places we could do that. Maybe they've been adding extra patrols for all the mail runs.

MULLANEY: They wouldn't have time for any other work if they did that. Did any of ye boys tell anyone?

FARRELL: Are you accusing us?

MULLANEY: Ye might have let something slip … innocently … in passing like.

O'REILLY: What do you take us for?

MULLANEY: Even in the pub after a few drinks? *(To O'Reilly)* I know, O'Reilly that your tongue can get fairly loose.

O'Reilly angrily approaches Mullaney.

O'REILLY: Watch what you're saying! Commanding officer or not, I'll have no man accuse me of being an informer.

MULLANEY: I'm not accusing any of ye. It only takes a little slip. That's all I'm saying.

O'REILLY: There's no need for talk like that.

MULLANEY: It's hard to know who to trust these days.

O'REILLY: Well you know you can trust us.

Pause

MULLANEY: You're very quiet Sean.

SEAN: I'm thinking.

MULLANEY: About what?

SEAN: I'm thinking that you're very quick to point the finger at everyone else.

MULLANEY: I wouldn't go there, Sean.

SEAN: You said yourself that you can't trust anyone these days.

MULLANEY: Be careful now, Sean.

SEAN: You went away from the plan when you hid the guns there last night.

MULLANEY: I explained that.

SEAN: Maybe you left them there as a sign or maybe you didn't leave them there at all. It's just a story you made up.

MULLANEY: *(Annoyed)* Why would I warn ye off? I could have let the raid happen.

FARRELL: He's right Sean.

MULLANEY: Damn right, I'm right! The only person outside this group that knew about the raid was Ernie O'Malley. I had to get approval from him to go ahead with it.

O'REILLY: Then it might be someone in division headquarters?

MULLANEY: Maybe, but I suspect the informer is closer to home.

FARRELL: Unless the walls have ears …

MULLANEY: I wasn't going to say this but as we're being open and honest here Sean, I have a thought. What about Tomas?

SEAN: My brother is no informer.

MULLANEY: You would say that.

SEAN: He was one of your most trusted Volunteers.

MULLANEY: We all know he's for the Treaty. If he's not with us, he's against us.

SEAN: He doesn't want to take sides.

MULLANEY: He already has.

SEAN: What do you mean?

MULLANEY: Don't let on you don't know.

SEAN: Know what?

MULLANEY: That he's applied for one of the National Army jobs?

SEAN: He wouldn't.

O'REILLY: Maybe you don't know your brother as well as you think?

SEAN: Shut up, O'Reilly. How do you know this, Mullaney?

MULLANEY: We have our own informants. *(Sean is speechless)* If I'm right, he may have been an informer all through the war.

SEAN: Mossie Kinsella was identified …

MULLANEY: Kinsella was a mistake. We never felt we got the right man. This proves it.

FARRELL: I can't believe that Tomas could be an informer.

O'REILLY: I can. I always thought there was something off about Tomas, no offence Sean. And you know what, it was Tomas gave us the information about Mossie.

FARRELL: Mossie was acting suspiciously though.

O'REILLY: According to Tomas. Mossie may have been a decoy to throw us off the scent. He was a good choice, no one liked him.

SEAN: Tomas would never...he wasn't even at the meeting.

MULLANEY: But he knew about it?

SEAN: *(Growing frustrated – worried)* I asked him to come along. You told me to!

MULLANEY: He knew what we were planning and how we operate. He's a clever lad. It wouldn't take much for him to figure it out.

FARRELL: It does all fit Sean.

SEAN: You all know Tomas and what he's done for the cause over the last few years. Sure, he even shot an RIC man.

O'REILLY: He wasn't all that keen to pull the trigger.

MULLANEY: We thought we'd be killing Dwyer that night, but it was his lackey we got. And Dwyer was a friend of your family, wasn't he? Who's to say he wasn't forewarned not to go out that night?

O'REILLY: And afterwards, Tomas wasn't even lifted for questioning.

SEAN: I know my brother. We may have our differences but he's no informer.

MULLANEY: Who else could it be?

SEAN: I don't know but I'm telling ye, if a finger is laid on Tomas, you'll have me to deal with.

MULLANEY: We can't ignore this Sean.

SEAN: Maybe … there's another way of finding out.

The men ask 'what / what do you mean / what way.

SEAN: We go directly to the source.

MULLANEY: Source?

SEAN: The informer is passing on the information to someone. If we can find that someone, they might lead us to the informer.

MULLANEY: *(Sarcasm)* So we just walk into the Civic Guards station and ask them if they wouldn't mind telling us who their informers are.

The men laugh.

O'REILLY: That should work!

SEAN: Not the Civic Guards. If it's been the same informer all the way through who else will know? *(Pause)* Well?

O'REILLY: The RIC?

SEAN: Exactly

FARRELL: They've been disbanded for months so they have.

SEAN: Some of the men are still around.

O'REILLY: Dwyer.

SEAN: I bet he could tell us a few stories

The men consider this.

MULLANEY: You might be on to something there.

SEAN: It's worth trying and there's no risk. He's just an ordinary civilian now.

O'REILLY: We'll pay him a visit so.

FARRELL: What if he won't talk?

SEAN: I'm sure he can be persuaded. *(To Mullaney)* Can you get us a revolver?

MULLANEY: I can. We need to do this soon.

SEAN: Tomorrow night?

MULLANEY: All right, here's how it'll work. O'Reilly, Farrell, I want you boys to meet each other at the church at seven tomorrow evening. When ye see me and Sean passing into Main Street from the College gates, follow us at a distance. It will look too suspicious if the four of us are walking along together.

FARRELL: Grand. What then?

MULLANEY: Sean and I will pay the Dwyer's a visit and you two take up position close by. I'll call if I need ye.

SEAN: You don't need to tell Ernie O' Malley about this. It's just the four of us. Agreed?

MULLANEY: Agreed. Right boys, until tomorrow night.

O'REILLY: Aye, we'll see you then. Seven.

MULLANEY: If this doesn't work, we'll still have to investigate Tomas.

SEAN: It'll work.

MULLANEY: And if we discover that it is Tomas?

SEAN: There's only one way to deal with informers. I'll not stand in your way.

MULLANEY: Aye. See you tomorrow.

They all bid each other goodnight and door/ footsteps as they leave.

SEAN: Tomas, what the fuck might you have done?

Sean looks worried. He waits a short while then exits

END OF EPISODE

EPISODE 42 – INFORMER REVEALED, MAR. 1922

Scene 1 - Outside, a park.

TOMAS: Just think, Lizzie, in two weeks time, we'll be married and living in Sligo.

LIZZIE: And you'll be in a uniform and I'll be baking cakes for you.

TOMAS: I won't be expecting that, I'm not like your brothers. You can sit around doing nothing all day if you like.

LIZZIE: I love you, Tomas Barry.

TOMAS: And I'm fierce fond of you, Lizzie O'Neill.

LIZZIE: *(Pretend indignation)* Oy!

They laugh.

VOICEOVER: Fractured – March 1922

Scene 2 - Dwyer's House

It is early evening in the kitchen of the Dwyer's house. Dwyer is sitting at the table which is covered in papers. He has a pencil and is making notes. Betty enters and starts setting the table.

BETTY: Move your arm there, Tom. *(Sets a plate)* Thanks. Will you be much longer?

DWYER: Just finishing up the Leixlip list.

BETTY: I want to get supper on the table.

DWYER: I won't be long, Betty.

Pause as she looks at him

BETTY: You're spending an awful lot of time on this,

DWYER: I have a lot of catching up to do.

BETTY: You're out all day and then you're up half the night.

DWYER: It'll get easier, I promise.

BETTY: I saw more of you when you were in the RIC so I did.

DWYER: *(Trying to make light)* This job is safer.

BETTY: With the Treaty signed, you could get a position with the new Irish Civic Guards.

DWYER: We've been through this.

BETTY: Would you not give it a try?

DWYER: No.

BETTY: But you'd be an Irishman working for the Irish Guards.

DWYER: Stop now Betty.

BETTY: You worked as a policeman all your life. It's a job you were good at.

DWYER: Hughes and Stiff died on my watch. I wasn't that good.

BETTY: It was hardly your fault. Would you not at least apply?

DWYER: *(Slams hand on table)* For Christ's sake Betty! *(Beat)* Sorry, Love. Sorry. *(Beat)* I did apply.

BETTY: Oh? And?

DWYER: I wasn't wanted.

BETTY: They said that?

DWYER: They said they weren't sure where my allegiances lie.

BETTY: What?

DWYER: They said that I never showed any sympathy for the Volunteers during the struggle so they owed me nothing.

Footsteps as she crosses to him.

BETTY: Oh Tom, love, why didn't you tell me?

DWYER: Maybe … I felt a bit ashamed.

BETTY: There's no shame in that. It's their loss.

DWYER: I don't mean ... look, I think...in that moment, I saw myself as they did. An Irishman who took money from the English to fight my own people.

BETTY: You were trying to uphold the law.

DWYER: English law! We told ourselves we were just doing our job but...I don't know.

BETTY: Maybe we should just leave here and make a fresh start.

DWYER: I have this insurance job now.

BETTY: You hate it.

DWYER: I'll get used to it and Liam Costello said he made a good living on it.

BETTY: *(Tactfully)* He wasn't ex- RIC. How many people will drop away when they realise that you were.

DWYER: They'll forget in time.

BETTY: Like the new Civic Guards forgot? It'll always hang over you. *(Pause, he has no answer)* Promise me you'll think about it.

Furious banging on the door.

DWYER: *(Pushing back chair, standing)* It better not be those little gurriers again shouting their insults.

BETTY: That's what I mean. People won't forget.

DWYER: *(Footsteps)* They won't forget when I get my hands on them, that's for sure.

BETTY: Go easy, they're probably just children.

Dwyer footsteps into hall to door. Opening of door. Distant commotion. Mullaney and Sean push him into the room. They are both wearing caps and scarves over their faces. Mullaney is holding a gun.

MULLANEY: In! Now!

A struggle.

DWYER: What the hell are you doing? Let me go!

Door slams closed.

BETTY: What's going on...who are you two?

MULLANEY: Get in there. *(Pushing him)* I've a gun. Get in!

BETTY: Jesus, Mary and Joseph. What is it ye want?

DWYER: Get out of my house.

SEAN: Not until we get what we came for.

BETTY: And what's that?

MULLANEY: Information, missus and we won't go until we get it.

SEAN: You won't be harmed if you cooperate.

DWYER: Ye come in with your faces covered, waving a gun and you're not going to harm us!

SEAN: Not if you cooperate.

DWYER: The scarf didn't fool me when you raided the station that time and it's not fooling me now. You may as well take it off Sean.

Sean looks at Mullaney.

BETTY: Sean Barry? Brigid's son?

DWYER: It's a sorry state of affairs when a neighbour's son bursts into my house. Take off the scarf.

Sean uncovers his face.

SEAN: Makes a change from you bursting into my mother's house to arrest me, doesn't it?

BETTY: That was his job back then, he has nothing to do with the RIC anymore.

SEAN: If I hadn't got the tip off, your husband, my Daddy's good friend, would have been very happy to throw me in a jail cell.

DWYER: And did you never wonder where the tip off came from?

Sean looks at him puzzled.

SEAN: What?

DWYER: I sent that girl to your house, you fool. I was hoping you'd be quick enough to get out before I arrived.

MULLANEY: Did you hear that, Sean? A likely story. Sit down the both of yous.

DWYER: I'll do as I like in my own house.

He remains standing.

MULLANEY: *(Click of gun)* Sit down! *(Chairs scraping as they sit)* We want the name of your informer. The one who has managed to scupper all our plans of the last while including one as recently as two weeks ago.

DWYER: That's all done with now.

MULLANEY: Not for us, it's not.

DWYER: I know nothing about any informers.

SEAN: You ran the station in Maynooth for years.

DWYER: I did.

MULLANEY: And you received information regarding Volunteer activities? *(No answer)* Didn't you?

DWYER: I had no dealings with any informers.

SEAN: You're telling us that in all that time, you never met or weren't aware of any informers?

DWYER: Yes.

MULLANEY: We brought the gun with us for a reason.

DWYER: You're not going to shoot me.

MULLANEY: Not just you, no.

DWYER: You touch my wife and I swear to God , you will have to use that gun.

SEAN: Just tell us what we want and we'll be gone.

DWYER: I know nothing.

MULLANEY: I'll ask again. Did you ever receive information about Volunteer activities?

Dwyer doesn't respond

BETTY: For God's sake Tom. Tell them what they want and be done with it.

DWYER: *(He hesitates)* Information was passed to me but it was always indirectly.

MULLANEY: Who passed it on?

DWYER: We'd mainly get word from Naas and sometimes from Dublin.

MULLANEY: An informer living in Maynooth would go to Naas or Dublin to pass on information?

DWYER: I suppose so.

SEAN: My arse. You just sat at your desk waiting to get the word?

DWYER: I didn't know any informers.

SEAN: I don't believe you, Mr. Dwyer.

DWYER: I'm telling you.

SEAN: Was Mossie Kinsella an informer?

DWYER: *(Laughs)* Ye wasted a bullet there. He was no more an informer than I was.

SEAN: You just said you didn't know any informers. How come you know that Mossie wasn't one?

DWYER: *(Trying to cover)* I meant that ... well I knew Mossie ... he was always in and out of the station complaining about one thing or another. He hated everyone.

MULLANEY: That doesn't rule him out. We're staying until we get the information we came for. Sit down there, Sean. *(They pull out chairs. He picks up a saucer)* You've set the table all nice, Mrs. Dwyer. *(A smash, Betty yelps)* Whoops.

DWYER: Leave my things alone! By God, I'll - How many times do I have to tell you. I don't know.

SEAN: Did they get paid for passing on information?

DWYER: Why does anyone do anything except for money?

SEAN: That's the difference between you and us. *(Pause)* Who would this informer talk to in Naas?

DWYER: There's no point in asking me.

SEAN: And then you'd get ... what? ... a letter or a phone call passing on the information?

DWYER: Yes.

SEAN: Which? A letter or a phone call?

DWYER: A phone call.

SEAN: From the same person?

DWYER: The officer in charge.

MULLANEY: It all sounds very vague so it does.

DWYER: I've told you all I know.

SEAN: Where are all the RIC records?

DWYER: We were told to burn them all.

SEAN: That was handy, wasn't it? And you didn't keep any records of your own?

DWYER: I did not.

SEAN: Not even as a memento? Something to remind you of your great days in the RIC. *(Dwyer doesn't respond. Sean sees all the papers on the table)* What are all those papers on the table?

DWYER: They're private … none of your business. *(Sound of Sean sifting through them)* Don't touch them.

SEAN: Oh, names, addresses, quantities of money paid. Maybe this is a list of informers.

DWYER: Put that down. It's got nothing to do with you.

SEAN: I wonder if we called on *(Reading)* James Ryan, number. 6, St Catherine's Park in Leixlip, would he be able to give us any information?

DWYER: No he wouldn't. *(Dwyer hops up, footsteps, pulls paper from Sean)* It's for my new job. Leave it.

SEAN: You be careful now.

BETTY: Don't you touch my husband.

DWYER: Just stop your playacting and go.

MULLANEY: We'll go when we're done.

Another cup is smashed.

BETTY: Jesus!

MULLANEY: You know more than you're letting on.

BETTY: He doesn't know anything! Just leave my house. Now.

SEAN: I'm going to search upstairs.

DWYER: Don't you dare.

SEAN: Mullaney, Cover them.

He exits upstairs. Mullaney holds the gun on Dwyer and Betty.

DWYER: Come back down here … now.

A lunge towards the stairs

MULLANEY: Don't move, old man.

BETTY: Listen to him, Tom. Don't .

DWYER: But I can't just …

BETTY: They'll be gone as soon as they know there's nothing to be found.

MULLANEY: Listen to your wife, Dwyer. Sit back down. Now.

Dwyer sits. Upstairs we can hear Sean pulling out drawers etc.

MULLANEY: What's all the paper on the table for anyway?

BETTY: My husband sells life insurance. They're his customers.

DWYER: Betty!

(Mullaney breaks out laughing)

MULLANEY: Him? An insurance salesman? Who'd have thought? I wouldn't say you have many customers in Maynooth, what? *(Laughs again)* That's a good one!

DWYER: It's honest work. *(Noises from above)* What's he doing up there?

MULLANEY: If you do know something, you'd be better off telling us. Sean won't give up easily. The place will be smashed to bits.

DWYER: Am I to tell you til I'm blue in the face?

Footsteps as Sean comes back down.

MULLANEY: Anything?

SEAN: Fuck all.

DWYER: There's nothing to find. And don't use that language in front of my wife.

SEAN: Oh, pardon me. Here's the deal, I know you know. And unless you tell us, we will shoot you. Won't we comrade?

MULLANEY: We won't have a choice.

DWYER: Sean, I have known you since you were a small lad -

SEAN: And now I'm a big lad and I'm not stupid enough to believe your lies. *(Lunges at Dwyer)* Name of the informer. Now.

BETTY: Sean, please don't hit him. *(To Dwyer)* If you know anything, tell them. Nothing is worth this.

SEAN: Listen to your wife.

DWYER: I'll not have anyone's blood on my hands.

SEAN: It never bothered you to have Volunteer blood on your hands.

DWYER: You'll have to shoot me.

BETTY: Don't say that, Tom. Sean, please. What would you mother say?

MULLANEY: Maybe I'll shoot your wife.

Betty screams.

DWYER: Don't touch her!

He makes a lunge. Sean knocks him to the ground. Furniture goes flying.

SEAN: Don't try that again, Dwyer.

MULLANEY: *(To Betty)* If you've any prayers to say, Mrs, you'd better say them now.

BETTY: *(Pleading)* Tom?

SEAN: He means it! I can't stop him.

DWYER: Oh Jesus....

SEAN: Just the name.

DWYER: Let my wife go first.

MULLANEY: Tell us. Then I'll let her go.

DWYER: All right.

Dwyer is struggling. He can't bring himself to say the name.

SEAN: We're waiting

MULLANEY: Tick-tock

BETTY: Just tell them.

DWYER: God forgive me. It's … it's Lizzie, Lizzie O'Neill.

Silence

MULLANEY: Lizzie?

SEAN: I don't believe you.

DWYER: You've got your name. It's not my problem if you don't like it. Now, let my wife go.

MULLANEY: Go, you bitch.

Betty is released, sobs. Dwyer comforts her.

SEAN: You're sure it's Lizzie O'Neill? Why would she …

DWYER: The truth hurts. *(Gloating)* She played ye well so she did, you and your little brother. She's a clever girl.

Sean can't believe it.

SEAN: No. She likes Tomas.

DWYER: You got what you came for. Now, get out of my house.

BETTY: *(To Sean)* I don't know how you can be your mother's son. You're a disgrace.

SEAN: Says the bitch of an RIC man.

BETTY: I'll tell everyone about this.

MULLANEY: No one will believe you. And if either of you warn Lizzie what's coming, you'll never rest another night easy in your beds.

DWYER: You bastards.

MULLANEY: *(To Dwyer)* And here. *(He takes a coin from his pocket and places it on the table)* A shilling. You were paid for the information.

He and Sean laugh. Footsteps as they make their way to the door. Betty sobs, Dwyer comforting her. They exit.

Scene 3 – Outside on street.

Running.

MULLANEY: What are we going to do about Lizzie?

SEAN: Leave Lizzie to me.

END OF EPISODE

EPISODE 43 – FIGHTING CONTINUES, APR. 1922

Scene 1 - UaBuachalla's house

UaBuachalla and Sean are bent over a map.

UABUACHALLA: This is the plan, first we make our way up on the train - *(A hammering at the door)* There's the girl now. She's reliable. Get the door, Sean.

Door opens.

GIRL: What d'you want Mr. UaBuachalla, sir?

UABUACHALLA: Deliver this letter to Father Dempsey, into his hands, no one else's, alright?

GIRL: I will.

Tucking it away.

SEAN: And I want you to go to the O'Neills in the back lane, do you know the place?

GIRL: I'm scared of them men, so I am.

SEAN: You won't meet them. *(Passing over more letters)* Post these letters in. Let no one see you. Here's a penny. *(Footsteps as she runs off. Door closes)* What was that you were saying about a plan, Domhnall?

VOICEOVER: Fractured – 12th April 1922

Scene 2 - Barry's pub.

Joseph is stacking bottles and Brigid is moving chairs. Footsteps as Tomas arrives in, he's on his way out and is in a hurry.

BRIGID: You're hardly leaving yet? Brid hasn't been in and -

TOMAS: I'm not leaving yet, Mammy. Sure, there's at least forty minutes before the train. I'm on my way to Lizzie's is all.

BRIGID: If you ask me, she should be the one making it her business to wave you off.

TOMAS: She was only coming up from Sligo last night, Mammy. She was most likely tired and slept in. Or maybe she -

BRIGID: Well for her, sleeping in.

TOMAS: *(Rising above it)* I'll be back soon. If Colgan calls -

JOSEPH: We'll tell him where you are. Go on. *(Tomas leaves. To Brigid)* Can you not just pretend to like the girl?

BRIGID: I was never an actor, Joseph. If it wasn't for that strap, he wouldn't even be thinking of joining the National Army.

JOSEPH: Tomas doesn't do anything he doesn't want to. Rumour has it he takes after his mother for that.

BRIGID: It's just…I've a terrible feeling about it all.

JOSEPH: He'll be grand. And you can't stop the lad from living his life.

BRIGID: Sligo is awful far away, Joseph.

JOSEPH: Won't Sean still be here? And Mary?

BRIGID: Having one son won't replace the other.

JOSEPH: Don't go upsetting yourself.

BRIGID: I'm not upsetting myself. He's upset me. Him and Colgan and that Lizzie one, turning his head - he was perfectly happy until she got her claws into him.

JOSEPH: He's perfectly happy now, Brigid and don't you want that for him?

BRIGID: Happy? He's arguing with Sean night and day and I know there's something gone wrong between him and Mary.

Joseph turns away, not wanting to reveal what happened between Tomas and Mary.

JOSEPH: They'll come around.

BRIGID: How? If he walks into a room, Mary walks out. She's not even here to say good-bye. There was a time she would have cried her eyes out over him.

JOSEPH: There's a blessing then. Bad enough you doing it.

BRIGID: I don't want him to go, Joseph. I don't want any of them to go anywhere anymore. Losing Moll..

JOSEPH: Aw Brigid – *(He walks to her. Hugs her)* Come here.

BRIGID: I've tried to accept it, Joseph, but I can't. My arms ache with all the mothering I want to give her. Half the time, I'm walking about in a daze, still thinking that it's not real but the whole world is going on as if it is. And, then, it dawns on me, over and over, every day, each day worse than the last, that she is gone. Forever.

JOSEPH: Aye...

BRIGID: In all my life, as long as I live, I have to accept that I will never see her smile again or hear her voice or her laugh or see her grow. She will never grow up, Joseph

JOSEPH: Aw Brigid..

BRIGID: Our little girl, who'll never kiss us again, Tomas will never call for Millie Mollie May again and her little friends will move on and get married and the loss of her will stab me afresh each time I see them. How can I be expected to bear such pain?

JOSEPH: I feel it too. I might not say it, but I feel it too.

They embrace. Beat.

BRIGID: That's why, for Tomas to go..it's tearing me up. I don't think I can bear it.

JOSEPH: He'll return, so he will.

BRIGID: Aye, but...I thought, once the Treaty was signed that it was over. That we could go back to what we were.

JOSEPH: Tomas was never going to be happy running this place. I think, deep down, we both knew that.

BRIGID: But to join the army, Joseph. I couldn't bear to lose another one.

JOSEPH: It will all settle down, you'll see.

BRIGID: Maybe if I explained to him -

JOSEPH: You could. And he'd probably stay. And he'd be miserable.

BRIGID: Just for a while and then he might -

JOSEPH: The lad can't live his life to please you.

BRIGID: *(Beat)* Aye.

JOSEPH: Tomas would be wasted in the bar. He'll do well and he'll be with Colgan -

BRIGID: Colgan is half-cracked! Weren't you listening to Sean's stories about him at all up in Ballykinlar? *(During this Colgan arrives in and listens in amusement. Joseph spots him and tries to interject)* He was making people go by false names to confuse the British and then Sean said, those same people were getting taken out and tortured. Not content with that, he was making the men into an army right in front of the English guards. Colgan just invites trouble on his head.

JOSEPH: Ah .. now Brigid, he's not that bad, I -

BRIGID: He's worse. And I was talking to his mother, Anne three days back, her heart is broken between his brother Pearse and himself and -

JOSEPH: Colgan is a grand lad.

BRIGID: Does a grand lad go off running about the countryside and not a word to his mother for weeks on end?

JOSEPH: You always liked him -

BRIGID: I never did. I'm not in the habit of liking troublemakers and rebels and -

401

JOSEPH: *(Desperate)* You always said he was grand.

BRIGID: He's about as grand now, Joseph, as your…your arse.

COLGAN: And a very fine arse you have there too, Mr. Barry. Hello, Mrs. Barry.

BRIGID: *(Unabashed)* Mr. Colgan.

Scene 3 - UaBuachalla's house

UABUACHALLA: And The boys up there will meet us in Broadstone.

SEAN: That's grand. And will we have guns?

UABUACHALLA: O'Reilly is getting them from Ellen Kenny.

SEAN: O'Reilly's joining us?

UABUACHALLA: He is.

SEAN: And Mullaney?

UABUACHALLA: He's needed in Celbridge. But my son, Joe, is coming.

SEAN: Great.

UABUACHALLA: Sinead wouldn't have said that - she'd have tried to lock him up, God rest her.

SEAN: My mother'd do the same.

UABUACHALLA: Brigid was never one for the Volunteers.

SEAN: *(Affection)* Never one for fighting unless she's at the centre of it.

UABUACHALLA: She's a force, is Brigid Barry.

SEAN: She is that.

UABUACHALLA: Did you manage a 'goodbye' to her today at all?

SEAN: I've told Ellen Kenny to let her know once we're in Dublin.

UABUACHALLA: You might regret it. In '16, I made every fellow go home before we left.

SEAN: And some of them weren't let back, I heard.

UABUACHALLA: That's true. Did you manage a 'goodbye' to Joseph at least?

SEAN: Sure, he'd only tell me mother. Anyway, what with Tomas joining the army, I left well enough alone. Now, enough, what's the plan once we're in Dublin?

Beat

UABUACHALLA: I'm fierce sorry about you and Tomas.

402

SEAN: He's a stubborn little fecker. Always was.

UABUACHALLA: He probably says the same about you.

SEAN: He says a lot worse. *(Studying map)* Is this where the Four Courts is on this map?

UABUACHALLA: Aye. The plan is to take it tonight, along with some other buildings around the city, in the hope that we can bring both factions of the IRA army back together.

SEAN: It's a miracle you'll need for that. The split's getting terrible, so it is. I've read of houses being raided for arms and people being shot dead and -

UABUACHALLA: Which is why we need some decisive action now. Force things.

SEAN: How will that work though?

UABUACHALLA: Think about it. The British will hate it, us taking over an important building like the Four Courts. They'll demand action and sure Mick Collins is never going to use his new army to shell his old comrades.

SEAN: He believes in the Treaty.

UABUACHALLA: So does your brother. Would he shell you?

SEAN: I suppose not.

UABUACHALLA: There you are then. We're all Irishmen. All brothers. O'Connor believes that the British will most likely take it upon themselves to shell us -

SEAN: No Irishman would let that happen.

UABUACHALLA: The boy has got it!

SEAN: And we'll be united.

UABUACHALLA: Maith an buachaill. Look here now at this map of the four courts. *(He unfolds another map)* There are four buildings on the site - the Four Courts proper, the North Block, the Public Records Office and the Land Registry. Our headquarters, according to GHQ will be right here, on the edge of the north block.

SEAN: So any shelling from the Bridewell police station -

UABUACHALLA: - across the road -

SEAN: Will have to go through the Land Registry building before it hits us.

UABUACHALLA: Lovely and simple.

SEAN: It's brilliant! How are we getting in?

UABUACHALLA: The word is that there will be one policeman -

SEAN: One?

UABUACHALLA: Aye, poor divil won't know what hit him. We'll go in late, some of the boys will scale the railings, take him prisoner and let the rest of us into the building.

SEAN: And we'll be fortifying the place?

UABUACHALLA: Yes, all the windows will be barricaded and defended.

SEAN: Supplies?

UABUACHALLA: That's what I have you down for. While I'm getting into the Four Courts, you'll be with another group. It's riskier, you'll be taken to the Four Courts Hotel, here *(He points it out on the map)* and ye will raid their stocks. Take everything you can.

SEAN: No better man for getting food!

UABUACHALLA: An army marches on its stomach.

SEAN: It'll be a grand adventure.

Scene 4 - Barry's pub

BRIGID: You make a martyr of my son, Patrick Colgan, and I'll be after you so I will.

COLGAN: He's only joining the new National Army, Mrs. Barry, not nailing himself to a cross.

BRIGID: May God forgive you for that.

COLGAN: Is the martyr in, is he? I don't have much time.

BRIGID: He's gone to visit Lizzie, to say his good-byes. A fine girl she is, lying in bed half the day and her sweetheart going to the army.

COLGAN: When he gets back, tell him I'll meet him at the station on the quarter hour.

JOSEPH: We will.

COLGAN: *(Footsteps, pause)* He'll be grand, Mrs. Barry. I give you my word.

Brigid nods, emotional.

JOSEPH: Thanks, Pat. Be safe yourself now too.

COLGAN: I will. Goodbye now.

On his way out, he passes Poor Brid, bustling in with Colm.

POOR BRID: Hello Pat, are you off today too?

COLGAN: I am, Mrs. O'Sullivan. Come in there now and I'll close the door after you.

POOR BRID: Grand. Grand. The best of luck to you, Pat. Come on in, Colm. *(Door closes as Colgan leaves)* I got held up terrible in UaBuachalla's, Brigid. He had the shop closed early, so I had to go further afield to get the tablets for Mr. O'Sullivan's indigestion. Anyway, that's by the by. Where is the soldier?

BRIGID: Gone to get Lizzie O'Neill out of her bed, she couldn't even bother herself to come over and say goodbye. And her professing undying love.

JOSEPH: Brigid now -

POOR BRID: Is she back from Sligo? Her brother was storming up the Main Street just now. He got a letter to say she's gone for good.

JOSEPH: I wouldn't blame the girl, staying away from those boyos. Maybe that's why she wasn't over, ey, Brigid?

BRIGID: Aye. Maybe.

POOR BRID: Wait until you see what Colm has made for Tomas.

BRIGID: *(To Colm)* You made something for Tomas, Colm? Aren't you the great chap?

POOR BRID: Show them there now, Colm.

Colm unfolds a picture. It's a soldier with an enormous gun. A man lies bleeding at his feet. Brigid and Joseph don't quite know what to say

POOR BRID: Isn't that marvellous now? *(Jabbing picture)* That's Tomas with the gun and that's the enemy lying bleeding on the ground with his guts out. Wouldn't you know exactly what it is?

JOSEPH: It's fairly graphic, all right.

BRIGID: Very…nice, Colm.

BRIGID: He's a dab hand with the pencil. You'd want to see the drawing he did of the dead cat last week. The detail on the maggots was amazing.

Door opens. Tomas enters. He's a lot more subdued than when he left.

JOSEPH: There he is now, Brid. Tomas, Pat Colgan was in looking for you. Said he'd meet you at the quarter hour down at the station.

TOMAS: Aye, I met him coming up the way with another lad. I'll go upstairs, get my things.

BRIGID: Would you not say hello to Brid? She called in to wish you the best. Colm has a present for you.

TOMAS: *(With a big effort at cheer)* Hello, Brid. Sorry...a present for me, have you, Colm? *(Takes paper. Tomas takes it and is taken aback)* That's a great drawing altogether. Thanks.

POOR BRID: You'll be missed behind that bar, Tomas Barry. Come here and give me a hug.

TOMAS: I'll miss you Brid but I'll be back.

POOR BRID: Aye.

TOMAS: Next time ye see me, I'll be in a proper uniform.

POOR BRID: I'll have to learn to salute.

TOMAS: You will!

POOR BRID: I'd best be off. Mr. O'Sullivan is waiting on his tablets. You take care, d'you hear now.

TOMAS: You too. And Colm, be a good boy for your mammy. Do everything she tells you, just like I did when I was a lad.

Brigid laughs half-tearfully. Brid exits. Door opens, street, closes. Silence. Tomas stares after them.

BRIGID: You better hurry up, Tomas. Time is getting on.

TOMAS: Aye.

He still makes no move.

BRIGID: Now, Tomas.

TOMAS: Aye.

JOSEPH: Is...is everything alright, son?

TOMAS: I, eh..just thought, you should know that, I won't be going to Sligo now. I'll be staying in the Curragh.

BRIGID: But your heart was set on Sligo. I hope you're not doing it for me, Tomas. You have to go to Sligo.

TOMAS: No, I don't Mammy. I have to go where I'm wanted. I'm not talking about it.

Footsteps as he leaves.

Scene 5 - Uabuachalla's house

UABUACHALLA: Word has it that some of the Civic Guards will mutiny and give over their weapons.

SEAN: Marvellous.

UABUACHALLA: We could be there for the long haul.

SEAN: I don't mind once we get a result.

A knocking

UABUACHALLA: I'd say that's O'Reilly, let him in there.

Footsteps, door opens, closes. O'Reilly enters. Breathless.

O'REILLY: I ran slap-bang into Dwyer on the way here and me with guns hidden in me pockets.

UABUACHALLA: What odds, his sort don't count for anything anymore.

O'REILLY: He's leaving Kildare soon by all accounts.

UABUACHALLA: And good riddance. *(O'Reilly lays guns on the table)* That's some selection of arms you have.

O'REILLY: That Ellen Kenny is a fine soldier. *(Lays more down)* She had bundles of them buried all over the college.

UABUACHALLA: I hope ye weren't seen. The College is about to come down hard on us, I heard.

O'REILLY: They were never really behind us. All that support was just because the rest of the world approved. But no, we weren't seen. *(He distributes the guns)* Here Sean, that's yours. UaBuachalla, there you go. Take an extra one for Joe.

UABUACHALLA: Thank you. *(Taking gun)* I have to ask, did you sort out the O'Neill girl, Sean?

SEAN: I did, she admitted all.

O'REILLY: Did Tomas have an inkling, d'you think?

SEAN: I'll not dignify that with an answer.

O'REILLY: I mean no offense -

SEAN: You've just accused my brother of being a traitor.

O'REILLY: You've got to wonder -

SEAN: Do you? Do you wonder, Domhnall?

UABUACHALLA: Tomas is a fine boy, a good soldier.

O'REILLY: If he's so good a soldier where is he now?

SEAN: Doing what he thinks is right.

O'REILLY: And maybe he thought siding with loud mouth Lizzie was right too, ey?

SEAN: He knew nothing about Lizzie. He still doesn't.

O'REILLY: You never told him?

SEAN: There wasn't any point to it.

O'REILLY: She ruined a lot of ambushes, Mossie Kinsella was killed in her place -

SEAN: Maybe Mossie informed as well. You weren't too quick at finding the mole, were you?

O'REILLY: Because your brother, he was the one told us to hold off, told us to plant false information to see if we could catch the fecker and in the meantime, Lizzie is ruining all. I just think questions -

UABUACHALLA: The girl was exposed, dealt with, isn't that enough?

SEAN: Aye and for your information, she swore to me Tomas had nothing to do with anything.

O'REILLY: She would say that.

SEAN: She was telling the truth. My brother -

O'REILLY: I hope you made no allowances for her on account of your brother.

SEAN: She's gone, I can guarantee it.

O'REILLY: And when did all this take place. I saw her not three weeks ago, bold as brass, flaunting herself about town.

SEAN: It took place less than three weeks ago. She's gone, I said.

UABUACHALLA: Didn't her brothers call into the shop yesterday moaning that she'd taken off, wondering how they were going to manage at all.

SEAN: They think for the moment that she's at her aunties in Sligo.

O'REILLY: And Tomas?

SEAN: Same.

O'REILLY: I wouldn't want to be around when everyone finds out the truth.

SEAN: That's taken care of too. Should happen anytime now. There's a girl delivering a few letters to them.

UABUACHALLA: Good man, Sean. Now -

O'REILLY: She was one of our best women.

UABUACHALLA: Or one of the worst, depending on what way you look at it.

O'REILLY: Aye.

UABUACHALLA: Let's just put it behind us, focus on what we're doing now.

SEAN: Instead of looking for trouble by bringing it up.

UABUACHALLA: Sean.

SEAN: Sorry, sorry…it's just..

Beat.

O'REILLY: I'm sorry too, alright. I've never quite…understood Tomas, if I'm honest.

UABUACHALLA: There's no law says people have to get on with each other or understand each other. But we have to have one another's backs.

O'REILLY: Aye. (*He holds out a hand*) Shake on that. (*They shake*) There's an end to it now.

SEAN: Aye.

O'REILLY: No hard feelings.

SEAN: No.

O'REILLY: And if this works out, we'll all be together again.

UABUACHALLA: Did you say your goodbyes, O'Reilly?

O'REILLY: My what?

UABUACHALLA: Your goodbyes? To your family and that.

O'REILLY: Ah no…

UABUACHALLA: This could be a long haul.

O'REILLY: Sure, who would I say goodbye to?

UABUACHALLA: I thought you'd parents and a wee sister?

O'REILLY: I had three sisters, Domhnall. They died, one after the other in 1918 with the flu. My parents too. God rest them.

SEAN: You never said -

O'REILLY: Aye. Well…not much point in dwelling on it all. The youngest girl wasn't much older than your Moll.

Beat

UABUACHALLA: You parents would be proud of what you've done for the cause, I'd say.

O'REILLY: I like to think so but they were simple people. Not political at all.

UABUACHALLA: What made you -

O'REILLY: After they died, I thought, what sort of a fecking country is this where people are so grateful for a leaky roof and a bit of land? I felt they should have had more.

SEAN: They should have had.

UABUACHALLA: And they would have had if the Irish had governed the Irish. It's foolishness to expect a foreign invader to care about us.

O'REILLY: Right you are. Show me the plans. Is that the Four Courts?

Scene 6 - Barry's pub

BRIGID: It has to be that Lizzie one. Why else would he stay up here? I'll brain her.

Door opens, street, closes as Mary enters. See their confusion.

MARY: What's the matter?

JOSEPH: Do you have any idea why Tomas has suddenly decided to stay here instead of going to Sligo, Mary?

MARY: *(Cold)* I'm only here to collect my sandwich.

Footsteps as she goes to move on past them.

BRIGID: I don't know what's happened between the two of you, but I know you should at least wish your brother the best in his new life.

MARY: You're right, Mammy, you don't know what's happened.

BRIGID: He was your pet, d'you not remember? He'd follow you everywhere.

MARY: He was three, Mammy. He grew up. Now can I get my sandwich or not?

JOSEPH: There's something up, Mary. He's not going to Sligo and he won't say why. He'll talk to you if you ask him.

MARY: I don't want to ask him.

BRIGID: Do it for me, Mary. Please. Haven't I been through enough? I need to know what's upset him.

MARY: That's not fair asking me to talk to him.

JOSEPH: Maybe not.

Brigid gives a sigh of despair. Mary, hating this, reconsiders.

MARY: I'll see what I can do.

Scene 7 - Uabuachalla's house

UABUACHALLA: And then the – *(Furious knocking)* Who is it?

FR DEMPSEY: It's myself, Father Dempsey, Domhnall.

UABUACHALLA: Aw grand. You got my letter, Father.

FR DEMPSEY: It just said to come at once, that you had a request to make of me.

UABUACHALLA: Aye. You must keep it to yourself, Father.

FR DEMPSEY: If this is some fool's errand to go kill more people, that I do not wish to know.

SEAN: It's an errand to unite people, Father.

FR DEMPSEY: You don't unite with guns, Sean Barry.

UABUACHALLA: Hear us out, Father. *(Beat as the priest nods)* Tonight, a number of men opposed to the Treaty are planning to take over a number of buildings in Dublin city centre. It will be done as peacefully as possible and -

FR DEMPSEY: Whatever for? We have peace now. We have a treaty now.

UABUACHALLA: We have an army split down the middle, Father. We have two factions of Irishmen trying to run the country. We need to unite them.

FR DEMPSEY: By taking over buildings. Causing trouble?

SEAN: There'll be no trouble, Father. Not unless it's from the other side.

FR DEMPSEY: You expect Mick Collins and his new army to do nothing?

O'REILLY: We expect the British to act, Father and there is no way our pro-Treaty old army comrades will stand for that.

FR DEMPSEY: Then you under-estimate the support for this peace, boys. *(Beat)* What am I doing here?

UABUACHALLA: We want to ask your blessing.

FR DEMPSEY: Absolutely not. No.

UABUACHALLA: Why?

FR DEMPSEY: Because we live in a democracy, boys. We have fought for this democracy and in the democratic Dail, your Dail, Domhnall, the government of this country voted for the Treaty.

UABUACHALLA: By a slim majority who are running scared of the British.

FR DEMPSEY: In your mind. In mine, they are men who want peace, who want this country to start building herself up again.

UABUACHALLA: We can never do that under the terms of the Treaty as they are now.

FR. DEMPSEY: Your fellow politicians are not stupid, they are as informed as you are. What DeVelara is doing is utter madness.

O'REILLY: Trying to save us from becoming British subjects is utter madness is it?

411

FR. DEMPSEY: What is needed now is rational debate, not more war.

UABUACHALLA: And we will have that debate. In time.

FR. DEMPSEY: What you and these men are doing is taking action without any authority from the state. You have no moral right to do that. It's military dictatorship and is an insult to civil liberties.

UABUACHALLA: Taking the Four Courts is not an act of War, Rory O'Connor assures us of that.

FR. DEMPSEY: Pull the other one. If your side is angry about anything, let it be the atrocities' in Belfast. Catholics being attacked. Burned out.

UABUACHALLA: Will you bless us or not, Father?

FR. DEMPSEY: I will not.

UABUACHALLA: Then you better go.

FR. DEMPSEY: If you kill anyone, it'll be murder.

O'REILLY: It wasn't murder to kill six months ago, Father.

UABUACHALLA: How can it be murder to kill an Irishman and not an Englishman, Father? Does the sin of murder have a nationality now?

FR DEMPSEY: You know fine well it doesn't. But if a reasonable peace is offered, then it should be explored and killing people is not acceptable unless it's been given a chance. Sean, this will break your mother's heart.

SEAN: I can't live my life to please my mother, Father.

FR. DEMPSEY: I buried little Moll a bare four months ago.

SEAN: I know you did and I wish I thought different, but this is how I feel, Father. I can't deny my conscience.

FR. DEMPSEY: And I can't deny mine. There has been too much loss. Have any of ye any idea what it is to sit in a confessional and listen to your flock ask forgiveness for the most grievous of sins? It almost destroyed me. Day after day I had to give that absolution. I gave it because there was no alternative to what these boys and girls were doing. But now there is. There is a way and we have to try to make it work. I will not condone another killing.

O'REILLY: I thought your sort weren't meant to judge, Father.

FR. DEMPSEY: I have never judged, just tried to understand. With understanding comes forgiveness. But this…

UABUACHALLA: Then you'll understand how we feel, Father, when we try and fail to understand the logic of the other side.

FR DEMPSEY: You will damn your souls.

UABUACHALLA: But in the process, hopefully we will free Ireland.

O'Reilly and Sean turn away from the priest.

FR DEMPSEY: Oh aye, turn your backs on me. On peace. On the church. You will destroy this country, do you her me. Do ye? *(No reply)* So be it.

He leaves.

Scene 8 - Barry's pub

Tomas enters from upstairs.

TOMAS: I can't find my bible, so I took yours, Mammy, is that alright? *(Stops at the sight of Mary)* Mary.

MARY: *(Long beat)* Tomas.

TOMAS: I'm heading away now.

MARY: Aye.

TOMAS: Is there a chance, Mary that -

BRIGID: Don't be afraid to come back if you don't like it, Tomas. They'll always be a bed for here for you.

TOMAS: Thanks, Mammy.

BRIGID: And Sligo, just -

JOSEPH: Me and your mother will see you down at the station, Tomas. Come on, Brigid.

BRIGID: My purse.

JOSEPH: Don't be worrying about your purse, I've got money here. Come on. *(Door opens, street)* See you soon, son.

They leave. Long pause

TOMAS: *(Raps the bar. Hesitant)* D'you remember how that nick in the bar happened?

MARY: Aye.

TOMAS: You had me on your back and you fell and I hit -

MARY: *(Short)* I remember, I said.

TOMAS: And then the glasses behind the bar all smashed and I told Mammy that it was my fault. My idea.

MARY: *(Cold)* Weren't you the great lad?

TOMAS: And Mammy smacked me from one end of the pub to the other and my head streaming in blood from the glass.

MARY: Aye.

413

TOMAS: What I'm trying to say, Mary, is that I would have lain down and died for you.

MARY: I don't want to talk about any of this.

TOMAS: I'm so sorry, Mary.

MARY: You've said that.

TOMAS: And I'll keep saying it until you forgive me.

MARY: Why aren't you going to Sligo?

TOMAS: *(Wrong footed)* What?

MARY: Mammy said you weren't going to Sligo now.

TOMAS: That's true.

MARY: You were going not four hours ago.

TOMAS: That's true too.

MARY: Are you staying for Mammy?

TOMAS: No, but I thought she'd be pleased.

MARY: She's worried is what she is. One minute you're swanning off west and the next you're staying in Kildare. What are you trying to do to her?

TOMAS: Nothing.

MARY: Is it something to do with Lizzie O'Neill? *(Tomas reacts, upset)* What is it, Tomas?

He pulls out a letter and hands it to her.

TOMAS: Her brother got this letter this morning. I - I don't understand.

MARY: *(Reading)* 'Dear Tomas…really sorry..not coming back…met a man…' She met a man? Jesus.

TOMAS: A farmer from Donegal she says.

MARY: But, I thought….

TOMAS: So did I.

MARY: Oh, Tomas….

TOMAS: I don't believe she wrote it.

MARY: But sure who else…?

TOMAS: I don't know, something is just not right.

MARY: Like what?

TOMAS: I don't know.

MARY: *(Beat)* Lizzie was never….you know…

TOMAS: What?

MARY: The most reliable girl.

TOMAS: She was different with me.

MARY: Maybe you think so but …

TOMAS: I know so. She was different with me. We were getting married.

MARY: Aye, maybe you were but then a better prospect came along. That's just Lizzie.

TOMAS: No. That's not just her.

MARY: Wake up, Tomas. She was chasing Sean for ages and then when he was put away, she was after you.

TOMAS: She was never chasing Sean.

MARY: She was so. Me and Cissy used to laugh at the way she'd be waiting outside the pub with her tongue hanging out after him.

TOMAS: Shut up, Mary.

MARY: Lizzie O'Neill liked the soldiers, everyone knew that.

TOMAS: *(Beat)* Not me.

MARY: Then you're a fool.

TOMAS: You know nothing about the real Lizzie.

MARY: By the looks of this, you didn't know her too well yourself.

TOMAS: *(Beat)* Just…just go.

MARY: Now you know how I feel. You thought you'd have a lovely life with the person you love and bang, all gone. *(Tearful)* Enjoy feeling like that, Tomas.

Footsteps as she crosses the bar, opens the door and slams shut.

Scene 9 - Uabuachalla's house

We hear O'Reilly, Sean and Uabuachalla singing the English version of the national anthem and laughing as they get themselves prepared. We hear packing and slamming and finally a door opening.

ALL: 'Soldiers are we,
Whose lives are pledged to Ireland,
Some have come from a land beyond the wave,
Sworn to be free, no more our ancient Ireland
Shall shelter the despot or the slave;
Tonight we man the Bearna Baoil
in Erin's cause come woe or weal,
'Mid cannon's roar and rifle's peal,
We'll chant a soldier's song.

415

UABUACHALLA: Ready.

O'REILLY: Ready

SEAN: Ready

Door closes.

Scene 10 - Barry's pub

The 'Soldiers song' can play through this small scene too. Tomas unfolds Lizzie's letter.

TOMAS: Met a man .. oh, God, Lizzie.

Hammering on door.

COLGAN: *(From outside)* Tomas Barry, hurry up would ya!

TOMAS: *(Forced cheerfulness)* Coming, Colgan.

He picks up his bag.

COLGAN: *(Distant)* Come on then. The train won't wait forever and neither will I!

Tomas tears letter in half and half again.

TOMAS: *(To himself)* And I'm done waiting too. *(Raised voice)* I'm ready, Colgan. *(He opens the door)* I'm ready.

Door closes.

END OF EPISODE

END OF SERIES

BONUS – COUNTY COUNCIL MEETING, JUNE 1920

NOTE: This episode was written to follow on from the Council elections in June 1920 to add some historical colour. We had hoped to perform it in the Council chambers in Naas. When Covid forced us to convert the series into podcast format, we decided to omit this episode as it did not progress the main storyline. We present it here for your enjoyment.

The first meeting of the newly elected Kildare County Council after the 1920 local elections took place in June 1920. In attendance were the 21 elected Councillors, two co-opted Councillors, a deputation from the Gaelic League plus 4 Council officials (Secretary, Surveyor, Assistant Surveyor and Accountant). The final Council numbers were 17 Sinn Fein, 5 Labour and 1 Independent. In trying to dramatise these events, the challenge was how to deal with so many people. The approach here is to capture what was said rather than who specifically said it. There are specific instances where some comments have to be associated with a particular speaker due to past events etc. So the piece was limited to 8 speaking parts with audience members making up the balance. At the beginning of the scene, the Council area is unoccupied. William Coffey, the Secretary of the Council enters and addresses the audience.

COFFEY: Good morning everyone. I'd like to welcome you all to the Council chamber. We do have a large number of new Councillors so for those of you who do not know me, I am William Coffey and I am the Secretary of the Council. My main duty during Council meetings is to record the minutes and assist the Chairman in running the meeting. I hereby call upon all elected members to acknowledge their presence and take their seat in the Council chamber.

He produces his list and reads the names. Characters and audience will take a seat in the meeting area.

COFFEY: In alphabetical order; Donal Buckley, TD, Sinn Fein; Mark Carroll, Sinn Fein; Hugh Colahan, Labour; James Cregan, Labour; Joseph Cusack, Sinn Fein; Patrick Dooley, Sinn Fein; Francis Doran, Sinn Fein; Thomas Doran, Sinn Fein; John Fitzgerald, Sinn Fein; Michael Fitzsimons, Independent, returning ; Nicholas Hanagan, Sinn Fein; Thomas Harris, Sinn Fein; William Mahon, Sinn Fein; Richard McCann, Sinn Fein; Eamonn Moran, Sinn Fein; Arthur Murphy, Labour; William Murray, Sinn Fein, returning; James O'Connor, Sinn Fein, returning; Patrick Phelan, Sinn Fein, returning; Michael Smith, Labour; Christopher Supple, Labour

After all have taken their position, Coffey takes his position behind the top table.

UABUACHALLA: Before you begin Mr. Coffey, can I request that you use the Irish version of my name; UaBuachalla.

COFFEY: As you wish sir. Again, welcome gentlemen. As the outgoing chairman and vice chairman have not been returned .. *(Some laughter)…* we must elect a chairman for this meeting before we can proceed. Are there any proposals? *(Silence)* The meeting cannot proceed without a chairman.

PHELAN: I propose Domhnall UaBuachalla.

COFFEY: I need someone to second that proposal.

CUSACK: I'll second that.

COFFEY: Mr. *(hesitates)* UaBuachalla

UABUACHALLA: Is mor an onoir ata deanta agaibh orm etc etc ……

As he is speaking, there may be a few looks among some of the Councillors. When he is finished, there is an embarrassed silence for a few beats followed by a some muted coughs.

UABUACHALLA: What I mean is that I am honoured to be asked but I would prefer if some other member would take the role of Chairman as I have no experience in the running of such meetings.

CUSACK: Sure most of us are new here and we're all more or less in the same position.

UABUACHALLA: What about one of the returning Councillors?

PHELAN: There's only four of us and I can only speak for myself but I'll stick to my original proposal.

COFFEY: Any other proposals? *(Silence)* All those in favour of Mr. UaBuachalla chairing this meeting, raise your hands. *(All raise hands)* Unanimous. Mr. UaBuachalla, please take the chair.

Applause as UaBuachalla moves to the top table and takes his position. Coffey hands UaBuachalla the agenda for the meeting.

COFFEY: This is the running order for today's meeting. The first item is a request from the Kildare Gaelic League for permission to address the meeting. They have a deputation outside. The Council generally receives deputations first before the general business begins.

UABUACHALLA: The Gaelic League! Close to my own heart. I certainly have no objections. Any objections from my fellow Councillors? *(General murmurs of consent)* Very well, show them in.

Coffey exits the room.

UABUACHALLA: As I myself am a member of the Gaelic League, I will remain impartial during this.

Coffey re-enters followed by a deputation of 1 to 4 people. Only one, Art O' Connor TD will speak.

COFFEY: Mr. Art O' Connor, TD and his colleagues from the Gaelic League.

UABUACHALLA: You are all very welcome.

ART O'CONNOR: A chairde etc etc ....

He speaks a few sentences in Irish until interrupted by UaBuachalla.

UABUACHALLA: May I interrupt you with the greatest of apologies? Could I ask you to continue "as bearla" for the sake of my colleagues less versed in Irish.

Embarrassed laughter.

ART O'CONNOR: That indeed saddens me but will strengthen our resolve to pursue our goals with greater vigour.

COFFEY: If you wish, you may address the Council from the podium.

He takes his position on the podium.

ART O'CONNOR: May I first thank the Council for giving us this opportunity to present our case. We're here to ask the Council to help push the Irish language ahead in the country. We feel that one of the best methods of getting Irish into its proper place is to make it the customary language in meetings such as this and in schools. It is within the power of the Council now to make this a reality.

COLAHAN: May I comment?

UABUACHALLA: Certainly

COFFEY: On a point of order Mr. Chairman, it is customary to allow a delegation to present without comment and the proposal will be discussed later on in the meeting.

UABUACHALLA: Very well. Proceed Mr. O'Connor.

ART O'CONNOR: We would ask the Council to ensure that any new members of the clerical staff would have a proper knowledge of Irish. This should not cause any injustice to existing members of staff who through no fault of their own might not be conversant with Irish. We feel that an immediate action could be the decision to have the Council cheques, paper headings and the like in Irish. The Council can do a lot in getting Irish into schools by insisting that teachers being appointed should have a knowledge of Irish and that Irish should be a regular subject on the schools programme and not just taught after school hours. We humbly ask that the Council seriously considers our proposals.

UABUACHALLA: As you know, I am of one mind with the deputation in this regard. This is a discussion that should be held in every council chamber in Ireland. I know that the assembled Council here will seriously consider your recommendations. The Gaelic League is doing great work in promoting the Irish language and Irish culture and I urge you to continue in your endeavours.

ART O'CONNOR: Again, I would like to thank the Council for their time. Go raibh maith agaibh.

UABUACHALLA: Go raibh maith agat.

The deputation leave the chamber.

UABUACHALLA: *(Consulting his notes)* Next item is the co-option of two additional members. Mr. Coffey, can you elaborate?

COFFEY: Of course. The elected Council members are allowed to co-opt two additional members to the Council. If more than two nominations are received, a vote would have to be taken. Prior to this meeting, Councillors were asked for nominations. I only received two so both will be co-opted. The two additional members are Mr. Nicholas Travers, Sinn Fein proposed by Mr. Mark Carroll, seconded by Michael Fitzsimons and Mr. Henry Fay also Sinn Fein proposed by William Mahon and seconded by Eamonn Moran.

PHELAN: Henry Fay said he wouldn't be able to come to the meeting but Travers is outside. Will I bring him in?

UABUACHALLA: Thank you Mr. Phelan.

Phelan exits.

COLAHAN: Another two Sinn Feiners! Have ye lads not got enough on the Council?

General laughter.

CUSACK: There was nothing stopping Labour making a nomination.

COLAHAN: Ah will you stop. With only five of us, what chance would we have?

CUSACK: It could be worse. You could be like poor Fitzsimons here, all on his own.

More laughter.

FITZSIMONS: Gentlemen, I appreciate your sympathy but I'm well capable of looking after myself and anyway, didn't I second Travers's nomination.

CUSACK: I don't think we would have had any trouble finding a seconder.

Laughter.

UABUACHALLA: Alright gentlemen, settle down. We have a meeting to run. *(As he is speaking, Phelan returns with Travers)* You're very welcome Mr. Travers

TRAVERS: Thank you.

Travers and Phelan take their seats.

UABUACHALLA: Next on the agenda is …. *(Hesitates)* election of Chairman? We've already done this so next item is ….

COFFEY: No Mr. UaBuachalla

UABUACHALLA: What?

COFFEY: You may have misunderstood me. The first election was for a Chairman to chair this particular meeting. Usually, the Chairman or Vice Chairman are returned during elections but this time … it was different. We needed to appoint a Chairman to start the meeting.

UABUACHALLA: So, what's this?

COFFEY: This is to elect a Chairman for the coming year. It couldn't be done until the entire Council had been assembled hence it comes after the co-options.

UABUACHALLA: Typical British bureaucracy!

Laughter.

COFFEY: That's the way it's always been done.

UABUACHALLA: Exactly! It's not for today but I propose that for the future, we examine the ways we work and move it as far away from the British system as possible.

General approval "here, here" etc.

PHELAN: We've wasted enough time on this. I will remain with my original proposal and propose Domhnall UaBuachalla. I don't see any necessity in giving a reason for this but suffice to say that he nearly doubled the quota required in north Kildare at the elections.

Cheering, applause.

CUSACK: And I second the proposal.

COFFEY: All in favour? *(All raise hands)* Congratulations Mr. UaBuachalla.

UABUACHALLA: Thank you and I will give my commitment to do all in my power to ensure that the work of this Council is efficiently carried out. *(Applause again)* Back to the agenda. Election of Vice Chairman. Any nominations?

CUSACK: I nominate Eamonn Moran.

PHELAN: I'll second that.

Pause.

UABUACHALLA: Any other nominations? No. All in favour? *(All raise their hands)* Unanimous. Mr. Moran is elected as Vice Chairman. *(Applause)* Next item – Dail Eireann authority.

O'CONNOR: Yes. I included that on the agenda. I wish to propose the usual resolution acknowledging the authority of Dail Eireann as the duly elected government of the Irish people.

General assent from the council.

CUSACK: I will second that.

ALL: Here here

FITZSIMONS: May I speak, Mr. Chairman?

UABUACHALLA: Certainly Mr. Fitzsimons.

FITZSIMONS: While I do not wish to appear as a dissenter, I have to state that I will be unable to support this motion.

UABUACHALLA: May I ask why?

FITZSIMONS: You are all aware that I fought the recent election on a different ticket to the rest of you in the chamber.

O'CONNOR: That might have not been your best decision.

Laughter.

FITZSIMONS: The people who voted for me did so on the basis of my election campaign. If I agree with this resolution, I will be placed in the same position as the rest of the members of this Council.

O'CONNOR: Would that be so bad?

FITZSIMONS: I always believed there was a better way. I understand of course that I am in a hopeless minority on the Council.

PHELAN: Why don't you throw in your lot with the rest of us?

FITZSIMONS: You have to realize that I am in a curious position here.

PHELAN: You are a citizen of the Irish Republic as well as anybody else and I'm sure you recognise it?

FITZSIMONS: I am an Irishman and I hope I have always been a good nationalist. I ask my friends and colleagues on the Council to respect my feelings in this case and I assure you that I will do my best to support the Council but I must stick with my principles.

UABUACHALLA: I'm sure I can speak for my colleagues on the Council when I say that we will bear no ill will against you. The motion is before the Council. All in favour, raise your hands.

All except Fitzsimons raise their hand.

UABUACHALLA: All against? *(Fitzsimons raises his hand)* The motion is carried. Next on the agenda is the munitions strike. I understand Mr. Colahan that you have a proposal?

COLAHAN: Yes. I propose that this County Council express our approval and admiration of the action taken by the Irish railwaymen and dockers in refusing to handle munitions of war intended for the destruction of our fellow countrymen.

General assent from Council "here here" etc.

COLAHAN: We should pledge ourselves to help them by every means in our power and we should call on all classes in the country to give their moral and financial support to these men in their fight against self-extermination.

Applause.

O'CONNOR: I will gladly second that proposal and I suggest that we add 'and the Council form themselves into a committee to collect funds in support of the railwaymen'

COLAHAN: Absolutely. This is not just a trade union fight but a fight for the nation. I will volunteer to act as treasurer for such a committee and I know my labour colleague, Michael Smyth will help me in this regard.

UABUACHALLA: Indeed. These men must be applauded for their actions. I put the resolution to the Council. All in favour, raise your hands

All raise.

UABUACHALLA: The resolution is adopted. The next item is the Irish language. I presume Mr. Coffey that this refers to the Gaelic League submission.

COFFEY: Yes

COLAHAN: May I make a comment?

UABUACHALLA: Certainly

COLAHAN: Meaning no disrespect to my Sinn Fein colleagues, but I would urge caution in implementing some of the Gaelic League proposals.

UABUACHALLA: Please elaborate.

COLAHAN: While I do have a "cupla focail", I am not as proficient in Irish as I'd like to be or as some of the other members of the Council are. I am sure that I am not alone in this?

Muted mumblings from some of the Council.

UABUACHALLA: The Irish language is our heritage. It's what separates us from the British.

COLAHAN: I agree. But I feel that a gradual implementation would be advised. We want the best people in office and on the council staff. The lack of ability to speak Irish should not exclude us from picking the best. How effective would this Council be if half the members couldn't fully follow the proceedings?

UABUACHALLA: I see your point but ..

COLAHAN: If I may, we are all republicans here no matter what party we belong to and surely our first priority is to build a Republic with good people in charge.

UABUACHALLA: We cannot neglect the Irish language.

COLAHAN: I'm not saying we should but we should implement changes gradually.

O'CONNOR: While I can't agree entirely with Mr. Colahan, I can see his point. I would like to propose that as a starting position, the Council does all in its power immediately to further the teaching of Irish and Irish history in schools. I also feel that Council cheques and paper headings could easily be changed to Irish.

UABUACHALLA: I imagine that could be done.

O'CONNOR: I also propose that the Council minutes should be signed in Irish and the Council should give preference in relation to advertising etc. to newspapers that publish Irish speeches and give Irish a fair show.

COLAHAN: I would gladly support that as a starting point and will happily second Mr. O' Connors proposals.

UABUACHALLA: I feel more should be done.

COLAHAN: Yes but everything doesn't have to be done immediately.

UABUACHALLA: Very well but this is a subject that I feel strongly about and I personally will not abandon it.

COLAHAN: That's as it should be.

UABUACHALLA: Very well. Can we vote on Mr. O' Connor's proposals. All in favour?

All raise hands.

UABUACHALLA: The proposal is adopted. Mr. Coffey. How will we proceed in getting the paper heading and cheques in Irish?

COFFEY: I will have to check with the office but I imagine we will first need to use up the current stock. I will report back at the next meeting.

UABUACHALLA: Thank you. Next item is Mr. Cusack's proposal to rescind the Council's condemnation of the Easter week rebellion. I am aware of this but perhaps for the benefit of the other Council members, you might elaborate Mr. Cusack.

CUSACK: Certainly. I was horrified to learn that this Council passed a resolution in 1916 condemning the Easter week rebellion. I cannot believe that Irish men whatever their politics could do such a thing. I now propose that this council immediately rescind this and strike it from the records.

General mutterings of disbelief from the Council.

UABUACHALLA: It is difficult to imagine how such as proposal could have passed

PHELAN: I do not think that the council passed such a resolution at all. I certainly have no recollection.

UABUACHALLA: Mr. Coffey. Do you have the minute books from that time?

COFFEY: I do. *(Gets book and goes to appropriate page)* Will I read the motion?

UABUACHALLA: Please do

COFFEY: Council meeting 29th May 1916. The motion reads - That we, the members of the Kildare County Council, strongly deprecate the recent deplorable action of a section of our countrymen in resorting to force of arms. At the same time we strongly appeal in what we consider the best interests of this country, and the empire as a whole, to the government to extend the greatest possible clemency to the rank and file, who we believe were deceived into taking part in the rising. That we take this opportunity of again recording our unabated confidence in Mr. J.E. Redmond and the Irish parliamentary party, and we thoroughly endorse the attitude they adopted during the crisis we are passing through.

Loud murmurs from council.

CUSACK: That should be ripped from the records.

UABUACHALLA: I agree. And Mr. Coffey, this was passed unanimously by the Council?

COFFEY: It was. The motion was proposed by John Healy who is no longer on the Council and was seconded by ... *(Hesitates)* Partick Phelan.

General shock. Phelan looks uncomfortable.

COLAHAN: *(Laughing)* Is this the same Patrick Phelan who a minute ago had no recollection that such a motion had been passed?

CUSACK: There was hardly another one.

PHELAN: That was four years ago.

CUSACK: Now, Paddy. How could you forget something as significant as that?

O'CONNOR: I was on the Council at that time and I was not aware of this resolution was adopted. I may not have been in the chamber at the time … *(Laughter)* At that time Councillors were in the habit of going out for refreshments … *(More laughter)* It is possible that in their absence, a resolution could be passed.

CUSACK: *(Sarcastically)* Oh, quite possible but Paddy here seconded the resolution.

PHELAN: Very well. I am deeply shamed to have been associated with that resolution and while it was only four years ago, we all know that those were very different times. At that time, I truly believed that the rising in Dublin was wrong but times have changed. I cannot nor will I try to say anything to support my actions at that time but my opinions have changed very much over those four years. Today, I believe no man can remain outside the movement in view of the feelings of the country.

Applause.

UABUACHALLA: The Council appreciates your honesty Mr. Phelan.

PHELAN: If I may, I would like to second the motion to rescind that resolution.

Cheers from Council.

UABUACHALLA: Can we vote on that motion? All in favour? *(Unanimous)* The motion is carried unanimously

CUSACK: Can I further propose that the page in question be ripped from the book and burned.

Cheering and applause.

COLAHAN: While I agree in principle, I feel the minute book is the formal record of Council meetings and I would not agree with defacing that record. Also, we may not like what happened but it is part of our history and we should not forget. Can I suggest that we cancel the resolution by drawing a line through it with red ink.

UABUACHALLA: I think that's acceptable. *(Murmurs of assent)* Mr. Coffey, will you see to that?

COFFEY: Yes. Mr. UaBuachalla *(He does so to applause)*

UABUACHALLA: Next on the agenda is a proposal from Mr. Supple that smoking be allowed in the Council Chamber during meetings.

COLAHAN: I will gladly second that proposal.

Laughter.

FITZSIMONS: If that proposal is accepted, I would have to leave the chamber.

COLAHAN: May I ask why?

FITZSIMONS: I cannot stand the smell of smoke and it makes me cough.

Laughter

O'CONNOR: Perhaps we could have all the smokers sit at one side of the chamber.

PHELAN: I am a non smoker myself and I would not oppose the proposition on that ground. However, I do think that the business of the Council would be transacted with greater decorum if the members refrained from smoking during meetings.

FITZSIMONS: Here, here. We do not want the meeting to resemble a gathering on a street corner.

COLAHAN: Sure it's only a bit of smoke. Smoking never did anyone any harm.

UABUACHALLA: The proposal is before the Council. All those in favour?

All except Phelan, Fitzsimons and O'Connor raise their hands.

UABUACHALLA: Those against?

Phelan, Fitzsimons and O'Connor raise their hands.

UABUACHALLA: Majority in favour. The motion is carried.

Cheers from the majority.

COLAHAN: Thank God for that.

He produces cigarettes or a pipe. Laughter.

FITZSIMONS: Mr. UaBuachalla, as it appears that this proposal will be instantly implemented, can I suggest that we take a brief break in proceedings. I'd like to get a few mouthfuls of fresh air!

Laughter.

UABUACHALLA: Of course Mr. Fitzsimons. Can I ask members to be respectful of their non-smoking colleagues. We will reconvene in fifteen minutes. Thank you.

The Councillors wander off.

END OF EPISODE

Printed in Great Britain
by Amazon

71506697R00251